"She pay wi...

"Something better, Doc. S... Carol Anne plucked sor... ...er and dropped the tiny object ... ...palm. "Here's how she paid. She said to send her the change care of this address—" she waved a piece of paper at him "—once we've hocked it."

Tag lifted the ring to the light. "A diamond!"

"If you believe that, Doc.... It'll be a zircon, I guarantee, worth fifty if we're lucky."

They both looked up as headlights swept the room, followed by a second pair, then a third. Brakes yelped in the parking lot. Doors slammed.

As Tag threw open the door to the clinic, another car wheeled in off the road.... No, this was a van. With the logo of the local TV station emblazoned along its side. It was a media frenzy. With its prey in sight.

"Dr. Taggart! Why did you perform unauthorized surgery on the finest racing sire ever bred in America?" Voices receded into the yammering din of white noise. Somewhere, Susannah Mack was laughing at him. Laughing at him while his life ended up in ruins.

"No comment." He'd save his comments and his own questions for the one woman who could answer them. He gazed into the cameras, because he knew she'd be watching. *Read it in my eyes, Susannah. You can run. You can hide. But I'm gonna get you, if it's the last thing I do!*

Dear Reader,

"She's from Texas," my oldest friends roll their eyes and say whenever I stick out my chin, take the law into my own hands and charge off to seek Justice—and usually find Trouble instead. Like the time I dognapped one hundred and twenty pounds of bellowing mutt that was terrorizing our neighborhood at 3:00 a.m. and tied him to the police station back door, with a doggy confession looped round his shaggy neck. (*I've been barking again.*) Or the time this five-foot-two-inch woman got indignant and tried to stop a large and irate shoplifter all by herself—*not* one of my better ideas.

And maybe my friends' explanation is the best one—call it a mental holdover from the Wild West days, when Texas Rangers were few and far between. So if a lady wanted justice—or revenge (which we all fondly imagine to be the same thing)—well, she just had to find it herself.

Whatever, this Texan found it easy to imagine a woman like Susannah Mack, who needed revenge—shoot, she earned it!—and who was spunky enough, indignant enough and reckless enough to fight for it against overwhelming odds. And then to imagine her ideal partner in adversity—Dr. R. D. Taggart, a man practical, tough and tender enough to see his Texas Pistol safely through her wildest schemes to the happy-ever-after ending she so richly deserved.

So here's Susannah's story. I had a lark writing it, and I hope you will reading it. All the best!

Peggy Nicholson

DON'T MESS WITH TEXANS
Peggy Nicholson

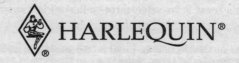

HARLEQUIN®

TORONTO • NEW YORK • LONDON
AMSTERDAM • PARIS • SYDNEY • HAMBURG
STOCKHOLM • ATHENS • TOKYO • MILAN • MADRID
PRAGUE • WARSAW • BUDAPEST • AUCKLAND

ISBN 0-373-70834-3

DON'T MESS WITH TEXANS

Copyright © 1999 by Peggy Nicholson.

This edition published by arrangement with Harlequin Books S.A.

® and TM are trademarks of the publisher. Trademarks indicated with ® are registered in the United States Patent and Trademark Office, the Canadian Trade Marks Office and in other countries.

Look us up on-line at: http://www.romance.net

Printed in U.S.A.

This book is for my mother, Marguerite Grimes, the first horsewoman I ever knew. Her endearing spunk and stubborn gallantry inspired my heroine, Susannah Mack. It's also for Ron duPrey, only my sun and moon and a northwest breeze at dawn.

With special thanks to John Civic, D.V.M., for his kind advice on veterinary procedures. Any technical mistakes this author may have made were despite his bemused help—*You want to what?*—rather than because of it.

CHAPTER ONE

SIX HOURS AFTER SURGERY, the tomcat was looking like a keeper. "Gums couldn't be pinker," Tag assured him. So he wasn't bleeding internally. He let the cat's upper lip drop and the tom slashed at his leather glove, then retreated to the back of the cage. Reflexes coming back nicely after anesthesia. His pupils were equally dilated and no wider than they should be. "So what day of the week is it?" Tag murmured, and got a sing song growl in reply.

"Wednesday, right. First week in January, last year of the century." The car that hit him last night must have just grazed him, breaking his jaw as it tossed him aside. But his brains didn't seem to be scrambled. "And who's the president?"

The tom's ragged ears stayed flattened to his furry skull. Another subsonic moan issued through wired jaws.

"Who cares? You wouldn't give three fleas and a dead rat for every politician in the country," Tag translated. "Can't say I blame you." Neither would he. Politics was a pastime for comfortable people with time on their hands and steady paychecks coming in. For his and the cat's kind, survival was the name of the game. And living well was its best revenge.

Still, to live well this stray would have to learn to tolerate humans. Because as soon as he mended, Tag meant to find him a home. He hadn't spent half the night patching him up just to boot him back out on the street when he was healed. He shut the cage door, then lingered, talking soothing nonsense till the cat stopped growling.

"Got time for a paying customer, Doc?" Carol Anne

Kopesky, Tag's medical technician/receptionist, frowned at him from the doorway leading to the front of the clinic. Hired some twenty years ago by Tag's senior partner, Dr. Higgins, and trained by that grimly practical gentleman, she took his same dim view of charity cases. And now that Higgins had suffered a mild heart attack and taken a leave of absence, Carol Anne was watching their bottom line with even more than her usual zeal. Tag was earning for two now, till Higgins returned to the Green Mountain Veterinary Clinic next Monday. And even then he would only be practicing part-time.

"Mrs. Allen's in room one," she briefed him as Tag stretched his tired bones to his full six feet, one inch. "With her Irish setter, Jebbie, for his yearly checkup and vacs." She lowered her voice. "A month late. I was afraid we'd lost them to you-know-who."

A new practice had opened in Bennington, twenty miles to the west, last summer. Their competition was a small-animal man with glitzy new facilities and all the toothy charm of a TV game-show host. Higgins had brought Tag in as his junior associate to counter that threat.

A bell rang as the clinic's front door opened.

"That'll be Mrs. Rafferty with Gigi," Carol Anne added as a *yap-yap!* like two strokes of an ice pick to the skull rang out from the reception room. "Here to have her toenails trimmed, and don't even *think* of suggesting we knock her out to scale her teeth. Gigi has a delicate constitution." She rolled her eyes and departed.

"Right." Let the day begin. Tag rotated his shoulders under his white coat and headed for exam room one. Four hours' sleep last night, and five the night before, with that false alarm out at the Great Dane kennel on the edge of town. A first-time mother's delivery, except that she hadn't. No doubt she'd drop tonight—about the time he dropped off.

Three dogs, two cats and a molting parrot later, he heard a truck rumble down the driveway. Tag injected the last c.c.

of distemper vaccine into a squirming Lab puppy and glanced up in time to see a dusty two-horse trailer, hitched to a pickup, glide past his window and on to the barn. Damn. Somebody who hadn't heard that Doc Higgins was out of commission.

Higgins ran a mixed practice, serving small animals and large, for what had been a rural farming community. But dairy farms were giving way to computer analysts' country retreats, where the largest animal in residence was more likely an English sheepdog than a sheep. Tag, in keeping with changing times, was a small-animal specialist. Unless the occupant of that trailer had a very simple problem, he wouldn't be much help.

"You'd better go see," he advised Carol Anne as he set the syringe aside and took hold of the puppy before it could leap off the table. "Paws like pie plates, he's going to be a bruiser," he added to the proud owner. "Have you thought about obedience school?" The bell chimed at the front door. Driver of the truck and trailer, he supposed.

While Tag gave his views on various trainers around the state, he listened with half his attention to the voices down the hall. Carol Anne's was rising and taking on a hard edge. Some sort of disagreement going on out there? Her opponent's responses were barely audible, a low liquid murmur and pause, insistent for all its softness. A woman, he thought. Any man would have recognized Carol Anne's no as no and stomped off by now.

"So Carol Anne can give you Mrs. Dearing's number." He eased patient and owner out the door and down the hall toward the debate. "I believe she has a class starting next month." He gave the puppy a farewell ear scratch. "Meantime he's looking terrific. You're doing a great job with him."

As they reached the reception room, a girl—woman—spun away from the desk to face him. Hair the color of marigolds, flying out from her head as she swung. Cheeks pink with emotion, big eyes meeting his own like a slap. "Are you the doctor?"

High-heeled boots rap-tapping on the linoleum, she came at him. For a moment Tag thought she'd march right into the puppy's owner, but at the last instant the women do-si-doed and she was toe-to-toe with him, looking up. Despite three-inch heels, she stood no higher than his heart. Pointy chin, lush lips. "You're Dr. Taggart?" She caught his sleeve.

An emergency, that was clear. Half his mind was already listing the instruments and meds he might need—tourniquets, splints, horse-size syringes, painkiller? The other half was taking her in the way a punch-drunk boxer takes it on the chin, one hit after another, with no time between blows to recover. Drawl like hot honey in spite of her urgency. Her hair wasn't standing on end; it just seemed that way. Eyes blue as a summer thunderstorm, pink-rimmed with recent tears or maybe lack of sleep, long-lashed in gold. A faint scent of flowers overlaid with a whiff of…bourbon? Maybe it was just some component of her perfume.

She tugged him toward the door. "Would you please, please, please help me?"

He would, in a heartbeat.

"I tried to tell her," Carol Anne said angrily from behind the counter, "that Dr. Higgins is out. That if she'd just drive to Bennington, I'm sure she could find somebody who'd—"

"I haven't got *time!*" his captor snapped without turning. She transferred her grip from his sleeve to his forearm. Slender fingers, and strong. "If you'd just come see…"

"Of course. Show me."

"Doctor! Honestly, I never—"

The door slammed on Carol Anne's reproach and they burst out into cold, crisp air—a warm day for January in Vermont, low forties with sunshine. Her breath smoked. "He's around back." She couldn't weigh more than a hundred pounds, but she was all leg in her tight blue jeans and short denim jacket. Matching him stride for stride, she tugged him down the drive, and he went willingly, wanting to laugh, in spite of her urgency, because of her fierceness.

"*What* an old dragon! I thought she'd chew me up and spit me out before you showed up. Though she's right, this is terrible, me landing on you out of nowhere like this, 'thout an appointment, but I…" She shrugged and smiled up at him for the first time in apology. Beautiful teeth, something Nordic in her blood with that high coloring. She pronounced her long *I*s as *ah. Ah thought…Ra-aht,* instead of right…

Georgia, he guessed. What was she doing up here in the cold north? "How did he hurt himself?" And if she could smile like that, how terrible could it be? Half of him hoped for a false alarm, an easy fix. The other half wanted something serious that he could heroically cure. *Dr. Taggart at your service, m'lady.*

She shook her head. "He's not hurt. Not yet." Her smile faded and she darted ahead. "Here he is." She threw a bolt on the trailer and swung open the rear door. "My baby." She pronounced it *mah.* "Hey, Pookie, sweetheart!" She tipped her head in from the side, to peer past a dark brown flank and black tail. "It's gonna be okay now. Ollie, ollie oxen free. Dr. Taggart's gonna fix you up jus' fine."

Pookie was enormous, or maybe it was the confines of the trailer that made him seem so. Horses always looked enormous to Tag. Had ever since he was a boy back in Boston and saw the mounted cops' animals, unpredictable and dangerous as their riders, with steel-shod hooves that could mash a mouthy slum kid's feet to jelly. Though he'd handled horses at veterinary college, first impressions were hard to lose. Why couldn't she have had a cow in need? Cows weren't half so intimidating.

She bent over, denim stretched tight around trim curves, and Tag's attention swerved sharply and stuck fast. Clearly he hadn't been dating enough these past five months. Too busy, with Higgins dropping like a stone not six weeks after Tag bought into the practice. And even if he'd had the time, he hadn't seen a woman up here he wanted to chase. Till now.

Metal rumbled as she slid a gridded ramp down to the ground. Tag found his voice. "Wait a minute. If he's not hurt, what's the problem?"

"Not a problem, exactly. I mean it *is,* but—" She vanished into the empty stall to the right of the horse. Hooves thudded on padded metal, then the horse, a stallion, backed ponderously down the ramp. Tag retreated several hasty steps. Miss Blue Eyes reappeared, holding the animal's lead, then clattered down to ground level, caught his halter beneath his chin and turned him around. "Ta-da!"

The stallion tossed his dark head and she staggered, then laughed and flattened a hand high on his glossy neck. "Pookie, meet Dr. Taggart."

The stud's head towered high over her red-gold ripply curls. Horse-mountain. Dark eyes focused on Tag with an almost human curiosity. The stallion snorted, and the gruff *"Huh!"* sounded like an opinion.

"What precisely do you want me to do for…Pookie?" All half-ton-plus of him?

She gave him a dazzling smile. "I want you to Bobbitt this ol' boy for me." She slapped the stud's shoulder for emphasis.

Oh, boy. "You mean…"

She nodded vigorously. "I mean fix him. Geld him. I bought him for riding and he…" Her eyes slid away to follow a crow winging over the barn, then back to Tag's face and she shrugged. "His octane's a bit high." Her chin tipped up a notch. "I mean I can handle him, but…"

Tag didn't know much about horses, but he knew this one was no lady's ride. One toss of his head and the beast could have flipped her over the barn. "Um…if he's Pookie, then you're…?"

"Susannah," she said, and held out a fine-boned hand. "Susannah…Mack."

He liked her strength as they shook, liked even better that his hand dwarfed hers. She had calluses, just enough that her touch was interesting. "Susannah, if you just bought him… He's a looker, but isn't he a bit more horse than you need? Maybe you should consider taking him—"

Her eyes went steely. "There isn't anything on four legs I can't ride. That's *not* the problem."

"Then the problem is…?" And why the rush?

She stared at him unblinking as the tomcat he'd saved last night, then looked down at her toes. "Problem is we're new in town. Just up from…the South."

Tag glanced automatically at the trailer's license, but it was too muddy to read the state. Looked like they'd forded a river on their way.

"We drove all night, and now we get here—" She scuffed at the frozen dirt "—I find the stable where I'd made arrangements won't take him. I forgot t'mention he was a stud. They have only one turn-out pen, lots of mares, and they're afraid he'll…" She laughed.

"He will." Tag rubbed the back of his neck and sighed. The last time he'd gelded a stallion, it had been a Shetland pony who'd almost returned the favor. He'd sported a tiny, blue-black hoofprint on his upper thigh for a month. He'd gone along to watch Higgins on a Saturday and that canny veteran had taken one look at the pony, then pressed Tag into service. The time before that had been in vet school. "What about some other stable?"

She looked up from her boots. "I want *that* one. And it's just going to be the same ol' story, wherever we go." She drifted closer and put a hand on his arm. "Please do it? I don't know where I'll go or what I'll do if you don't help us.''

When she put it like that... And she was determined, that was clear, and he was damned if he'd have her turn to any other man—any other vet— for help. ''All right, then.'' *Let's get it over with.* ''When did he eat last?''

''Not since 'bout ten, last night.'' She let Tag go and backed off a step, still holding him with her storm-cloud eyes.

''Good. Then his stomach's clear.'' The clinic barn was clean, with a freshly bedded stall waiting for the patients Higgins might never see again. And the older man's instruments were stored in the surgery. ''If you could walk him around the grounds for fifteen minutes or so, settle him down, I'll turn on the heat in the barn and set everything up.'' And snatch a quick look at his text on equine procedures.

And face down Carol Anne's outrage when he told her to postpone his first two afternoon appointments. Luckily Susannah had descended on him at the start of his lunch break. An experienced vet could geld a horse in half an hour or less. But he'd want to take his time, measure twice and cut once, as the saying went. *Oh, boy.* Tag turned and headed for the clinic.

CHAPTER TWO

FIFTEEN MINUTES LATER, hands freshly scrubbed and jaw clenched tight on all the words he'd not said back to his assistant, such as *Who's the vet and who's the med tech here?* Tag stomped out the back door of the hospital, his home-visit bag swinging at his side.

"You don't know her from Adam, that's not your specialty, and she didn't even make an appointment!" Carol Anne had protested, the last apparently being Susannah's greatest sin. "Just waltzes in here, flaps those big eyes, says pretty please and you jump. *Men!*"

There was nothing like a little opposition to make him cast his own doubts aside. Tag stopped to scan the fields beyond the barn and his cottage, which he rented from Higgins. No long-legged lovely with King Kong horse. His gaze swung to her trailer and he frowned. Something about it... He spun on his heel as Carol Anne leaned out the back door of the clinic.

"I phoned Doc Higgins, but he's not answering. But I left a message that if he came in anytime soon, he should call you on the barn line and—"

"Cancel that." Tag didn't need him or want him for this. And Carol Anne should know by now that he sometimes took advice, but he never took orders. They glared at each other for an ice-cold, unbending minute, then she banged the door shut.

He needed to calm down. Animals could sense your tension before you felt it yourself. Tag took a slow breath. Bedside manner of quiet, sunny confidence, that's what was wanted here. Piece of cake, really, this procedure. The premise remained roughly the same whether you did tomcat or elephant. Laying him down would be the scariest moment. Horses were more fragile than they looked. And the danger cut both ways. A horse like that, toppling, could smash a man flat. His eyes lit on the barn door, an inch or so ajar when he'd left it tightly closed. Ah.

They were waiting for him in the corridor outside the stall. The stud lifted his head and pricked his ears as Tag entered the barn. Susannah didn't stir. She stood at his shoulder, face pressed to his chocolate-brown hide, one arm hooked over his withers. Asleep on her feet like a horse? "Susannah?"

She swung her head lazily Tag's way, mouth, nose and forehead sliding across the stallion's sleek coat. A sleepy, sensual move as if dragging her face across a warm pillow. *To face a bedmate.* The hair lifted along his arms. She was something! Cheek resting against the horse, she smiled at him. Her eyes glistened.

Had she been crying? "Susannah?" He reached for her, but Pookie thrust his nose out between them. Tag switched his attention to the stud, who had teeth the size of dominoes, offering the back of his hand for inspection, fingers curled away, ready to dodge. But the horse was satisfied with a lusty whiff of him, not a chunk. "Good Pook, nice Pookie." Tag got a hand on his halter, rubbed his neck, turned to study her. "You all right there?"

"Um." She nodded and pushed off from the horse. The hand that had been hidden from view held a small silver hip flask. "Just fine." She cleared her throat and her voice gained conviction. "Finer than fine." She thrust the flask at him. "Like a sip?"

"Not while I'm working." He took the container and sniffed—bourbon—closed it with the cap that dangled from a silver chain. This was beautiful workmanship, with the name "Brady" engraved elaborately across its face. *Who's*

Brady? He tucked the flask into her jacket pocket. She was shivering, all the feverish vivaciousness of their first meeting faded to a braced stillness. And her eyes were much too bright. "You know," he said, "we don't have to do this right now. We could board him here for a day or so, if no stable will take him." Of course, that meant Higgins would insist on doing the job once Carol Anne reached him.

Her lips slowly parted—and Tag's brain went blank for half a dozen heartbeats. Then thought returned as his blood flowed north again and she shook her head.

"Nope. I've made up my mind. Let's do it."

Then he'd better get on with it. He had a full slate of patients this afternoon, beyond the two appointments he'd made Carol Anne reschedule.

He decided to give the stallion his first shot right there in the corridor. A tranquilizer, intramuscular injection. Susannah gripped the stud's sculpted nose with one hand, held the halter tight with her other. If he reared, she'd go flying. Tag slapped Pookie's neck smartly, the impact supposedly disguising the following prick, then inserted the needle. Pookie let out a grunt of surprise. But no fireworks. Tag had treated poodles that struggled more. "Good boy."

Then a quick exam while he waited for the preanesthetic to kick in. Pulse, taken at the submaxillary artery along his lower jaw, was thirty-six. "Good…" Tag placed his stethoscope on the left side of the stallion's chest just behind the elbow to check the heartbeat, then over the lungs for the respiratory rate. Ten breaths a minute, average for a horse at ease. He glanced at Susannah. "Any idea if he's had a tetanus booster lately?"

"It's up-to-date."

She looked dead certain of that, so he left her stroking the stud and crooning endearments while he went in to check the stall. He spread more hay from the new bale in the corner, though the bedding was clean and deep enough already. Nerves. "Okay, you can bring him in now."

Filled with a seventeen-hand stallion, the stall seemed the size of a shoebox. "Can you put him up against the wall there, head toward the door?"

She could, handling him as deftly as a trucker backed an eighteen-wheeler alongside fuel pumps, one small sure hand flattened to the monster's ribs as she shoved him over. Pookie allowed himself to be parked, his left side nearly touching the wall, then turned his head to look at her with a snort of surprise while Tag swung the gate around. This was a hinged device Higgins had built years ago, a wide padded rail that hemmed the horse in against the wall. "Duck under, Susannah." She ducked and he swung the rail all the way parallel to the horse, then dropped the front fitting into its reinforced slot. Let out a breath of relief. Not that the stud couldn't still kick his way free if he took the notion.

She grabbed a lapel of the leather jacket Tag had thrown on over his lab coat. "You're gonna put him to sleep, aren't you? I don't want—"

"It's okay, Susannah." He caught her wrist. Unlike her stallion pal, her pulse skittered wildly and her skin was clammy-cold. "He'll be sleeping like a baby in a minute. Won't feel a thing." You could do a stud with a local, but he'd just as soon this brute was safely in dreamland when he stole the family jewels.

"The gate lets him drop straight down, nice and easy. We don't want him falling sideways." He rubbed a thumb across her silky skin, then had to consciously pull away to stop. "Why don't you sit on that bale while I get organized?

"You wouldn't know what he weighs, would you?" he added over his shoulder as he spread out a sterile sheet, then laid out his surgical pack, the various antiseptic scrubs, several pairs of gloves.

"'Bout twelve hundred an' fifty-five," she drawled.

Tag blinked at the precision. How many owners knew to the pound? He glanced back and saw she'd pushed up her sleeve to consult a man's wristwatch, one of those ugly black, multifunction sportsman's timepieces that dwarfed her slender wrist. Her long legs were crossed and one lizardskin boot jiggled nonstop. "Won't be long now," he assured her, deciding to leave the special gelding tool out of sight till he'd banished her from the stall. "He's a thoroughbred?" He didn't know much about horses, but big and rangily graceful as this one was...

"Yeah."

"How old?" He drew the bottle of short-acting barbiturate from his bag and shook it. "Twelve?" Pookie's teeth weren't those of a young horse.

"Fourteen."

Based on the weight she'd given, Tag calculated the dose and filled the syringe. He detached the 18-gauge needle and held it between gloved fingers. "Has he ever been raced?" A lot of clapped-out racers ended up as hunters or riding hacks, the lucky ones that didn't go to the dogs.

"Um...few times." She sprang to her feet and went to the horse's head. "We gonna *do* this or not?"

"Right now." Joining her at the stud's forequarters, he swabbed the jugular furrow with alcohol, then pressed down on that vein, nearer the heart. The vessel swelled with impeded blood. He smacked it with the back of his hand, then inserted the needle. No objections from Pookie, who was looking mellower by the minute. "He's going to go down almost at once when this hits his bloodstream. Keep your hands and feet out of his way." He attached the syringe, checked that the needle was still in place, then slowly depressed the plunger. "We'll lay him down, then I want you to wait outside. Won't take long at all."

"Nope, I stay here."

"But—"

"I want to watch."

Great. He'd be happier fumbling his way through this without an audience, but one look at the angle of her chin, and he knew better than to argue. "Okay. Here we go." He withdrew the needle. Pookie's ears pricked, then wobbled. He let out a whuffling breath and swayed on his feet. The gate creaked ominously. "Hands out of the *way,* Susannah."

While the stud folded slowly, majestically, front legs first, she crooned wordless sympathy and cupped his muzzle, supporting his massive head as it drooped. Tag bent to watch his back legs, folding nicely, all in order, good…good… That high, whimpering sound scared him for a second, then he realized it was the woman, not the horse. Pookie grunted and settled into the straw with a sleepy grunt.

"Oh, Jeez *Louise!*" She collapsed bonelessly beside his head.

"He's fine, Susannah. Don't worry." Tag glanced at his watch, then swung the gate out of the way. "Now we've got to roll him onto his side."

They had to brace their feet against the side wall, straighten their legs and put their backs into it. Once Pookie lay limp as a beached whale, Susannah returned to the stallion's front end. While Tag changed his gloves, she stripped off her jacket. She levered the horse's head onto her knees—"Lord, he's heavy!"—slid the jacket beneath, then settled him again. "Oh, Pookums…"

It wasn't that warm in here, but Tag couldn't stop now to give her his own coat to wear. And the stud's lower eye was protected from the straw, something he should have thought of himself. "Watch his eyes and ears for me, Susannah. If you see any signs he's waking…" There wasn't a chance of that, but it would keep her occupied and out of his way.

Still, after a minute's wordless crooning, she demanded, "What are you doin' now?"

"Scrubbing him down." Betadine, alcohol wipe, then Betadine spray. While that dried he checked the stud's pulse at the back fetlock—slowing, but still well within acceptable range. Then his breathing—shallow, steady and slow. No worries there. *Time to rock and roll.* Tag reached for his scalpel, then glanced up—to see her small, greenish-white face staring at him from the far end of his patient.

With her pupils dilated, her eyes looked black, not blue. The irises were ringed entirely in white—and locked on the razor-sharp blade in his hand. He'd been an idiot to let her stay. "So here we go," he murmured in the same soothing voice he saved for scared animals.

"Yeah..." She swallowed audibly. "Y'know, I think... maybe this is—" She vanished from view beyond the stallion's bulk. Straw rustled.

"Is what?" But she didn't continue and Tag's focus narrowed to the task at hand. *Steady, steady, easy there, gently...* Time was of the essence now. Half his attention was focused on the dark skin under his gloved fingers, half envisioned the vital structures he knew lay beneath it. *Nice and easy now...*

He didn't think of the woman again till he reached for the emasculator. If she hadn't liked the scalpel, she'd like the look of this tool even less. "Won't be long at all," he murmured comfortingly, sparing her a glance.

Beyond the dark rise of the stallion's shoulder, then the descending curve of his neck, he saw an upturned hand, like a starfish flung down in the straw. A swath of red-gold crinkled silk spilled over a mound of dried grass, then vanished from sight. "Susannah?" He couldn't see more from this angle without standing. Her fingers curled limp and unmoving. "Susannah?"

There came a faint sigh and a murmur. Her hand flexed slightly, then relaxed. Out as cold as her four-legged friend.

And speaking of which, the clock was ticking. Tag had seen enough people faint in vet school not to worry about her. She hadn't fallen far, and she'd fallen on straw. And if she was this squeamish she'd be happier out of it. *Teach me to let amateurs in the op room!* He grabbed the special stainless-steel pliers and went back to work.

Eight minutes later when he set the instrument aside, she still hadn't stirred. Tag did his final cleanup, a last inch-by-inch inspection, a quick stick of long-acting antibiotic to the rump, then nodded. A good job, if he said so himself. Even fussbudget Higgins would have had to agree.

"Susannah?" He hid his tools from view, then stood, stretched and had to smile. *Oh, Susannah!* She was as irresistible as a basket of golden retriever pups. She'd toppled straight back into the straw, one arm flung overhead, the other resting below her small breasts. She breathed deeply, easily, soft lips barely parted. Faint had flowed straight into sleep, it looked like. *Drove all night,* he remembered. He knelt beside her and clamped his fingers on his knees to keep from smoothing her hair.

It was like a run of rough water on a mountain stream, riffling and rumpling and cascading down sunstruck rocks, an eddy of smooth gold here, a swirl of copper and sunshine there. It almost begged a man to thread it through his fingers, use it to tip back her head for a—

"Bad idea," she muttered without opening her eyes. "Oh, *real* bad!" She scowled, wrenched her head to one side, her lashes shivering.

Damn, was she psychic on top of all else? Tag hadn't blushed since seventh grade, the time that little redheaded substitute teacher caught him peeking down her— "What is?" he said guiltily.

"Don't!" She opened her eyes, stared blankly at a world of straw for a second, then swung her gaze up to his. "Don't do it. I changed my mind!" She latched onto his jacket lapels, hauling him down and herself to a half-sit, their faces mere inches apart.

"You mean...?" His stomach did a slow, nasty somersault,

and it wasn't just her breasts nearly grazing his chest or the tip of her tongue glossing delectable lips. "Susannah, you mean don't do your stud?"

She nodded violently. He slipped an arm under her shoulders before she choked him. "Uh, Susannah…it's a bit late for that now." *All the king's horses and all the king's men, babe…* "The Pook'll be neighing tenor from now on."

"Ohhh…" She squeezed her eyes tight and simply lay there, letting him support her weight for a long moment. "Oh." She drew a shuddering breath and opened her eyes. "Right."

He blinked, then realized. She meant "right," not "rot." She gave him a wavering smile and shrugged as he lifted her upright. "Oh, well, it was just a thought…"

Tag was having second thoughts, too. Malpractice suits against vets weren't as rare as they once had been. Trusting idiot, he hadn't even made her fill out the forms beforehand as he should have. If she wanted to claim otherwise, he had no legal proof that she'd requested this procedure and not a tonsillectomy. Higgins would have called him twelve kinds of lust-struck idiot for this oversight, thinking with his—

"Never mind." She braced her arms behind her and he let her go. She glanced around. "How is he?"

"Couldn't be better." One dark ear twitched at their voices, then flopped again. He'd finished in the nick of time. Tag brought his gaze warily back to her face. Her color was returning to normal, well, maybe a bit pinker than normal, but whatever she was thinking he was pretty sure it wasn't lawsuits. He pulled a wisp of straw from her hair and she gave him a shaky smile. It would be all right, thank God. She might be a waffler, but she wasn't a blamer. "You're from Georgia?"

Her foxy brows drew together. "Texas." A two-and-a-half syllable word, the way she said it. "Te-exas," pronounced with pride and mild reproof, as if he'd asked an angel for her address. *Left hand of God, of course, silly. Where did you think?*

Was it an ethical blooper to kiss your patient's owner? And did he care? Tag wasn't the outlaw he'd been in his youth, but he still followed his own counsel more often than not when it came to rules.

On the other hand, one of his personal principles was that you didn't kiss a cornered woman. Not the first time, anyway, before you knew how she felt about it. He helped her to her feet, stood looking down at her. Her eyes weren't blue in this light, but violet. "If you're from Texas, then what's a blue norther?" He remembered puzzling over the phrase in a paperback western he'd read that summer he'd spent locked up in reform school.

She laughed. "Big winter storm, comes whoopin' down out of the Panhandle. The whole sky goes purply blue and the horse trough freezes over. Why?"

"Dunnow. Just crossed my mind." Pookie lifted his head and blew, and the moment passed. They helped him roll awkwardly to an upright position. After he'd considered that woozily for a minute, he snorted and struggled to his feet. Stood wide-legged and swaying.

Out in the corridor, the phone rang. "Be right back." If that was Higgins, he was too late.

It was Carol Anne. "*Doc*tor Taggart. Mrs. Hazard and her Rotweiler have been waiting to see you for *ten* minutes."

"Tell her five more." Tag returned to Pookie's owner. "He needs to be quiet for the next hour or two, Susannah. So why don't you come up to the clinic? Carol Anne can find you a cup of coffee and—"

She shook her head. "I'd rather keep an eye on him."

"Suit yourself." She was a stubborn little cuss, but that was part of her charm, the variety—softness and toughness, flashes of fire and hints of tenderness. He shrugged out of his leather jacket as she turned back to her horse. He probably shouldn't do this, but… He settled his coat around her, smiling down at her as she glanced back over her shoulder, surprised. "Meantime, this'll keep you warm."

Her lips parted as if to protest—then closed again and curved softly. She put up her arms like a trusting child and he helped her into its sleeves. Then she rotated under his hands to face him. "I want to thank you, Dr. Taggart."

"It was my pleasure." He shouldn't push it. She had to be beat if she'd driven all night, but he didn't want to let her get away. She was new in town and he meant to stake his claim before another man spotted her. "Once you've settled Pook into his new home, how about coming out to supper with me? Something simple. I know it's been a long day and you…" He paused as her face closed down. *Stupid, you should have waited!*

Her shoulders stiffened under his fingers, subtly shrugging him off. "That's most kind, Doctor." Her drawl was more pronounced, as if she drifted southward away from him. "But truth is…I'm married." She dropped her chin and fumbled with the zipper of his coat. "B'sides, I don't much like men, now'days. Not that way." She scuffed a boot in the straw. "But I appreciate the offer." She looked up suddenly, jaw set, eyes direct and purply blue, the color of a freezing Texas wind.

"Right." He felt as if she'd slapped his face. No, he'd run head-on into her hand—she hadn't raised it against him. He'd been the one who'd come on like a half-grown, bumptious puppy, sniffing after his first bitch in heat. She'd simply needed a doctor. Married, standing there straight and small in his jacket. "Right, well…" *Crap.* Stick your neck out this far, there was no way to retreat without looking a fool. He headed out the door. "Come up to the office if you need anything. I'll check back in an hour, see how he's doing."

Or you could always come up and pay. If it wasn't love at first sight, then he supposed it was business. Carol Anne would certainly see it that way. For all he cared, Susannah Mack could have a freebie.

CHAPTER THREE

HE TURNED UP THE HEAT on his way out, stalked past her trailer. Something odd about that... He looked back and saw what his subconscious must have noted an hour before, then skated blithely past in favor of a honey-mouth drawl and a pair of big, anxious blue eyes. There was more mud on the license plate than there was on the trailer.

Fortuitous splash when she drove through a puddle? Or... He'd used that trick himself a few times, back in his car-collecting days that summer he'd turned thirteen. Not that every cop didn't know it, too.

Tag walked back to the trailer and brushed his fingers across frigid metal. Dried mud sifted down. A Kentucky plate. But Susannah had said ''Texas'' like she meant it, the way a U.S. Marine said ''America.''

She hadn't mentioned where from down south she'd departed yesterday, he reminded himself. Just because she was a Texan didn't mean she still lived in sight of the Alamo. Maybe he was imagining things—there was nearly as much mud splashed on the truck as the plate. *Nothing but hurt pride talking,* he mocked himself. *There's no crime in turning down a date, is there?*

He put her deliberately out of mind for the next half hour. Then she was driven out in a rush, as Champion Ophelia's Flowers of Elsinore decided to drop her first litter of blue-bloods. Though the brindle Great Dane was in superb condition and gave no indications of needing a vet's assistance, Elsinore Kennel was Green Mountain Clinic's most valued account. Tag had promised months ago that he'd attend the blessed event.

Stopping only to scribble a prescription for Pookie's pain-killer, he left Carol Anne to cancel the rest of his appointments, then roared off to the kennel. The afternoon blurred into a succession of squirming, squeaking, blind furry bundles, each needing its nostrils wiped clear and its ribs gently massaged with a soft cloth before it was presented to the anxious mother and her exuberant breeder.

Normally Tag loved whelpings, but this time, tired as he was and still smarting from rejection, he simply gritted his teeth and endured. Sometime between the eighth and ninth puppy he began to watch the clock. By now it would be safe to move Pookie. Carol Anne could give Susannah her post-op instructions, but had she gotten the name of the stable where Susannah would be keeping her stud? *Gelding,* he reminded himself.

Because even if the woman was now off-limits, Pookie was still his patient. If Susannah didn't bring the horse back for Tag's inspection tomorrow, he'd have to hunt her down. There were only five stables he could think of in the neighborhood.

The sun had set and the cold clamped down like a vise of black iron when he escaped the kennel. Numb with fatigue, he paused by his truck, wondering where he'd left his jacket, then remembered. Susannah. She'd have left it with Carol Anne, he supposed, and felt a moment's quickening. Would it now smell of her—flowers, horse and bourbon?

Get a grip, Taggart! Jaw clenched to keep his teeth from chattering, he drove toward the clinic and his cottage behind. Past suppertime and he'd skipped lunch, he realized. There were store-bought pizzas in his freezer. Flip one of those in the oven, down a beer or two tonight—he deserved it—then to bed. Tomorrow was anoth— He took his foot off the accelerator.

Light glowed in the clinic windows, though it was past six. And Carol Anne's ancient Ford was still parked out front. As he came through the door she looked up from the other side of the reception counter. "Emergency?" He supposed he was good for one more.

"Not...exactly."

"She left her horse here?" he guessed, and felt a sudden, ridiculous surge of hope and pleasure.

"Huh! They drove off not half an hour after you left."

He frowned. "You didn't tell her it would be better to—"

"I did and she wouldn't. Said she had to hit the road and that was that."

He'd met plenty of self-centered owners these past few months. He'd not have put Susannah among them. He supposed her horse would be all right as long as she took the curves carefully. Still, he didn't like it.

"She asked me the best road to take for Boston," Carol Anne added.

"Boston!" Two hours to the southeast? What the hell had she been doing up here, if— "She didn't say anything about a stable here in town?"

Carol Anne shook her head with grim satisfaction.

Well...that was that, then. He might as well have dreamed her. No, she'd left him—or actually taken—one thing to remember her by. Tag stared at the coatrack standing in the corner beyond the file cabinets. "Where's my coat?" He *liked* that coat, an old leather bomber jacket, Second World War, which he'd found in a Boston army-navy store his last year in high school. He'd shed blood for that coat once in a bar, the time a drunken biker took a fancy to it. And now Susannah had it off him for nothing but a smile? *Left it in the barn,* he assured himself, swinging toward the door. She wouldn't have—

"That was *your* jacket she was wearing?" Carol Anne gave a cackling laugh. "Well, *that's* the topper on a day to remember! You sure can pick 'em, Doc.'' She turned toward the rack to pull down her own quilted overcoat.

''She pay with cash or a check?'' If she'd paid by check, he could track her down through her bank. He wanted that jacket back, by God, and more than that, he wanted one last look at her face. Clearly he'd missed something the first time.

''Oh, no, something better.'' Carol Anne shrugged into her coat. ''She was fresh out of cash, is how she put it. And I told her we don't take out-of-town checks.''

''You could have made an exception.''

''Ha! I said she could put it on a card, and she gave me a butter-wouldn't-melt look and said something seemed to be wrong with her cards.''

''And so?'' He wasn't going to like the punch line if Carol Anne had stayed past closing to deliver it.

''So I said, let me try, anyway.''

''And she didn't have any,'' Tag muttered to himself. She drove around the country, ripping off gelding services from sucker vets? What kind of a con was that?

''She had an American Express and two Visa gold cards.''

But? Tag crossed his arms on the counter and waited for it.

''Every one of which had been canceled.''

''Right. Canceled.'' He rubbed the back of his aching neck. ''So you told her goodbye and God bless?'' She could have had his services for the asking. Could have had much more than that, if she'd wanted. There'd been no need to rip him off.

''You must be kidding. I asked Ms. Colton just how she intended to pay in that case—''

''Colton.'' He was missing something here. Had missed a whole truckload of somethings. Must have left his brains in bed this morning, when he rolled out at 3 a.m. to take that call about the cat. ''Colton? Her name was Mack.''

''Susannah M. Colton, according to her cards. I wrote it down here, along with her address.''

Tag stifled an impulse to lean across the counter and strangle his assistant. Nothing was wrong, nothing really. Susannah *had* left him a way to reach her. Had no doubt been too flustered by Carol Anne's evil eye to remember his jacket. She'd drop it in the mail when she'd reached her destination. ''May I have it?'' He tried for exaggerated patience, but it came out closer to a snarl.

''You surely may.'' The med tech plucked a sheet of paper from an under-counter drawer, then something shiny. ''And *here's* how she paid.'' A cold, tiny object was dropped into his outstretched palm. ''She said to send her the change care of this address—'' Carol Anne waved her paper and smirked ''—once we've hocked it.''

Tag lifted the ring to the light. Fire glimmered, then flashed. ''A diamond!'' he said blankly. Big enough to choke a goose. Engagement ring, he supposed. Married, but she didn't like men, she'd said, not that way.

''And if you believe that, Doc, you shouldn't be let outdoors alone. It'll be zirconium, I guarantee, worth fifty if we're lucky.''

Had she been wearing this ring when he met her? No. He'd have noticed. Tag snatched the paper from Carol Anne's fingers and read:

Susannah M. Colton
Fleetfoot Farm
RR 1
Versailles, KY 36502

Fleetfoot Farm. It rang a distant, somehow ominous, bell.

''*Five* cancellations,'' Carol Anne muttered. ''Doc Higgins will have kittens when I...''

They both looked up as headlights swept the room, followed by a second pair, then a third. Brakes yelped in the parking lot. Doors slammed. Footsteps approached at a run.

Tag groaned. As Carol Anne had said, this was a day to remember. And clearly it wasn't done yet. He dropped Susannah's ring into his pocket and clenched his fingers around it. Three cars at once, so this wouldn't be a run-of-the mill vet's emergency—an injured cat or a puppy with fits. Another car roared into the lot. He drew a breath and headed for the door. You heard of such crises in vet school. They were every beginner vet's worst nightmare, a what-if scenario that if you were lucky, would never happen to you: *A car wrecks on a nearby road—something messy and terrible, a head-on involving a school bus or a motorcycle.*

And the way the nightmare always plays out, the local M.D.'s away or falling-down drunk. So they turn to the next best thing, a veterinarian. *So here we go.* People were just big furless animals, at heart, and if there was one thing he did well in life, this was it. He could help.

As Tag threw open the door a fifth car wheeled in off the road… No, this was a van. With the logo of the local TV station emblazoned along its side. Lights flashed in his face— he blinked and took a step backward. Not a wreck—a media feeding frenzy.

With its prey in sight. "Dr. Taggart?"

"Dr. Taggart!"

"*Sir!* How does it feel to have gelded Payback, the finest racing sire ever bred in America?"

No. No way. Not possible.

"Doctor, were you aware that Payback was insured for some sixty million dollars with Lloyd's of…"

Pookie. Pookums. *Payback.* He'd never been to a horse race, but even he had heard that name.

A brunette in a tailored suit stormed the steps, fluffed her hair and spun toward the onlookers. Red lights gleamed like weasel eyes as cameras rolled. "We're talking tonight with

Dr. Richard Taggart, small-town veterinarian in southern Ver-mont,'' she declared, and thrust a microphone under his nose. ''Dr. Taggart, when America thinks horse racing in the twen-tieth century, only three names come to mind. Secretariat. Ruffian. And greatest of them all, the stallion Payback, Triple Crown winner, five-time Eclipse Horse of the Year, sire of some nineteen millionaire offspring, crown jewel of world-famous Fleetfoot Farm in Kentucky, who up until today com-manded a stud fee of *four hundred thousand* dollars per mare! So would you care to explain to racing fans everywhere why you gelded…''

Voices receded into a yammering din of white noise. Tag stared blindly into the blaze of lights. As if she stood just beyond them, meeting his gaze—and laughing. Laughing at him with her honeyed, lying, beautiful mouth and her eyes like a Texas blue norther. Well, she'd sure blown *his* life away! Seventeen years of it, since the day he'd decided to become a vet, instead of a car thief.

''Sir, Stephen Colton, owner of Payback, states that you were never authorized to perform this procedure, which ren-ders his stallion utterly worthless. Would you care to explain why you—''

''No comment.'' *Not for you, bitch.* He stared out past the lights. *Not for any of you vultures!* He'd save his comments and his own questions for the one woman who could answer them, once he got his hands around her lovely neck. He winced as another flash went off, then gazed steadily into the cameras. Because somewhere out there, she'd be watching. *Read it in my eyes, Tex, wherever you are. You can run, you can hide, but I'm coming to get you. Gonna get you, babe, if it's the last thing I do!*

CHAPTER FOUR

PAYBACK WAS THE LEAD story on the eleven o'clock news that night, and the network anchor reported it with a stern, semisorrowful expression that failed to hide his glee in relating such a juicy scandal.

Phone off the hook and with emergency bottle of scotch near at hand, Tag shoved a tape into his VCR, gazed owlishly at all its buttons, then nodded to himself and hit Record. Facts could be weapons and he didn't mean to miss a single one.

"In a bizarre and still-breaking story," intoned the anchorman, "NBC News has learned that sometime late last night, Susannah Mack Colton, wife of bluegrass millionaire Stephen Colton, secretly removed the world famous thoroughbred stud Payback from his stable at Fleetfoot Farm in Kentucky. The former exercise girl drove the Triple Crown winner and five-time Eclipse Horse of the Year to a small town in Vermont, where she paid veterinarian Richard D. Taggart to...geld the famous stallion." Brief pause to let the magnitude of this outrageous act sink in around the nation.

"Seen here in his unforgettable Kentucky Derby victory, headed home eighteen incredible lengths ahead of the competition—" the camera shifted to a clip of a chocolate-brown stallion covering the ground in gigantic, effortless strides, a jockey crouched high on his withers with whip hand unmoving, while in the background a grandstand seethed with silently screaming racegoers "—Payback has long since retired to stand at stud at Fleetfoot Farm, renowned racing stable in the Kentucky bluegrass." The view shifted to an overhead shot, showing the rest of the Derby field laboring farther and farther behind, then Payback sweeping smoothly under the wire at the finish line, while the anchorman continued off camera, "As top racing sire in America for the last eight years, Payback commanded a stud fee of four hundred *thousand* dollars...per mare."

The camera returned to the studio and the anchorman. "And in an average breeding season, the stallion serviced one hundred of the finest thoroughbred broodmares in the world." The newsman lifted his craggy brows to fix his audience with a significant gaze. "Meaning, folks, that this equine Romeo's earnings averaged out to some forty *million* dollars per year!"

The anchorman touched the tiny receiver in his ear and his smile broadened to a blissful grin, immediately stifled. "In fact, NBC has just learned that one of the holders of a lifetime breeding right in Payback is Qeen Elizabeth II of England, herself an ardent racing fan.

"According to owner Stephen Colton, Payback was insured by Lloyd's of London for *sixty* million dollars. But with his gelding today, this stud of the century's value has been effectively reduced to...zero.

"The question that racing fans everywhere are demanding be answered tonight is *why?* Why did Susannah Mack Colton, er...pluck this four-legged golden goose?"

The camera shifted from the newsman's wounded perplexity to a shot of Susannah, standing somewhere in a parking lot, gripping Payback's halter. The camera lights made her eyes seem enormous, bruised by shadows, but her chin was tipped to a familiar angle of defiance. "When Mrs. Colton, Payback at her side, was asked that question during a press conference she called in Boston earlier this evening, she had only this to say..." The sound switched to a taped recording, and Tag winced at the hunting-pack yammer of four reporters shouting questions at once.

An insistent tenor rose above the others as a microphone

was thrust into the picture. "But *why,* Mrs. Colton? Why did you have Payback gelded?"

The gelding's ears flattened back and he lunged teeth-first at the encroaching mike. Susannah staggered, then dug in her heels and hauled his nose around. "Why don't you go ask my husband?" she cried over her shoulder. Payback shook his head again, shaking her like a rag doll.

The view swung wildly, showing reporters scattering like a flock of panicked pigeons, then steadied on Susannah, who stood poised and alert, facing Payback as he reared. When his flailing forefeet touched earth, she closed in and caught his halter, backing him away from her inquisitors.

"*Damn,* Susannah!" Tag muttered. If the horse yanked her under his hooves…

But she had him under control again and she glanced back at the cameras. "Now that's enough! He's tired and ya'll got what you came for."

"Just one more question, Mrs. Colton!" called the tenor, a short, hatchet-faced man. "Who did the actual gelding?"

"I *told* ya'll, that doesn't matter. What matters is—"

"You phoned the *Boston Globe* this afternoon from the Green Mountain Clinic in Vermont."

"H-h-how—" She stood, blinking in the harsh lights, mouth ajar.

"Caller ID, you nitwit!" Tag groaned and gripped a handful of his own hair. She'd set up her news conference from the barn phone—and obviously never stopped to think that any half-competent investigative reporter would surely have—

"So if you know-it-alls know it already," she cried, then staggered as Payback sidestepped, "what are you asking *me* for? Oh, what's the—" She wheeled her horse in a circle. The picture wobbled as the cameraman retreated from Payback's wicked back heels, then the scene ended—to be replaced by Tag himself, scowling from the top step of the clinic.

"Good God!" Tag thought. He looked like *that*? Ax murderer at bay?

"We asked the same question of Dr. Richard Taggart. Why would a reputable veterinarian agree to geld the finest racing sire ever bred in America—and without consent of his owner?"

"No comment!" Tag's image snarled at the camera.

Tag moaned and dropped his head in his hands. With a few final words promising to keep viewers informed of late-breaking developments, the anchor wrapped up—to be replaced by a cheery jingle assuring Tag that if he used a certain breath mint, all his troubles would be over.

Tag grabbed the remote, slapped the mute, groped blindly for his Scotch. *Reputable vet!* Funny how they could say one thing and mean precisely the other. And once they'd put their spin on the situation... Maybe he should have talked when they were hollering their idiot questions.

His stomach revolted at the thought of himself, pleading his innocence to those carrion pickers, while half the country gleefully watched. *Don't whine, and never explain to strangers* was more his style.

"Tomorrow," he consoled himself. He'd talk with Glassman, the lawyer he'd consulted when he'd bought into Higgins's practice. And he'd talk to Higgins—if the old man hadn't suffered another coronary tonight watching the news.

He looked up at the TV in time to see a hulking policeman palm the top of Susannah's crinkled-silk head, then tuck her neatly into the back of a patrol car. "Crap!" He snatched up the remote, jabbed buttons.

"—on charges of horse theft," concluded the announcer, while behind glass, Susannah lunged for a nonexistent door handle, then rapped furiously on the window. "Just one more twist in this bizarre tale about a legendary racehorse, a jockey's beautiful daughter from Texas and a bluegrass millionaire,'' observed a voice-over as the police car set off.

The camera closed in greedily on Susannah's face. Her lips were moving—she was calling someone? Cursing someone? Her husband, her lawyer, God…all three at once? Her expression was angry and urgent and somehow forlorn. The car turned a corner, and the camera cut away to a hotel fire in Chicago.

"Serves you right, babe. Lock you up and throw away the key, for all I care." Not that they would. Some five-hundred-dollar an hour lawyer would be getting her out on bail in no time. Millionaires' wives didn't spend the night in jail.

"More's the pity." Tag lifted his glass to take another swallow—then deliberately set it aside. What he needed tomorrow was a clear head.

Today he'd taken it on the chin, but tomorrow was his turn. Time to start punching back. Susannah Mack Colton might be a career wrecker—a walking one-woman demolition derby!—but he'd worked too hard these last seventeen years to go down without a fight. A street fight, South Boston style. He might have cleaned up his act since his teen years, but he hadn't forgotten a move. "Messed with the wrong vet, Blue Eyes, I'm telling you."

So to bed, then tomorrow.

TOMORROW WAS EVEN WORSE.

It started with *The Today Show* and an exclusive interview with Stephen Colton, Susannah's husband. Hearing the intro, Tag dashed in from the kitchen where he was scrambling eggs. A wide-eyed woman, he couldn't recall her name, leaned toward a man sitting at ease in the network's New York City studio. She rested a commiserating hand on the sleeve of his perfectly tailored suit. "I understand that your marriage was an unquestionable love match, Mr. Colton. Oh, may I call you Stephen? Yes, well, I believe Susannah was an exercise girl in your stables, Stephen, when you first met?''

Colton shook his head. Razor-cut dark blond hair, shining and flawlessly parted, didn't stir. The guy looked to be a few years older than his own age of thirty and Tag supposed women would think him handsome, in spite of those wire-rim glasses. *Pretty boy,* would be the male opinion. Certainly it was his.

Colton's smile was gently nostalgic. ''In the stables of a business associate of mine in Texas. I flew down to buy a promising filly.'' His eyes crinkled. ''Came home with two, instead.''

''Self-satisfied ass!'' Tag sat and turned up the sound while the interviewer chuckled appreciatively, then switched back to Deeply Concerned. ''It sounds like Cinderella and her prince! A girl who loved horses and a man who bred and raced some of the nation's finest. So what went *wrong* with this perfect fairy tale?''

Colton shrugged his pinstriped shoulders. ''Why do people fall out of love? Who's to say? We came from entirely different circumstances…''

''Different worlds,'' crooned the woman.

He smiled sadly. ''Mint juleps in silver goblets versus Lone Star beer in longneck bottles. I suppose I was a fool to think she could ever…'' He shrugged again. ''Anyway, we gave it our best shot for two years, but it was time to move on. At least…I thought so.''

The woman leaned forward, hanging on his every word, her expression avid. ''You mean…?''

His good humor faded. ''I mean, I asked Susannah for a divorce two nights ago.''

The interviewer quivered like a springer spaniel with a rabbit in sight. ''The night that she…took Payback and drove away?''

''She *stole* Payback later that night. Yes.''

Tag swore softly, savagely. *You used me for that, Susannah?*

"So it was your asking for a divorce that triggered her..."

"That and the news—which I suppose I didn't deliver as tactfully as I might have done. Perhaps that bit could have waited till later. I also told her that I planned to remarry. That I'd fallen in love with another woman."

"Ohhh..." The interviewer sounded halfway to orgasm. "I see. *Yes.* So this was an act of...spite!"

"Spite, malice and revenge," Colton agreed in his Kentucky gentleman's drawl. It was quicker and more mannered than Susannah's breezy twang.

"Payback, Texas style!"

"I'm afraid they do believe in getting their own back down there. Don't mess with Texans, or however it goes. I certainly knew Susannah had a temper and I suppose I expected...some sort of tantrum. Maybe a few dishes smashed or possibly the whole table service, but..."

"But to...*smash* the finest racehorse you ever bred! That anyone in *America* ever bred! Payback was a national treasure. I think you could say he belonged to...*all of us.*" The interviewer held that thought for three beats of nationwide mourning, then cocked her head and wrinkled her charming nose. "You know, Freud's somewhat out of fashion nowadays, but might one argue that there's almost something...symbolic in a scorned wife's *gelding*—" she giggled "—her husband's most treasured stud."

Colton's eyebrows shot up, but apparently he decided not to take offense. His smirk was confiding. Merrily roguish. "Ah, but I have others!"

"And a spare set of gold-plated balls for dress occasions, rich boy?" Tag snarled.

The interviewer giggled. "Other *stallions,* you mean!"

What had Susannah seen in this...this... Tag's head jerked

around at the smell of— *"Damn!"* The eggs! He bolted for his smoky kitchen.

THE DAY SLID STRAIGHT downhill from there. Reporters were camped out at the back door of the clinic when Tag went in to work. He had to wade through the baying pack, hands jammed in his pockets to keep from punching the eager faces thrust into his own.

"Dr. Taggart!"

"Dr. Taggart, would you care to comment on—"

"Dr. Taggart, were you aware that—"

"Move it or *lose* it, pal." He gained the back door and unlocked it, opened it wide enough to slide in sideways—

"Taggart, how much did Mrs. Colton have to pay you to get you to geld Payback?"

An ice cube slithered down his spine. They *couldn't* think he'd— He halted, half in, half out the door. "We charged her our standard fee for—" His heart dropped a beat as he remembered. At least they'd *tried* to charge her the usual fee for that procedure. God, Susannah's ring! *Let it be zirconium, oh, please God!*

He had a feeling God had gone south on vacation this week.

He slammed the door on his own aborted statement and locked it. Fists pounded, voices rose indignantly. Did they think they owned him? If Payback was a national treasure, then what was he? National whipping boy? He half ran toward the office. "Carol Anne!"

She sat behind her counter with a stunned and mutinous look on her face, her hair escaping its pins. Beyond the locked front door, he could hear more of the same mob. "Carol Anne, did you tell anyone about the ring? Her ring?"

"And good morning to you, *too,* doctor."

"I'm sorry, good morning. The ring—did you tell anyone?"

Her glower turned to a blinking stillness. She sniffed, opened the appointment book and buried her nose in it.

Control, control. If he shook her she'd quit. "*Who,* Carol?" She flipped to the next page, as if today could simply be skipped over. He leaned above her, a silent growl vibrating deep in his throat. She hunched her shoulders. "Doc Higgins, okay?"

Higgins wasn't so bad. Higgins was as stingy with his words as he was with his gauze pads. He wouldn't—

"—and my sister," she added in a mutter, not looking up.

Wonderful. "All right, I want you to toddle straight out that door and tell her—"

"She's already gone in to work. Her shift starts at six."

Carol Anne's sister was a waitress at the best place—the only place—in town to get an early breakfast. At six this morning the diner's counter would have been lined elbow to elbow with newsmen, sucking down coffee and local gossip. "Cripes. Then I want you to call her and—"

"Call—ha! I unplugged the phone. Somebody's got an automatic dialler locked in on us. You can't call in or out." She rubbed her nose and looked up. Her eyes were red-rimmed. "And you know what's on our answering machine from last night? Loonytunes calling in from all over, threatening to burn us down, or blow us up, or do to you what you did to that stupid nag!" She snatched a tissue from her pocket. "If you'd only listened to me…"

All right, forget the ring. By now that horse was out of the barn. "What did Higgins say?" He'd not been able to face the old man last night. Nor call, not with his own line jammed with incoming viciousness.

"He said you should've listened to me."

Tag counted backward from ten, then slowly up again. "What else?"

"He said you'd better get yourself a good lawyer and it better not be on his dime."

"I was going to phone Glassman at nine. Guess I'll have to go see him, first break in the schedule I get."

That break came earlier than expected. The first appointment of the day was a no-show. Simply forgot, or something more ominous? The second, Mrs. Wiggly and her cat, Sherman, arrived on time, but after they'd run the gauntlet of newshounds, Mrs. W was near tears and Sherman was doing a Persian variation of the Saber Dance.

When the third and fourth appointments were no-shows, it began to look like a trend. The fifth was an overweight dachshund, who bit a newsman on his way in the door. The reporter threatened to sue. Tag came out and offered to punch his nose for him, which seemed to cheer the reporter and his photographer no end, after which Tag completed Bismarck's exam, then declared the clinic closed for the morning. He hung a sign in the window and left Carol Anne trying to phone out to cancel the rest of their appointments.

Because even more than loyal patients Tag needed a good lawyer.

He took the long way into town, which was down a logging road, then up over a rocky hillside pasture, thankful that his new truck had four-wheel drive. By the time he reached Main Street he'd lost his pursuers. Shutting the outer door to Glassman's office behind him, Tag breathed a sigh of relief—Ollie, Ollie oxen free—then grimaced as he remembered who'd said that last.

Glassman's receptionist looked up with a smile. It froze on her face.

"Hi, Barbara. I know I don't have an appointment, but..." He gave her his best grin. They'd had a flirtation going while Glassman had been drawing up his contracts to buy into Higgins's practice. He'd considered asking her out, but somehow couldn't see himself ever telling Barbara about the car collection he'd started at age thirteen. Barb believed in The Law, not the unbearable beauty of Porsches.

"I'm afraid—"

"Barb, if he could see me for even a minute. I'm in the soup. I guess you know, if you saw—"

"I did." She shot a glance over her shoulder toward the inner office. "But I'm afraid we—he—can't help you." She lowered her voice. "He took a retainer this morning. The other side."

Tag stared at her blankly.

"Colton. *Stephen* Colton," she hissed. "He's retained us."

Colton? Here? "To do what?"

"I've no idea, Tag, and if I had, I couldn't tell you. Colton's man showed up waving a check for five thousand half an hour ago. They're in there now, so if you don't mind…"

"Yeah. Sure." Just like that, wave a check and he was the enemy? Well, hell, there were other lawyers.

THERE WERE THREE OTHERS in town—and Colton had retained all three. For a pretty boy, he played dirty. Outside the office of the third and last, Tag stopped to rub his aching neck. Okay, so now what? Drive to Bennington?

But would a small-town lawyer do the job, if Colton intended to go for blood? Maybe he should hire a Boston heavy?

But a big-time legal shark would do his own bloodletting, and Tag had zip to spare. He'd used every dollar he'd saved since graduation to buy his first slice of Higgins's practice.

And surely it was too soon to be talking lawsuits? First he should talk to the guy. Colton might be a snob, but he hadn't looked stupid or unreasonable. And his real quarrel was with his crazy wife, not an innocent bystander. Find a phone then, that was next. Once Colton had heard Tag's side of the story…

It took him eighteen tries to get past a busy signal. When someone picked up the phone at last, Tag drew a thankful breath.

"May I speak to Mr. Colton, please?"

"I'm afraid he's not available just now." Another pattering Kentucky drawl—a woman's, sweetly professional. "But may I take a message?"

He wasn't leaving his apologies and regrets with a secretary. "Yes, um, would you tell him Dr. Richard Taggart called and that I urgently need to talk with him? I'll keep calling on the hour, every hour, till we connect." No use giving his own number, since the line was jammed with crank callers.

That done, and maybe a call was all it would take to straighten this nightmare out, Tag headed back to his clinic.

Where Carol Anne's car was no longer parked in front of the building. Gone home to lunch, he supposed. But like piranhas gathering, the number of reporters had increased. They turned as one when he parked, beamed as they recognized him, but rather than rushing to meet him, they held their ground by his front door.

As Tag reached the steps, he saw why. A burly stranger was screwing something into the clinic's doorjamb—a steel hasp. "*You!* What d'you think you're doing?" He jabbed an elbow in someone's ribs, shoved another aside, gained the top step—just as a second man snapped a padlock in place.

Locking him out of his own clinic! For a roaring moment, the world went bloodred. Tag grabbed the lock man's collar with both hands. "You bastard!" He hauled him up on tiptoe.

"I wouldn't!" squeaked the man. His helper loomed at Tag's shoulder. Laying a hand on Tag's biceps, he dug in stubby fingers and breathed meaningfully in his ear, "I *really* wouldn't, Dr. Taggart. You've got trouble enough already."

So what's a little more? Still, Tag let go of Squeaky. "What the *hell* d'you think you're doing, locking my—"

The other man—a lawyer, who else would wear a three-piece suit in this town?—shook his head. "Not anymore, it isn't. Dr. Higgins sold out."

Sold out? Tag stood, sucking for a breath that wouldn't come. Sold, just like that? That fast? "To...to whom?" But that was obvious. How many millionaires had he pissed off this week?

"The FYA Corporation of Delaware."

Colton's cover. Had to be. "Higgins didn't own it all to sell! *I* own—"

"One-fifth of the goodwill—and none of the property. Yes, we know that. And you're welcome to take your share of the patients and practice anywhere else in this town, or any town you please."

Right, practice small-animal medicine without a clinic? Without supplies, instruments, exam rooms, a phone? Using what for money in the meantime?

Higgins's accountant had divided the business that way for some arcane tax reason that Tag had never bothered to follow. The deal had required that Tag first buy the clinic's patients, its goodwill, while he rented use of the facilities from Higgins. Once he owned a hundred percent of the goodwill, they'd agreed that then he'd start buying the property, using his share of monthly earnings to do so, while the old man phased out of the business. In five years he'd have owned it all.

The lawyer turned to his heavy. "Leo, if I may have that box?" The thug scooped up a box that had been sitting on the stoop by his size fourteen feet and passed it over. The lawyer presented it with a tiny smile. "We cleaned out your desk for you. And your diplomas. When you wish to pick up your share of the patient files, and one-fifth of the Rolodex, then please call my office." He placed a business card on top of the box Tag had automatically accepted. "We'll be keeping the books for a few weeks while they're audited. But once that's done, then—"

"Sure." Oblivious to the flashes going off as cameras recorded the awful moment, Tag watched the pair go. Just like that, they could chop him off at the knees?

He could feel a howl rising in his throat. Could see himself tossing the box aside—all that remained of his hopes in one pathetic box?—and hurling himself on the departing shyster's back. Dragging him down. Ripping and tearing and gouging as he'd learned long ago on the street....

What d'you think this is for, Taggart my man? Knuckles gently rapping his forehead. Tag blinked, the words drifting back over the years one more time when he needed them. Jake talking, the big young counselor at the reform school, been-there smile, words that could cut through Tag's rage when no one else could reach him. *You use that to think with, kid. It's not decoration. Fists are for fools and losers, and that's not you, Taggart.*

So Tag drew a breath and nodded to someone not there. Fists jammed in his pockets, he stood by his padlocked door while the cameras probed his face. While his bright future drove away in a shiny blue BMW. Blinking hard, he looked up at the lowering sky. Once upon a time, he wouldn't have been able to resist a car like that. But he was somebody else now.

At least, as long as they'd let him be, he was.

A flake of snow drifted down…then another. Winter.

CHAPTER FIVE

A PHONE CALL to Carol Anne, Tag told himself, as he strode up the walk to his cottage. Remind her to feed the stray tomcat while he was away. Presumably Higgins could get her past that padlock. Then throw together a couple of days' change of clothes. It might take that long in Boston to find the right lawyer.

Once he'd hired his big-city shark, he'd worry about shark feed. Somewhere in Boston he'd find a jeweler to buy Susannah's ring. Because if Colton had given her that rock, it wasn't zirconium. With any luck—if there was any luck left anywhere in the world—he'd get enough to pay his lawyer. *And no, Susannah, I won't be sending you back your change, care of Fleetfoot Farm.* Her bill was higher than she'd dreamed and mounting by the minute.

And if he couldn't salvage his career, then her ring would be just the first installment on all she owed him.

A letter was taped to his front door. Tag took it inside with him, ripped it open, then wadded it as he cursed aloud. A notice from the FYA Corporation, terminating his tenancy in their cottage, effective a month from today. Teeth clenched till they ached, he stalked to his TV. He'd set the VCR to record the noon news before he left the house that morning.

The twelve o'clock lead came as no surprise. The cameras showed Susannah Colton, sometime earlier that morning, coming down the Boston courthouse steps with a grim-looking suit—her lawyer, according to the voice-over. Besieged on all sides by reporters, she looked tiny and dog tired.

More teenager than woman in her jeans and a man's leather bomber jacket that hung down to her slim thighs.

Tag growled as he recognized it, but still, something twisted inside. She was wearing the same clothes she'd worn yesterday when he met her. She'd spent the night in jail, after all?

The newscaster confirmed it as reporters blocked the couple's way. With one arm draped protectively around her shoulders, seeming almost to hold her up, Susannah's lawyer was doing the talking. As for his client, a night in a cell seemed to have knocked the stuffing, all that Texas grit and sass, out of her. She looked fragile, stunned. Less like a desperado horse thief or a vindictive wife than a scared little owl, staring out from shelter with those wide, haunted eyes and her feathers all ruffled.

A woman having second thoughts was what she looked like, and unpleasant ones. *A little revenge seemed like a good idea at the time, huh, Tex?* But now she was realizing. *Bit off more than you could chew, did you, darlin'?*

Or maybe she only needed a good night's sleep to regain her spunk—and her spite. Looking at Susannah, Tax had missed most of the lawyer's statement. He rewound the tape and this time focused on her designated knight.

"Mrs. Colton has no statement at this time," that gentleman said grandly if predictably.

The surrounding pack resumed their yelping. Susannah put her head down and allowed her companion to steer her to a waiting car. The anchorman switched back to the studio.

He interviewed an expert on equine insurance, who hemmed and hawed and finally hazarded a guess that Lloyd's of London would decline to pay out on Payback's policy because, one, the horse had not been killed but only altered, and two, that horrendous act had been instigated not by some crazed outsider but by Stephen Colton's own lawful wedded wife.

Tag attempted a whistle, but his lips were too dry. Sixty million dollars irretrievably washed down the drain? Even a millionaire might miss a sum like that! If Colton wasn't the forgiving sort, and it looked less and less as if he was...

The question was, once he'd had time to cool down, who would Colton blame?

BY THE TIME Tag checked into a Boston hotel the tabloids had the story.

Revenge of the Century! shrieked the one in his hotel lobby, in two-inch type above a picture of Payback and one of the Coltons, kissing at the altar.

Payback, Texas Style! blared one of the rags he saw in a drugstore, walking back from supper at a cheap fishhouse down near the docks.

Don't Mess with Texans! warned another.

By morning the *Boston Globe* had dug deeper. *$30,000 Payoff to Geld Payback!* yelled its banner headline. Ice in his guts, Tag told himself that at least now he knew what to ask for Susannah's diamond. Assuming the jerks hadn't made up that sum along with the rest of their facts.

By the time he'd hired his lawyer, the evening papers were out and somehow they'd dug up his juvenile records—which his lawyer had spent the past two hours assuring him were sealed. Buried forever. Not to worry.

Ex-Car Thief Took $30,000 Bribe to Ruin Payback! was how one headline put it.

Why bother with lawyers and the courts? He'd been tried and convicted already, and he could guess the sentence.

SHE SHOULD HAVE BROUGHT an umbrella. The collapsible one she'd bought in Paris was up at the big house along with the rest of her stuff. Her lawyer was still working on retrieving all that.

She should have bought, at least, a raincoat, one of those

cheap plastic things. But she'd be counting her pennies from here on out. So the bomber would have to do. Leaning back against Brady's pickup, Susannah Mack Colton tipped her Stetson to let the rain run off, folded her arms and snuggled her nose below the collar of Doc Taggart's old jacket. She sucked in a breath of cold, damp Kentucky air, savoring with it the scent of man and leather, oddly comforting on this comfortless day.

Beyond the white board fence, a hundred yards up a low hill, the crowd was still gathering. A good-sized group, Brady would have been pleased. Black umbrellas, dark clothes, like a bunch of mushrooms sprouted in the rain.

She wondered suddenly what they were burying Brady in. Should have been his old jockey silks, the ones he wore winning the Derby on Payback. But they'd never fit. He'd put on the pounds since he'd quit the track and stepped down to stallion groom.

"Never mind. They'll give you fresh ones upstairs," she drawled softly, and dug in her pocket for his flask.

One swallow left since the night he'd given it to her. "That's for warmth, not for whoopee," he'd warned as they parted. "You save me a drop."

He'd never come for it. She hadn't had a sip since she'd found out why, that awful night in a Boston jail.

The crowd was bigger now. A wall of darkness ringed the grave. She tipped her brim to hide all that and looked down at his name on the flask. Brady, engraved in curly letters on old silver. A fine, fancy gift from a grateful British bettor, that time Brady won the Epsom on a five-to-one shot.

She had to struggle with the cap. Last closed by Dr. Taggart's big, capable hands, she remembered with a rueful grimace. She held up the flask to the dripping sky. "Here's to you, Brady." Something warmer than a raindrop ran down her cheek and she brushed it away. "If they have horse races in heaven, then you and Daddy must be runnin' neck and neck 'bout now. God bless…and Godspeed.'' She held the last taste on her tongue, fire and sweetness, then welcome warmth around the heart. *G'bye, ol' friend.* She buried her nose in the jacket again and breathed deep.

When she heard the sound of a car stopping behind the truck, Susannah didn't look up. *God give me strength!* If it was more reporters… One more stupid question, just *one* more, *and it's Katy, bar the door!*

''Miss? I'm afraid you can't stop here, Miss.''

Oh, one of them. Eyes narrowed, shoulders squaring for a fight, she turned her head slowly. This was a public road even if Stephen would never admit it and had convinced the county he had the right to patrol outside his own fences, bully anybody who dared look at his farm.

Her muscles eased as she recognized the approaching guard. ''Hey, Randy.'' Randall was one of the few decent ones who didn't give her the creeps. Most of the security guards her husband hired seemed to be angry, disappointed men. As if life didn't give them enough opportunities to use those guns that dragged down their belts.

''Miz—!'' The guard yanked off his hat from long habit, then stood there twisting it. ''Mrs. Colton, ma'am! I didn't recognize—''

''Hardly surprisin'.'' Stephen had always insisted she dress her part around the farm. If she must wear pants, then it had to be jodhpurs with a silk shirt or a tweed jacket. Hair up in a snooty French twist. Only when she rode out with the exercise boys at dawn was she allowed to wear jeans and let her hair fly free. Funny that Stephen fell for her, looking like that, then had to change that first thing once he got her.

The guard glanced from her to the distant ceremony. ''Oh. I guess he wouldn't let you…?''

''Nope.'' She'd had her lawyer ask, since Stephen wasn't taking her calls. Word had come back promptly from on high.

Translated from Houlihan's tactful legalese, the word was, "Not in this lifetime, sugarbabe!"

Funny how little you could know a man in two years. She'd known Stephen was tough. Kentucky hardboot, they called a shrewd horseman hereabouts. But just how hard his boots were, she'd only begun to learn these past few days. She had a feeling the lesson wasn't done yet, either.

"Sure was a shame," Randall observed, putting his hat on and coming to stand beside her, facing uphill. "Surprised the heck out of me when I heard. That old man was so tough I'd have said Brady'd bury us all."

"Yeah." She'd thought so, too. But then, her own father had gone in seconds—one horse stumbling in front of his own, then the pileup from behind. Winged hero to smashed cripple in less time than it took her to scream and rush to press her hands to the TV screen, as if she could lift those tiny, flailing bodies off him. For horse folks, life usually happened fast, and it happened hard.

"But that plate in his skull, a fall on that…" Randall heaved a hound-dog sigh. "And they say he must have knocked it more than once, tumblin' down a whole flight."

"Yeah." *And Brady wouldn't have been hurrying so, 'cept for me.* She swallowed hard and blinked at the distant funeral.

Movement up there, looked like they were almost done. Dropping red Kentucky clay on his coffin, one by one, then trudging off over the crest of the hill.

A tall man dressed in black stepped apart from the dwindling crowd and stood staring down at them, something ominous in his stillness.

"Oh, Jeez, is that the boss?" Randall took two long steps away from her, spun toward his truck, then back again. "If he saw I was talking to you…!"

"You're just tellin' me t'beat it, that's all. He can't blame you for that."

"Oh, can't he?" Good jobs were hard to find out in the

country. A job at Fleetfoot Farm was golden. "But you're not going."

"Not till it's over, I'm not."

"Look, Mrs. Colton, I'm *real* sorry, but—" the guard grabbed her arm and hustled her toward the pickup's door "—get out of here, will you? Please, ma'am? It's my job if you don't."

"*Ouch,* dammit, lemme go!" Even a week before, if Randall had dared lay a finger on her, he'd never have worked again in the bluegrass. Now she was fair game for anyone. The door scraped her shins as he yanked it open. He grabbed her waist and tossed her up on the seat. "You son of a bitch!" She slapped his hands aside.

He shut the door carefully on her, then held it shut, one-handed, while he stooped for her fallen hat. She gave up pushing and rolled down the window. "Bastard!" The tears that had been threatening all day brimmed and overflowed. Her face burned with the shame of it. She didn't cry easily or often. Never before strangers.

"Ma'am, I'm *real* sorry, but y'know, you started it all."

"Ha!" She rubbed her nose and glared past his shoulder. Stephen hadn't missed the show. Thank God she was too far away to see him grinning! *He who laughs last*... It was a phrase he'd always been fond of, trailing it off with a little smirk and a shrug.

"I don't blame you for wanting your own back," Randall was saying, brushing off her hat. "Lot of us had a good laugh when we heard what you'd done."

Maybe the guards and the house staff had. But not *her* people, the grooms and the trainers and the exercise boys down in the stables. They weren't amused. She'd met a groom on the streets of Lexington yesterday and he'd spat at her feet.

"Serves him right, I say. But he's a hard one and they say he *never* forgets if you cross him. I was you, I wouldn't hang around here. I'd want some miles between.'' He offered her the hat with a pleading smile.

It was good advice. Advice she'd already given herself. She'd only stopped to say goodbye, and now there was no one left by the grave but her husband.

A word that wouldn't apply much longer.

She took the Stetson, saw the muddy bootmark on its brim—*well, damn*—and sat blinking frantically. *Don't be such a stupid crybaby!* She dropped it on the seat and started the truck.

''Where're you headed for, ma'am, if y'don't mind my asking?''

''Texas, where else?'' *This kid's had enough of the high life.* Her sister would be waiting for her in Houston, with that big old terry-cloth robe she always loaned Susannah when she came calling, and endless cups of hot chocolate. They'd stay up talking all night, and Saskia wouldn't judge.

She couldn't get back to Texas soon enough. Careful not to look toward the distant watcher, Susannah set her eyes on the open road and drove.

CHAPTER SIX

JUNE IN KENTUCKY. Beyond those towering, wrought-iron gates, Fleetfoot Farm looked like a slice of paradise. More than a square mile of prime bluegrass, according to Tag's guidebook. Hill upon hill of lush emerald green—bluegrass wasn't really blue, so go figure—stitched with white board fences. Flashes of chestnut and bay as thoroughbred yearlings chased each other around a distant pasture. A shady avenue lined in century-old sycamores, rising toward a glimpse of far-off roofs, which would be Colton's antebellum manor.

So it was her upcoming expulsion from this Eden that Susannah had been avenging when she brought him Payback to ruin. To have risen this high, then to lose it. Tag could almost feel pity for the lying little bitch.

Almost. *Has he ever been raced?* Gullible fool, had he really asked that?

Few times, she'd drawled, and looked him straight in the eye. God, she must have been laughing fit to burst!

A heavyset guard paused in the open door of the gatehouse. Piggy eyes moved over Tag's rusting and battered vehicle, an ex state police car he'd recently bought at auction. Its big V-8 engine burned oil and sucked gas at an awesome rate, but as long as you fed the monster, at least it still had some speed. The guard swaggered over to its window, his smile dismissing both man and car. "You here for the tour?" A driver of a heap like this might be allowed to press his nose to the glass, catch a peek of heaven, was the unspoken assumption, but he'd have no real business with the high and mighty.

''Yep.'' Tag dragged his own eyes away from the gun on the man's hip—more firepower than he'd have expected out here in the country—as he mustered a smile. Smiling was his best disguise these days. Since January, not a single gossip rag or network newscast had caught the infamous Dr. Taggart with a smile on his face. ''The tour.''

Like many of the big racing stables and stud farms of the bluegrass, Fleetfoot Farm opened its barns and grounds to its admiring public in the summer months. And the only way he could hope to gain admittance to Susannah's ex's estate was if he was disguised as a lowly tourist.

Because in six months of trying, Tag hadn't managed a meeting with Stephen Colton face-to-face. Nor had he even talked to the elusive bastard over the phone. But for the few glimpses he'd had of the man on TV, his signature on the blizzard of lawsuits that drifted down on Tag's head, his endless army of legal minions, Colton might have been a figment of Tag's worst nightmare. An invisible hand dealing cards of misfortune.

And it was you dragged me into the game, Susannah. But for you, I'd still be— He blinked as the guard thumped his fender.

''...the *bus,* mister,'' he growled, apparently repeating his words. ''See it?'' He jerked a thumb at the gates. Beyond them, halfway along the tunnel of trees, a tour bus chugged uphill. Trailed by three cars and a van, it rounded a bend and disappeared. ''Follow that bus. Stay right at the first and second forks in the drive, then you'll see the parking lot. Just stay with the tour, y'hear?''

Was it branded on his forehead that he was different? Dangerous? Did he look what he felt, lean and angry, like a coyote who'd missed his rabbit three days running? Tag showed his teeth in what he hoped passed for a smile, nodded and steered his beater through the massive green gates, swinging open in electrified silence.

Halfway through, the car died. Twisting the key, he swore and pumped hard on the gas—blue smoke blatted out the back. Time for another quart of oil. He bucketed on through the gap without looking toward the guard, who'd be grinning. Blast this wreck! Blast the woman who'd brought him to this!

He'd lost his beloved pickup, the first and only new wheels he'd ever owned in his life, in the second month of the disaster. He'd sold it to pay his mounting legal fees, since his lawyer had known better than to work for him on credit. But not to worry, Atkins had assured him each time he handed Tag another bill. Come his day in court, it would be obvious to even the densest jury that Tag was innocent of any wrongdoing. He'd operated in good faith, believing Susannah's assertion that she was the owner. Colton could sue, but he'd never win.

Yeah, and the meek shall inherit the earth.

Whatever advice Tag had been buying, Colton obviously had bought better. Or maybe he'd simply known how the game was played. Because each time Tag's lawyer prepared a painstaking defense encompassing hours of depositions, reams of paperwork, phone calls, assistants, charges, countercharges and consultations, the suit would be dropped at the last possible instant. Leaving Tag with more bills to pay.

He'd scramble to meet those debts—then a new lawsuit would loom over the horizon, winnable in the end, ruinous in the desperate meantime. And even knowing the score, Tag had to respond to charges, no matter how ridiculous. You couldn't ignore a lawsuit. Death by law. A slow, nibbling death.

So I don't play that game anymore. No more depending on lawyers. On anyone but himself. It was the way he'd grown up, after all, on the streets of South Boston. In the years since, he'd tried his best to play by society's rules—

and he'd gotten both hands smashed in a drawer for his efforts. From now on it was back to his own rules.

Round the bend he came to a fork in the road. The right-hand choice followed the shoulder of the hill, curving gently around the unseen manor. The track and stables would be at its back, he supposed.

Tag chose the left fork, which burrowed into a glossy dark wall of rhododendrons, then burst out the other side into sunlight. Across a lawn smooth and wide as a golf course, beyond a spouting fountain encircled by red roses, the white columns and tall chimneys of Fleetfoot Farm reached for the sky. Tara north. *My old Kentucky home, be it ever so humble.*

He parked on the raked gravel sweep before the portico, feeling as if a hundred eyes watched him from the French windows to either side of the door. After all his months of trying to make contact, surely it couldn't be this easy? Where was Colton's wall of lawyers, his bodyguards, his secretaries?

The door knocker was a polished bronze horseshoe, mounted curve-down to hold the luck. What must it be like to be born lucky, a fourth-generation millionaire? To never once in your life have gone to bed hungry, wondering how you'd pay the rent? Did Colton have a clue how the other half lived? Two savage knocks and the door swung silently open.

"Yes, sir?" Except for the drawl, the speaker might have been snatched from Central Casting. The perfect English butler. Silvery hair, crisp white sleeves, a black waistcoat and trousers. No doubt he'd been polishing the sterling when interrupted. Eyes fixed respectfully on Tag's face, though Tag was sure his best suit had been noted and found wanting.

Go ahead, tell me to apply at the back door, pal. But this one was too old to punch. "I'd like to see Mr. Colton, please." *Please let him be home.*

There was no guarantee. In the first weeks of the scandal Tag, along with everyone else in America—had learned more

than he'd ever wanted to know about the reclusive millionaire, thanks to the tabloids. Colton had his own jet, another
house on a private island off Miami, inherited rights to the
finest salmon fishing in Scotland. If his horses were racing in
Europe this week he'd be there to collect the trophies. If not,
he might be off shopping for broodmares in Japan or gambling in the Bahamas.

"Whom may I say is calling?"

By God, was it possible? "The name's Taggart. R. D. Taggart."

"Ah." The butler didn't pull an Uzi out of the porcelain
urn to the left of the door, but his eyelids quivered. Trained
in the very best butlering schools. "Yes, sir."

Tag kept his face relaxed, his hands in view. *Don't call the
cops, old man. I just want to talk.*

The butler pulled a chain and a gold pocket watch slid into
his palm. He consulted it with pursed lips. "Mr. Colton will
have finished his barn rounds, I b'lieve. You might try down
at the office."

An elegant dodge while he called for reinforcements? Or
the truth? Tag was tempted to shove past him and find out.
But once he'd crossed the line into open belligerence, there'd
be no going back. So he thanked the man, then followed his
directions to the office, which turned out to be an entire building, painted white, trimmed in forest green to match the gigantic barns that dotted the hills beyond the manor.

A receptionist, blond and beautiful, was just cradling her
phone when he found her on the second floor. "Yes, Dr.
Taggart?"

So much for surprises. "To see Mr. Colton, please."

"Of course, but I'm afraid he's in a meeting. If you'd care
to sit over there? And could I bring you a cup of coffee?"

So easy, so civilized, this reception, he thought, taking a
seat. It felt all wrong. All these bitter months, though he'd
boxed only shadows, he'd still sensed the presence of an en-

emy casting that shadow. Someone derisive...intelligent...
merciless. Could that all have been his own paranoia? Colton's ignorance of what was really happening to Tag's life?
An unfortunate misunderstanding blown up into a legal vendetta, like the classic case of two spouses who wanted a
friendly divorce, but ended in a bankrupting brawl, thanks to
their lawyers? As he sipped Colton's excellent coffee, for the
first time in months Tag allowed himself the barest of hopes.
Perhaps a truce might yet be reached.

An hour passed and the hope cooled with the coffee. "How
much longer do you think he'll be?"

The blonde gave him a sunny smile. "Shouldn't be much
longer."

Half an hour later he asked, "Where's this meeting taking
place?"

Her blue-shadowed eyes flicked to the mahogany doors on
her left. She smiled. "I'm *sure* they're almost done. More
coffee?"

He'd give it another fifteen minutes, not a minute longer.
Tag prowled from a Palladian window overlooking a broodmare paddock—spring foals butting their dams in the udder
or loping alongside them on comically spindly legs—back to
blond-and-beautiful's desk. She looked more anxious each
time he made the circuit. He turned from the window at fourteen minutes to find her whispering into her phone.

So give it five more.

The double doors opened at minute nineteen and another
blonde stepped through, this one at least ten years older than
the receptionist. Polished to a metallic gleam. Soft lips, hard
green eyes. She approached with hand extended. "Dr. Taggart? Claire De Soto, Mr. Colton's assistant. If you'd come
through to my office?"

She led him to a corner room. DeSoto had pull, apparently.
She put some effort into the hospitality, insisting he take the

most comfortable armchair, offering him a mint julep, which he refused. "Now how may we help you, Dr. Taggart?"

"By getting me Colton." He was out of patience. Smelling rats.

She lifted a plucked eyebrow. "He'll need to know in regards to what before seeing you, Dr. Taggart. So...?"

So talk or get out, huh? All right. *I want my life back.* "I'd...like to know what he wants. These lawsuits...they aren't going to bring back Payback's—" *million dollar balls* "—his potency. There's no way I can give that back to him. And it doesn't look like Colton needs my money." Tag glanced wryly to one side. Through the window on the right, he could see a half-mile exercise track in the distance. In the foreground, a groom led a prancing colt across a courtyard. "So what does your boss want from me?"

Tag had apologized last winter, in a letter passed from his lawyer to Colton's. There'd been no acknowledgment. Still, he'd be happy to apologize for a second time. Because if Payback was the best horse Colton had ever bred, then Tag could sympathize with the man's outrage. His disappointment. The stud had been much more than an oat-burning money machine. He would have been the foundation of all Colton's hopes for future generations of wonder horses.

Tag sincerely regretted the part he'd been tricked into playing in blasting those hopes. But surely Colton could see that Susannah had screwed them both. "If it's an apology he wants..."

"I'm sure he'll tell you."

That was all that Tag wanted or needed. To meet Colton face-to-face, without lawyers or tape recorders. Without witnesses. So that he could hear the man out, try one last time to apologize.

And then explain to him calmly and clearly where they were headed if they couldn't reach a truce. If Colton couldn't back off, wouldn't back off, then Tag would have to kill him.

It was as simple as that. *I want my life back. And I don't mean to live it looking over my shoulder.*

But you didn't make that kind of threat to lawyers or assistants, then ask them to please pass it on to the boss. Statements like that might be a basic man-to-man truth, but in the eyes of the law, they constituted assault. Seventeen years ago Tag had spent a summer behind bars, and that was enough for one lifetime.

"Is there anything else you need from Mr. Colton?"

One thing. "Susannah Mack's address." Her divorce had become final two months ago, he'd learned from the gossip rags, shortly after the charge of horse theft had been dropped. That was the last mention of her he'd been able to find anywhere. The bitch had dropped off the face of the earth. Gone to ground in Texas, maybe? Or some place much fancier? Wherever, she'd be enjoying her pay-off in the unbreachable seclusion that only big money could buy, he supposed. Because the tabloids also noted that, though the terms of her divorce had been settled privately, they were said to be exceedingly generous. Ten million was the figure whispered most often.

Whatever amount Colton had paid her to go away, Tag figured at least half of it was his.

"Oh…" DeSoto hadn't expected that one. "I see." She rose. "Well. If you'll wait one minute, Dr. Taggart…" She shut the door behind her.

One minute turned into ten. Twenty. *Enough.* Tag stood, and standing, glanced up at the far corner above the chair that DeSoto had chosen.

The lens of a camera gazed blankly back at him. Hair prickled at the nape of his neck. A security camera within an office? Aimed at the window, surely? He turned. No, aimed at his chair. "You son of a *bitch!*" Had he been watching all this time?

"Dr. Taggart?" DeSoto stood in the doorway, an odd little

smile curving her lips. "Mr. Colton won't be able to see you today, after all."

Two hours on ice. Suckered into hoping again. And all for what? For the same reason children pulled wings off flies—because they could?

And, clever boy, Colton had used women to do his petty work. Much as Tag needed to punch somebody, he didn't punch women. "Where is he?"

"Why, there he is now!" DeSoto nodded at the window. "He must have stepped out the back."

Out in the courtyard between the office and the nearest barn, a man stood by the door of a red Ferrari convertible, looking up. Gold wire rims, impeccable seersucker suit. As their eyes locked, Colton grinned, waved jauntily, got in the car.

Tag started for the door, the roar of a big engine reaching him faintly through the glass. He swept DeSoto out the exit before him, then swung to look back. As he'd thought, she couldn't have seen Colton from where she'd been standing. A setup from start to finish. "Where's he going?" And by God, she'd tell him!

Out in the corridor, DeSoto smiled demurely from beyond a wall of muscle—two guards built like linebackers, each with a hand resting on a holstered gun. "Would you show Dr. Taggart to his car, please, Peterson?"

Tag wanted a fight so badly, he could taste its blood in his mouth.

The smile on the larger guard widened. He rocked on his heels. *Come on then,* his eyes invited. *You and me.*

With pleasure! Tag took a step forward—and saw beyond his mark another camera, tucked up in a far corner of the hallway. If he fought these two, he'd be fighting for Colton's entertainment. And if he lost, Colton would see him beaten.

Tag pulled in a shaking breath. *I play by my rules, you bastard, not yours.*

"Thank you," he said, and no two words had ever come harder.

CHAPTER SEVEN

THEY ESCORTED HIM in smirking silence to his car, then tail-gated him all the way to the front gates, the grill of their outsized pickup filling his rearview mirror with glinting chrome. Swearing helplessly, Tag gunned his engine as he shot through the gates, but the truck was faster. "Crap!" His head snapped backward as they bumped him. "*That's* it." He swerved to the shoulder and stopped. "You want a fight, you got it."

As Tag stepped out, the driver popped the truck into reverse. With the shotgun rider waving cheerily through the windshield, it roared backward down the road, past the gates, then shot forward and through. The gates closed behind it. The truck tootled farewell as it vanished up the avenue of trees.

Bastards, bullies, thugs! Somebody's going to pay for this! Someday, somehow... But not today. He glared at the white board fences extending either side of the entry. Electrified, naturally. So-o-o... "Later."

Fingers clenched on the steering wheel, he headed back toward Lexington. What now, what now? And using what for money? He had four hundred left in cash, the remains of his final paycheck from the dog pound in Buffalo. That job had ended three days ago, when the pound had run out of funding for his position. Third job that had fallen out from under him in the past six months.

When that final, dreary attempt to get on with his career aborted, something had snapped. Never mind the lawyers, he'd thought. He'd deal with Colton himself. Reach a truce somehow, then ask for Susannah's address. No reason her ex should protect her, he'd figured.

He'd figured wrong every which way, regarding Colton. *Petty bastard.*

A horn sounded behind him and his teeth snapped together. Didn't they know when to back off? The truck behind, Fleetfoot green like the guards' truck but smaller, beeped again. "All *right* then, dammit!" He pulled over, climbed out and stalked back to where the truck had stopped on the shoulder behind him.

The driver didn't step out to meet him. A small, stocky man. Sandy hair, pug nose, Irish face. Shrewd gray eyes studied Tag through his rolled-up window.

"What d'*you* want?" The guy looked too short to make a satisfying opponent, though Tag knew well enough from his Boston years how fierce the Irish could be.

The window rolled down an inch. "I heard you might be looking for Susannah."

Yes! "Who's asking?"

"I'm a trainer back at Fleetfoot. Friend of her and Brady."

Brady? An image of a silver flask skated across his mind—*that* Brady? "Who told you I was looking?" He was in no mood to trust, but still, to get his hands on Susannah...

The window rolled the rest of the way down and the trainer grinned. "Ah, they sneeze up at the big house, we're wiping our noses in minutes down in the barns." He glanced over his shoulder. "I can't stop long. If anybody sees me—"

"So you know where she is?" *Don't look too eager.* If this guy was her friend, he wouldn't want to send her trouble.

"Yeah, d'you mean to go see her?"

He must believe, as the rest of the world did, that Tag and Susannah had been conspirators. The sleaziest tabloids had even speculated they were lovers, supposing this was how she'd recruited him for the dirty deed. "Thought I might look her up," he said casually. "But I haven't heard from her in a few weeks and I was afraid she might have moved on."

"She has that." The trainer checked the road behind them again. "Look, I have this message from Brady, but I don't trust the mail. It's got to be delivered personal, put straight into her hand. And I can't get away myself."

"Be happy to take it." Finally, *finally,* something was going his way. "Where'd you say she was?"

"Southwestern Colorado. Little town outside of Cortez. Dawson, it's called." The Irishman drew a crumpled envelope from a back pocket. "Here's the message." His fingers tightened on one corner as Tag took hold. "I have your word you'll deliver it to her? To Susannah and no one else?"

"You got it, pal." He might stick it in her sexy little ear, but she'd get it, all right.

The trainer nodded and let go. "Makes no sense to me, but I guess she'll know what to do with it. Tell her I found it tucked inside his hatband, the one he wore that night. I was thinking I'd see her at the funeral, but—"

"Brady's dead?"

The gray eyes narrowed. "Deader than doornails. Fell down some stairs last January. Didn't you know?"

"No, I..." *Think fast.* This guy could still contact her, warn her that her hideout was blown. "That was a crazy time for me," Tag improvised. *To put it mildly.* "Guess she didn't want to bother me with it." Thoughtful Susannah. "I'm very sorry to hear it."

"Yeah, just about broke my heart, it did." The trainer started his engine. "Well, I can't be stopping. Give Susannah my best, will you?"

"Will do." For the first time in six months, Tag's smile was genuine as he waved farewell. *Nothing but the very, very best for little Susannah!*

MESSAGE FROM A DEAD MAN. Lurking in a booth in the far corner of Moe's Truckstop outside Dawson, Colorado, wait-

ing for a grilled cheese sandwich he didn't want, Tag drew
Brady's message from its envelope. Unfolding the smudged
strip of paper, he studied the penciled scrawl for the fiftieth
time in the past three days.

For the fiftieth time, it read as pure gibberish. Was it possible that Brady, owner of a whiskey flask, could have been
a raving drunk? That might account for this nonsense and
might also, come to think of it, explain his fatal fall. The
words were scribbled with blithe abandon or possibly haste,
t's uncrossed, spacing ragged.

> Susie, what we were talking about. Decided it might
> come in handy for leverage. Got it, but couldn't make it
> to your car. If you get this, the honey's where…

Several words were crossed out here. The writer had borne
down so hard on his pencil, he'd ripped a hole.

> Remember that time I called you a begonia raper? Take
> care, kid.
>
> > Brady.

"Begonia raper"—what kind of nonsense was that? Tag
frowned as he folded the paper and put it away. And
"honey"—every time he read that word, he tried to make it
come out money. His four hundred had dwindled to two and
most of that spent for gas, not food or shelter. Till he tapped
into Susannah's bank account, he was counting pennies.

*But if she's loaded, what's she doing working in a dive like
this?* When he'd reached Dawson late this afternoon, he'd
stopped at the tiny post office, casually asked its ancient postmistress if she knew where his dear friend Susannah Mack
might be staying hereabouts?

Stomach growling all the way west, sleeping in his musty

heap every night to conserve cash, he'd cheered himself on by picturing the coming reunion. He'd imagined finding his quarry smug and cozy in some new lover's hideaway, a rustic timber-and-glass ski lodge à la Aspen, which wasn't so far to the northeast. Or maybe luxuriating in a retreat for the rich and too-famous, an upscale dude ranch or an exclusive health spa, secluded somewhere up in the mountains north of Dawson.

To keep himself awake on the road late last night, he'd fantasized catching Susannah at such a spa, facedown on the massage table and half-asleep, her slender body draped in nothing but a sheet. He'd pictured himself booting the masseuse out of the room, locking the door, then taking her place. He'd rubbed Susannah's velvety back till she purred and stretched like a cat—then he'd given her shapely rump a resounding whack.

She'd whipped around, losing most of her sheet as she rolled—to reveal big blue eyes blazing up at him from the midst of a gooey, inch-thick, coffee-colored mud pack. Baring his teeth as he leaned over her, he'd pressed a forefinger to the tip of her muddy nose. Had waited while righteous indignation faded to doubt. Then just as her eyes widened in horror, he'd snarled, "Hey, *babe!* Remember me?"

"Here y'go!" Tag jumped half a foot as his waitress smacked a plate down on the table. "Can I get you anything else?"

"This'll do. Thanks." He'd drunk three cups of coffee already in the hour he'd been waiting. His waitress had told him when he asked that Suzie Zack worked the night shift, nine to dawn. He glanced at the clock over the distant counter. Eight-forty. Twenty minutes till he learned if the postmistress had been correct in claiming that the only newcomer to the county with a name remotely resembling Susannah Mack was Suzie Zack, that new little waitress down at Moe's Truckstop.

But what the blue blazes would Susannah be doing working

in a truckstop? Checking it out from the inside with a notion to buying it?

He was reaching. The tabloids had reported that, according to unnamed sources, Colton had given her a cool ten million and dropped the charge of horse theft—in exchange for Susannah's granting him a swift, uncontested divorce. *Ten million!* With bucks like that, she'd be investing in stocks and bonds and diamonds, not truckstops.

The logical explanation was that Suzie Zack the waitress was not, and never had been, Susannah Mack, rich and vengeful hellcat. Still, he sat here sipping coffee and hoping. Because if Susannah wasn't here in Dawson, then where on earth was she?

Quarter to nine and all that coffee was making itself felt. Leaving his sandwich to cool on the table, Tag tugged the bill of the baseball cap he'd bought for disguise lower over his nose. He headed down a narrow hall that he guessed led to the rest rooms. It did—and also to the phone.

His waitress stood with its receiver jammed to her ear. She smacked the side of the pay phone and swung half-around. "Well, then, where *could* I—" Her mouth rounded to an *O*.

Tag gave her an innocent grin and resumed walking. She spun away, stood silent with shoulders hunched till he'd shoved through the door to the men's room.

Where could I what? he wondered while he took care of business. *Where could I score some dope?* But a big, motherly rawboned woman in her forties, she didn't look the sort. Or... His smile faded. *Where could I reach Susannah?* He slammed out the men's room door. She'd been giving him looks ever since he'd asked when that new waitress, the little one from Texas who'd served him last week—what was her name, Suzie?—came on duty? He'd figured that was a safe way to pose the question. Because if Zack proved to be Mack, then no doubt all the men were asking for her.

But now he thought about it, his waitress had vanished down this hall only minutes after his first inquiry.

No one stood at the phone now, but the door beside it was just closing. Hell, to lose Susannah now when he was so close! He'd been too impatient. Should have simply watched and waited even if it took her a week to show. Tag opened the door and leaned out to scan a potholed patch of pavement.

A cool, sage-scented mountain wind was blowing. Rolling before it, a beer can tinkled eerily, then came up short against a rock. Somewhere out in the dark a coyote yipped. Nothing else stirred. Whoever had come this way had moved on. Either gone back to the kitchen or to the parking lot out front.

Swearing under his breath, Tag turned back to the eating area. He could leave, then lie in ambush outside the kitchen door, but if for some reason she entered by the front or side door, instead... As he reached the end of the hall he skidded to a stop.

A short, slender woman stood at a table across the room, facing away from him. Taking the order of three trucker types who grinned up at her.

Thank you, God! His heart drumming a hunter's beat, Tag ambled over to his booth and slipped into it. He pulled the bill of his cap down to his nose and slouched till his eyes barely cleared the back of the opposite banquette. *Susannah Mack, as I live and breathe!*

Waiting tables. She wore a white butcher's apron tied over a blue work shirt and jeans. She seemed thinner than he remembered—she turned to take the third man's order and the overhead lights threw an elegant cheekbone into stark relief. But he'd have known her anywhere, even without those lizardskin boots. She'd pulled her marigold mane back into a prim braid, though wisps of it escaped already to feather her cheeks. She swiped a forearm up across her brow as if she could feel the heat of his eyes, nodded coolly at something one of the customers said, then swung back toward the kitchen.

As she moved away, the biggest trucker grabbed an apron string. The perky bow at her hips unraveled and she stopped.

You— Tag found himself halfway to his feet. He dropped abruptly back into place. He couldn't walk over there and heave that jerk across the counter without Susannah noticing. And he'd promised himself their first encounter would be private. On his terms. *So easy. Cool it.*

Besides, his Texas hellion needed no man's help. She turned with graceful deliberation, said something that didn't carry to Tag's ears. Her admirer sat back and clasped his hands on the table, schoolboy with knuckles rapped. Chin high, boot heels clacking, she marched off to the kitchen. When the door swung shut behind her, the trucker's friends tipped back their heads and roared.

So now what? For six months this had been his fondest, his only dream, the moment he confronted Susannah. But in every version of his fantasy, from gotcha-at-the-health-spa to gotcha-at-Monte-Carlo, their confrontation occurred in private. *Just you and me, babe.* He meant to savor every minute while she tried to explain, to apologize, to plead for his understanding and forgiveness. Let her bat those big blue eyes and cling to his knees, if she wanted. It was her turn in the dock. His turn to be judge and jury. His turn to pronounce sentence. *Payback time!*

Now that he knew Zack was Mack, he'd best get out of here before his own waitress told Susannah she had another admirer across the room. Once outside he'd check around back, see if a new car had joined the two he'd scouted before entering. The latest arrival should be Susannah's. He'd find the best spot to park his own car where he could watch it, then be in place to follow her home at dawn.

The door to the kitchen swung open. His waitress steamed out and headed his way, brandishing a coffeepot in each hand.

"Which would you like this time, honey, caf or decaf?" Without waiting for a decision she filled his cup. "So what's wrong with the sandwich?"

"Nothing. Could I have my check, please?"

"You let it get cold, no wonder you don't like it. Cook'll stick it back on the grill for you." She whisked his plate away.

Blasted, bossy woman. "And the check," he called after her as she detoured to the truckers' table.

Something moved at the corner of his eye. Without turning his head, Tag glanced toward the kitchen. Was the door shuddering against its jamb, as if it had just this second swung shut? Or had he imagined— His own waitress bumped it with her hip and shoved through. The door swung back into place, bounced twice, came to rest.

Even if that had been Susannah looking him over, all she could have seen from that distance was his cap and maybe his eyes. Nothing alarming, just another admirer, shyer than her bow tweaker.

There was no way she could guess that someone was hot on her trail. No way on earth she'd be expecting Dr. Taggart, sucker extraordinaire, to pop up in Colorado. He bet he hadn't crossed her mind once since the day she'd wrecked his life. He'd been a mere pawn she'd used to check a king.

The door swung again. Bearing an overloaded tray, his waitress rotated out into the room and made for the truckers. She set out their orders, then returned to the kitchen. Damn, where was his bill? "My tab," he demanded five minutes later when she brought him his reheated sandwich—now scorched around the edges.

"Oh! Forgot t'write it up. Be right back."

While he waited, he ate the sandwich. He finished, then sat, foot tapping, watching the truckers grow more and more restless, till the bold one sauntered over to the swing door and stuck his head through. "Hey! Can we get some more coffee out here?"

And another crack at Susannah, Tag imagined.

They didn't get it. It was his own waitress who bustled out, lips pursed with indignation, coffeepot held like a lethal weapon. She splashed the big one's cup to overflowing—he shoved back hastily from the table. The other men pushed their cups across to her side and smiled meekly while she poured. "What about you?" she demanded, bearing down on Tag with her pot.

"Just my bill. Please." *And...* His nerves were suddenly jumping. "What happened to the other one? To...to Suzie?"

"It's a slow night. Cook asked her to clean out the walk-in. I'll tell her you asked."

"No! Don't bother her. I'll catch her next time."

"*No* bother." She sailed back to the kitchen.

Wonderful. Tag tugged the bill of his cap lower. Now what? If Susannah came over to his table, he supposed he could grab her, hustle her straight out the door to his car.

But one yelp from her, and her three admirers would be on him like pit bulls on a soupbone. And though given the provocation he wasn't opposed to kidnapping, he'd rather not try it in public. *So get out of here.* Tag pulled out his wallet. He had four fifties left, nothing smaller, and it really hurt to leave one behind. Thanks to Susannah, he'd sunk to that. *Call it an investment,* he told himself as he retreated toward the exit. Once he got his hands on Susannah, she'd repay it with interest.

"Oh, mister? *Mister!*"

He turned to find his waitress waving the fifty at him like a hanky. "*Thank* you! You're a prince!"

Prince of fools, more like. He nodded a grim good-night, then paused. Behind his waitress, the largest trucker must have decided he had an opening. Three long, stealthy strides and he was at the kitchen door, then halfway through. He halted, backside in the dining room, the rest of him in the kitchen, while his friends, Tag, then the waitress as she swung to follow Tag's gaze, watched.

Thirty seconds for a thorough survey of the far room, then the trucker reappeared. "Hey, where's the cute one?"

Tag winced. The waitress squared her broad shoulders and grew half an inch. "Went home sick half an hour ago." She turned to include Tag in her sour triumph—and tucked his bill in her breast pocket.

Shit! Tag spun and bolted for his car. So she'd spotted him, after all! Idiot, fool, sitting there like that other luststruck moron, smugly assuming he had his prey cornered! Letting her friend lull him with cups of coffee while Susannah Mack headed for the hills. God, women were devious!

He stopped in the midst of the front parking lot to turn a frustrated circle. Out beyond the lights was a darkness like none he'd ever seen in the east. There were hundreds of foothills out there to head for. Mile upon empty mile of mountain beyond that. Once Susannah started running, how far would she run?

Didn't matter how far. She could run to California—to the ragged ends of the earth, and he'd follow. "Gonna get you, girl, if it's the last, the very last, thing I do." *So move! Go!* She had at most thirty minutes on him, more like twenty, he thought. And the night was crystal clear. You could see fifty miles or more from the top of any rise. Let him catch one glimpse of her fleeing headlights—

Yanking his keys from his pocket as he ran, he ducked into his car. The engine roared...stuttered... He cursed, pumped the pedal and it caught. He swerved past a big rig parked near the pumps, another idling in off the two-lane highway, then braked at the exit, peering both ways.

Off to the left was Dawson, its meagre lights twinkling in the desert-dry air. To the right was a ribbon of blacktop, vanishing into the dark. No street lights in this wide, desolate world. "Which way, Susannah, goddam you. Which way?"

Something hard and cold touched the back of his neck, making him jump violently. The unmistakeable chill of steel—there was nothing colder—shot down his spine. Goose bumps stampeded after.

"Go right," a bleak little voice drawled at his ear.

CHAPTER EIGHT

ROT? "SUSANNAH!" He reached without thinking for the gun.

"Hands on the wheel! *Now,* you son of a bitch!" The gun jabbed him for emphasis. "Both hands and don't you move 'em! Now turn right and *drive.*"

He'd wanted her. Well, he'd found her. Tag let his breath out between gritted teeth as he turned onto the highway. But in seeking her, he'd forgotten one teeny, tiny detail. A woman who'd done what she'd done must be crazier than Ned's hatband. "What d'you—"

"Shuddup!"

Not just crazy, but madder than a swatted hornet. His speedometer passed twenty, steadied at thirty. If he drove too slow, then maybe some highway patrolman would—

"Faster!"

He looked for her face in the rearview mirror and saw roof, instead. She must have swiveled it before he'd entered the car. Crazy-but-not-stupid was even worse. "Where are we—"

"One more peep out of you, mister, and I'll blow your ear off. I've had it up to *here* with you people, up t'my eyeballs, and I'm not takin' any more. You pushed the wro-o-ong woman."

You people? *Me and who else?* Totally psycho. The speedometer needle touched fifty. He could brace himself on the steering wheel, then stomp on the brakes, put her through the windshield...

He wasn't going to do that. Not unless he had to.

"I mean it's one thing messin' with me. But my sister? She loved her job. And that poor old man back in Houston? What'd he ever do t'anybody 'cept hire me? That shabby ol' stable was his life. You bastards ever think about that? Care about that? Canceling his liability so he had to close? That was low. Mighty low."

"What are you—?" The gun barrel jabbed him and he shut his mouth.

"Tapping my phone, followin' me everywhere, stealin' my mail." Cold steel nudged his spine. "Step on the *gas,* slowpoke, I mean it. Drive sixty or die."

When you put it like that... The fence posts to either side ticked past faster and faster, striding backward into the night. Where the hell were they going?

"Then my job in Austin. At least you paid off that sorry sadsack. You can tell Stephen I was almost grateful when he fired me, but still... Oh, slow down now."

The headlights hit something white, hung on a fencepost ahead. A cow skull, eyesockets gaping, teeth grinning, horns pointing the shortest way to the hereafter. He hardly noticed. Stephen? As in Stephen Colton?

"I said slow *down!*"

"Would you for Pete's sake make up your mind, woman?" He let the car coast till the needle touched forty. Strung between the posts, barbwire silvered in his headlights, twisted black and cruel as the lights swept on. A car raced to meet them, flicked its beams to low and shot on by. No help there.

"My mind's made up. No more. I'm entirely sick of this. Sick of waiting for the next boot to drop. Sick of runnin' and hidin' and changin' my name. I mean when is enough gonna be enough?" The gun barrel prodded his nape.

"You're asking me?"

"I'm *telling* you. Now. Tonight. It ends here."
Ends how?

"Turn right." A dusty lane led off the highway, winding out into trackless black.

"Here?" His breathing accelerated. *Ends how, Susannah?*

"Here and now, you creep. Turn!"

Maybe he should grab her gun as they turned? The cold steel at his neck abruptly withdrew. If she'd sat back in her seat, he'd never reach her in time. The car bounced through a shallow ditch, rumbled over a cowcatcher that spanned a gap between gateposts, lunged on through. His lights swept a pair of ruby eyes, which blinked, then vanished as a shadowy form scuttled for cover. Stones clattered under the tires.

"When I saw you t'night, sitting out there smirking, well, that was the last straw. I don't know how you found me this time, mister, but you're gonna wish you never did."

Colton was hounding her, too? Not in person, of course, not Mr. Clean Hands Colton, but by proxy? Well, maybe there was justice in the world, after all! The road twisted and rose through the dark, his lights bouncing off brush and low trees. "Susannah?"

"Hush!"

"Look, you've got to—"

Click-*klack!* "No, I don't."

God, she cocked the gun! Something big, by the sound of it. Probably an automatic. His hair was standing straight on end and quivering, as if it wanted to take flight from his luckless skull. Cold sweat trickled down his cheek.

They mounted a hill, circled a higher one, rattled down into a valley. Mountains loomed in the near distance. Where the hell were they? There wasn't a light to be seen anywhere. "Susann—"

Boom!

His elbow slammed the door, his head the roof—
"Ouch!"—his backside hit the seat again. "Goddammit!"

Cold wind trickled through a bullet hole somewhere
overhead. "I said hush and I meant it," she drawled in a
voice of sweet reason.

Whatever the lady wants! Careful to make no sudden
moves, ears ringing, he steered the car back onto the track.
She'd answered his next question anyway. The gun was
loaded.

They came to a fork in the trail. "Go left," she purred
at his ear.

"You know this is none of my business," he said,
speaking even faster when the gun touched his earlobe. "I
don't give a *damn* about you and your ex's feud. Who
wins, who loses. *Believe* me." *To hell with both of you.*

"I know you don't, lambchops." She drew the side of
the gun barrel across his cheek, a kiss of cold steel.
"You're just in it for the money, right, big man? Well, in
my book that makes you lower than skunk turds. Lower
than doodlebug droppin's, hurtin' people for money. And
if you're tryin' to tell me you're for sale to the highest
bidder, then forget it. Stephen'll trump me every time. You
know it. I know it."

Where the hell was her ten million? Surely with that,
she could hire bodyguards to counter Colton's harassers?
She could buy a whole new identity and drop down a
rabbit hole, if it came to that.

"Stop!"

"What!" He jammed on the brakes. The car shuddered
and died.

"Shut off the lights."

He pushed a knob and it was like falling down a well,
darkness imploding.

"Don't move, don't breathe, don't turn your head, you

creep.'' The door behind him opened. His eyes swiveled to the max. He caught a glimpse of a thick ugly barrel with a black hole in its end. One-eyed death, staring hungrily at his temple. He could hear his own breath bouncing off the windshield, fast and infinitely fragile. He jumped as the door slammed.

What now, Susannah?

''Hands on the wheel,'' she commanded, voice fainter beyond the glass.

He could duck down on the seat, but it wouldn't do any good if she meant to do him. Could slam his door open, but if she dodged it, then—

Blam! His head hit the roof again. *''Shit!''*

Bam!

The car settled gradually, wearily to his side. His tires. She was—

Boom! Coming from the right rear, this time.

Bitch!

She moved into view, faced his right front tire—and blew it to kingdom come. Air hissed. His hands on the wheel were shaking. The shadowy little figure out there slowly lifted her head. Their eyes locked through the glass.

You, babe... Maybe this was what he'd felt from the moment he'd met her, first looked into those blue norther eyes. His fate, come to blow him away. *So do it, then, you bitch, before I beg!*

''Don't let me ever see you again,'' she drawled. Then, back straight, head high, she stalked off into the night.

''GOD ALMIGHTY.'' Tag closed his eyes and sat, shaking all over. He felt sick to his stomach. *Thank you!* His head hit the headrest and he sagged, savoring the sound of his breath—continuing.

Suddenly the car was too small, a shabby tin coffin that

had almost claimed him. He shoved the door wide, stumbled out.

His knees wobbled. He didn't bother to close the door. The interior dome light had died weeks ago, so it threw no light to reveal him. Breath smoking, he looked up at the stars. Millions...upon *billions*. Bigger, brighter, more beautiful than any stars he'd ever seen in his life before. *Thank you!*

He looked down at his tires—and gratitude ebbed away. The tide reversed, rage flooding inward, a blood-warm tide, rising gradually at first. He rounded his car on legs stiff with outrage. One tire shredded... Two gone, three and then four. He'd never make it back to the highway on his rims. He stopped to turn a slow circle. Where the hell *was* the highway?

And more to the point, where was his raving hellcat? *Susannah, by God...* He turned another circle. Silence, like he'd never heard before. How far could she have— His head snapped around as, far out in the dark, something rattled.

A stone rolling under a boot heel? The direction he was staring, a long, low ridge cut the stars. A faint line of silver defined its ragged shoulder, promise of moonlight to come. He was looking east.

Movement stirred at the edge of his vision. He shifted his eyes, then caught it again, halfway up the nearest hill. A small figure, maybe a hundred yards out, striding purposefully for the moon. Without one look behind or one thought, he started after. *Lunatic, hellcat...it ends tonight.*

Wreck my life without a second thought, will you? The ground was rough underfoot, but he was wearing track shoes, their rubber soles silent on stone. *Exploiting my wish to help you, dragging me into your spiteful, childish feud with your worthless husband...*

He brushed through a stand of low bushes, came out the

other side. Making me the laughingstock of every last vet in America? The fool who gelded Payback? He spotted her as she topped the rise.

Taking my home, my reputation, my clinic… His eyes were adjusting to the dark. He could see her clearly now— saw her as she stumbled, her hands flying out to balance herself. Her gun was outlined for a second against the sky. *Geez*—it was a mother!

Wouldn't have mattered if it was a bazooka. If she drove a tank. *Gonna get you, girl.* He stumbled himself, fell to one knee and swore. Looked up. Had she heard?

She whirled, moon-silvered braid flying out like a comet's tail. Was she staring back down the hill? Could she see him kneeling? "Bastard! You keep away from me!"

In your dreams, babe! Tag leaped to his feet as she vanished over the top. He tore straight uphill, reached the crest and paused, panting, eyes sweeping the darker slope below.

"C-come any closer and I'll shoot!" she shrilled, from not far away.

Stealing my future… Stealing my Truck! His eyes lit on the small, frozen form downhill and he lunged for it.

Blam!

His hat flew away. He put a hand to his head, remembering he was wearing it at the exact moment it became history. Man, she could shoot like that? And how many shots remained?

Four for the tires…one for the ceiling shot…then this one that nearly took his head off, he reckoned, stumbling after her.

She squeaked like a rabbit and fled.

Six shots, an automatic often had eight. He skidded to a backpedaling halt as she turned.

Blam!

That made seven. He let out his breath and went for her. *Scare me half to death, will you?*

Pistol raised and held two-handed, she backed away from him, shaking her head. "D-d-don't make me do it!"

Shoot out my tires? He didn't even have enough money left to replace them! He kept on coming.

Blam! The bullet slammed stone at his feet, whined off into the night—and Tag launched himself with a snarl.

He hit her hard and low and they flew backward into bushes. Twigs snapped and scratched. Susannah shrieked and hammered his shoulders as shrubbery collapsed beneath them. He scrambled astride her and sat. She writhed, clawed at his thighs, drew a gulping breath—and reached between his legs.

"The *hell* you do!" He captured her wrists, pinned them to the ground and leaned over her, panting, their faces not three inches apart. *"And where's my jacket?"*

"Wh-wh-*what?*"

He bared his teeth. "My jacket, babe!" Damn her! All these months rehearsing the first thing he'd say to her, and he'd blown his script already. His jacket was the least of—

"Y-your— I don't have— You're *crazy!*" She kneed him in the back.

"Ouch, dammit, you little hellion!" He wrenched her arms together over her head, clamped both wrists with his left hand, then reached back and grabbed a booted ankle as she slammed him again. "Quit, dammit!" He hooked his elbow under her knee and leaned forward, panting. *"Quit!"*

She wriggled once, then froze.

He could feel her small, flat belly heaving against his groin. Felt himself respond as his eyes moved irresistibly to her breasts. *Dear God, not now!*

If not now, when ever? He'd hunted her down and now he had her. His to do with as he pleased, his darkest instincts clamored. His by every right and desire. *And she owes me.*

Shuddup!

She shuddered violently. "You even *think* about it, mister, and I'll k-kill you."

He laughed incredulously. Squashed flatter than a bug and she was still giving him orders? "You think you got any say-so here?" He let go of her knee and pressed a taunting forefinger to the tip of her nose. "What about please, Texas?"

Whack! She nailed him between the shoulder blades.

Damn! He recaptured her leg and brought it forward, trying to shield his back with it. "You ever heard the word quit?" If he couldn't have one kind of surrender, by God, he'd have the other! "Say uncle!"

"Fff—y-yuh…uhhh…"

"Uh—*huh?*" He leaned closer, smiling evilly. "I didn't quite hear that. What'd you say?"

She licked her lips, not trying to be seductive, but still his eyes were captured, his mouth yearning to follow. All he had to do was lean forward an inch— Damn and blast her, who had whom here? "You care to retract that?" *Or don't.* Lady's choice tonight.

She nodded eagerly—and the moon inched above the horizon at last, silvery light sweeping westward. Touching his face.

Her mouth rounded to a delectable, stupefied *O*. "Doc…tor Taggart?"

CHAPTER NINE

WELL, AT LEAST she remembered him. That was something, anyway.

"Wh-wh-what are *you* doing here?"

Feeling suddenly embarrassed on top of lustful, a mix that only made him madder. "Hey, I can be anywhere. It's not like I have a clinic to tend to these days." Warily he let her leg go, then found he had no place to put that hand. It cupped instinctively to... He flattened it hastily against his thigh. "And I had this question..." He'd wondered for months. "How'd you happen to choose me?" *Was it something I did in some previous lifetime? You're karma with curves, sent to smash me personally?* Or was she just a random disaster, looking for a place to happen?

"I...took a wrong turn somewhere. I was looking for Canada."

And found me, instead? He wouldn't ravish her—he'd strangle her!

She made a tentative movement with her hands, but he ignored the hint. "Your...your clinic's gone? You mean Stephen...?" She bit her lip when he nodded. "I'm sorry."

"I can't tell you how much better that makes me feel!"

She winced. "I really am. If I'd known what he... I mean, I knew he held grudges, but to carry on like this... I never thought—"

"Now *that* I believe." She tried to move her hands again and his grip tightened.

"I'm *really* sorry. Truly, truly, I am."

"Good. That's very sweet. So now you can make amends." His thighs pressed her ribs as his body had its own thoughts of how she could do that.

She stiffened and her chin tipped a haughty notch. "Such as?"

Flat on her back and still defiant, she was…something. "Such as show me the money, lambchops."

"For gelding Payback? I gave you my ring."

"Which your better half sent a lawyer to take back not a week after the fudge hit the fan. Seems it wasn't yours to give in the first place. Colton family heirloom, the documents said, yours only on loan." He'd wondered at the time about that. A man giving the woman he loved an engagement ring on loan?

"And that's only the first item on your bill. There's also six months of legal fees on all those lawsuits your husband brought against me. And one canceled career as a vet. Plus eight years of college tuition down the hopper. Not to mention pain and suffering." To say nothing of pummeled pride. "Oh, and one leather jacket, used but never abused. I figure my bill's about…ten million dollars."

"Ten…" Her breath whooshed out on the word. "Ten…" Her body was shaking between his thighs. She was laughing? "Ten million! W-w-would you take an IOU?"

He scowled and shook his head. "Cash on the barrel, babe."

She laughed harder. "I've got f-forty-two dollars and a horse left and you want ten *million!*" She bucked beneath him, giggling. The moon rose a degree and she burst into tears—moonlight streaming down her cheeks. "Here S-Stephen's tryin' t'take his sixty million out of my hide and now you—*hic!*—you want ten-*ic!*" Hiccups on top of giggles on top of tears. And now she was coughing, pushing desperately at his knee. He growled and rolled off her, pulled her to a sitting position and thumped her back. She sucked in a shivering breath. "Ten-*hic!*" She collapsed, forehead pressed to her knees, chortling helplessly.

He'd liked it better when he was on top and she was terrified. She drew in another quivering breath and held it. He prodded her shoulder. "What happened to your ten million?"

That set her off again, hooting and hiccuping while he glowered, feeling like the designated driver at a New Year's Eve champagne bash. At last she sat up and wiped her eyes. "N-never had it to start with."

"But the papers said—"

"You b'lieve everything those buzzards print?"

After all those lies they'd printed about him? Still... He'd been homing in on her fortune like a compass needle to true north. *I needed to believe,* he realized. If he let it go now, what hope was there? "What about your divorce settlement?"

Hands clasped around her booted ankles, she propped one cheek on her upbent knees. Her smile was wry. "Know what a prenuptial agreement is?"

"Little idiot!" He realized he'd spoken aloud when her head came up.

Her shoulders squared. "I married for love, thank you."

"Yeah, and look where it got you. You didn't read the fine print?"

She shrugged and gazed haughtily off toward the moon.

He reached to poke her, then pulled his hand back. "So how much *did* you get?" Even a million would do him, he supposed.

"Forty-five thousand," she muttered without looking around. "Twenty for every year we stayed married was how it worked. Since we lasted two years and three months, then—"

"That's ridiculous!" *As much as that slimeball has?* "But I'll take it. At least it's something."

"That's what my lawyer said when he took it."

"Your lawyer."

"Seemed like a pretty good deal at the time, keepin' me out of prison for horse theft, handlin' my divorce..." She shrugged.

"Then what about gifts your husband must have given you, furs, jewelry, all that?" There had to be—*had* to be—something to salvage.

Her shoulders jerked again. "Jewelry's long gone. Hocked it months ago. And the furs—that fancy sable coat he gave me for Christmas...and the lynx, it was brand-new, since I never wanted it. Wouldn't wear it." She tipped her head back, as if consulting the rising half moon.

"What about them?" A sable would bring thousands, and a lynx, much as he believed that lynx fur belonged on lynx, not women, would—

"I threw 'em in the dump."

You lunatic little bitch! Maybe she could afford grand, cut-off-your-own-nose gestures like that, but he— Thanks to her he didn't have enough money left to buy four tires. Hell, he didn't *have* tires, thanks to her! "You mentioned a horse," he said, his voice husky with rage.

She nodded at the sky. "A twelve year old broodmare. Sheba. All I got left, but she's an ol' honey. Secretariat's her grandsire twice over, bred to a Nijinsky mare on her sire's side, and to a *full* sister to Ruffian on the other. No race record, she bowed a tendon when she was a yearling, but her foals..."

"That's nice," he cut in, though it was Greek to him. "What'll she bring?"

Her head swung around. "Bring?"

"When you sell her to pay me back, Susannah. What's she worth?"

"Ohh, no." Shaking her head, she scrambled to her feet. "Uh-uh."

No way did he feel safe sitting, with Susannah Mack standing over him in pointy-toed boots. Tag stood up, too.

"You think I'd sell a granddaughter of Secretariat's? She's probably the last fine thing I'll ever own."

"You should have thought about that before you started feuding with your husband. Before you tossed your sable, babe. Before you brought me a stolen horse to geld!" He loomed over her, a finger jabbing home each point.

Toe-to-toe with him, she cocked her chin. "I'm *not* selling her!"

"Want to bet?"

"You're on!" She backed away from him, paused, tugging at her braid, then glanced down. Started circling.

"Where is she?"

Humming something under her breath, Susannah shrugged and drifted into a wider circle. "That's for me t'know, big guy, and you to find out."

"And by God I will." It hit him suddenly what she was looking for—just as she stooped. Three strides and he caught her by the back of her belt, swung her, squeaking, aside. "Allow me." He bent down and picked up the gun, then stood, holding it. "A *.45!*" He went cold, then hotter than he'd been all night. "Do you realize what this would have *done* to me, woman?"

She held out her hand for the gun. "I aimed over your head."

"And took my damned hat off."

"Just lucky, I guess."

You or me, babe? Nailing his hat was no lucky shot. So that was one more lie she'd told him—among how many?

She still had her hand out for the gun. He grasped it and started east, gave a good tug that brought her stumbling after. "Where were you headed?"

"Someplace." She tugged back, tripped, then gave up as he laced his fingers through hers and towed her on.

Someplace east of here. She'd been laying a beeline when he tackled her. "Tell me when we get there." Otherwise, he'd just keep walking till she caved. Given her choice of footwear and his, he bet he'd outlast her.

HALF A MILE of rough going, covered in irate silence, brought them to the long ridge he'd seen from the car. Too steep to climb, but a trail no wider than a goat track hugged its base. "Left or right, Texas?"

She shrugged and half turned away, pulling against his hand like a bored and sulky child.

Stubborn, stubborn. He'd met mules who weren't half this stubborn! "Fine." To their left, the trail meandered north the length of the long ridge, with no relief in sight. To their right—*rot,* he corrected himself—the trail looped around the sheer end of the ridge and disappeared. Rot would be right, then. Her madness was not without method, he was learning. She would have had some destination in mind when she forced him off the road.

"Fine." He turned left and felt her instant resistance. Smiled to himself. "This way looks good." For blisters. He dragged her on a few halting steps, then she dug in her boot heels.

"It's th'other way."

"Ah." He couldn't keep the smirk out of his voice and her head shot up.

"Smartass."

His grin widened. With a wordless little snarl she spun on her heel. Yanked his hand smartly to make him follow.

He did, savoring his small triumph and the swing of her slender hips in the moonlight. As they rounded the ridge, the trail grew rougher and broke down into slithering scree, shards broken off the cliff face above. He glanced up at it uneasily. *Where are you leading me this time, babe?* Cute as she was, it was hard to remember the danger. *Think bear cubs and baby cobras,* he told himself.

She glanced back for a second. "You got a name b'sides doctor?"

"Tag." She'd occupied his every waking thought for six months, haunted his dreams. Somehow it seemed she should have known it.

"Tag? That's it?" A woman with three syllables to her own handle, she sounded scandalized, and faintly pitying.

"All I'll answer to." Richard was only slightly more acceptable than Donald. And R.D. sounded like Arty with a head cold. "Just Tag." *Doctor* rubbed him raw these days.

She trudged on in silence for a while, then, "Tag, I've been thinking."

"Uh-oh."

She tossed her braid, but forged on. "'Bout my mare. If I could raise the money for a fee to a good—a really good—stud…"

"Like the one I gelded?" he couldn't resist snarling.

Her shoulders hunched and her fingers tensed within his, but she pushed on. "If I could breed my mare and she had a wonderful foal—and with her bloodlines, there's no way she wouldn't—in three years it'd be ready to race. And if it did really well, then, well, I could pay you back some of what I—" She stopped as he laughed aloud and swung back to face him. "Well, what?"

"Sell her *now*, Susannah."

"But—"

"I'm not up for any pie-in-the-sky partnership with *you*, babe. You have to sell her."

"Sure…if that's how you feel…I'll just do that." Her drawl dripped with honey. "When they serve ice cream in hell."

"A bit sooner than that, babe. Like tomorrow."

"Hah!" She turned and stalked off, dragging him behind. The trail climbed steeply up the cliff face for another fifty yards, then she stopped so abruptly that he caught her shoulder with his other hand for balance.

A wide valley swooped away from the far side of the ridge. At its bottom, maybe a quarter mile distant, a thread of silver wound between dark stands of trees. Beyond the stream, the land rose again in a series of giant steps, slopes of meadow and forest, with the last of them tilting up to form a mountain, slabs of raw granite gleaming pale in the moonlight.

Beautiful. His fingers tightened half consciously on softness, traced the delicate ridge of a collarbone, the silky hollow below. "She's down there?" Down in the trees something gleamed. Moonlight reflecting off weathered wood, it looked like—a barn, maybe? Let him get his hands on the mare and he'd sell her himself.

She twisted away from him and yanked her hand free. "She's someplace safe."

"Not with me in the world, she isn't." He didn't take Susannah's hand again. She held her shoulders just as straight and her head as high, but her steps wove a little as they started downhill. Still spunky, but definitely fading. If she tried to run, he'd catch her easily. It was well past midnight, Tag estimated. No lights showed in any of the ranch buildings he began to pick out on the far side of the creek.

They crossed the water by a series of broad stones. A mountain stream, narrow and rushing, with the fresh scent of ice melt. The main house was built on the hill beyond, high enough to be safe from spring floods. An old house, two storied, with a steep tin roof and a broad porch. Susannah paused before it and turned. "Thank you for seeing me home." She held out a small, fine-boned hand and tipped up her chin. "I'm real sorry about the mix-up tonight and about what…happened to you. And that we can't agree 'bout my mare."

For the first time he could see her as mistress of Fleetfoot Farm. She had the grit, if not the polish. If Colton had only been patient, kept her a few more years… Still, he couldn't help but laugh. "Nice try, but you're not rid of me that easily. Where do we sleep?" He was as beat as she looked.

"For all I care, you can sleep in the horse trough!"

So much for the lady of the manor. He grabbed her elbow and started for the front steps to the ranch house. "Here?" And who else lived here? For all he knew, a lover. *Good.* Somebody to punch out, at last, maybe. He was tired of boxing shadows, haggling with women. *I drove halfway across the country for this?* No ten million, just a snake-mean, mule-stubborn little Texas hellion, who looked like she hadn't had a square meal in months?

"Not here—no! Lemme go!" she whispered frantically.

"So where, then?"

Growling a continuous little growl, she turned and limped off around the house. They passed a barn, leaning drunkenly in the moonlight. A corral built out from its rear, where horses snorted and kept pace with them on the other side of the rails. Up past a small cabin set back in the trees, then another with a car parked outside. "This is some sort of motel?"

Susannah sniffed. "Dude ranch."

Ah. They crossed a meadow, tall grass swishing their legs, then came at last to a stand of pines surrounding a tiny cabin, its tin roof patterned with moonlight and shadow. Three sagging steps led up to a shotgun porch, splitting the structure front to back into two. Susannah paused before a door on the right. "This is my place."

"And what's yours is mine." *Get used to it.* He opened the door for her, then waited, grimly ironic, utterly immovable, till she sighed, cocked up her chin and led him inside.

CHAPTER TEN

IF SHE'D BEEN in any kind of a forgiving mood this morning, it would have been hard not to forgive Dr. Taggart. *Tag,* Susannah reminded herself, dropping to her heels beside the couch. He must have tossed and turned plenty last night— hardly surprising, considering her old swaybacked sofa was a foot too short for him—and had kicked his blanket halfway off. He lay bared to his boxer shorts, with his hard, furry stomach rising to a wide, hairy chest, a temptation to any woman. Her palms tingled just looking at it. One nicely mus- cled arm was thrown over his eyes, and a sweet, dopey smile tipped the corners of his mouth. Dreaming a sweet dream, it looked like.

Keep right on dreaming it, she told him silently and lifted a corner of the blanket off the floor. She shifted to her knees and peered under the couch. Now where— "Erk!"

She popped upright again, helped by the big hand on her braid, to find herself nose to nose with her uninvited guest. No longer looking sweet and dopey. He looked surly as a prodded bear in February, if bears had hazel eyes. And day- old beards.

"D'you mind?" She tipped her head back, but he didn't take the hint.

His fingers slid down toward the end of her braid. He brought the tip up to tickle her nose. "Not at all, Blue Eyes. How can I help you?"

She batted his hand aside. "I want my pants back." *And some panties.* Having to ask made her temper flare anew.

He'd confiscated her jeans last night—threatening to come get them himself if she didn't hand them out her bedroom door— leaving her with only her work shirt and underwear to sleep in. And before he'd done that, he'd collected the two drawers of her bureau that held the rest of her wardrobe—precisely two pairs of jeans, four T-shirts and two pairs of shorts—all to keep her from bolting.

For a moment she saw her walk-in closet at Fleetfoot, as big as this cabin and five times as grand, with its beveled mirrors and its varnished cabinetry and its white wall-to-wall carpet. Stuffed with rack upon rack of designer clothes, and now here she was, begging for a pair of jeans?

"Sure you weren't after your pistol, hotshot?" Tag patted the pillow his head was resting on. "Got it safe and secure for you right here."

"Hey, if I'd wanted to cash your check for you, I'd have taken a skillet to your sorry skull." She jerked her chin at the cast-iron frying pan sitting on the stove across the room. "Now gimme my pants! *And* my boots." He'd taken those, too.

"So take 'em." He rolled onto his side to watch as she groped under the couch, then drew a drawer out from under-neath—her underwear drawer.

Heat rose in her cheeks. She had nothing to impress the nosy son of a gun. Six months ago her lingerie drawer would have been full of gaudy silks and frothy lace, enough to sat-isfy the pickiest peeping Tom. On their first trip to Paris, Stephen had insisted she outfit herself, a whole bride's trous-seau right down to black garter belts and stockings made of the sheerest silk, with seams up the back.

Now she owned just eight pairs of cotton bikinis briefs and… She pulled a shimmer of crimson silk out of the pile, then a bra to match. And the one set that had survived her divorce, since she'd been wearing them the night she'd left Fleetfoot. She sat upright, clutching them defiantly to her breast, then realized, *I was wearing these the first time we met!*

"Nice." His eyes lifted from the splash of color in her hands to the tilt of her chin. One side of his mouth tipped up, and his hand reached lazily for her braid, where it dangled on her shoulder. She sniffed and leaned back, but by accident or design he'd hooked a finger into the rubber band. The elastic slid off the braid's end and fell away. "Very nice…"

She whipped her braid back over her shoulder, the last of its strands untwining and rippling free, then sat back on her heels to glare at him. Now she needed her jeans. "You're not making this easy."

"Why should I? Life's been nothing but not-easy for me since the day I met you."

"And I told you I was sorry." She started to set her lingerie on the floor, then thought better—the mice ruled the chipped linoleum and she'd been too squeamish to set traps. She dumped her things on top of his blanketed thigh. Shoved back the first drawer and drew out the next one.

And she really was sorry. "Sorrier than sorry." For all the good that did him. Sorry that she'd leaped before she'd looked and dragged him helter-skelter into the mudhole after her. Then sorry that she'd hadn't known, hadn't guessed, that Stephen had been punishing him, too, all this while.

All this time whenever she'd thought of him, which was each and every time she put on his old jacket, she'd pictured Dr. Taggart as still being up in Vermont, steady and smiling and capable, happy in his clinic. There when she'd needed him. Nobody she could or would ever go back to, but simply…*there,* a bright spot in her memory in this present world of dreary gray.

If she'd thought it through for one minute, she'd have known better. But these past six months had presented darn few moments for peaceful contemplation. Since the night Brady had thrown pebbles at her bedroom window, she'd felt as if she was running in front of a steamroller, with the steam-roller gaining. You looked back once in a while as you ran, but you didn't look up, down or sideways and hardly ahead. You ran for dear life.

She selected a fresh T-shirt and a pair of jeans, then looked up to find that Tag had drawn her gun out from hiding. He'd nosed its muzzle under a strap of her bra and now dangled the contraption before his face, inspecting a 32B cup as if he'd never met one before. "*Give* me that!"

He lifted it up and away out of her reach. She'd have to lean across his stomach to follow. "Where'd you get this?"

"Paris. On my honeymoon." If he really had to know.

"How'd you sneak it through customs?"

"They don't—" She stopped. "Oh, you mean the gun? I took that off a man in Austin."

"Stole it, you mean?" Tag swung the .45 back her way, allowing her to snatch her brassiere.

She tucked it under a fold of denim in her lap, then shrugged. "He owed me a whole week's pay when he fired me. Claimed I was stealing out of his cash register at his café, so he didn't have to pay me anything. Said I was lucky he didn't call the cops, have 'em throw me in the slammer."

Jail. She found that her arms had crept up to hug herself. *The sound of steel gates clashing behind her like a trap, the groans and cries in the night, the smell of vomit and worse things…* That one night in Boston was all the sample she'd ever need of jail, thank you.

Tag's eyes had narrowed beneath their level black brows. He aimed the gun at a waterstain on the ceiling, casual, utterly detached. "And were you stealing?"

"What d'you think?" Still, it hurt, his asking that. More than it ought to have done. He was nobody to her, really, just one more stranger judging her. *Well, join the crowd, buddy!* The whole world, it seemed like, some days. *They say even the Queen of England hates me, and I wouldn't know her if she sat in my lap!*

"Hey, what do I know? A woman who'd steal a sixty-million-dollar stud, why would she balk at a few greasy fivers?"

So think what you like, big guy. Claiming you were honest was like going around telling everybody you met that you were sane. The more you insisted, the loonier you sounded. She shrugged and let it go. "Anyway, I knew where he kept this hidden under the bar and I was starting t'feel like I could use one, so I took it and called us square." She stood and turned toward the bathroom.

He snagged one of her shirttails and she stopped, her skin tingling where the back of his hand brushed her bare thigh. If he lifted that hem even an inch... She narrowed her eyes in warning.

"Use it for what, Susannah?"

"Oh...for things." *Things like somebody slashing the tires on my car, back in Houston.* Then, once she'd moved on to Austin, somebody breaking into her apartment one night while she was working, taking all the cash Saskia had lent her plus the little she'd managed to put by. And those phone calls late at night, somebody telling her by his heavy breathing that he knew where she lived, could come get her whenever he chose. *Things like men.*

It was funny, all her life she'd grown up around men. Was comfortable in their rowdy, easygoing company. She'd never once stopped to think that, all that time, she'd been under this or that man's protection. First her dad and his partner in the old days back at their ranch, then more recently Stephen, making her untouchable. Free to go where she pleased without a care or a thought. But now, out on her own... *I don't like men so much nowadays.* "Just for things."

The back of Tag's hand brushed her leg again, sending heat creeping up her thigh, warm honey sliding down her insides.

She smacked his hand away, then backed out of reach. "Now if you'll excuse me..."

"Or not." Still, his eyes followed her all the way to the bathroom door.

Which had no lock on it, Susannah realized as she shut it. She propped the tin wastebasket against it—that way at least she'd know if he entered—stripped her shirt off over her head, then turned on the taps in the shower.

Not that he would, she told herself. If Tag was the kind of man who'd take advantage, he'd have done so last night.

Skimming her underpants down her thighs, she remembered the warm, solid weight of him, pinning her to the cold ground. Her skin shivered on her bones and roughened. Her nipples rose and hardened. She growled wordlessly under her breath and stepped in past the shower curtain. *Forget it!*

Ten minutes later Susannah stepped out of the steamy bathroom to the smell of fresh coffee. She turned toward it automatically even as resentment rekindled. *Thinks I'm a thief, but there he is, scrounging through my cupboards.* "Hey, just make yourself right at home."

"I intend to." Busy pouring out a mugful of brew, Tag didn't look up.

Oh, yeah? Still, he did look as if he belonged, standing there in her kitchen, wearing nothing but his jeans, which were old and faded and rode low on his lean hips. Big bare feet, dark hair still tousled from his pillow, sorely in need of a shave. Anybody seeing him would assume he'd spent the night—and spent it in her bed. Except that neither of them was wearing a silly grin this morning.

His hand hovered over the sugar bowl. "How do you take it?"

She blinked. That mug was for her? "One sugar. Please." She found a can of evaporated milk in the fridge and added a splash of that. In twenty-seven months of marriage to Stephen, she couldn't remember him fixing her coffee for her, not once. Not that they'd exactly hung around the kitchen at Fleetfoot, with that snooty French chef ruling the roost.

She retreated to the table and sat. Holding the mug just below her nose, she closed her eyes and inhaled. Her hot shower had made her sleepy again. Seemed she was always tired these days, between her day job and her nights as a waitress.

And today she was muddled, on top of tired. She would have been coming home from the truckstop about now, if this had been an ordinary day. She'd have had her breakfast before she left Moe's—that was one of the perks of the job— and would now be tumbling into bed for a few hours' shut-eye before rising at noon. She sighed and took a sip of coffee, nodded blind approval, then opened her eyes to the sounds of chopping.

Tag had found her onions and the potatoes. He was making breakfast? Her stomach rumbled enthusiastically even as she frowned. Pushy, like most Yankees she'd met. She set her mug aside and pulled a comb from her hip pocket, started working on the snarls in her wet hair.

Tag glanced over at her for a moment and his hands stilled. Their eyes locked, hers defiant, his...intent, darkening as his pupils widened. He looked back down at his chopping. "Last night..."

Let's not think about last night. But watching his big, capable hands on that knife, how could she not? She remembered them on her wrists, holding her effortlessly. Her helpless, frantic rage, before she realized who had her.

"Last night you didn't recognize me at first, so who did you think I was? Somebody sent by your husband?"

"My ex," she corrected him, and broke away from his troubled gaze to stare off at the far wall, tugging the comb through her hair.

"You said something in the car about your sister losing her job?"

"Saskia, my older sister." Susannah set down her comb to reach for her coffee. "She's— She *was* a teacher at a private high school in Houston. They let her go. Said they didn't have enough money to keep her on next fall." *My fault. If I hadn't run to her...*

"And you think Colton arranged that? But that happens all the time, doesn't it, jobs folding?" Tag moved to her fridge, found the butter and eggs and her last chunk of cheddar.

She smacked her mug down too hard—coffee slopped out onto the tabletop. "Not to Saskia, it doesn't. She'd been there for six years. They loved her, the kids and the administration both. But now...now she can't find another job to save her life, even in slum districts where they're cryin' for English teachers. Each time she gets an interview for a new job, everything goes wonderful. Then they send off for her references and *phttt!* Forget it. After that, they wouldn't hire her for janitor."

Tag cracked an egg into a bowl, tossed the shell in the trash, reached for another. "You ever consider that she might be a lousy teacher? And her old boss is saying so now he's rid of her?"

"Never crossed my mind once. Not for one single, solitary minute." She tipped up her chin and forced the comb through another snarl.

"And what about that old man you mentioned, something about his insurance?"

She nodded and pulled hard on the comb. The pain in her scalp felt...right. No more than she deserved. "Ike...he had a run-down ol' stable on the edge of town. I went to work for him when I got t'Houston. Teaching kids to barrel race, leading trail rides. He lost his liability insurance two months after I came. No other company would pick up his policy, so he had to close down." *My fault...*

"That kind of thing happens all the time, Susannah."

"Sure does, if you hang around me." *I'm a walking Jonah. Look at you.*

Beating the eggs to yellow froth with a fork, Tag scowled. "So after your job at the stable went south, what then?"

"I'd figured out which way the wind was blowin' by then. And there was nothing left for me in Houston." Saskia had already given up job-hunting. By now she'd be biking across Europe, looking for someplace to settle down and teach English. She'd always had a talent for ducking trouble, while Susannah always seemed to ram it head-on. "So I moved on up to Austin." She hadn't dared go back to the home ranch and ask her father's old partner for shelter, not if trouble was following her like a tin can tied to a mutt's tail. "Changed my name. Got a job waitin' tables in a café…"

A sizzle went up as Tag dropped the onions and potatoes into hot butter. He adjusted the heat beneath the cast-iron skillet and turned. "Where you were fired for stealing from the cash register."

She opened her mouth, then closed it again. Felt the tears start. *Too tired for all this.* She ducked her chin and let her hair swing down to curtain her face, ran the comb through from crown to ends. *Think what you damn well please. You will, anyway.*

Their silence stretched tight, filled with the sizzle of frying vegetables, the smell of browning butter. "How long did you work there?" he asked finally.

"'Bout two months. That seems to be about how long Stephen gives you to settle in before he pulls the rug out from under. I guess he wants you to start hoping again. Thinking this time it's over."

"Two months." Tag stood stone still, staring at the wall, then jerked his head abruptly. He poured the eggs on top of the frying vegetables, sprinkled cheese, found a spatula in her utensil drawer. "So then you had this…misunderstanding with your boss at the café, and he fired you. What makes you think Colton was behind that one?''

''Well, for one thing, I didn't steal anything, and for another, Stephen called me that night. To make sure I was getting the message.'' She shuddered, remembering waking to her phone ringing. Groping for the sound with dread in her heart. Saskia? Nobody called you with good news at three in the morning. Lifting the receiver—to find a laughing, familiar voice on the other end, soft and furry as a tarantula snuggling into her ear. A voice she hadn't heard since Boston. Hadn't thought she'd ever hear again.

Tag dropped his spatula in the pan and turned to stare at her. ''What did he say, Susannah?''

''Oh, lots of things…'' *You're finished, sugarbabe,* said with a smile in the voice. Said the way any other man would say *I love you.* ''''You bother to get up and I'll just knock you down again,'—he said that. And…'' Meeting Tag's eyes, she felt the blood rise in her cheeks. She bit her bottom lip and looked down. *And don't even think about taking a lover. Not ever. You had your chance, and you blew it.*

If Stephen saw her here with Tag like this, he'd think… She shivered. And it wouldn't be just her he'd want to punish.

Tag touched her shoulder with one fingertip. ''What, Susannah?''

She shook her head. ''Just ugly, gloating things. 'Cause what good is revenge if you can't claim it? If your mark doesn't know you delivered his bad luck up-close and personal?''

The smell of burning singed the air. Tag swore and spun to the stove, grabbed the pan off the flames—let it crash back to the burner. ''Damnation!''

While he ran cold water over his burn, Susannah found a pot holder and retrieved the smoking skillet. The top layer of eggs looked salvageable. She raked it out onto two plates. ''You all right there?''

"Just...wonderful." Tag stood, staring down at the sink, absently rubbing the fingers of his injured hand together. "Couldn't be finer."

Yeah, he looked fine. She found forks and knives for them both and refilled their mugs with coffee.

"Tell me one thing, Susannah." His mouth twisted wryly. "Your stud. Pookums. Colton bred and raised him, I hear. But who named him?"

"Named him Payback?" She handed him both plates, collected their mugs and led the way out to her porch. "*Now* you're gettin' the picture."

CHAPTER ELEVEN

THEY ATE THEIR BREAKFAST sitting on the top step of the porch. A late breakfast, though the sun was just rising over the mountain to their east. Susannah stopped with fork halfway to her mouth to follow the path of a bluebird across the meadow, then sighed with pleasure. "I've been missing the mornings, working at Moe's." She stretched out her long legs and wiggled her toes, sighed again.

Tag grimly shoveled in mouthfuls of burned egg, the taste of ashes and disaster. He got the picture all right. Finally. He was screwed.

Fourteen years ago, Colton had named the finest horse he ever bred Payback? It wasn't just a catchy name to psych out the competition at the racetrack, he was finally realizing. It was a credo, a way of life!

A twisted way of life that Colton, with all his millions, could indulge. Revenge was too expensive for most people, but this man had the means.

Tag had lost three jobs in the past six months—at roughly two-month intervals. Once he'd been accused unjustly of incompetence, then fired. Twice he'd been told that the money for his position had run out. He'd assumed it was just the way his luck was running since Susannah blew into his life, not *engineered* bad luck.

But if those setbacks had been Colton's doing, if Susannah was telling the truth, then Tag had seriously underestimated his problem.

All these months he'd been picturing Colton as a petty,

petulant rich boy. Spoiled rotten from having his way all his
life, but too soft to do his own dirty work. A man who'd send
in his lawyers or his secretary, where another man might use
his fists. A man who might be too small-minded to forgive
Tag's mistake, but who'd eventually grow bored with his legal vendetta and wander off to other pursuits, other enjoy-
ments.

But if revenge *was* his enjoyment? His hobby? If payback
was his reason for living? If he wouldn't rest till he got it?

You only have Susannah's word on all this! Susannah,
straight-faced liar, admitted thief. He hoped to God that this
time she *was* lying!

Susannah, whom Colton had chosen for his soulmate. No
accident that, any more than Payback's name. You could see
the pattern working, once you knew to look for it. Colton had
chosen Susannah, a Texas pistol with a hair-trigger temper—
who'd go to any extreme to get her own back? One of the
tabloids, that first week of the scandal, had labeled Susannah
"Most Spiteful Woman of the Century." Talk about two people who were made for each other!

And here he was, caught in the middle. Smack dab in their
crossfire. If he had any sense he'd run for his life—except
how far would he get, running on his rims?

While he'd been brooding, Ms. Spiteful had wandered off
into the meadow. She leaned down to pick something, her
hair cascading around her shoulders in a bright waterfall. She
wandered on, stooped again. Nothing wrong with *her* world
this morning, it looked like, from her drowsy smile.

She padded back to the steps and held up a bouquet of
wildflowers. "Nice, huh? These spiky ones are columb—"

"Where's your damned horse?" A broodmare with Secretariat bloodlines—she ought to bring something. Enough for
four tires, anyway. And maybe a plane ticket out of the country? If Susannah was telling the truth about Colton, then all
his plans had changed.

Smile fading, Susannah tossed her flowers over her shoulder. "I'm not telling you that."

"But you will, babe, you will."

"Hah! And here I thought…" She collected her plate and mug and started up the steps past him.

As her foot hit the step he sat on, he reached down and caught her ankle. She stopped, and for a second Tag thought she'd crown him with her plate. *I wouldn't if I were you, Susannah!*

She must have gotten his message. Eyes flashing blue fire, she swung the plate behind her back, her other hand whisking her mug from view, as if she tucked temptation behind her. With the movement her small, shapely breasts swelled against her T-shirt and his anger fused with a different kind of heat. Damn and blast her!

Every time he worked up a good reason to hate her, she'd do this to him, and he'd swear she wasn't trying.

"I think it's time you went away, Taggart," she drawled, voice quivering with the effort to hold it steady. "I've got work to do and you…you've worn out your welcome."

"Dream on, Lambchops. I'm staying till you pay what you owe me."

"Might take a while, with me making minimum wage on my good days. I should have your ten million saved up, oh, in a thousand years or so."

Meantime, I'll take it in trade. Something told him if he said that, she'd smack her mug upside his head. Still it was a nice thought for a moment, a thousand years' worth of Susannah.

But he liked his women willing—and sane. Two strikes against this one. "So I'll stick around."

He had his whole life to rethink, anyway. He'd intended to take several million off Susannah, then set up a new clinic somewhere. Start his life over. But if she was to be believed, there were no millions for the taking. And if he did find some way to finance his clinic, Colton would only knock it down. He needed to think.

"No. You won't." She stepped up to porch level with her free foot, then pulled against his hold on her other foot. He allowed that foot to lift—then held on, leaving her balanced on one leg. "Dana won't let you," she added, scowling.

"Who's Dana?" He lifted up slightly to correct her wobble. Damn, he shouldn't like holding her this much.

"Woman who owns this ranch. Do you *mind?*"

He let her go because she thought he wouldn't, then followed her inside. "Guess I'll have to ask Dana for a room. Is the one next door vacant?" He hooked a thumb toward the cabin on the far side of the porch.

"She won't rent to you."

"Why not? I'm a dude."

"I'll tell her not to, *dude*. That's why not." She thumped her dishes down on the counter, then turned and found herself at bay. She leaned backward till she couldn't lean any farther. His hands landed either side of her, pinning her there.

"Fine. You tell Dana...and you know who I'll tell? And what I'll tell?"

"What?" A pulse fluttered in the hollow at the base of her long, delicate throat. She no longer smelled of bourbon and expensive French perfume, the scent he'd remembered all these months. She smelled of soap and an elusive, delicious something that must be the woman herself. He ached to put his nose on the soft spot, there where her shoulder joined her neck. *"What?"* she half-whispered.

"I'll call every tabloid I can think of. The TV tabloids, too, and all that sniggering gang. Nobody's run a good piece on you in three months or so, Susannah. It's time for a follow-up, don't you think? Something along the lines of 'Whatever happened to the most spiteful woman of the century?' Living quietly in the country, is she? Well, let's take our cameras and go see for ourselves, shall we? Inquiring minds would sure like to know. Can't you just see them swarming out there in your meadow?''

''You bastard!''

''And your husband. I mean your ex. I'm sure ol' Stephen wants to stay in touch. Have you dropped him a postcard lately? *Ooof!*'' A small fist landed square in his middle, rocking him back on his heels. Tag caught her wrist as she swung again, then her other wrist as she tried a hook. ''Whoa. Quit!''

''Lousy, rotten Yankee!'' She burst into tears and he froze—this was more reaction than he'd wanted—and her knee shot up, nearly unmanning him.

He almost fell over, dodging it. He let her go and backed off. ''Yankee's not an insult where I come from.''

''So why don't you go *back* there?'' She swiped at her cheeks with both hands. Tears hung like crystal in her sandy lashes. Her lips were trembling. He could almost feel them quivering against his own, soft as damp silk, salty with tears. He wanted to kiss her till she stopped crying and smiled.

She spun away and slammed dishes into the sink. Then stood there, back proud and straight, splashing water halfway up the far wall while she washed. And Tag stood behind her, hands jammed deep in his pockets, jaw clenched on an apology she didn't deserve, but that he couldn't quite drive from his mind.

He hovered for a short while but Susannah paid him no more heed than she did the refrigerator. Okay. Fine. He could always use a shower while she sulked. But then he paused beyond the kitchen, thinking. There wasn't much here to hold her once he let his guard down, was there? She'd run before, she could run again. And somewhere she surely had some sort of wheels for running. Which would be parked where? Down at the barn?

Then it hit him. Behind Moe's, he'd bet his last dollar. The truckstop was too far from the ranch for her to have walked it last night. She must have driven to work. *So if she left her wheels there while she hijacked me, she left her keys...?*

In her jeans pocket, of course. But they hadn't been there last night, when she handed her jeans out the bedroom door. Which meant...

"What the devil do you think you're doing?" Susannah demanded some ten minutes later from her bedroom doorway.

Tag dragged his arm out from between the mattress and box springs to dangle a key ring. "Looking for these." He dropped the keys in his pocket and smiled.

"Son of a sneakin' bitch!" She spun on her heel and went back to the couch, found a pair of socks in the drawer beneath, then her boots. Stomped her way into them, then grabbed her Stetson off a hook by the door.

"Where're you going?"

No answer, not even a farewell scowl. The sound of boot heels clattering down porch steps. Then silence tiptoed cautiously back.

Tag grimaced. What was he feeling guilty for? She'd blown his life apart like a child kicking a castle made of blocks across a room. If she didn't like his face around here, she could hand over her horse.

Not his stubborn Susannah. Something told him he'd have to find the mare himself. Now what else should he do to nail Ms. Blue Eye's sweet fanny to this cabin till he'd done so? She needed wheels to flee—he'd scotched that. And she needed money. Forty-two dollars she'd said last night, an amount too small to bother banking—if she'd been telling the truth. Where would she hide it?

AN HOUR LATER, Tag strolled down the meadow toward the barn. A soft wind teased his hair, still damp from a shower. Back at the cabin everything was now as secure as he could make it. He'd hidden her .45 and her keys under a floorboard in the vacant cabin that mirrored her own. Susannah's money stash, precisely forty-two dollars as reported, he'd found concealed in an orange juice can in her freezer.

He could have pocketed the roll as fair payment—it would pay for one tire for his car—but he hadn't been able to make himself do it. Instead, he'd buried the stash at the bottom of her flour cannister. Just as long as she couldn't use it for running. *So now, Susie Q, where are you?*

He found her in the corral back of the barn, wrangling dudes, a pair of them. The middle-aged woman was mounted and sedately walking her mare along the far side of the corral. Meanwhile Susannah was encouraging a short-legged, anxious-looking man in his efforts to mount a long-legged horse with a dubious expression. "Goood—yeah, that's the way," she drawled from her place at the horse's head. "Get your foot right up there."

The man scrabbled frantically for the stirrup, shoved his foot into it, looked at her helplessly.

"Great, Henry. Now grab the horn, give a little hop and up you go."

Up, Henry didn't. He made a halfhearted lunge at the saddle and came scrabbling down again. Doubtful no longer, his horse, ears swept back, sidled away from her would-be burden, pivoting neatly around Susannah.

Left foot caught in the stirrup, Henry hopped desperately after.

"Stop that, Ladybird!" Susannah ducked under the mare's chin to give her a smack on her shoulder. Ladybird stopped and rolled her eyes, but by now her rider had lost his stirrup. He stood there, flushed and shaken. "I d'know, Susie, maybe I'm not cut out to be a cowboy."

"Oh, sure y'are! You've got great balance, I can see that already." Susannah glanced around, eyes narrowing to blue slits when she spotted Tag.

As Henry turned to follow her gaze, Tag scrubbed a hand

across his grin. Not that he had any right to laugh. Mounting a horse was probably harder than it looked.

"Let's use the block this time, why don't we? We'll work on mounting later on, once Lady's settled down again." Susannah nodded at a tree stump set along one side of the corral. "Step up on that and I'll bring her over."

Tag waited while Henry clambered aboard. Susannah shortened his stirrups, gave him a few tips about how to hold his reins, then sent him ambling toward his mate on the far side of the corral. Thumbs hooked in her pockets, she stood watching, the stiffening of her shoulders being the only indication that she heard Tag's approach.

"You're very patient," he observed, stopping beside her. More patient than he'd have expected. But then, she'd been an exercise girl when Colton found her, he reminded himself. Anyone who worked successfully with animals had to have patience.

She shrugged tightly, not looking his way.

"That wouldn't be your Secretariat mare, would it?" He nodded toward a little black, saddled and waiting with reins dragging the ground. She looked a cut or three above what Susannah's dudes were riding.

"Huh!" Susannah headed toward the mare, her strides lengthening as he kept pace. "Look how short she's coupled. And her butt—quarterhorse as they come. You don't know much about horses, do you?" Reaching the black, she rubbed a glossy shoulder with its hairless scar. "And didja ever see a thoroughbred with a brand?"

Two R's, Tag realized, back to back, making an image much like a ribbon tied in a bow.

"Dana's brand, the Ribbon R." Susannah gathered the mare's reins and mounted, long leg arcing gracefully over the saddle. Her boots found the stirrups as she glanced down at him contemptuously. "I'll give you a hint, big guy. You'll see that brand on every horse on this spread. My girl's elsewhere." She spun the little mare on a dime, then set her loping gently across the corral toward her dudes.

CHAPTER TWELVE

FOREARMS PROPPED on the top rail of the corral, Tag watched the riding lesson for a good half hour. Walk, trot, don't hold the saddle horn, then *whoa!* Practice in neck-reining, circles and figure eights, playing follow the leader behind Susannah's prancing little mare. She made it look fun, encouraging and teasing her pupils on, raising her demands just a little each time they'd mastered a skill, applauding their efforts till they beamed.

"All right, folks, we're outta here," she announced at last as she sidestepped her black up to the corral gate. "Time for some rough-riding."

Tag moved to open it for her.

"Don't bother." Susannah flipped a loop of rope off the top post, then nudged her horse into the widening gap, forcing Tag to stand aside. Hands in his pockets, he watched with envy as Susannah led her dudes up the flowering meadow toward the high country, not once looking back.

He gave himself a shake and glanced at the sun. About two o'clock, it looked like. He had a feeling that Susannah had not been bluffing when she'd assured him he wouldn't find her broodmare at the dude ranch. Still, he'd be a fool not to check.

A quick walk-through showed him there were no horses stalled in the barn, just riding tack and an ancient tractor, with hay in the loft above. He made the acquaintance of a barn cat, however, a big, young gray tom, more his sort of animal, who gravely accepted his due in back-scratching. And who then accompanied him on his stroll through a fenced pasture that stretched east from the barn.

Tag counted another nine horses dozing in the shade beneath the trees. Every one of them was marked with the Ribbon R on the left shoulder. "So now what?" he asked the cat mincing along at his side.

"Yeowr," his companion observed, and peeled off toward the barn.

"My thought exactly." This wasn't going to be as easy or quick as he'd hoped. Meantime, he'd best line up some food and shelter for tonight, something a bit more inviting than mice and a hayloft or Susannah's man-crippling couch.

Down at the ranch house, his knock on the kitchen screen door brought no response. Walking around to the front porch, Tag found a boy, early teens, tacking a paper to the door. He grabbed a fly rod, turned—and halted. "Oh." A towheaded, good-looking kid, with something sullen about him. Obviously not pleased to see a stranger.

"Hi," Tag said easily. "Is your mother around?"

The sullen look settled into a scowl. "You mean Dana?"

Not his mom, he meant. "That's right. Is she at home?"

"Went to town." The boy started determinedly down the porch stairs.

It was street reflex to settle the question of dominance between males and do it quickly. Tag took a step sideways into his path. "And she'll be back when?"

"Uh, anytime now." The kid paused on the last step and shuffled his oversize feet, then seemed to realize that the eight-inch elevation was a compensation, if not an equalizer. He stuck out his chin and met Tag's gaze squarely.

Good for him. "D'you know if there're any vacancies? I need a room for a few nights."

"Um, cabin one's open this week. Seventy bucks a night or three hundred by the week. Includes all meals, family-style."

A bargain by eastern standards, but too much for his underfed wallet. "What about that other half of the double cabin at the top of the meadow?"

"Roof leaks. We don't rent it." The kid leaped sideways off the steps. Cocking his rod over his shoulder, he started toward the stream. *Not intimidated, you understand,* said his sauntering retreat. *But I'm a busy man.*

"Thanks," Tag called after him, and received a shrug in response. He glanced at the note on the door.

"Yes, we have vacancies," it read. "Please wait."

Tag occupied the time waiting by making a slow circuit of the house. He might not have money, but he had skills this place could use. Paint was peeling everywhere, and bits of porch trim sagged here and there. *No man about,* this house cried silently. A thirteen-year-old kid with a chip on his shoulder wasn't up to the job. Tag sat down on the porch steps to wait.

Some time later he jerked out of a sun-induced doze as a car door slammed. A blue van, parked just down from the house, with a man and woman already starting toward him and two children erupting out its side door. The boy let out a whoop and lit out downhill for the stream. The little girl skipped after her parents and caught her mother's hand. Not Dana, Tag realized, rising. Tourists. Dudes.

"Jerry Zimmer," the man announced, pumping Tag's hand. "From Chicago. We saw your sign out on the highway and decided to take a chance. Got any rooms left?"

This was the duty the kid had skipped out on, Tag realized. He could tell them to wait for Dana, but Jerry's wife was already noting the house's shabby exterior with her eyebrows drawn together.

As she plucked at her husband's sleeve, Tag made up his mind. "You're in luck. We've got one cabin left, a nice one." At least he hoped it was nice. "Ninety a night or four hundred by the week, including meals. Like to take a look at it?"

The little girl bounced up and down on her toes. "Do you have ponies?"

"We've got the prettiest ponies in all Colorado. And a real cowgirl who can take you on trail rides," Tag assured her. "Want to come see 'em?"

An hour later, when an old pickup rattled up over the top of the hill, Tag was again waiting on the top step. A dark-haired woman waved at him from its window and pointed around the side of the house.

Following the truck to the back, Tag found its driver sliding down from the high seat. Dana. Younger than he'd pictured her, maybe thirty, with hair cut boy-short. Tired-looking, and as she turned sideways to lift a bag of groceries from the seat, he saw why. Four or five months pregnant, he estimated. She swung around and gave him a smile of equal parts warmth and worry. "Hi, I'm Dana Kershaw. Were you wanting a room?"

"R. D. Taggart. I'm a friend of Susannah's." He lifted the bag of groceries from her arms, saw a second waiting on the seat and collected that, as well. "I did want to ask you about lodging, but first I have a confession to make. I put a family of four in your number-one cabin. For three-fifty for the week. Is that all right?" He'd let Jerry bargain him down from four hundred and feel good about doing it.

Her surprise was fading to delight. "All right? That's... It's..." She shook her head dazedly. "*Thank* you! What did you say your name was?"

SHE'D BROUGHT HER DUDES safely back down the mountain, given all three horses a quick rubdown, then fed the herd in the home pasture. Then spent the rest of the afternoon searching her cabin and the vacant one alongside.

She'd found her .45 under a floorboard and hidden it this time where Tag would never find it. And her car keys were now tucked safely in her jeans pocket. Susannah stalked downhill, wondering where the skunk had wandered off to. Not half far enough, something told her.

She found him in Dana's kitchen, making the supper salad. Usually Susannah's job. "Nice ride?" he asked, looking up from slicing a cucumber.

"Only kind there is." She selected a knife from the chopping block, since he'd already snagged her favorite. "Where's Dana?" And why had she ignored Susannah's plea?

"She's setting the table." Tag drew a folded note from his pocket. "By the way, I found this on the counter when I brought in her groceries."

It was the note she'd left for Dana this afternoon, begging her to tell Tag he couldn't stay, to pretend that all the cabins were booked for the next month and promising to explain why when she saw her.

"Nice try, Tex, but it's too late now." Tag wadded her note and lobbed it across the room, scoring a clean basket in the trashcan by the stove. "Dana and I have a deal. I'm resident house painter, carpenter and kitchen helper for as long as I want."

"I'll tell her to cancel it."

"Do that and I drop a dime to the tabloids, I promise you."

"Creep!" She stabbed her knife into his chopping block and spun away. Walked aimlessly to the fridge and opened it. Focused finally on the iced tea pitcher. More was needed. She filled the kettle, then moved to the stove, keeping her back to him.

"Speaking of notes," Tag said behind her, "I've been meaning to tell you. I have this—"

"Oh, there you are!" Dana cried, bustling into the room. "We've got an extra four for supper, Susie, thanks to Tag. Did he tell you? I thought we'd skip the garlic bread and make biscuits, instead. Then I'll bake tomorrow, instead of Sunday."

"Sounds good." Susannah cocked her head to study her

friend's flushed cheeks. She'd known Dana for six weeks now. The woman put on a brave face always, but this was the first time Susannah had ever seen her approaching happy. *Nothin' like a good-looking man underfoot, skunk or no, to cheer a lady up.*

"Have you seen Sean anywhere?" Dana asked, reaching up for her big mixing bowl.

"Here, let me get that." Tag nudged her gently aside and lifted the bowl down off the top shelf. He moved back to his salad, oblivious to Susannah's sudden stillness.

There it was, the kindness she'd remembered all these months whenever she thought of Dr. Taggart. She'd spent her whole ride up the mountain, convincing herself that she must have imagined it. That she'd needed something nice to believe in these past few months with the rest of her life going down the tubes, and so she'd made him up. That the real man was nothing but a selfish skunk, no better than Stephen. But no, here it was again.

Just not aimed my way this time. Something dark fluttered inside her, like a blue rag flapping in a cold wind. The kettle whistled. She squared her shoulders and turned to it. *So what?*

"Um, Sean?" she repeated, recalling the question. "Nope, he wasn't up by the barn." Dana's stepson would hang around horses when they sprouted wheels and chrome tailpipes, not before. Meantime, she had her own questions for Dr. Taggart. He'd had her too flustered to think at first, but the ride had cleared her head.

Susannah didn't get a chance to ask during supper, even though Dana placed Tag in the seat next to her. With ten sitting down to baked ham, sweet-potato pie and cheddar biscuits at the long dining room table, conversation stayed loud and general. Henry was regaling them all with a description of the elk they'd seen up on the mountainside. His wife, Lynn, was going on and on about the wildflowers. The Zimmer girl was pestering Susannah—could she please, please, have that red-spotted pony for her riding lesson tomorrow? He—indicating Tag—had thought that would be fine.

The Appaloosa? Two-year-old Tamale would toss her over the moon! "Well, honey, I was hoping you'd help me out with this little paint pony, Guapo. He's been awfully sad since we bought him. He's 'bout your age, eight, and I reckon he misses his mommy. Anyway, I was hoping you could cheer him up for us." Catching Tag's grin from the corner of her eye, she kicked his ankle under the table. *Mess me up now, and I'll saddle* you *for her, stud, that's a promise.* One more thing she'd have to get straight with him, the pushy damn Yankee. She was the wrangler here and all four-legged decisions were hers.

While I'm here. She paused, glass midair. Not much longer, she'd decided today. That rag flapped again in her mind, scudding before the cold wind, snagging on the barbs of a fence, ripping a bit, then blowing on.

Because if Tag had found her, then Stephen could find her. And since Dana would never take Stephen's bribe to kick Susannah out, he'd have to hurt her to get his way, the way he'd hurt Ike. And Dana would be such an easy mark—she was hanging on by a thread here. She couldn't do that to Dana. *'Bout time to move on.* She shivered and set down her glass.

Tag's big fingers encircled her elbow from behind, where no one else would see. "Cold?" he murmured.

"Yeah." To the heart. She could have made something here. She and Dana were *simpatica*, and Dana desperately needed a knowledgeable partner. They could have built something here, together.

While the others tucked into Dana's peach pie with vanilla ice cream, Susannah went out to the kitchen to start on the dishes. A few minutes later Tag loomed alongside her and reached for a dish towel. She'd give the man that, anyway. When there was a job to be done, he didn't sit on his hands, waiting to be asked. They worked in surprisingly comfortable silence, elbow bumping elbow, till finally she broke it. "I've been meaning t'ask—how'd you find me?" She'd been so careful, leaving Austin at rush hour the morning after Stephen had phoned her. She'd tied its hectic freeways in knots, dodging round and round the cloverleafs, watching for a tail, before she'd finally skipped town. Then she'd driven like a crazy lady, driven all that night, eyes on her rearview mirror. She'd have sworn that nobody followed.

And nobody could have guessed where she was headed, since she hadn't a clue herself. She'd ended up in Dawson purely by chance, because she'd been too beat to drive farther, and it had seemed as good a place as any.

Better than any, it had turned out.

His rag paused on the dish. "I found you the same way I'll find you again if you run, Susannah."

But how? She wanted to grab him by his broad shoulders and shake the answer out of him. Because till she knew that, there was no knowing how to plug the leak. How to disappear better next time.

Till Tag popped up like a bad-tempered jack-in-the-box, she'd have sworn only one person in the wide world knew who she was and where she was—her father's partner, Jake. As soon as she'd decided to stay in Dawson, she'd dropped Jake a letter.

Because Jake was her one fixed point in a world spinning right off its axis. Jake would tell Saskia where to find her when she asked. And Susannah had told him that if Cam ever called, wanting her, to let her know. Cam had been so torn up after Brady's death, she couldn't cut him loose entirely. He was getting old. Might need a friend someday.

So Jake knew where she was, but Jake would never betray her. He'd been her second father all those years, keeping her back at the ranch when her dad was off on the racing circuit.

And he'd been an absolute rock, once her dad took his last fall and came home for good, paralyzed from the waist down.

But Zelda? Jake's wife was as good-hearted as he was but without his shrewdness. She'd trust Satan to pass the collection plate and be shocked when it came back empty. Usually Jake kept important details to himself, just so she couldn't give them away to anyone who asked. But maybe this time…? "Did you stop by my dad's ol' place, west of Kerrville?"

The ranch was no secret. The papers and the TV scum had told the world everything there was to know about her, and then some. It had sickened her so she'd stopped reading the papers or watching the tube by the second day. The woman they were talking about was nobody *she* knew—or needed to know.

"No." Tag took another plate from her, stood for a moment, not wiping. "I stopped by Fleetfoot Farm." He glanced down at her as she flinched. "And I met an old friend of yours there, a trainer, said he was your friend and Brady's."

"Cam." So Cam must have called Jake, talked to Zelda, instead, and helpful Zelda had told him where to find her. Three people could keep a secret if two of them were dead, her dad used to say. *But what else could I do?* If she'd told no one in the whole world how to find her and then something happened—either to her or to someone she loved… That fluttering feeling moved through her again. She'd be nothing but that rag, tumbling across the plains, blowing nowhere. Without connections you were nothing. Nobody to no one.

But through her connections is how Stephen would track her down. Might be tracking her down already. *I've gotta move on.* Tonight, she decided. She handed Tag a plate, then couldn't let go—as if the floor had dropped out from beneath her boots and her grip on that plate, Tag's strong fingers on the far side of it, were all that kept her from falling out into the windy dark. Out into starless space. Out, out and gone.

Tag peeled her fingers from the plate, set it aside and cupped his palm to her cheek. "What's the matter, Blue Eyes?"

His fingers were hot and damp from the dishwater. For a foolish moment she had the feeling that if she turned her head and pressed her lips to his big, rough palm, he wouldn't move. Wouldn't laugh at her. She blinked rapidly and turned back to the sink, water going gray with grease. "Nothin' in the whole, wide world." He'd come to her for money, not from caring, she reminded herself. *A smart man knows his friends,* was another thing her dad used to say.

She remembered the night she'd told him, out on their porch, that she meant to marry Stephen. *"I know you love him, honey,"* he'd drawled after a long, long silence. *"But will he make you a best friend when the fire dies down?"*

"Why, yes," she'd said. Absolutely. You bet—and rammed her head straight into trouble. And her dad wasn't sitting on the porch now to go back to, to say, "You were right and I was wrong one more time, Daddy." He'd passed on three months after her wedding and she missed him yet.

"We're not making much headway here." Tag caught her arms from behind and eased her over to where he'd been standing. *There's that gentleness again,* she told herself as he put his towel in her hands. "So let's try this." He picked up her scrubber and a plate.

After a moment she got her fingers moving. "Cam," she said as she dried. "How was he?"

"Looked fine to me. Said to give you his best and..."

She glanced up to find him frowning at the saucer he held. "And?"

"And he gave me something to bring you. A...message."

Her fingers stopped moving. If Stephen was hurting Cam, too! *How far does it go? He's going to get every last person who ever smiled at me?* "What'd he say?"

"It's a written message. From Brady."

She threw down the towel. He was making this up, but for what reason? "Pull the other leg—it jingles. Brady's dead, big guy."

"I know that. But Cam said he found it hidden in his hatband. The hat Brady wore the night he fell."

An image of Brady's battered old fedora filled her mind. She turned it this way and that, mentally fingered its fraying green ribbon. He'd tucked all kinds of notes inside his hat's inner band—his grocery list, phone numbers of women he met in bars, a reminder to send his youngest niece a china horse for her birthday. "Where is it?" she said finally.

"I have it."

Anger flared, spread like the roiling flames below a launching moonrocket. "Why isn't it here in my hand, then? If Brady had something to say t'me…" *Something about that night?*

"Because I'm proposing a trade," Tag said evenly, swinging to face her. "I give you the message, Susannah, and you…you hand over your broodmare."

The glasses to be washed were lined up along the back of the sink. She scooped one into the dishwater and splashed its contents straight in his face. "*Pond* scum!" He'd hold a last message from a dead man hostage for his own uses?

Water dripped from Tag's nose, beaded in his long, dark lashes. He shook out his hands, then wiped his face—slowly, deliberately. She bit her bottom lip and waited for the explosion to match her own. "Don't do that again," he said, his voice way too quiet.

"Then don't *you*—" She turned as the door to the dining room swung open and Henry pushed into the kitchen.

"You ready to head into town, Susie?"

She'd asked him for a lift to Moe's this afternoon, since her car was still parked there. "Sure thing. Be right with you."

"Got room for one more?" Tag said as he dropped a heavy

hand on her shoulder. A gesture that meant *Don't even think about protesting.*

"More the merrier!" Henry assured him. "See you at the car in ten minutes?"

CHAPTER THIRTEEN

THAT HE HALF AGREED with her only made Tag the madder. Bargaining with Brady's message did seem lower than low, but what were his options? *Let's try to keep in mind just who damaged whom here.* Considering that she'd willfully leveled his life, why should he flinch at throwing her a hardball?

He'd cheered up when he stopped by his cabin to grab her keys from his hidey hole—and found them gone. Along with her gun. *Here we go again.* It was their brief truces that confused him. As long as they both knew this was war, he was fine.

His eyes skimmed over her slender figure as she stepped from Henry's car in front of Moe's. No room in those jeans for anything but sweet Susannah. She wouldn't shoot him tonight, anyway. They waved cheerily as Henry and Lynn drove off toward Dawson in search of a real cowboy bar, then turned warily to face each other, smiles slipping.

"If you're planning to mooch around Moe's all night, you better think again," Susannah said. "Judy knows you're no friend of mine and—"

"Judy?"

"The other waitress—she warned me about you last night. I told her that if any strangers ever came askin' for me, t'let me know."

"So *that's* how you spotted me."

"Yep. Which means from now on, if I were you, dude, I wouldn't drink Judy's coffee or try t'eat here."

And let's not even think about that sandwich last night,

Tag decided, suppressing a shudder. "Fine. I'll just wait around back in your car." He held out his hand. "The keys, please?"

"Over my dead body!"

"Kinky, Lambchops, but there're easier ways." He patted her cheek and ambled off around the side of the building. "Have a nice night."

He didn't need to break into the battered old Ford with Texas plates. Somebody had long since smashed its driver-side vent. Shoving his hand through the plastic taped over the gap, Tag opened the door. Though he hadn't hot-wired a car in seventeen years, it was one of those skills like riding a bike. Once learned... In five minutes he was tooling merrily out of the parking lot.

WHAM!

He'd been having a very nice dream, Susannah and him rolling around in the straw of the clinic's stall, with Payback sprawled in the hay beside them, watching their antics through sleepily approving eyes. Payback was a stud again, Tag remembered that, as he opened his own—

Whop!

Looking up, he found the object of his dream—the human one—apparently upside down and scowling at him through his dusty side window. Not looking half as pleased with him as she'd looked in his dream.

Whump! Whump! Whump!

She smacked the roof of his car and kept on smacking till he sat up and opened the door. "Yeah?"

"Where's my car?" By the pink light of dawn, Susannah looked half-dead on her feet—and downright dangerous. Eyes like a roaring blue norther, horse troughs freezing solid from the Panhandle south to Galveston.

"Ah." Tag swung his legs out of the back seat onto the ground and stood, feeling safer immediately. It was nice to have almost a foot on your opponent. "Did you notice my new tires?" Good luck was such a rare event these days he'd hardly been able to believe it. Plus a moon like a silver dollar to work by, then that dream on top of all. And now, the look of incredulous outrage on her face as she stalked slowly around his car, hands on her hips. "Look familiar?" Who said revenge wasn't sweet?

"You mean...?"

"A perfect fit." Retreads like the ones she'd shot out, but these days he wasn't asking gift horses to say "Ah." It was enough to have wheels again. A man without a car was like a woman without a wiggle. Powerless in a cold, cruel world. "And don't worry, I put yours up on blocks. When you earn enough for four tires, then we can—"

"Shut up." She flounced around to the passenger side and got in. Tipped back the seat, stretched out her long legs and slid down till she was nearly prone. By the time Tag climbed into the driver's seat, her eyes were closed and her hands were clasped over her flat stomach.

"Home?" he asked, and the word was both strange and sweet on his tongue.

"I guess..." A down-hearted sigh of a sound. She didn't open her eyes till they turned off onto the unpaved road, marked by a sign proclaiming the way to the Ribbon River Dude Ranch, four miles. Guests Welcome. "What d'you think you're gaining by all this?" she murmured without opening her eyes. "Why're you hangin' around? You know if I had money I'd give it to you."

"Kind of you, babe."

"Kind? The pleasure'd be all mine, believe me, if I could see the south end of you headin' north." She opened her eyes and sat up as they crossed the low concrete bridge that spanned the stream. "But I haven't got the money and I never will. So can't you let it go?"

"Sure. Like you let it go when your husband told you

he was dumping you?'' They drove past the house and he waved at Dana, out on her porch.

"Dumping me?" Susannah pulled the elastic off her braid, shook her hair out. "What're you talkin' about?"

"Dumping you for another woman." The car bumped up the track alongside the meadow to stop below their cabin. "What started this whole moronic feud, remember?"

Susannah's peal of laughter was vivid as the streak of cloud overhead, blazing flamingo-bright from the sun rising beyond the mountain. "You got it all wrong, Doc!" She opened her door, stepped out, then leaned back in, her smile wide and mocking. "Stephen wasn't leaving *me*. I was leaving *him!*"

Before he could catch his breath, she'd run lightly up the steps and ducked into her cabin. Uncontested winner of this round—Ms. Susannah Mack.

Letting her have the last word—for now—Tag turned his attention to his own cabin. Which could use it.

The furniture had all been shoved into the kitchen, then draped with a plastic tarp. Buckets and bowls stood here and there on the floor, testimony to the leaks that Sean had mentioned, though the layer of dust that covered every surface showed it hadn't rained in quite a while. Part of the deal he'd worked out with Dana was that he'd patch the tin roof.

Tag found a broom in the closet off the kitchen and set to work. Two hours of sweeping and mopping and carrying out mice nests banished the worst of the grunge. He moved the furniture back in place, using Susannah's arrangements next door as his model. By then it was nearly eleven. The mattress could use a ten-minute test-drive, he decided.

When he opened his eyes again, it was past noon. He lay blinking sleepily up at points of sunlight showing through the tin. Out his bedroom window a bird whistled a three-note call he'd never heard before, and somewhere far off a horse whinnied.

Susannah. He went to his car for a change of clothes, showered, then knocked on her door. No answer.

He found her down at the corral, cleaning a saddle she'd thrown over a sawhorse. Within the enclosure Katy, the Zimmers' daughter, straddled the paint pony. Guapo wore a halter, instead of a bridle and a stirrupless pad was cinched around his stocky barrel. The pony wandered at will. The child's face was a study in dazzled contentment. Her hands rested on her plump thighs, and if the paint paused too long, she nudged him gingerly in the ribs with her heels. "Look at *me*, Tag, I'm learning to ride!" she yelled from the far side of the pen.

"I can see that! Way to go, cowgirl!" He stopped beside Susannah. "You start her without a saddle?"

"Yep." She gave him a brief unfriendly look, then dipped her rag in the can of saddle soap and bent back to her job. "I'd start her bareback, the way my dad taught me, if she was my own kid. But Mrs. Zimmer looks like the type who'd complain if I sent her back smelling like a horse, so a saddlepad will have to do."

"Doesn't give her much to hang on to." Though Susannah might be a pistol-packing maniac in her personal life, he didn't doubt for a moment that she knew her stuff when it came to horses. But she was angry at him again about something, her foxy-colored brows drawn together in a cool frown. *Talk to me, babe. I've got more questions than a three-year-old.*

"I don't want her starting out depending on a saddle horn," she drawled, turning to check the girl. "Ridin's all about balance. 'Bout hanging on with your legs, not your hands." After that she clamped her soft lips into a straight line and refused to be drawn out again. When the saddle was buffed to a satiny glow, she hoisted it easily.

"Here, let me carry that."

"*No,* thank you." She marched off toward the barn.

Tag shrugged and went along. "You're mad at me," he said when she'd thrown the saddle over a rail inside, then dragged down the next in line.

"Just 'cause you stole every dollar I own? Silly me." She headed for the bright square of sunlight at the end of the barn.

Tag caught the saddle horn, bringing her to a halt. "You mean your forty-two dollars?" She must have tried to add last night's tips to her stash. "It's in a safe place, Susannah."

"Yeah? Well, I don't believe I appointed you banker."

"But that's what I'll be till I get some answers. I don't want to wake up some morning and find you've skipped town."

"I don't owe you any answers." She tipped up her face to follow a barn swallow, swooping above them into the loft.

"You owe me plenty." He wanted to touch the point of her upturned chin, trace the delicate line of her throat down to the curving softness just showing at the V of her T-shirt. Unable to do that, he rocked the saddle by its horn, making her sway gently on her feet. "Like what the hell was this all about, Susannah? If your husband wasn't dumping you, then why spite him by gelding Payback? I don't get it."

The saddle creaked as she shrugged. "Had my reasons."

"What? Tell me."

"Tell *you?*" She let her arms drop away and stepped back, leaving him holding the load. Attached to forty unsupported pounds of saddle, he staggered, then caught it just before it hit the ground. "Now why would I trust a money-grubbing Yankee who'd trade the last words of my dying friend for his own gain?''

Put like that, he couldn't think of a reason that would convince her. He followed her back outside and swung the saddle up on her sawhorse.

She attacked it with rag and saddle soap, the rich, masculine smell rising between them, sun warming their backs. Sweat darkened her shirt between her breasts, making the cloth cling to her heated skin. He could no more have walked away from her at that moment than he could have flown to the moon. Tag found a second rag she'd draped over the rail, dipped it into the can and started copying her actions, soaping the other side of the saddle. Susannah ignored him completely.

''You can stop this anytime,'' he reminded her finally. ''Sell your broodmare, pay me off and I'm outta here. History. You can have Brady's message and God bless.'' For all the good it would do her.

''Don't hold your breath.''

No way he could have. His breath was coming faster, just being this near to her. He could have dipped his head and buried his nose in her silky hair, drawn in its scent. Fresh-cut hay and marigolds, he imagined. ''What would you get for her if you—when you sell her?''

She snorted and shoved his rag out of the way to jab her own back in the soap. ''I bought her at auction, practically stole her from a farm that was going under. Paid twenty thou' for her. Might get double that if I was lucky.''

Say they realized thirty thousand, with his luck. And he couldn't beggar her, no matter what she'd done to him. When he thought Susannah was worth ten million, he'd always figured he'd settle for five in the end. So half of thirty thousand was...dismal.

''What would you do with all that money if I did give

it to you?'' she murmured, working her rag around the silver conchos on the saddle skirts.

He'd given that some serious thought, last night, while he changed tires. ''I'd get out of the country. Go find me a shack on some beach in Thailand or someplace like that. Be a beach bum. Eat fish and coconuts for five years, chase dusky maidens. And hope your ex forgot about me, meantime, found somebody else to pick on.''

It was that or kill the man. Tag had no doubt he could do that, but looking up at that magical moon last night, he'd decided he'd do almost anything to avoid it. He meant to live his life free. That had been the whole point of his life ever since he could walk or form a thought. But if he killed a man, he'd spend the rest of his life looking over his shoulder, worrying about the law. And he'd never be free of his own conscience.

So running was smarter all the way round. Find a beach and lie low. Kick back for a while, take the time off he'd denied himself for the last seventeen years, building his career. Even if Colton was the king of revenge, surely no man could sustain a grudge for five years.

''In other words, you'd run like a rabbit?'' Susannah hammered the lid down on her can of saddle soap, set it aside.

Tag reached for the saddle just as she did, and it came up between them, almost levitating. He reeled it into his chest, which brought her in, too, nearly within kissing range. Definitely in range, if he leaned closer. ''So what would you have me do, Susannah?'' He couldn't focus on her blue eyes. His gaze kept dropping to her lips. The tip of her tongue flicked out to wet their softness and he almost groaned aloud. Was she doing it on purpose?

''Hey, Susie!'' Katy and her pony stood on the other side of the fence, staring at them through its rails. ''Guapo's bored. Can we go outside?''

"Soon as you know how to use a bridle, honey. Did you bring him over here the way I showed you? Using your knees?" When the girl nodded, Susannah said, "Then you're ready. Be right back." She let go of the saddle, leaving Tag to lug it along behind her.

THAT NIGHT, washing the supper dishes together, he remembered to say, "I found my jacket in your car last night."

"Oh…yeah." Susannah kept her head bent to the pot she was scrubbing.

"It's one thing I wondered about. Why'd you take it?" Compared with everything else she'd done to him, stealing his bomber was nothing. But Tag had always found you could judge people by the little things. Never trust a man who'd kick a dog. If your date's mean to the waiter, then walk and walk fast.

"I forgot I was wearing it." A patch of pink bloomed along her sculpted cheekbone. "Your ol' dragon of a receptionist was giving me the evil eye, what with my credit cards bouncin'. Stephen had canceled every last one of 'em by then. And I was scared silly he'd have some way of tracing me, once she called the numbers in. I knew Pook and I'd better hit the road, runnin'. So—" she shrugged and handed him the pot along with a defiant look "—I just forgot."

"Fair enough, you forgot." Maybe. A *big* maybe. "So what about later, once you had time to remember?"

"I…" The pink along her cheekbone was fading into an over-all rosiness. "Once I realized I'd kept it, it was such a ratty ol' thing, it seemed easier to write you than wrap it and send it back." She turned to face him, her eyes too wide, too innocent, her cheeks the shade of a tequila sunrise. "So I dropped you a postcard from Boston. Told you to deduct whatever you wanted from my ring for it—"

"The ring that wasn't yours to give me in the first place."

"That one, yeah." She made a face. "I didn't know that. More fine print I must have forgotten t'read before the wedding."

"I never got your card." If she'd mailed it at all. She was lying about something. Her gaze was too unblinking.

"Well, I sent it."

Truth or another barefaced lie? On one side of the question, he'd left town the day after she did. By the time he returned from Boston, his life was in shambles and he hadn't caught up yet. What with his moving and the clinic changing hands and the bags of hate mail that had descended on him, some of his legitimate mail might easily have gone astray. For all he knew, he could have lost dozens of letters. But that one? The one that proved her honesty? How convenient.

"I did send it," she insisted into his silence.

"Right," he said neutrally. *So why, babe, do you look guilty as sin?*

And why couldn't he simply accept that she was a lying, vengeful little bitch? Before Susannah, he'd have said that only a fool confused lust with trust. *But who's the fool now?*

CHAPTER FOURTEEN

A COUPLE OF DAYS' dancing around each other had gotten her precisely nowhere, Susannah thought, while she leveled her plastic crate below Tag's bedroom window.

She'd offered to teach him to ride in exchange for Brady's message. Face it, it would have been her pleasure to put Tag up on something he couldn't handle, Tamale maybe, then watch him clutch and wobble. *At my mercy, dude!* Now that would be a nice change. She was so sick of his holding every advantage on her—of size, strength, education. Brains that at least matched her own.

But no dice. The only thing that Tag was willing to trade for was her broodmare, and Sheba was a nonnegotiable. So housebreaking was Susannah's only remaining choice, short of a stickup. *So, big guy, here's hopin' you don't lock your windows.*

But he did, of course. Yankees weren't the trusting sort, Susannah was learning. *And how could you ever trust somebody who can't trust?* She hurried back to her cabin for a knife, stopping on the porch to look up at the moon—on the wane now—then down toward the ranch house.

The kitchen windows were dark. Which meant that Tag must still be in town. He'd dropped Susannah at the truckstop as he did every night now, picking her up again in the morning, then he'd driven on to the grocery store down-valley near Cortez. The shopping list Dana had given him should keep him busy for a good hour or so.

Once he returned, Susannah assumed he'd help Dana put

the food away. Then most likely she'd offer him a cup of coffee. *For all I know they hang around together every evening, talkin' till midnight.*

Or later. A raw, hot feeling moved through her and she rubbed her stomach absently. Not that it was any of her business if they did. Not that she really believed Dana had stopped missing her husband enough to actually notice Tag. She'd only been widowed four months.

But even if she didn't notice him, he'd notice her. Dana was very pretty. Awfully sweet. Any man would be a fool not to like her. To want to help her.

And any woman would be a fool to pass up Dr. Taggart's company. The man was pure, unadulterated hunk. A toe-curler. Mad as he often made her, Susannah could hardly keep her own eyes off Tag whenever he was around.

Yeah, and look where that got you the last time you fell for a pair of wide shoulders and buns to die for, she reminded herself, returning to his window at the back of the cabin.

But Tag had something Stephen lacked. Something she'd been too young and smitten to look for, going in, the last time. What her dad must have seen was missing, when he'd tried to warn her about Stephen that night out on their porch. Tag had kindness.

At least she thought so. The latch swiveled beneath her knife's prodding. She pulled the upper sash down, since the bottom one seemed to be painted shut. Stepped up from the crate to the sill. *We'll see how kind he is if he catches you climbin' in through his back window!*

But nobody yelled and nobody caught her as Susannah stepped over the sash and down to his bedroom floor. *So...if I was a message from Brady, where would I hide?* She drew a penlight from her pocket and swept its beam around the— "Uhh!" She leaped back, her bottom bumped the wall. She stood, plastered against it.

Two green eyes glared right back at her.

"Zorro!" The barn cat rose from Tag's pillow, to stretch, then stroll across the mattress to meet her. "You scared me within an inch of my life, you devil!" So Tag had taken to sleeping with him, had he? The tom had been following him around all week. Seeking free medical advice, Tag always claimed.

Now he dogged Susannah's footsteps, stropping her shins while she searched the drawers of Tag's bureau, the pockets of his shirts and jeans. She checked beneath his mattress—nothing. Looked below the floorboard where he'd hidden her keys and gun—was he that tricky that he'd use the same place twice?

Nope. She let out a vexed sigh and stood. "You think he keeps it on him night and day?" Tag knew how hot she was to see Brady's message. Seemed to know by instinct that she couldn't leave Dawson without it. That the curiosity was half killing her. "That's where I'd keep something safe, if I was big enough to know nobody could take it off me."

But he'd locked his cabin on leaving from the very start, which seemed to imply that the treasure was here. "Gimme a hint, fuzz-face."

No reply. The tom had wandered off somewhere. Susannah swept her light around the bedroom one more time, then followed him out. The drawers in Tag's kitchen would be her next— She stopped, her light catching the cat crouched by the door. "You want out, huh?"

"Merrrrr." He addressed that remark to the paneling, rather than her.

"Too bad. If I let you out, then Tag'd know somebody—" Through her boot soles, she picked up what Zorro must have heard much sooner—the vibration of someone coming up the steps to the porch. "Oh, Lord!" She spun—and her flashlight smacked the doorjamb, fell and went out.

Find it quick or he'll know! She knelt in the dark and groped frantically. The tom must have caught her panic. She felt the soft whisk of his fur as he dashed past. Her fingers closed on the flashlight and she bolted for the window just as a key turned in the outer door. *I'll make it! I'll just—* *"Oh!"* That soft ropy thing underfoot was—

"Yrrrrrreooow!"

—the blasted cat! Susannah sidestepped, tripped over the scrambling brute again to sprawl face-first across the mattress. *"Ooof!"* The flashlight went flying. *Forget that!* She sucked in a breath of Tag's scent and rolled. She was still in darkness. If he didn't come in the bedroom, then maybe… Lunging to her feet off the side of the bed, she made the window in two soft strides, stepped up onto the sill—

—and a pair of big hands closed around her waist. "Hold on, there."

"I was…just leaving," she said with all the dignity she could muster, given the circumstances, as Tag lifted her off the sill and set her down.

Too close to his warmth, her hips just brushing his thighs, his hands almost spanning her waist and none too gentle. He put his face in her hair and inhaled, then laughed under his breath. "Susannah."

"Last time I looked." She was breathing too fast—his hands on her and the fright of the last few minutes. Her face felt redder than red, so good thing he hadn't turned on the lights. "Now if you *don't* mind…"

"Oh, but I do. Trespasser." Fingers warm on her waist, he turned her around, holding her up when she almost fell over her own wobbly knees. Then stood there, a big shadow gazing down at her. "So let's start with the penalty. Excuses can come later."

"What pen—" His mouth covered hers and she gasped aloud—gasped into him, more like. *Oh, that one…* A wave of warmth broke over her as her hands crept up to his shirt and caught hold. *Oh, boy…* She opened her mouth wider in welcome and shuddered against him. He groaned, a deep, soft sound of pleasure and wanting. Now she was in for it. She stood slowly up on tiptoe, arching into him, senses opening to the delicious taste of him, his warmth and tantalizing hardness beneath her hands...

Susannah Mack, have you gone entirely crazy? She yanked her mouth sideways and free. ''Lemme go!''

''That's—'' Tag's mouth paused an inch above her lips. His voice was husky with laughter. ''*That's* what you're saying?'' His thumbs fanned the softness below her ribs.

''Yeah...'' *I think...I guess...* If she had any sense left at all. Which she did. She flattened her hands against his chest and straightened her arms, levering herself out of his hold. Her back hit the wall behind her. So much for getting away.

Tag let go of her waist and braced his arms on the wall to either side of her shoulders. Dropped his head till his forehead rested against hers. ''If that was no, then yes might scare me half to death. I think I see what—'' He stopped abruptly.

''See what?''

He shook his head lazily against her, then brought one hand to her face, palmed her cheek. ''Was...there something you needed in here?''

Like you, maybe? He was the last thing she needed. *And the first I want?* She wasn't that much of a fool, was she?

Rough, warm and gentle, Tag's fingers slid down her cheek to span her throat. The back of his hand nudged her chin, coaxing it higher.

One more kiss like the last one and she was done for. *It's now or never, Susannah.* There was always one instant when you were riding a big ride, a tough one. The moment when everything teetered in the balance, when somebody's will was the stronger. When you dug deep down and decided. She lifted her chin and squared her shoulders. ''You know what I came for, Tag, and it wasn't this.''

''I know.'' He let her go and walked back to the door.

Giving her a chance to scramble out his window. She didn't take it. "Brady's message is mine and I want it. Tonight."

"Hmm." Tag strolled on into his living room and switched on the lamp by the couch. Susannah followed and stood, arms crossed, toe tapping, while he found the cat waiting by the door, looking as fussed and bothered as she felt. Tag put him out. Wandered on into the kitchen.

Temper rising, she followed. She'd had the high hand for a moment there, but now the reins slid through her fingers. Back turned her way, he found a bottle in the cabinet, then brought down two glasses. "Scotch?"

Her dad and Jake used to drink scotch when they were feeling expansive, after they'd cut a fine deal horse trading. The taste was always a comfort to her, bringing sweet old memories from when the world was simple and right. "Sure, just a drop. With ice." She should repeat her demand for Brady's message, then go. Licking her lips, she tasted Tag on them—and stayed.

"How'd you get back here?" he asked idly while he fixed their drinks.

"Judy's cousin gave me a lift." Sam had been happy to please her. She'd told him days ago that Dana would be needing a wrangler any time now, and that when she quit she'd recommend him. Sam knew his horses and he was as gentle as Tag, though he hadn't Tag's edge, that hint of steel underlying the kindness. "I told Moe I had t'take the night off." Moe wouldn't put up with much more of her nonsense, but that didn't matter now. She had one foot out the door already.

Because she could *feel* Stephen coming. Feel him breathing down her neck, his hardboots stomping closer and closer these past few days. This was her seventh week in one place. It was time to move on before Dana was hurt by her presence. All she needed was her message from Brady, then she could go.

Presuming I find a way to give Tag the slip. The thought

of doing so didn't give her the pleasure it should have. "What are *you* doing back here?"

"So inconveniently?" He handed her a glass. "Dana had something on her grocery list about cream for Susannah. I wasn't sure what she meant. Hand cream? Cream for coffee?"

Susannah made a face. "Whipping cream. I told her I'd make strawberry shortcake this week."

"Ah. Well, anyway, I called her to ask, but Sean said she was in the bath. So I tried to phone you at the truckstop and Moe told me you'd gone home sick. At which point…"

"You smelled a rat and came roaring back. Of all the rotten luck!" She sat next to him on the couch, then slouched down in disgust, stretching her legs out before her till her bottom nearly slid off the cushion. Bad move, she realized instantly, feeling his eyes on her. She brought her boots primly together. Balanced her glass on her stomach and closed her eyes.

Ice clinked in his drink beside her. "You were wasting your time, anyway."

"Yes?" She took a considering sip of her own, and with the taste, was yanked back years and miles to the home ranch—to see her dad laughing as he fanned a winning poker hand out on the kitchen table, Jake throwing down his cards in pretended outrage. He and Zelda used to drop by to play with them Friday nights, knowing how her dad loved the game, how bored he got, confined to his wheelchair. "So it's in your wallet?"

"Could be."

Is. A wave of raw frustration swept through her. She could see herself rolling over to kneel astride him, grabbing two fistfuls of his shirtfront, shaking him and demanding what was rightfully hers. "It's mine, Tag, and I want it." She wasn't leaving this room without it.

Ice clinked beside her. "Tell me about Brady. Was he your lover?"

She snorted and drank. "Hardly. Brady was..." she smiled slowly to herself "...my friend. As cantankerous an ol' hardboot as ever came hammerin' down the backstretch. Used to be a top jockey. He and Dad were rivals way back in the good ol' days. One would win Jock of the Year one year, then the other the next. Brady took the Derby on Payback the year my dad came in second on Arcturus. Fact is, Dad came in second in almost every race that year, what with Brady and Payback takin' the Triple Crown and everything else they entered."

She took another sip of scotch. Smiled. "By the time I met Brady, he'd stepped down to stallion groom at Fleetfoot. He was getting creaky and sick of starving himself down to ridin' weight. And he had this plate in his skull from a bad fall..." Her smile faded to bleakness.

"He was Payback's groom?"

"That's right. Oh, they were a pair of hell raisers, those two. Then when I showed up, Brady sort of took me under his wing, made it a threesome." There she'd been, awkward and shy and alone. Neither fish nor fowl. Married to Stephen, but not fitting in up at the big house, what with her country ways. She'd have been more at home with the folks down in the stables, but they were wary, assuming she'd report anything they said back to her husband. It had taken her more than a year to win their trust, and meanwhile, in that first lonely year, Brady had been there for her. Teasing her at first, bragging how much better he'd ever been than her daddy. Then later advising her, once she realized that he knew more about the ways of the rich after riding for them for forty years than she ever would.

Brady had been a godsend. She'd wanted desperately to fit in that first year, but Stephen wouldn't help her—seemed almost to enjoy it whenever she made a fool of herself in high society. As if her isolation and her insecurities somehow made her more his and his alone. *My little diamond in the rough,* he'd called her once at a Keeneland auction party, patting her bottom as he said it for all the world to see. As if she was a high-class call girl hired for the night, not his wife. So it was Brady she'd run to when she had questions or troubles. Kentucky without Brady would have been downright unbearable.

And now, when Brady was trying to speak to her one last time from beyond the grave, Tag stood between them. "I want his message, Tag."

"And you know what *I* want." Reaching out, he caught a strand of her hair and wound it around his finger.

"Sheba?" *Or tonight, maybe me?* Either way, her answer was the same. "Sure thing, when pigs pilot jetplanes." She had to keep in mind that he was here for his own purposes. That he bore her a grudge and maybe rightly so. And though the man might kiss like a five-star dream, she'd be a fool to give herself into his hands. Her trusting days were just about done. She'd grown up since Stephen.

"Seeing as how I don't want to wait that long," he said, "how can we settle this? Thumb wrestle?"

"Huh!" He'd kept on reeling in her lock of hair till his hand floated only inches below her chin. Looking down at it, she had to smile. "No way, José." *Never trust a man with big thumbs.* She shook her head lazily, liking the prickly feeling at her scalp from the tug of her hair. The sensation feathered softly down her spine. Holding in a shiver, she felt her nipples rise, instead. She maneuvered her glass past his fingers and drank.

"Flip a coin?" Tag looped another coil of her hair onto his forefinger and tugged gently, tipping her head back against the cushion.

"Don't think so." He was going to kiss her if she didn't move. Heat coiled in her stomach. Her bones felt as if they were melting like sun-warmed chocolate. Inadvisable to stand, with melting bones, she decided. She narrowed her eyes at him. "Let go, Tag." *Now. Before I let you kiss me.*

He let her go, leisurely, unwinding her hair coil by coil, then turned to pick up his glass on the side table. Set free, she felt a slow welling of disappointment. That wasn't what she'd wanted, either. *So make up your tiny mind, Susannah Mack. What do you want?*

She closed her eyes and sipped—and the answer came, nonsensical, undeniable. *I want him to hold me.* Not make love to her, just hold her for a little while. She'd been such a long time scared. Lonely for longer than that. To close her eyes and burrow her face against his solid warmth and heave a great big sigh, then just rest for a while with his strong arms walling out the world—was that so much to ask?

She knew the answer to that one. *You bet your boots it is.* If she asked Tag to hold her, it wouldn't end there. Not after that kiss they'd shared. And she didn't need the rest of it. *He came to get his own back. To take my mare away. Not to love me, or save me, or even give me a hug when I'd about hock my soul for it. Got that, Susannah?*

Got it. She watched while he got up and strolled off to the kitchen, then came back with the bottle of scotch and a deck of cards.

"Found these in a drawer the other day," he said as he refilled her glass. He sat a decent distance away from her this time and set the deck on the cushions between them. "Draw for high card?"

She smiled and cut the deck. Held up an ace of hearts. "Beat that."

"Your deal, cowgirl." He set the deck beside her thigh.

Shades of old good times, scotch and poker. Two wasn't enough to make a real game, but still… "Playin' for what stakes?"

Tag had a killer smile when he needed it, lazy and knowing. "How about Brady's message...set against your Secretariat mare?"

Don't bet what you can't afford to lose, her daddy had always said and she couldn't afford to lose Sheba. On the other hand, this might be her fastest route to Brady's message. She wasn't a half-bad card sharp. "How 'bout Brady's message against I *tell* you where Sheba is?" Because knowing wasn't the same thing as laying his hands on her. One phone call, and she could have Sheba shipped halfway across the country.

As he weighed the counter offer, she widened her eyes and tried not to blink, striving for a look of limpid innocence. Tag's gaze dropped to her lips and stayed there. "Good enough," he said finally. "But I'm afraid no poker chips came with the cards. So what do we use for bets?"

"I'm using my money you swiped. Where's my forty-two dollars?"

Here came that killer smile again. "Bottom of...your flour cannister, Lambchops."

It would be a waste of good scotch to dump her drink on his head, Susannah decided regretfully. She gave him smile for smile, instead. "Well, don't go 'way then. I'll be *right* back." *To take you straight to the cleaners, you smart-ass Yankee dude!*

CHAPTER FIFTEEN

YOU'D THINK WITH AS MUCH practice as she'd had, she'd be a better liar, Tag mused, while Susannah kicked off her boots and they cut again for first deal. She'd promised to tell him where her mare was if she lost. Translated from Susannah-think, that meant she had some way of moving the horse before he grabbed her.

Never say die, that was his stubborn darling. But as usual, she wasn't thinking it through. Once he knew where to look, he'd simply do whatever was required to prevent Susannah from reaching a phone till he could play equine repo man.

If I win, Tag reminded himself. And truth be known, he didn't care that much if he lost. As long as he withheld Brady's message, guilt would nag him. He was ready to lay that burden down.

"It'll take five t'sit down to this game," Susannah announced with gleeful authority, laying a bill down between them. "So ante up, boys!"

Great, he'd been thinking quarters for bets, tops. If luck ran against him, his remaining 110 dollars wouldn't last long.

The cards riffled and ticked as she shuffled, then began dealing. "This game's five card stud, gentlemen. No cards are wild. Minimum bet's a dollar. Max—sky's the limit."

"How will we know who's finally won? Winner of a certain number of hands? Eleven, say, or twenty-one?" Not that Tag felt any hurry to settle the contest with Susannah sitting barefoot and cross-legged on his couch, eyes bright as Venus at sunset. No hurry at all.

She gave him a gunslinger's smile. "Hey, when I've stomped you, dude, you're gonna know it. You'll go home wearin' a barrel."

"Brave words, hotshot." But she hadn't a poker face to match. As she examined her hole card, the tip of her tongue flicked out to wet her lips, while her slender throat moved in a slow gulp. *Bad hand, huh?* Tag checked his own hidden card—a queen to go with his jack, showing. Not much, but— "I'll bet one." He put out a dollar.

"I'll see that." Her bill was crumpled. A hard-earned tip, he realized with a twinge of remorse.

Third card was dealt faceup, and Tag's second jack took precedence over Susannah's three of spades. He grinned unsportingly and bet four dollars. "You'll stomp me when?"

She growled under her breath and matched his bet, then dealt their fourth cards, faceup, a ten to Tag, another three to herself.

A pair of jacks beat her pair of threes any day. He bet a fiver.

Her sigh came up from her toes. "I'll...see you." She matched him, then dealt their last cards, giving him a queen of hearts to pair with his hole-card queen. "Well, darn!" Susannah glared at her own ten of diamonds.

"We've got some nice barrels in size eight," he assured her, laying out another five dollars.

"I'm a size six, thank you very much." Susannah matched his bet, then...she laid two bills on top of it. "A-a-and I'll raise you...thirty." Her eyes were wide and innocent as a china doll's.

"Thirty." The woman was bluffing. Had to be.

She batted her long lashes at him. "You could always fold, hotshot."

With his twenty dollars already consigned to the pot? Not a chance. "I'll see that thirty."

"Not for long, you won't!" She flipped over her hole card. "Three threes—read 'em and weep."

"Why, you little…!" He laughed in spite of himself at her unabashed triumph and her wicked, bubbling giggle. Damn, but she'd suckered him! And she'd almost halved his stake in one game. "You won't do that again."

She didn't. The next time they played five card draw, his choice—and she beat him fair and square. Cute as a kitten, a killer at cards.

And lucky on top of it. By the end of an hour, he'd won a few hands, but where he played with cautious skill, she plunged with blithe abandon. He should walk away from this game—or run. His stake had dwindled to thirty-six dollars. It would be foolish to let her skin him. But Tag's pride was on the line now, as well as her broodmare.

And he wouldn't have stopped her giggling for the world. Because whether she was raking in the pot or watching him claim it, the woman giggled like a contralto canary. She was having a fine old time tonight.

And he couldn't blame her mood on the liquor, with which, hard pressed as he was, he'd have plied her shamelessly if he could have. She sipped like a bird—a canary who savored scotch. Susannah set her glass aside and gave him an evil smile. "Y'ever play Cincinnati?"

"Um…" A drop of gold glistened on her full lower lip. Tag gripped the top of the sofa, fighting down an urge to lunge across the cards, to tip her back against the armrest behind her, then lick that drop away. To keep on kissing till he'd covered her rosy face with kisses. That kiss at the start of the evening no doubt explained his bad playing. His mind kept abandoning the cards to circle on back to that. It had been a kiss like a head-on collision, both of them rushing for weeks—no, months—toward that fateful—

"Cincinnati," she repeated, her fingers rising to her mouth

self-consciously. "You do it this way…" She shuffled and dealt.

And beat him again. Then beat him at spit in the ocean and again at Mexican stud. He switched back to five card draw to make his cash last longer, then she chose seven card stud—and halfway through that hand, his wallet ran dry.

"I bet five," she said, and smiled up at him expectantly.

"I…can't." The humiliation was sudden and complete. A man was measured by his money. Shouldn't be, but was.

"You're quitting?" She looked stricken as a child who'd just been told the truth about the Easter Bunny. "You can't! It's not even midnight. I haven't stomped you half hard enough!"

"Too bad, babe, that's all I can afford to lose." Actually, he'd passed that point an hour ago.

"But…but… So I'll take an IOU! Where's a pencil and some—"

He caught her shoulder as she started to rise from the couch. "I couldn't pay it back later. Not till I find a job."

"That's all you had? Why didn't you *tell* me?" She grabbed two fistfuls of her winnings. "Then here, why don't you—"

"No!" He caught a slender wrist to keep her from shoveling money at him. "I said, *no*, Susannah."

"But—" her eyes filled slowly with tears "—I don't want t'stop. I haven't had such fun in…" She paused, thinking, her lips pursed in a delectable pout. "So bet something else, if you're too darned proud to gimme your marker."

"Like what?" He couldn't help touching her lips.

She leaned back and crossed her arms. Owl-eyed and solemn, she studied him. Then a slow, wicked smile curled and grew. "So bet me your tires, then. My car sure would like some."

If he had no money, then he had to have a working vehicle.

As it was, he'd have to start seeking a paying job of some sort tomorrow. "No way. A man needs his wheels."

"Tag, you are just no fun at all!" She caught a lock of her hair and brushed her lips with it, frowning. "Okay. I'll bet dollars for questions."

Those he had in plenty, starting with *Where did you ever learn to kiss like that?* "All right," he said at last. "I suppose." He didn't want the evening to end any more than she did.

Susannah found pencil and paper and wrote "One Question" on it. Tag matched her bet with that—and additional markers when she bet and raised again. By the time she'd won the hand, he was three questions down.

"Question One," she chortled, raking in the pot. "Lemme see now…"

"You're collecting now?" He felt a sudden stab of dismay. Somehow he'd pictured himself interrogating her, not the opposite!

"You bet your big boots I am."

"Getting hot in here." He retreated to the door and opened it. Then he slouched against the jamb, staring out at the moon, which kissed the tops of the pines to the west.

Susannah crossed to stand beside him, looking out. "Question one," she purred at his shoulder. "How'd you come to be a vet?"

"Why I became a vet…" That one he supposed he could handle. "I was sent to a…reform school, when I was thirteen. For a summer." He heard her suck in a breath beside him, but he kept his eyes on the sky.

"I'd never been out of the city—Boston—before that. So it was…different." Mind-blowing, for a cocky kid who'd thought he knew all there was to know about the world— only to discover that his world had been just a few square miles of greasy pavement. A world of hard knocks and small-time thinking. "I almost overdosed on grass and trees, that first week. And the stars, I'd never seen stars before, Susannah, not really. The city lights block them out. And there was a—'' He smiled, remembering. "A counselor, a young guy who managed to convince me I wasn't as bad as I thought I was. And that bad wasn't the achievement I'd always assumed it was.''

She laughed softly and touched his back. "But a vet?''

"Umm…'' He couldn't speak for a moment, with all his senses spiraling inward around that touch. *She just meant it to be friendly.*

She might as well have dripped gasoline down his spine, then struck a match. "Yeah…well, one day I found a hawk with a broken wing. I guess he'd dived after prey and hit a tree branch or a wire on the way down. A simple fracture. I splinted him up—took a few gouges doing it, before I thought of hooding him. But I didn't do a half-bad job, looking back on it. Kept him all summer, managed somehow to coax him to eat. He healed about the same time my release date rolled around. I took him out in a field behind the school, took the splint off and he just…flew.'' He felt the sting of old tears again. The pride and the soaring joy. "I thought if I could do that, I could…'' *Do anything! Fly away from an old shabby world to make myself a new one.* He shrugged. "That's why.''

"I like that why.'' She touched his back again, then turned away.

He followed, aching for her to touch him like that again. And again. *I want you, Susannah.* It scared him, how much wanting was starting to feel like need.

She was in the kitchen, freshening their drinks. "Question *two*,'' she said cheerily. "Why'd they stick you in reform school?''

"Ah…'' He propped one hip against the table. "To celebrate my thirteenth birthday—'' *there being no other cele-*

brations scheduled "—I swore that before I turned fourteen, I'd drive every kind of car there was worth driving."

She turned to look over her shoulder, her mouth rounding to a soft *O*. "You mean you stole cars?"

"Borrowed 'em. Joyriding. I'd already had a Porsche and a Jaguar and a BMW and a Corvette. The night I was busted, I was trying to sneak a Rolls-Royce Silver Cloud out of a restaurant parking lot past the valets. Turned out it belonged to the senator from Massachusetts. Not my smartest move."

She laughed as she turned to hand him his drink. "Last question. Where was your family during all this?" Looking up at him, her smile faded.

"There was only my father by then. And he'd have been where he always was. In a bar somewhere. Or passed out in a gutter on his way home."

"I see." She stood on tiptoe to kiss his cheek, lips soft as a butterfly's wing. "I'm sorry."

He didn't need pity kisses from anybody, not even her.

"I'm not." He took his drink and led the way back to the couch. "Everything turned out fine." Or at least it had till she'd driven up to his clinic with one simple request. "Now come back here and play poker. I'm feeling luckier."

He won two hands in a row. Susannah stopped feeling sorry for him and turned mock indignant, then mock dismayed as his luck held and he steadily won his way back to parity. She giggled and lost and threw new games at him—baseball, lowball, then something so silly that she trilled nonstop all the way through it. One-eyed noogie, in which each player wore one unseen card on top of his head, which the other could use for making up his hand. When Tag took that one, too, he realized he'd found the way to beat her. She couldn't giggle and think at the same time.

They played two more hands and as he raked in the last pot, he said, "Ready to cry uncle?" It had to be past one and

Susannah's lashes were drooping, giving her the look of a drowsy child. He wanted to carry her off to bed. His.

"Hah! In your dreams, dude." It was her turn to deal, but now, apparently, he couldn't lose. By the end of that hand she was out of cash and he'd won two questions off her.

"So, first question," he said while he shuffled. "That night I first…caught up to you, you told me you'd thrown your furs in the dump. Why'd you do that, Texas? Sheer cut-off-your-nose spite?" The waste of that still got to him every time he remembered.

"Well…" She reddened slowly under his waiting gaze, then shrugged. "Well, my lawyer had t'lean pretty hard on Stephen's shark to get my things back. My personal stuff, clothes and all…"

"You didn't go back and pack yourself?"

She let out a yip of startled laughter. "Haven't been back to Fleetfoot since the night I left. You saw those front gates. They don't open for this woman." She took a hummingbird sip of her drink and set it aside. "Anyway, so my lawyer finally pried loose my things and had 'em all shipped to my sister's." She heaved a long sigh. "But when I opened the boxes and went to hang stuff in her closet…something was wrong with everything. My lingerie, all my clothes, the furs I told you about."

"Wrong?" She'd propped her elbows on her knees and her face on her hands. He hooked a knuckle under her chin to tip her face up. "Wrong how?"

"Oh, little holes… Tiny holes started showin' up in everything. I thought maybe moths at first, but after a few days the holes got bigger. Then everything just sort of…fell to shreds." She shrugged, unwound her crossed legs and stood. "But hey, have y'ever been to Houston? You try t'wear a fur in that climate, they'd take you either for crazy or for a bear that took a wrong turn from the Rockies. They'd throw you in the loony bin or the zoo, depending. So I just dumped it all." She spun and headed for his bathroom. "Now if you'd excuse me a minute…"

"Sure," he said to the closing door, then sat, staring at its panels, while an ice cube slithered down his spine. *Battery acid!* Or some such corrosive, sprinkled over all. Diluted enough so that it took a few days to start doing its damage. Sprinkled on her underwear, she'd said, as well as her furs. *God almighty.* This was hating on a scale he couldn't imagine. Petty, but painstakingly vicious. *This is the guy I crossed? That Susannah helped me cross?*

When she came out of the bathroom with a freshly scrubbed face, Tag didn't know whether he wanted to pull her into his lap and hug her—or upend her over his knee and smack her sexy buns.

Both, he supposed, but one impulse neutralized the other. "Second question," he said coolly. "Why were you leaving your husband, if his version's not the truth? If it wasn't another woman, what was it?"

The cards slithered and whispered in the silence. Susannah sighed and stood beside the couch. "You sure know how to poop a party."

"Tell me," he coaxed, shuffling.

She brightened suddenly. "I just had a thought. Be right back."

Minutes later she burst back through his door with a smile—and her pistol. Tag's hands froze midshuffle, the cards exploding over his fingers.

Susannah set her gun before him and he remembered to breathe. "You can have this, instead of that question," she told him, seating herself again.

Meaning the question's more valuable. For a moment Tag considered refusing. But, call him a chauvinist, if one of them had to pack a gun, he wanted to be that one. "Good enough." He checked its clip—empty—then set it on the floor behind him and picked up the deck. If his luck held he'd get another crack at his question and then the big one, as well.

But Susannah won the next hand and resumed giggling.

Then Tag won, a major pot, including one of her markers. He lifted the paper and tickled her nose with it. "So tell me, Blue Eyes…" Suddenly he threw away his game plan. *Start with the big one.* The one he'd been asking himself— asking her in absentia—since day one. "Why did you have me geld Payback?"

"Why…" She licked her lips. Shook her head. "Ask me another one."

"Questioner's choice, darlin', and it's that one. Tell me."

Her beautiful white teeth clamped her bottom lip. She wouldn't meet his eyes. She shook her head. "Sorry."

"Dammit, Texas, those are the rules! Loser pays up."

She shrugged. "Gotta welsh on that one. Sorry."

Why? Would she look that bad if she told him? *"Susannah."* He wanted to shake it out of her. They were back to square one. Ms. Stubborn, sitting there with her chin tipped, and Mr. Bewildered.

"You could take my car instead," she offered timidly.

"Yeah, a rust heap older than my own, sitting on blocks out in the desert if the prairie dogs haven't hauled it away? I want your *answer,* dammit."

"Well, you can't *have* it, all right?" she flared suddenly. "You can have anything else you can think of—IOUs from here to Christmas! I'll wash all the supper dishes every night, teach you how to ride, anything you want except—"

"Anything," he cut in.

"Ummm…" Again, the tip of her tongue crept out to wet her lips. "Well, anything within—"

"Ho, no, sweetheart, we passed reason about twelve miles back. You said *anything.*"

She licked her lips again and he could see the pulse hammering at her throat. "Anything like…what?"

He picked up the cards and shuffled. "You don't want to bet questions, okay. Fine. Let's bet clothes, instead."

"Strip poker?"

He shuffled again. "That's the name of the game."

"Ummm...I don't think..." She scowled suddenly as he made the sound of a laying hen. "I'm not!"

"You're chicken, Tex. Well, fine." He put down the deck. "So tell me where you've hidden your mare. Or do you mean to welsh on that one, too?"

"All right!" She snatched up the cards. "You asked for it, buster! But I don't want to hear any whining when I walk off with your socks."

"No whining," he said mildly as she shuffled. "But before you deal, there's just one thing."

She looked up, exasperated. "What?"

"If you're not going to answer my question, then you owe me one piece of clothing already. And it's my choice."

CHAPTER SIXTEEN

SHE GLANCED AT THE BOOTS she'd shed hours ago—then started to rise.

"Forget it! No additions before we start subtracting." She grimaced wordlessly and sat back. "So..." A feeling of luxurious...wealth was settling over him. He felt like a pashah surveying his harem, such wonders, his at the merest whim. "Let's start with your...brassiere, cowgirl."

Her brows flew together. "What about my earrings?"

"What about 'em?"

She groaned and started to rise and he caught her foot. "Do it here."

"Nobody said anything 'bout that!"

"I'll close my eyes," he offered with an evil smile. *Your turn to suffer, babe, my turn to enjoy.*

"You better."

He did, savoring the rustle of her clothing, her little humming growl like that of a cornered wildcat kitten.

"There," she muttered finally. She sat glowering, face the color of roses, her breasts soft and full beneath her thin, navy-colored T-shirt. The nipples hardened and rose at the stroke of his eyes.

Oh, sweet Susannah! He tried to speak and found his throat had closed. He gulped and tried again. "Where is it?" At her look of outrage, he added, "I won it fair and square, so give."

She drew her red silk brassiere from Paris, France, out from under a cushion and threw it at him. He caught it midair. "Was it your deal?" He really couldn't remember.

She chose five card stud again, a game with few rounds of betting. Still, by the time it came to show her cards, she'd bet two gold stud earrings and raised with her belt. They were getting down to fundamentals. Fanning three kings out before him, Tag couldn't decide which he'd demand first, her jeans or her T-shirt?

"Why, look at that!" She spread out a full house—and giggled.

Tag shuffled and scowled while she put her earrings back on, then her belt. But it couldn't be later than two. He had all night to turn this around.

Or lose. Luck was a lady and tonight she was siding with her own. Tag didn't see another inch of Susannah's skin for the next five hands as she drove his holdings mercilessly down, until... "I'll see that one," she drawled, laying out a dollar that had once been his, "and I'll raise you...five." She looked up at him through fluttering lashes.

"So be that way." He skimmed his own T-shirt over his head and dropped it on the pot. She sat, owl-eyed and frankly staring. He scratched his stomach self-consciously. "Your deal, Blue Eyes."

"Oh..." She dealt another round, faceup. "High card bets."

That was him, with an ace showing. "Check."

"Then I'll bet." Which was her right by the rules of the game, though with a four and a five of hearts showing already, a serious player would have passed. He sighed and bet his right sock.

Then his left sock on the next round, then waited grimly for the fifth and final card. Susannah had three diamonds now. If this one...

It was. The ten of diamonds dropped neatly on top of her pile. *"We-ell."* She reached to run a nail across his knee. "Nice pair of jeans y'got there, dude."

She was bluffing. Had to be. He'd gained nothing useful

with his fifth card, but he still held a pair of kings. Worse hands had toppled empires.

"High card bets," she prompted him.

"Pass." He'd wait for showdown, thanks all the same.

"Well, I hate t'do it, but..." She set out a twenty. "See me? Or fold?"

It would be him who'd be seen if he met that! "You devil, d'you really have a flush?"

"It'll take your pants to find out, big guy."

"You're bluffing." And he could fold right here. Keep his dignity, but lose the game. Concede the evening—and hand over Brady's message.

"Cowards may think so, but they'll never know."

"All right then, babe. Just remember you asked for it." He stood and reached for his zipper. "Close your eyes."

"I'd rather watch."

"Tough. Shut 'em." He had to unzip with the most exquisite care. He stepped out of the jeans and kicked them across the floor, stifled the urge to cover himself with his hands and said, "Okay."

Her eyes opened—then widened till white showed all around. Her mouth dropped. *"Ohhh..."*

He'd won after all, Tag realized, starting to grin.

"Oh, my, I..." She glanced up at him indignantly, then her eyes fell again. "Where's your shorts? I was gonna quit the minute I saw what kind you—"

"I'm sort of behind on my laundry."

"Men." She rolled her eyes. "Well...he's sure one perky son of a gun, isn't he?" Starting to smile, Susannah reached out—to touch his thigh. The back of her knuckles smoothed down the outside of his leg to his knee, then slowly up again, brushing through his hair. Raising goose bumps and all else raisable. "My, oh, my, oh, *my*. Do I get an introduction?"

His mouth had gone dry at her touch. He shook his head. He'd been in charge only while she was shocked. Now her touch ruled him. Her palm flattened against his thigh and glided down again.

"So I'll just call him the doctor," she murmured.

Cures what ails you? She was his only cure. And the fever, as well. His knees were shaking. He sat beside her on the couch before he dropped.

Her eyes widened and she leaned away from him—came up against the backrest and waited, lips parting shyly. He followed her in a rush, hands braced to either side of her head. "Sus..." Their lips touched and her name ended in a kiss. He buried his hands in her hair, pulled her head back and plundered her mouth. *Oh, Susannah, what you do to me!*

She didn't do it for long. One kiss like a free-fall into the sun—gravity sucking him down into raging flames—then she wrenched her mouth aside. "Tag, don't! *Please* don't!"

He stopped, panting, his lips pressed to the soft skin beneath her ear. "You...you can't mean that."

She did. Her fingers smoothed over his bare shoulders. Caressing. Apologetic. They flattened against him and pushed. "Lemme up."

"Of course," he said icily, and sat facing front. Then turned to hide his arousal, shameful now, if only *he* was aroused.

"I..." Her fingers feathered uncertainly over his back. He tensed his muscles against them. "I'm sorry. It's just that I—"

"Don't worry about it." *You still love your jerk of a husband. Or you like to tease. Or it's just that you're crazy. Or you don't know what you want.* Whatever her reason, he was too hot to hear it tonight. All he could hear was no, but that was enough. He wanted her willing or he didn't want her at all. The way she'd touched him there for a minute, he'd thought—

You thought wrong. He stood and went looking for his pants.

"Tag..." she called on a soft note of pleading.

"It's fine," he said without turning. And maybe tomorrow it would be, when he'd forgotten what tonight might have been. "You want to talk, let's talk in the morning." Women always thought talk would fix things. Talking only told you where they were broken.

His jeans weren't quite as hard to slide into as they'd been to shed. He zipped his fly and turned.

"I'm *sorry*," she repeated. "It's just that—"

"Hey, no apologies needed or wanted." He took her by the shoulders and eased her toward his door. He had no right to be angry, but that didn't stop the frustration. The razor-cut sting of rejection. For a moment there he'd have given her anything and everything in the world that was his to give. She hadn't wanted it. So he'd deal with this alone. Be a gentleman again by morning.

"Tag!" Maddeningly perverse as always, she wheeled at the door, unwilling to go now that she'd had her way.

Woman, I swear! He didn't know where the edge of his control was anymore. Knew only that he had to stay this side of it. "Let's call it a night. You beat me fair and square and— Wait." He'd hung his old bomber jacket on a peg by the door when he'd come in, hours ago. He reached now into its pocket, drew out his wallet. "And you won this." He pulled out the folded envelope that he'd brought all the way from Kentucky.

"Ohhh. Right, I... Yeah..." She opened it then and there, then drifted past him, back to the lamp by his sofa to read the penciled scrawl aloud. "Susie, what we were talking about. Decided it might come in handy for...for leverage?

"Oh, Brady, you...!" She dropped on the edge of the couch. "Got it, but couldn't...couldn't make it to your car." She looked up at Tag, eyes blazing. "Couldn't!"

"What is it, babe?" Trouble without a doubt, but what kind?

"Couldn't," she repeated, as if the word were the worst of obscenities. Her eyes fell to the message. "If you get this, the honey's where…" Her voice cracked. She brought the paper close to her nose, staring at the crossed-out words, shook her head finally and continued. "Remember that time I called you a begonia raper? Take care, kid. Brady."

"Susannah? Babe?"

He might have been calling her from the moon. She set the paper on the side table as carefully as if it were spun from cobwebs. Sat staring down at it, her brows drawing slowly together. She shook her head.

"Susannah." He wanted to touch her. She looked as if one touch would set her off like a bomb.

"'I *couldn't*…'" She reached out toward the message— and stiff-armed the table. It went flying past Tag, her glass on it falling, ice tinkling, crystal smashing. *"Damn you to hell and gone!"* she cried, leaping to her feet. She started for the door, barefoot, heedless of the broken glass.

He snagged her waist as she roared past, spun her around and into his arms. "Whoa! Wait!"

She hammered his shoulders. *"He couldn't make it t'my—"*

"Quit!" He pinned her arms to her sides and hugged her, praying she wouldn't knee him. "Settle down and tell me!"

"He—" She burst into tears. "H-h-he— Oh, I was blind, blind, so *stupid* and blind! That coldhearted son of a *bitch!* I knew he was cold, but I never thought he'd…that he'd…"

Tag scooped her up and carried her back to the couch and sat, cradling her. "What? Tell me. What is it, babe?"

She caught his shirt with both hands and burrowed her face against his throat. "Couldn't make it to my *car!* We…we traded cars, me takin' his truck to tow Payback. Brady got me through the back gate, then he was gonna follow in mine. We were s'posed to meet 'bout a hundred miles north, by one o'clock.'' She shuddered and pressed harder against him. ''But he never came, so I finally got scared and drove on...''

Tag kissed her hair, smoothed a hand down her back. She was trembling nonstop. Her fingers felt icy againt his chest. ''Tell me.''

''If Brady couldn't make it to my car, parked up at the big house, it was 'cause they stopped him. Must have been huntin' him through the grounds when he wrote this. I always thought...I *believed*, Tag, when they told me he fell by accident. I guess I wanted t'believe—needed to. But he killed him.''

''Who? Colton?'' He tried to look down at her face, but it was hidden against him.

''For the honey. I guess Brady hid it when he saw he'd never get away.''

''What did he mean by honey?''

''They must have tried t'make him talk. T'say where he'd hid it and where I'd gone.'' She shivered and wrapped her arms around his waist. ''But Brady was stubborner than a Missouri mule. You could beat him to hamburger and he'd never...'' She made a small, keening sound deep in her throat and shuddered. ''Oh, you *bastard!* I'm gonna *get* you for this...''

Colton, she meant? Tag gathered her up and stood. The night was growing cold and she was drifting on the edge of shock. He carried her into his bedroom and laid her on the bed—or tried to. She clung like a little monkey. He had to lie down with her. Pull the blanket up over them both. ''It's okay, okay... '' He held her, kissed her cheeks, her forehead.

She shivered and squirmed closer. ''It's *not* okay. It's—''

''Hush, babe...'' He rubbed her shoulders. She was so soft and so cold.

''It's *unforgiveable.*'' She shuddered again. ''I won't forgive that!''

''Hush...''

"He's gonna pay for that if it's the last thing I ever—"

"Hush!" He stroked her. She made a mewling sound half between sob and growl and burrowed closer. He rolled halfway onto his side to free one arm, taking her with him. Beneath her T-shirt her breasts flattened against his bare chest. She'd never put her bra back on, he remembered, feeling the nudge of her nipples, hardening as he realized. She murmured and pressed even closer, as if she could flatten every inch of her flesh against his own, a scared little flounder seeking comfort.

Her thigh nudged between his. He gulped and lay motionless, hard as a board. Much more of this and his zipper would do serious damage! But she was trembling, not teasing. Something wet—tears—fell on his throat. "S'okay, darling. Don't cry."

"No." She shook her head and shivered. "It isn't."

He smoothed a hand slowly down her back. His fingers reached her bottom and cupped instinctively. He wanted to grab her with both hands and snug her closer, roll and dive into her.

Not now. Think of something else, Taggart. Anything but soft, needy woman, his for the taking, if he was a selfish jerk. *Think about changing the oil in your car. Run the multiplication tables...*

She flattened a hand against his bare chest and stroked upward, her fingers brushing across his nipple, her touch an electric shock that nearly convulsed him. He bit back a groan. Think about honey, Taggart. Not Susannah's honeyed kisses, but the honey back in Kentucky. *Whatever it is, it's valuable.* Must be a treasure if a man had been killed for it.

A fortune hidden back in Kentucky, while here in Colorado, he lay penniless. She'd stripped him all the way to his skin tonight. Come morning he'd have to find a job. *Or the honey...* She shivered again and he tightened his arms around her. "What'd he mean by honey, babe? It's something valuable, isn't it?"

"Not compared t'that old man!" A sound twisted out of her, anguished, hurting. She rubbed her face helplessly back and forth against him.

"It's okay, darling, stop..." He caught her head and lifted it to his to kiss her cheeks, her forehead, the tip of her nose. She thrust her mouth at him and he took that, too. She wriggled fully up onto him, her lips as hot and eager as his own, tasting of salt and scotch and Susannah.

He tore his mouth aside. "Susannah, we've gotta..." *Stop,* he tried to tell her, but his tongue was answering her will, not his. "Stop, babe," he gasped when he could breathe again. "If we don't stop now, I can't—"

"Please, Tag..." She slid her long legs to either side of him, bringing them groin to groin. "I can't stop thinkin'...can't stop *seeing* them hurtin'..." She trembled violently. "Oh, make me forget! Take me out of m'self, and away. *Please?*"

That maybe he could do. Or die and go to heaven, trying. His hands slid down to her bottom and caught hold. Their lips met again and he groaned into her. *Oh, woman...* He rolled without breaking their kiss and as his weight settled upon her she arched beneath him. *Oh, Susannah!* Softer than he'd dreamed, sweeter than honey. He pushed himself up with one hand and skimmed her T-shirt up to her neck.

She grabbed it and whipped it off into the dark. They came together again in a shuddering collision—the delicious kiss of skin to fevered skin. His hands found her breasts and she cried aloud. He slid down to worship them with tongue and teeth—she caught his hair with both hands and sobbed, "Yeah, *oh* yeah, oh, Tag, oh, *please*... Now..."

This was no night for finesse, not this time. She was as ready as he was. He rolled to one side to strip off his jeans. She sat and touched him everywhere, hindering him in her eagerness to help. He laughed wordlessly and pressed her down again, peeled off her jeans, then settled into her embrace, groaning as she wrapped her arms and her legs around him.

"Make me forget!" she begged as their lips met and he slowly thrust into her, shuddering with delight and something that felt like terror.

We'll, he'd try...

SOMETIME MUCH LATER in the dark, Susannah awakened him. She lay fully atop him, hot and wet, silky-skinned and trembling. Her hands framed his face. He kissed her fingers, murmuring "Sorry, I didn't mean to—"

"Sorry!" Her body shook against him, but this time it was laughter. "Sorry for sendin' me to the moon?" She kissed his cheek, his lips, his chin. Drew her knees up, then sat up astride him. "Tag...oh, Taggart..."

Her fingers found his nipples, played with them till he growled and caught her hips. "To the moon wasn't enough, huh?"

She laughed again deep in her throat and, reaching down, took him in hand. "What if I said I wanted a round-trip ticket?"

"That, darling, can be arranged..." He cupped her beautiful breasts, teased their tips to a hardness that matched his own, till she arched her neck and gasped aloud. *Oh, Susannah...* And this time he'd take his time... Take her in time... Take all the sweet, slow time in the world...

THEY MADE SLOW, sleepy love one last time as dawn brightened the cabin. Slow-motion, wondering ecstasy. She was the lock, he was the key...a door was opening somewhere inside him, morning on the far side of it.... Something strange and wonderful and utterly final waiting for him in the sunshine just beyond it.

Afterward they lay on their sides, still joined. This time it was Susannah who floated on the edge of sleep while Tag smoothed his hand lightly down her supple spine to her velvety bottom, then lazily up again. His. So tiny and right in his arms. Her lips moved against his chest in a sleeping kiss and he smiled. His by right of laughter. His by surrender. She'd given herself into his arms and begged for forgetting and he'd delivered. Moved her past sorrow into this place of peace and joy...

Her lips moved against him again. "Ollie, ollie, oxen free," she murmured, and sighed. Her breathing deepened.

Ollie, ollie, oxen free. She'd said that once before, where and when? Tag's own eyes, drifting shut, opened suddenly. She'd said that back in Vermont, to Payback, not to him. *Meaning we've found the safe place?* Sanctuary? She knew it even back then?

Whatever she'd meant, she was safe from now on. His now. His to hold and protect, if only he knew from what. His arms tightened instinctively, shielding her from whatever was out there.

Honey...some treasure that Brady had died for...that men would kill for... But was it a danger to her? She'd have to tell him now, now that her troubles were his, to be faced and somehow fixed.

Her lashes shivered against his skin. She lifted her head to give him a drowsy smile. "I can hear the wheels goin' round and round up there. What're you thinkin' 'bout?"

He brought his hand to her face. Touched her lips, smiled as she nibbled his fingertip. "About the honey, darlin'. What is it?"

Her teeth paused midbite. Her lids drifted lower, the lashes hiding her eyes. After a moment she sighed, long and deep, her breasts lifting against him. Automatically he reached to cup one, thumbed her nipple as it rose to greet his fingers.

She shuddered and buried her face in his throat. "That...why don't we leave that till morning?"

"Fine by me." They had all the time in the world.

THE NEXT TIME Tag opened his eyes, morning had come and gone. He lay, blinking up at the ceiling, smiling without knowing why. Almost noon, it felt like. Memory crept back, a slow-motion, gaudy parade, and his smile broadened. He swung his head slowly so as not to wake her—and found her gone. Nothing but a storm-tossed sea of sheets and blankets to show where she'd lain.

In the bathroom, he figured. Tag sat up and stretched, yawned hugely. "Susannah?"

No answer. In the kitchen, he hoped, thinking of coffee as he sat up on the edge of their bed. He stood and stretched, looked around and realized her clothes were nowhere in sight. Gone out on the porch, then, or back to her own cabin to change. Was it later than it felt?

He detoured to the bathroom, then stepped gingerly through the broken glass on his floor and out to the porch, buttoning his jeans as he went. No smiling woman awaiting him out there. In her own cabin, then, or possibly gone wrangling already? His eyes swept down-meadow toward the barn—and paused. He blinked. *No.* Looked again.

His car was gone. *No.* The hair was rising along his arms, the chill of the morning and a worse chill. No, he was borrowing trouble. There were half a dozen reasons he could think of to explain why his car was gone.

They crumbled to dust as he walked through her cabin, noting the empty nail by the door where her Stetson should have hung, then the bureau in her bedroom—with its emptied drawers. "Susannah, you little...!" He spun and went back to his own cabin, dread rising.

On his couch, the cash they'd bet back and forth till she

won it all had been neatly stacked. Precisely half of the total was missing.

And the...? He stooped, didn't see it, then knelt, his hands sweeping under the couch. He sat upright again, ice skating down his spine, swearing helplessly. The .45 was gone.

Car, gun, money, clothes, woman—all gone.

And with her, she'd taken his...? Tag wasn't sure what, only that he could feel it reeling out into the distance, like a guitar string stretching from him to her. Wire stretching tighter and tighter, biting into his flesh as she ran. *Damn you, girl!*

She'd done it to him all over again. Taken everything he had that mattered and run. To where?

CHAPTER SEVENTEEN

TWO NIGHTS LATER and a thousand miles east, Tag crouched in darkness, his forearms propped on the lowest strake of a white board fence, his body concealed by the bush that grew just inside it.

Beyond his hunter's blind ran a two-lane country road, then a ditch, then more white boards and posts edging its far side.

That other fence was the boundary to Fleetfoot Farm, its backside, nearly a mile from the grand entrance gates he'd once used on the far side of the estate.

The headlights of a car brightened the road to his left, and Tag pressed back into the leaves, praying. *Come on, Susannah, you sweet hellion, conniving bitch, come to me. It's payback time, baby, and I'm here to collect.*

The lights swept on by, moving purposefully and away. Not Susannah in his car, but a dark pickup with white lettering on its side. A Fleetfoot green truck? Colton's security guards, patrolling his perimeter?

Let them. His quarrel wasn't with those thugs tonight. Tag leaned forward again, his eyes fixed on the far fence. To his right it dipped to follow the contours of a gully, then rose again beyond that depression. At the lowest point of the land lay the single breach he'd found in all Fleetfoot Farm's formidable defenses—a three-foot-diameter culvert running under the fence. Put there, apparently, to carry occasional runoff into the ditch that edged the road.

Come to me, darlin'. Because if Tag had guessed right, wherever in the wide world his hellcat roamed, she was homing in on this precise spot. Walking right into his trap. This was the single spot he'd found in his entire, painstaking circuit of the farm's boundaries, where a motivated trespasser might wriggle, undetected, past Colton's electrified defenses.

And whatever else she might be, Susannah Mack was motivated, he assured himself, seeing again that moment in his cabin when he'd stopped her from running barefoot through broken glass. Whatever else she'd faked that night, she hadn't faked that emotion.

And she'd taken her gun. To use on Colton? *Little maniac! Sweet liar!* He closed his eyes for a moment, remembering just how sweet.

And how treacherous. "Let's leave the honey till morning," she'd promised. *Oh, you liar! I shared everything, while you...* Susannah Mack took care of herself. If she didn't come to get Colton, then she'd come for the honey, the treasure, whatever it was.

Or maybe she'd come for both. But come she would, Tag was certain. And when she came, she'd find him waiting. And not in a forgiving mood.

His forehead bumped the board above. He awoke with a grunt and a start. Where was he? Oh. He'd slept for only minutes? Or for hours. Damn. He'd half killed himself to beat her back here, hitching rides both night and day, walking between rides, only to fall asleep on watch?

Tag hauled himself erect and stretched, then stood, peering through the leaves at the culvert. Nothing had changed since he—

A flicker of movement beyond the far fence—*there!* As if some figure had abruptly stood. He blinked, widened his eyes, but it was gone.

Maybe it had been nothing but a horse, grazing in the pasture beyond. But maybe it had been her. He thought it was her. *And if she gets away from me into the grounds!* A square mile of woods and meadows and buildings in the dark—and her with the home-court advantage? Tag scrambled over the fence, reached the culvert and crouched.

Then he grimaced. Were there snakes? Possibly. But if Susannah could do it, then so could he. *Whither thou goest, babe.* He drew a breath and started through. Dust clouded him as he crawled, cobwebs brushed his face. He fixed his eyes on a pale circle some twenty feet ahead...then ten...then— "*Ouch!*" He yanked his hand back—punctured.

Ears craning to catch the sound of slithering, he waited. And heard nothing beyond the thump of his own heart. At last he reached out his hand with wincing reluctance to touch sharpness—a fringe of cut wires all the way around the rim of the pipe.

So it hadn't been the easy route he'd assumed when looking from the road. There had been a wire screen, blocking access. And whoever had gone before him had brought cutters to deal with the problem. *Susannah!* She would have seen this pipe from the inside, at some point in her two years at Fleetfoot, on one of her rides. He scrambled through the breached barrier, then rose to his feet. *Where are you?*

Not here. He stood in a wooded ravine, all its native undergrowth cut back to leave only trees. There wasn't enough cover left to hide a fawn, much less a Texas hellcat.

He scrambled to the top of the rise and turned toward the distant, invisible manor and the dozens of stables that lay between. Whatever Susannah sought, it lay that way. And her lead on him was less than ten minutes. Cutting straight across a wide pasture, Tag settled into a hunter's soft, ground-eating trot. *Gonna get you, girl, if it's the last, the very last...*

A quarter mile on he caught his first glimpse of his quarry—a small figure clothed in black, climbing over the far fence of a pasture just as he mounted the near.

By the time he'd run across the field she'd vanished. He paused, panting, peering right and left down a tree-lined lane. Narrow private roads criss-crossed the farm, dividing all the paddocks. The trees that shaded them formed tunnels of impenetrable black. Hills also cut his view. He'd lost her. *Blast you, Susannah.*

Nothing to do but press on. Twice he had to stop and hit the lush grass when a truck idled past. Guards patrolled the farm all night long? With millions in horseflesh on the property, he supposed that made sense.

He walked through a pasture and roused half-a-dozen yearlings, who snorted and stood staring, then stampeded off into the dark. *And let's pray Colton doesn't raise prize bulls, as well!*

Gaining the first barn, he paused to survey it from the shelter of a fence. Hell, she could have gone anywhere! Inside this stable or into any one of the other massive buildings looming up on the hills beyond. He could see now how Brady might have eluded capture for hours. Could have stashed his prize in one of thousands of hiding holes, inside or out.

A faint sound brought his gaze sliding around—to find a figure standing motionless alongside a Dumpster, some forty feet from the barn door. Watching.

The guard stood, shifting from foot to foot for five minutes or so, then he turned and moved silently off along one side of the building. Was security always this fierce? Or had something set them on red alert tonight? Tag put the barn between himself and the guard as he cut a wide circle the other way. *Babe, this isn't the place to be.* If Susannah's guess was right and these men had killed her friend, then she was now moving straight into the lion's jaws. And the beast wasn't sleeping tonight. On a distant hilltop, headlights followed a road, then turned away—the motorized patrol making its rounds.

Tag's path skirted a half-mile training track, then took him up a slope to a larger barn surrounded by paddocks, each with a high double fence that would keep a horse in one pen well separated from the next. Stallion paddocks? Brady had been a stud groom.

But so what? Tag could have missed her a hundred times over by now. If luck didn't run his way—and run hard—he wasn't going to find her.

Lose her tonight and you'll never see her again. This farm and what she meant to do here this night was his only clue, his last connection. Once Susannah left Fleetfoot, he would have no way of tracking her. Her next destination could be Timbuktu for all he knew.

Assuming she got what she came for, then got safely away. Brady hadn't escaped. *Couldn't make it to your car...* Tag rubbed his arms, rubbing down goose bumps. This place was so damn big. They could take her and he'd never know she'd been taken. Wouldn't be able to help her. *You could beat him to hamburger,* she'd cried, *and he'd never—*

He slammed the door hard on that thought. But all in one night his hands had memorized her slender bones, her exquisite fragility. If they... *Damn you, Susannah!* If only she'd trusted him, asked for his help.

Well, she hadn't. Which meant he had to do this the hard way, blind and groping. And this barn looked as good as any to try. Tag drew a breath, then walked casually across the open square toward the door, illuminated by an overhead light. If any guard was watching, let him see a man without guilt. Fleetfoot was so large that perhaps its employees didn't all know each other. *I'm the new vet, if anyone asks.*

Within the barn a dimly lit corridor led the length of the building between spacious stalls. Tag stopped at each door. Looked in through its barred upper half at glossy, magnificent animals, some of them sleeping, others waiting with pricked ears for his appearance. *Somebody's been through here recently?* A guard walking rounds? Or his own lunatic lover?

Halfway down the aisle Tag noticed the nameplates fixed above each door. Paid in Full was the name on the next one he came to. A chocolate-brown stallion lifted his head from his water bucket to stare back at him with luminous eyes, muzzle dripping. "Hey there, boy." A nine-year-old son of Payback, he remembered reading in the tabloids. Winner of the Belmont and the Preakness, though unlike his famous sire, he'd set no track records and he hadn't taken the Derby, most coveted gem in the Triple Crown. And so far his offspring had proved as middling. Still, this stud was Fleetfoot's best hope now that Susannah had rendered their superstar worthless. *And speaking of which*—Tag turned away—*whatever happened to...* His eyes lit on the nameplate three doors down. Payback. *Son of a—* He stopped, staring into the stall, and drew a shaky breath.

Susannah stood with long legs braced, arms thrown around the gelding's massive neck, her face pressed to his dusky hide. The horse stood motionless, head propped on her shoulder, his chin resting against the back of her waist. His ears pricked as Tag gripped the bars. *"Huh!"*

About what he'd said the last time they met. *Here's where I came in,* Tag told himself, drawing the door silently aside. *If I'd only known then what I know now.*

Not that he knew a hell of a lot more—or if the more he knew helped him make any sense of all this. But whatever she'd done, whyever she'd done it, surely it hadn't been spite? Susannah loved this animal.

Or was she crazy enough to use an animal she loved to spite a man she hated?

And as usual, in her vivid presence he was forgetting his script, every vicious and ironic thing he'd meant to say when he caught her. "Babe?"

She whirled with a shriek of surprise. Payback snorted and jumped back, ears flattening, head tossing.

She'd tucked her .45 in the front of her belt, Tag saw as she spun. "Allow me." He jerked the gun free, absently blocking her with one shoulder when she yelped again and tried to grab it back. He checked the safety, then stowed it in the back of his belt. Looked up to find her scowling at him through tears.

She wiped her eyes and tipped up her chin. "What are *you* doin' here?"

"Dealing myself into this game, babe." His impulse to haul her into his arms was fading. She wasn't glad to see him. He was just one more roadblock on the way to her goal, whatever the hell that was. Never had been more than that. "And what are *you* doing here? Bees to the honey, honey?"

She shrugged wordlessly, then spun on her heel to stare toward the end of the barn where he'd entered. A stallion nickered. Payback snorted and moved to the door. "The watchman!" Susannah whispered.

"After us?" Tag drew her into a front corner of the stall that was out of sight from the door.

"No." Her breath warmed his cheek. "He makes the rounds of the farm all night long. Stops by this barn once every hour."

Wonderful. He could hear the man clearly now, speaking a low word or two to his charges as he approached. "Will he come into the stall?"

"Shouldn't."

But if he does. Tag drew the gun.

"Hey, Pookster," a male voice drawled from the corridor. "What are you doin' up this late?"

Tag thumbed the safety. Susannah's fingers clamped on his arm. He shrugged himself free.

Something orange poked through the bars. Payback accepted the carrot with a low rumbling sound and pulled it into the stall. "You're welcome." The man chuckled—and moved on.

Soft sounds of crunching carrot. A door closing gently in the distance. Susannah thumped a fist against her chest. "Phew."

"Yeah." Tag put the gun away. "So now what?"

She drew a deep breath and met his eyes. "So now you go back the way you came in and leave me alone."

"Right," he said pleasantly. She never gave up trying. "Did you come to shoot Colton?"

She didn't pretend to be shocked. "Should, but..." She shrugged. "There's other ways t'make him pay."

"So you came for the honey." Useful for leverage, Brady had thought.

"And that's where you come into this, isn't it?" Her drawl was laced with contempt.

His temper flared to match hers. "You got it, babe. There's that small matter of my career you deep-sixed. If you're coming into some money at last, I'm taking half. So what is the honey?"

She shrugged and gave him a cool "make me" look. Hell, he'd worried about the guards hurting her? He'd throttle her himself. "You've got no choice, babe. I'm here and I'm in and we'd better get on with it. Where is it? Here in this barn?"

"Nope." She moved over to Payback and stood stroking his shoulder. "I just dropped by t'say 'hey' while I was in the neighborhood."

He'd always figured he'd fall for a sane woman, if he ever fell. She was outside his every calculation. "So tell the nice horse goodbye and let's go, Susannah."

She rubbed her forehead against his hide. "He's *too* nice, Tag. Feels like something's missing. His sass, his drive..."

"It's called testosterone. Takes about six months after gelding for a stud's levels to drop."

"I miss it."

If he shook her it would end in a kiss. He was boss only while he kept his hands to himself. "You might have thought of that before you asked me to—"

"I know, I know, I *know!*" She turned, near tears. "But I *had* to." She shrugged. "He's not the same."

Tag caught her arm and drew her toward the door. "He's fourteen, darling, and what did he have, a hundred mares a season, year after year?"

She wiped her nose. "More, if you count the ones that didn't take the first time. That he had t'cover twice."

"That's more notches on his bedpost than most men get in a lifetime of trying. He can take up philosophy in his old age, write his memoirs, raise begonias…" *And speaking of which.* "What's a begonia raper, by the way?" He drew her out into the corridor and shut the door behind them.

She turned back and gripped the bars. Making low, whuffling noises, Payback moved to the window to lip her knuckles.

"A begonia raper, Texas. What's that?" He peeled her off the bars and hauled her on toward the exit.

"That's for me to know and you—"

"And I will, by God." He eased the door open an inch and peered out. If anyone was waiting in ambush, he couldn't see him. "So let's get on with it." Twining his fingers with hers so she couldn't escape, he pulled her outside. A light glowed above the door. His every instinct cried that he should hunch his shoulders and scuttle off into the dark like a cockroach. "Which way?"

"Hush!" Fingers tense and trembling in his, she drew him off to the right, walking casually. They reached a patch of shadow thrown by the next barn and her pace doubled. "Come on, then."

Ten minutes of ducking and dodging took them steadily uphill. Toward the big house, Tag realized with growing uneasiness. And security seemed to intensify as they moved toward ground zero. Three times they had to go to earth and let guards prowl past—and it wasn't the same guard, thrice encountered. "Is this the usual routine?" he whispered while they lay beneath a tractor, watching the beam of a distant flashlight probe the edge of a fence.

Her hair brushed his mouth. "Not while I was here."

But after she'd heisted his finest stallion, maybe Colton had learned to lock his barn doors?

"Used to be it was grooms that did the rounds," she added. "Horsemen who'd know if a stud was coming down with colic or a mare about to foal. But these guys…"

Looked like trouble. Felt like trouble. But why should they be expecting trouble tonight?

Susannah crawled out from under the tractor, reached for his hand and drew him on. They skirted the farm's clinic, peering in through glass walls at the swimming pool with its underwater treadmills, used to exercise injured racehorses. From the clinic's far corner, Tag could see the office where he'd once waited in vain for Colton, then the crown of trees that hid the manor itself from view. "Where are we headed?"

"To the greenhouses at the back of the big house. I used to hide out there when I wasn't down at the stables."

"Begonias?"

She laughed under her breath. "Brady didn't know a rose from a daisy. He'd call anything with petals a begonia, just t'tease me. He came looking for me there once, while I was potting tulip bulbs for forcing. I like grubbin' around in the dirt, but Stephen always got mad at me, said let the gardeners do it. Messin' with houseplants was 'bout all I could ever get away with." Her voice had gone flat, some emotion walled off behind it.

"Brady asked what I was doing and I told him—forcing bulbs so they'd bloom early. He pretended to be shocked, me forcing flowers. Called me a begonia raper and I threw a pot at him." She halted, staring at the wide courtyard that lay ahead, with the farm offices on one side and an L-shaped barn on the other. A cat padded purposefully across the bricks. The gas lanterns at each end of the square burned brightly enough to cast its flowing shadow.

''We can cut across or go around,'' she muttered, ''but it's a parking lot on the back side of that barn. No cover at all.''

''Your lead, cowgirl.''

''Lot before lights, I guess.'' They climbed a fence to reach the end of the barn, then circled it to the right. They stopped at the same instant to stare at each other. A car was coming and coming fast. ''This way!'' Susannah spun and skirted the barn toward the square.

The car was gaining. She sprinted along the side of the building, Tag at her heels, then yanked open a door. They dived through into darkness and shut it behind them. ''Phew!'' She groped his chest, caught a fistful of his shirt, and tugged him on. ''That was close!''

They were in a hall, Tag determined, dragging his fingers along a wall as they shuffled on. She opened a door and pulled him inside. Long slits of dim light—a window with half-cracked blinds, facing the courtyard. He could make out a desk, file cabinets. ''Whoever that was, could he be coming in here?'' Tag moved to the window to peer through the slats.

''Don't think so,'' she muttered, joining him. ''This is a trainer's office. He won't show till the exercise boys come in, 'bout five.''

If that was when the farm came alive, they had two hours at best to find the honey and go. Out on the square, a small truck was parked, headlights blazing. Its driver switched off the lights as Tag watched, then swung open the door.

A short man stepped out and walked away from the truck. Light on his feet, but wide shouldered and stocky, he moved with the athletic bounce of a pit bull. Hands in his pockets, he turned, scanning the night. Tag frowned. A small man, in a small truck. ''Hey, it's—''

''Oh, Lord!'' Susannah caught his arm, her fingers stabbing into him. ''It's—''

''Your friend. Cam.''

''The hell it is! That's Murphy! But what's *he* doing here

this time of…'' She glanced at Tag, eyes narrowing. ''Why'd you think…''

''You said his name was Cam,'' Tag said carefully. ''Your friend and Brady's. The guy who gave me Brady's note.''

''Son of a…'' Her whisper trailed off to hushed horror. ''*That's* who gave you the message? But you said it was—''

''No, *you* told me his name was Cam. All *he* told me was that he was a friend of yours. You filled in the rest, remember?''

''That's no friend of mine or Brady's! That's Stephen's personal bodyguard! His head of security—Murphy! Ex-IRA man, they all said, then a mercenary and a gunrunner in Africa. He's colder than a bagful of frozen rattlers!'' She gulped and shied back from the window. ''If *he* gave you that message—''

A setup! All Tag's alarm bells were clanging. Susannah retreated another step and he caught her arm. ''You're sure that was Brady's handwriting? His words?''

''Oh, yeah, it was Brady who wrote that, all right.'' Tears were streaming down her face. She swiped at them savagely. ''They must've taken it off him, when th-they… 'Cause if anybody questioned Brady, it was that rat-weasel-bastard out there. Stephen would watch and call the shots, but it'd be Murphy who did the hurtin'.''

And it was Murphy who… Tag watched her eyes widen as it hit her. He caught her arms as she tried to spin away.

''And *he* told you where to find me? In Colorado?'' Her voice squeaked on the edge of panic. ''How'd he know where I—''

''Your guess is good as mine.'' He pulled her back to the window, hooked an arm around her waist to keep her there. If there was a rattlesnake loose in the house with them, he meant to know where.

Murphy stood talking with a uniformed guard, who topped him by almost a foot. The way the big man bobbed his head, you could see who was giving the orders. "I'd've sworn on the Bible I shook them after Austin," Susannah whispered beside him. "But if he and Stephen knew all along where t'find me, then why not hassle me there? Why would they need to lure me back here?"

"Think about it." He felt her stop breathing as she got it.

"'Cause Brady died before they could make him talk." She made a small, gulping sound. "With that plate in his skull, if they hit him too hard…"

"Or maybe he did fall downstairs, babe. Running from them."

"I hope, oh, I hope so. But whatever, they found his message, so they know he hid it and he hid it here. But they couldn't find it. Which means…"

"They need a bird dog." Somebody to lead them to it. And for some reason Colton hadn't wanted to simply snatch her and strap on the thumbscrews. Maybe because he still loved her? Or because he knew Susannah—knew she was stubborn as three Bradys and they'd have to kill her to get their answer? And that with the tabloids joyfully digging into the scandal of the year, his ex-wife's death would be one death too many to explain away?

Or because this way is more amusing? Hope given, then hope taken away while Colton looked on from above and pulled their strings?

Whatever, she'd walked straight into the trap. And he—fool, then fool again—had followed. Suckered into trouble one more time by a honey-mouthed drawl and a pair of blue norther eyes.

CHAPTER EIGHTEEN

OUT IN THE COURTYARD, the guard bobbed his head one last time and moved off. Murphy looked after him, then reached for his belt. Unholstered a portable phone and spoke into it.

All this activity—they must know we're here. They'd spotted Susannah's—his—car, maybe? Tag turned to ask where she'd hidden it—just as she jerked the gun from his back. "*Hey,* what d'you think you're—"

"I guess I'm just comin' up t'speed, here." She edged away from him, aiming the .45 two-handed. "But back where I come from, we don't look for backstabbers. Stephen always said I should grow up."

His eyes had adjusted to the dark enough to see her thumb touch the safety. "What the hell are you talking about?" Hands down at his sides, he took a step closer.

She shuffled backward, her gun lifted to center on his heart. "I'm talkin' about who brought me that message. Stephen had to send it with somebody I'd trust. Or least, someone I wouldn't suspect. That's you, dude."

"If so, he was using me, Susannah." All his weight on one foot, Tag brought his other foot nearer, shifted his weight to it.

"Bet your boots he was using you! But the easiest way was to buy you, wasn't it? And Stephen knows all about buyin'. You cut some deal with him, didn't you, to get him off your back? He'd stop coming after you, if you gave him me. You Yankee Judas!" As she retreated step by step toward the door, Susannah moved through a shaft of light from the window. Tears glittered, then a bar of black hid them again.

"Pot calling the kettle, Ms. Lone Ranger." Her chin came up in protest and Tag gained another stealthy foot. "I don't see you cutting me in on *your* game. They never taught you how to share down in Texas?" She shook her head fiercely and that was all the margin he needed. He rushed her.

She squeaked and stepped back. Hit the door. Then he was on her, swinging her gun hand up to pin it above her head. She yelped and brought her knee up, but he was too close. He clamped her thigh between his legs...

And they both went instantly rigid. God! He was hard as a rock. He groaned as he slid his other arm around her waist. *What you do to me, woman!* Her breasts were shuddering against him. He turned his head to rest his lips against her temple. "Bitch."

"Tr-traitor." Her head turned with grudging slowness till her lips touched his cheek.

He trembled and moved against her. *Susannah? Here and now?*

She didn't say yes, didn't say no. Just sighed. Her pelvis rocked inward to meet him, an unwilling wave pulled up by the moon.

He nuzzled her ear. *You drive me insane, woman!*

"Money-grubbin' bastard," she muttered.

Yeah, but three minutes of coaxing would bring her around.

They didn't have a minute. Not with dawn coming, a treasure waiting, and a hired killer stalking them. He let his breath out slowly into her hair. "Use your brains, Lambchops. If I was part of this setup, what would be easier than to turn you in now? I've got the gun. I know the honey's in the greenhouse. All I have to do is march you out this door and hand you over to Murphy."

"So why don't you shut up and do it, then! I'm sick of talkin' about it."

Deep down, they always seemed to agree. ''No, thanks. I'd rather collect my own debts.'' And right now he needed an installment. He dipped his head, then paused. Slow as sunrise but just as surely, her chin rose to meet him.

She opened her lips to him and quivered as his tongue entered, arching herself against him. Her arms slid around his ribs and held tight. *Oh, Susannah, girl!* Every time he thought he was winning, she did this to him.

TWENTY MINUTES LATER Tag had cooled down enough to think again. And at least half his thoughts were on the matter at hand. The other half lingered on Susannah's hips as he followed her lithe form down a path through a greenhouse. This was the fourth she'd led him through, one built off the next in a gleaming, jungly maze, smelling of flowers and damp and peat moss. ''How much farther?''

''If I'm right…'' She paused before a wall, turned left along it. He followed, trailing fingers over stone gone velvety with moss. ''Watch your step. Stairs ahead.''

He followed her down, feeling his way step by step. Old steps. The wood creaked beneath his weight and smelled of rot. He stopped thinking of making love to Susannah and recalled her essential trickiness. If she wanted to trap him, here was the place. Luring him down into a pit, cold stone closing round…

''Guess we can risk a light,'' she muttered somewhere ahead.

He winced as a bulb flared at eye level—low ceiling—then stood blinking. A cellar of some sort, ancient rock walls. The greenhouse had been built over a much older foundation?

''Through here,'' she called from beyond a doorway. Another light threw her shadow back across flagstones. Tag found her standing in a dead-end room. The remains of a massive fireplace formed one wall, a long potting table littered with trowels and bags of bonemeal had been pushed up against another. A small rusty refrigerator, vintage 1950s, was shoved against the end wall. Susannah put her hand to it, sighed and nodded. "It's still runnin'."

Tag could hear its compressor chugging wearily as he neared it. "The honey's in there?"

"If my hunch is right."

"We came all this way, risked our necks, on a *hunch!*"

"Yep." She opened the door and sank to her heels. "It's not too little. And they must have searched here. I don't know how they'd have missed—*oh!*" She pulled out a clay pot. "Will you *look* at that?" She thrust it at him.

"What?" He held nothing but a cluster of pale, shriveled shoots sticking out of dry soil.

"That's my tulips! They never even got a chance t'bloom." She sniffled and handed him another ruined pot. Then another.

"What the hell, Susannah. What about the…" He dumped them in a corner on the floor, turned to find her dragging out a mammoth pot from the bottom-back of the fridge.

She set it down on the ground before her with a grunt. "Brady. That ol' man was *so* smart. My dad used to say if you gave Brady an inch-wide opening along the rail, he'd drive a train through."

"*This* is what we came for?" Maybe she *was* insane. And all her buddies, too—Brady and Colton and Murphy. A lunatic feud over houseplants?

"I think." Susannah gripped the dried-out shoots that sprouted from the middle of the pot and pulled. They came up easily, no roots clinging to the soil. "'Cause I didn't plant bulbs in this pot, but here they are."

Camouflage. Anyone peering into the fridge would see exactly what he expected to see, Tag realized, as Susannah tipped the pot on its side to pour dry soil out onto the stones. Only a few inches of soil. Something large and silver gleamed below it. She flattened her hands and slid them in along the sides of the pot, lifted gently. *"Yeah..."*

As if she were hoisting the crown of heaven itself, she held up a silver cannister. Made of stainless steel, looking much like a half-size keg of beer. He'd seen such containers in vet school, used for—

"The last of Payback," she murmured reverently. "Pure speed and can't-quit heart in a can."

Honey. *Sperm.* The last hurrah of the finest horse of the century, packed in dry ice. A treasure. "My god!" he said softly, and reached for it.

AN HOUR TILL DAWN and maybe a quarter mile to go to the culvert. Tag caught Susannah's arm and stopped her in the shadows along a fence, to let her rest for a minute. He'd set a brutal pace since the greenhouse, leaving himself no time or breath for the thousands of questions that sprang to mind. They'd have to keep till they were safely away.

"Cross this road," Susannah muttered, nodding at the lane beyond the fence, "then straight on through that pasture. Want me t'carry it a while?"

"No, thanks." She'd brought a nylon backpack for the cannister. Its straps bit into his shoulders, but he was happy under the load. This was his future he was carrying, a future brighter than he'd dared dream for weeks.

"Now who's the Lone Ranger?" Susannah climbed over the fence, Tag followed.

They were halfway across the lane when an engine revved in the distance. Tag spun around. Fifty yards down the tunnel of trees, something moved, gleamed, then burst into blinding light. Spotlights on top of a speeding truck, freezing them like jacklighted deer.

"Go!" They scrambled over the far fence and into the last pasture. *They were watching for us,* he realized, grabbing Susannah's arm and running through the dewy grass. *Night-vision goggles!*

Behind them, the truck squealed to a halt. A door opened, then banged shut. The truck roared off down the lane. "They let somebody off!" he panted. But where was the driver headed?

"There's a road beyond the pipe," Susannah gasped. She tripped and he caught her up again. "He's gonna be waitin' for us!"

While the one behind herded them into the ambush. *And how do they know where we're going?* That was simple, now that he knew about Murphy. The culvert had been easy to breach, not through carelessness, but by intention. If there was only one way in and out of a trap, you knew where to—

"Jeez!" A shotgun blast shredded the air overhead.

Maybe fifty feet behind, the guard bellowed, "Stop! Stop or I shoot!"

The gun scraped Tag's back as she wrenched it out of his belt. "Susannah!" She wheeled, tearing free of his grip. "Don't—"

"You shoot what we're carrying and Colton'll sack your sorry ass!" she yelled, bouncing up on her toes with defiance and waving the gun. "You big—" She squeaked as Tag grabbed the back of her shirt and yanked.

"Come *on!*" With night-vision goggles, their pursuer probably knew which of them packed the goods, which meant that Tag's big-mouthed darling was fair game. *"Go!"* He gave her rear a hearty whack. She yowled like a singed cat and ran.

Tag ran directly behind her, his shoulders cringing against the next blast. Ten yards…twenty, the shin-high bluegrass as hard to run through as knee-deep water, and still the shot didn't come. Maybe Susannah's lunatic threat had worked? Or the guard was content to wait for reinforcements. She stumbled again and Tag threw an arm around her waist and hustled her on. "We'll never make it to the culvert in time, babe."

"I know it, damn and blast 'em!"

"The electric charge on the fence, is it lethal?" If they could make it over the border and out of Colton's private kingdom—

"No, but it'll knock you on your can. Don't know if we—"

"We've got to. Lemme see your clippers." They came to a stream—maybe two yards wide—and leaped it side by side. A line of shrubs grew along its banks. Tag yanked her sideways to follow that cover. She wrenched the clippers from a pocket and handed them over.

Rubber-handled. "Bless you!" He shrugged out of the pack and pulled her to a staggering halt. "Put this on." Behind them, he heard the sound of a heavy landing—then a curse and a splash as the edge of the bank gave way. He grinned. The guard was a truck jockey. This cross-country event was costing him. Enough?

"B-b-but—" Susannah struggled into the backpack "—what are you—"

He thrust the clippers into her hands. "You can cut the hot wire with these. They're insulated." And for once in her life she was wearing rubber-soled sneakers, not boots. "Follow the creek for another forty feet or so, then head right for the fence." She should hit it some fifty yards this side of the culvert. "Be quiet about it and cut us a way through, then wait for me on the far side." He had no idea where she'd hidden his car.

"Here, take this!" She shoved the gun at him.

"Thanks." He'd forgotten it entirely, maybe because it was so pitifully useless against a shotgun. Still she hesitated. He caught the back of her neck, hauled her in to brush her soft, panting mouth with his own, then spun away. "Rain check, baby, now *go!*"

Running silently back the way they'd come, he slipped around a bush—and ran straight into the guard. A big man with a shotgun slung over the crook of one arm, his eyes fixed to night-vision goggles as he scanned off to his right.

So much for technology. Tag smashed the side of his gun into the lens of the binoculars, driving them back into the guard's face, while his free hand gripped the shotgun barrel and twisted. He flipped it off into the bushes and it must have landed butt-first. The gun went off with a roar. The guard yelled.

Hit? Tag stumbled backward. He hadn't meant to kill the guy.

He hadn't. The guard launched himself in a flying tackle and Tag went down. *"Ooof!"* The bastard easily outweighed him by fifty pounds. Hammering at his face and throat, he rolled. Brush crackled beneath. They were both sobbing breathless curses, kicking and gouging— The ground dropped out from under them. They landed in the creek and broke free, choking and swearing. Tag crawled out first, knelt on the bank and found that somehow he'd held on to the .45 all this while. He thumbed the safety as he aimed point blank. "That's...that's enough."

The guard froze, hands half raised, then slowly straightened from a crouch. There was enough light now to see his face. To see he was grinning.

Tag spun around and fired at the shadow looming behind and overhead, arm upraised. The gun clicked. He kept on squeezing and squeezing the useless trigger till the first blow landed—rolling back the dawn, slamming him backward into the night. *Susannah, didn't you...?*

WHEN HE CAME TO he was on his feet, held there, with arms pinned behind him. A fist crunched into his ribs.

"Where's the girl?"

Yeah, like I can tell you. Not that answers were really

wanted yet. This was payback time. The guard standing before him was the one he'd taken down—Peterson, he realized,
his pal from his last visit—and now it was Peterson's turn.

"Ooof!" It wasn't the pain, it was the lack of oxygen. He
sagged, shut his eyes and made the man holding him do the
work. If they didn't give him a chance to breathe— "*Uhh!*"
No, it *was* the pain. He wanted to kneel with it and weep,
but once he went down they'd use their boots.

"Where's the bitch?" Peterson grunted as he hit him again.

"You leave him alone!"

Dear God! Tag opened his eyes and saw her coming, small
and straight and hopelessly stubborn, forefinger pointing like
an outraged schoolmarm. *Susannah, you lunatic, get out of
here!*

The guards burst into startled laughter. "You're just in time
for the show, Ms. Fancypants," Peterson assured her, and
turned back to Tag.

"I said *stop* it!"

He sniggered again and wound up. "You wanna make
me?"

This one would be extra special. Tag clenched his teeth.
Don't cry out, don't— "*Uhhhhh!*" It would have been easier
to take without her. He didn't care if the guards heard him,
only—

"All right," Susannah drawled and reached behind her
back. A silvery shape cut a swishing arc through the air, ending in the *crack!* of metal against bone.

Peterson squealed—a high-pitched, whinnying sound. Cradling his right elbow, he tottered in a tight circle of anguish.

"Never did know why they call it a funnybone." She
swung the tire-iron at his left elbow—he yelled again and fell
to his knees. Wide-eyed and deliberate as a tigress, she
stalked on past him, her gaze fixed on the man holding Tag.

"Hey, *no,* lady, wait a—!" He shoved Tag at her, but Tag
clamped his arms to his sides as he fell, pinning his captor's

forearms to his back. They went down together, the guard writhing on top. Her tire iron thumped—once—on bone. He grunted and went limp.

For a moment Tag was content to simply lie with his nose in the grass and breathe. Then the weight was rolled off him. "Oh God, oh Tag, oh God!" Susannah chanted in a voice half an octave higher than normal. She sounded tearful and all of twelve. "Tag, *talk* t'me! Get up! Help me! They'll be *comin'!*"

Too true. And an ex-IRA man wouldn't be the pushover these clowns had been. He sighed and somehow she wrestled him to his feet. She jammed a slender shoulder under his armpit and stood. "Come on!"

The second guard was out cold. The first sat, rocking with pain and glowering through his tears. Didn't look as if he'd be hoisting even a beer bottle for weeks, but Tag staggered free of Susannah and wobbled over to him. No use inviting a shot in the back. "Just your gun," he assured him as Peterson cringed. He'd leave payback to those who needed it. Still, he almost cried out in pain as he bent to pull the gun from its holster. Something was cracked for certain.

"Come on!" Susannah pleaded.

They didn't speak again until they reached his car, hidden some fifty yards down a driveway on the estate that bordered Fleetfoot. Susannah tossed the tire iron into the open trunk, then slammed it shut.

"I'll drive," Tag said.

"Yeah, sure." She loaded him in the passenger side, buckled his belt, then slid in behind the wheel.

His pride satisfied with the offer, he slumped against the door. The car flew down the drive, paused at the public road, then roared off to the right. "You gave me an unloaded gun," he said after a minute.

"I did not!" She turned to stare at him. The car hit a bump and was airborne, then landed with a wrenching groan.

"Watch the road, dammit. You did! It wouldn't fire. I wouldn't have been in that fix if it'd worked."

"Did you take the safety off?"

"Holy hell, Susannah, what d'you take me for?"

"An ungrateful Yankee grouch! They must've scrambled your brains for you but good, back there. Why on earth would I come back for you if I'd slipped you an empty gun?"

Change of heart? Because you're not quite as ruthless as you want to be? "You realized you'd miss my unforgettable lovemaking?"

"*Ha!* In your dreams." Still she smiled. Her smile faded as they rounded a bend. "*Sssssshoot!*"

Tag looked up just as she stomped on the brakes and spun the wheel—saw the green truck blocking the road, then fences, bushes whirling past, then open road as the car spun 180 degrees in a bootlegger's turn. "*Jeez,* Susannah!" Rubber squealed and caught hold—the car roared into overdrive and it occurred to him to brace his feet. "Where'd you learn to do that?"

She laughed delightedly. "My dad was the winningest jockey in this country and Europe, too, in his day. You think he didn't love all kinds of speed? He taught me that one when I was twelve. My sister does it prettier, but…" She whipped the car into a lefthand turn. They were heading back down the private drive where she'd parked.

"There's a back way out of here?"

"Sort of." They burst from the thickets out onto a perfect five-acre lawn, dew glinting in the first rays of the sun.

The drive made a dramatic carriage sweep before a mansion as grand as Fleetfoot. They passed a herd of life-size bronze deer, bombed through the sheltered portico, then abandoned the road—to turn right across the lawn, bumping downhill past the house, then a lilypond with a spouting bronze dolphin. "I think," Susannah added absently, rolling down her window while they zig-zagged around flowerbeds ablaze with red and blue.

Kneeling beside a border of delphiniums, a woman in an elegant sunhat turned to stare in drop-mouthed outrage as they rumbled past, carving tracks through the perfect turf.

"Mornin', Mrs. Belden!" Susannah yelled cheerily and tooted her horn. Her smile as she glanced at Tag was blissful. "When she's not gardening, she and her husband ride t'hounds. She showed me their collection of fox tails once at a party."

"Ah." They did think alike. He enjoyed her wicked grin as they cut a swath across the estate's rolling back acres, beautifully manicured for the hunt, with just enough cover left to lull foxes into setting up housekeeping.

"So someone was collecting Payback's sperm," he said at last. "Colton?"

"At his orders, anyway." Susannah scowled at the fence they were fast approaching. A narrow gap had been left in it for members of the hunt who hadn't the nerve for a four-foot jump. "Not quite as wide as I remembered," she murmured. "Oh, well." She put her foot to the gas and swerved left toward a wider stretch between posts.

They blew out the boards for ten feet to either side, bumped through a ditch and back onto public road. "But why would Colton collect sperm when he already had the sperm machine?" he asked when they were up to speed.

"Why would he do it when it's entirely illegal?" Susannah countered. "You can't artificially inseminate a thoroughbred. The Jockey Club would tar and feather you and ride you out of the race world on a rail."

"It's illegal?"

"As all get-out. Club rules. Limit the matings and you keep the price up on stud fees. And it keeps the company pluperfectly exclusive. The Queen of England runs thoroughbreds. And the Arab royals. Japanese billionaires and Hollywood movie stars and my ex and his Wall Street buddies. You think those folks would want t'rub shoulders in the winner's circle with some guy who owns a gas station or two, who saved up his greasy nickels and dimes to buy one frozen pop for his second-rate mare? No way, José. When the Queen's mares came to Payback, they came by private jet and stayed for months. And if you have t'ask how much that cost, you can't afford it. And *that's* the way they like it.''

So much for his brighter future. If the sperm wasn't sellable… ''I don't get it. Why would he do it, then?''

She shot him a troubled glance. ''Stephen said he'd shut my big mouth for me for good if I ever talked. And it's nothing I can prove now that Brady's dead.''

In profile, the corner of her mouth curled delectably. ''Doesn't much matter now anyway. What matters is it looks like he wants it in the worst way—and *I've* got it. That man's going t'pay for Brady if it's the last thing I ever do. So I guess I'll use it on my Secretariat mare. Three years from now her colt'll whip Stephen's butt at the track with all his fine friends watching. Oh, that'll be sweet! I can just see my dad and Brady, elbowing each other up in heaven as my horse leads down the backstretch at Churchill Downs.''

''You said it couldn't be used legally,'' Tag said carefully.

''That's right.'' Her smile deepened. ''But it can be used if you set up a fake mating. Long as you don't mind runnin' a dark horse, a ringer.''

Bingo! He breathed a sigh of relief, winced at the twinge in his ribs, and smiled in spite of it. ''If you don't mind, then there'll be others who don't mind.'' Others with deeper pockets.

''So?'' She flicked him a glance, frowned when she saw his smile.

''So forget about your mare, babe. That sperm's for the highest bidder.''

''The hell it is! It's mine!''

''Mine now, darlin'.'' He looked up as Susannah stomped on the brakes—to see one green truck blocking the road ahead, while a second sat ready to chase. ''Or maybe it's theirs.''

CHAPTER NINETEEN

"I JUST CAN'T SHAKE 'EM!" Susannah muttered, sounding close to tears.

It wasn't for want of trying. In the past half hour, Tag had seen more hell-for-leather driving than he'd hoped to see in a long lifetime. Susannah had shaken their tails twice by cutting across country and once simply by outrunning them. But though they'd made it nearly to the outskirts of Lexington, they still couldn't lose the pursuit.

"Son of a bug-eyed baboon!" She hammered on the steering wheel as they stormed past a strip mall—and a familiar green truck pulled out from behind its far corner. "How do they *do* it?"

"I think I've figured it out. Hey, don't pass that—!" Too late. He planted his feet and squinched his eyes as she swung out around the car ahead. Teeth clenched, he could hear the bray of the airhorn on the oncoming eighteen-wheeler. The car swerved right and the truck thundered past, shaking them down to the chassis. Tag remembered to breathe.

"How?" Susannah demanded.

"Well, first, I think we'll have to decide how to use the honey later, honey."

"I *told* you how I mean t'use it." They were coming to an intersection with traffic lights and the light showing was green. Swearing under her breath, Susannah slowed down.

"So I see this two ways," he continued calmly. "Either we're partners to the end, Susannah Mack, and I'm the senior partner. Or it's every man for himself."

The light turned yellow and the car lunged ahead. Brakes squealed to either side as they shot through the intersection. The pursuing truck hit its brakes and skidded out into the junction—as the cross traffic started moving. Bumpers collided from three directions. Tag looked back to see car doors slamming open, irate drivers hitting the pavement. Susannah glanced in the mirror and chuckled wickedly.

"So, do we have a deal?"

"Sorry, dude. Not a chance." She sliced across the oncoming traffic and into a mall parking lot, wove her way through acres of morning traffic. She stopped to let a proud young mother push a grocery cart with toddler across the lane before them. Tag unclipped his belt, slid over and put his foot on the brake on top of Susannah's. She turned, lips parting in protest. "If it's every man for himself, babe, guess who's going to win?"

"Get your foot off me!"

He leaned past her, grimacing as his ribs complained, to open her door. "Do we have a deal—or do I shove you out here? Your ex's thugs should be along any minute now to give you a ride. While you're distracting them, I'll make a run for it with the honey."

"You coldhearted, money-grubbin' Yankee bastard!" Tears glittered in her eyes. She jumped as a horn sounded behind them. "Get offa me!"

"Which will it be, sugarmouth? Partners or loners?" He might as well know now, before he fell any further.

She slumped disgustedly against her headrest. The car behind pulled out and passed, honking its irritation.

"Which?" Tag insisted. Her bottom lip was sticking out half a mile. He couldn't resist stroking it. She bit him. "Ouch, dammit. Which?"

"Partners," she growled, glaring straight ahead.

He couldn't help grinning, unsporting as it was. "Good.

Now head around to the back of the building. They'll be on us again in no time.''

"I think this time I might have lost 'em.'' Still, she followed his directions, rounding the mall, then winding through traffic on that side.

"'Fraid not.'' He should have guessed it sooner. Night-vision goggles, a head of security sophisticated enough to have run guns overseas? Murphy would have the latest surveillance toys. "I visited Fleetfoot back in June, remember? Left the car parked for hours while they kept me waiting.''

"So?''

"So stop here and let me see if there isn't some sort of radio tracking gizmo stuck underneath somewhere. What do you bet that's how they knew we were dropping in for a visit last night?''

"Holy…!'' She swerved into a slot and stopped. "And if there's one on your car, then there's one on my car, too. That's how they tracked me after Austin!''

"Most likely.'' He found it inside the third wheel well he checked and held it up to her.

"Stomp that sucker to Kingdom Come!''

Here came the hard part. "I can do better than that.'' Even now, they were far from home free. So far, Colton had used only his own considerable resources to hunt them down. But if he called in the local police as backup…and no doubt the locals would be more than happy to oblige a hometown millionaire in distress. "We don't need to just drop out of sight, we need a decoy. And that's me.'' He'd taxi across town, find a truckstop out on the interstate, attach the beacon to some long-distance hauler. With any luck Colton's men would chase it halfway to Canada before they realized their mistake. "You, partner, take the honey and scram. To someplace your ex would never guess in his wildest dreams. I'll meet you there in three days.'' *If you're not a lying double-crosser.*

Her wonderful eyes filled again. "But—''

Over her shoulder, two parking rows away, he spotted a familiar shade of green—on a prowling pickup. "Here they come, babe, you've gotta go *now*. Where do we meet?"

Her throat convulsed, then she nodded. "Ask Judy at Moe's, in Dawson. I won't be far from there."

"They'll look at the dude ranch," he warned as she slid into the car.

"I know."

"Good." He straightened and checked. The truck was rounding the end of its row to turn down the lane one over, homing in on them. He leaned through the window she'd rolled down. "Drive a little slower, okay, hotshot?" She nodded tearfully and he kissed her, sweeter than honey, salty with tears. "And get your headlights fixed before dark. They're both broken."

"Oh, don't go!" she whispered against his lips.

"See you soon as I can. No more than three days," he promised. If she didn't take the honey and run. With the beacon in his pocket, he turned away and walked fast toward the door to the mall. Let 'em figure out that one.

NEAR MIDNIGHT, high up on the far side of Dana's mountain. And tonight made the fifth night. He wasn't coming. Sitting in an old tin tub next to the woodstove, Susannah poured a pot of warm water over her head. She set the pot back on the stove and reached for her shampoo bottle down on the floor. Closed her eyes and set to working up a lather. He wasn't coming, if he hadn't come by now. Water dripped down her spine and she shivered in the high mountain air. If Stephen's men caught him...

And forget about taking a lover, babe. You had your chance and you blew it. Stephen's voice, like acid dripping down the phone line and into her ear. This time the shudder rattled her all the way down to her tailbone. If Stephen knew she'd taken Tag for her lover...what he'd do to him...

He can't know, she told herself, and wiped soap off her nose.

Oh, but he could. If he and Murphy had known where she was ever since Austin, if they could put a radio doohickey on her car, they could have bugged her cabin at the dude ranch. Bugged Tag's half, too, which meant—

No, no, no, no! Shut up! You're just borrowin' trouble.

So, where is he, then? It's been five days. Time enough to hitch to Mexico City and back. That beating he'd taken back in Kentucky, could Tag have been hurt worse than he'd let on? If he'd collapsed somewhere…

Or maybe he just got smart. Decided I was way too much trouble, a walkin' Jonah. That life was a whole lot healthier with me not around.

No, even if Tag *had* decided that, he'd still come for his half of the honey.

If Stephen and Murphy didn't find her first.

Across the one-room miner's cabin, a tin cup fell over. Pebbles rattled out onto the floor. She gasped and sat up. Out on the porch, something had kicked her ankle-high string, which ran through a chink between two logs and into the cabin and so to the cup's handle. She hadn't wanted anybody sneaking up on her while she slept.

A board creaked outside and her breath hissed between her teeth. *You're just gonna sit here and wait for it, Susannah Mack?* She wiped the foam off her forehead and stood. Stepped out of the tub and snatched up the .22 rifle Judy had lent her.

Knock, knock, knock.

Not just a critter, then. At least not one that walked on four legs.

Tag would knock, she told herself desperately as she braced one shoulder against the front wall and aimed at the door.

So would Stephen, just to be cute. He'd be oh, so courteous and ironically smiling when he caught her at last.

The door creaked and a crack showed along it, somebody opening it with ominous care. Then the door was pushed silently wide. She drew a breath and held it. This wouldn't be Tag, not after five days. And she hadn't had time to blow out the candles across the room.

He rolled in so low and fast, for a split second she thought it *was* an animal, then she swung down her sights. The muzzle nearly bumped his nose. He flung up his arms and backpedaled. *"Hoo!"* She jerked the gun aside, then up to the ceiling, took her finger off the trigger and sat. Her knees weren't working.

"God, woman!" Tag blew out a breath and dropped to his knees.

"I n-nearly shot you, you big, stupid...! What did you think you were doing?" Susannah wanted to smack him.

"You didn't answer my knock."

"Yeah, like I'm gonna, dressed in nothin' but soapsuds!"

"How was I to know?" Tag started to grin. "I thought maybe Colton had found you somehow, beaten me back here, was waiting in—"

"And where the hell *were* you?" She set the .22 down and crawled across the rough boards. Took his face in her hands and kissed him fiercely. *I thought you weren't coming back!* Tears spilling, she kissed his nose, his bristly cheeks and started to laugh. He was here, he was real, bigger in her arms than she'd remembered.

She smoothed her hands down his back and he groaned and hugged her closer. Kissed her brow and recoiled. "Like kissing a bar of soap!"

"What you get for bargin' in on a lady in her bath." She stood on shaky legs and drew him up, too. He rose with an effort. "Lemme finish and then..."

"And then, and then, and then, darling." He held her hand as he followed her to her tub. As if he couldn't bear to let her go for one minute.

"And *then* a bath for you, too." She sat and smiled up at him. "You smell like a horse." He smelled wonderful, sweaty and dusty and all man.

"That's not an added attraction?"

Just like that, five days apart, and it might have been five minutes. There was an ease here between them that she'd never known with Stephen, ease and at the same time, a simmering excitement, her body humming with anticipation. *Welcome back. Oh, welcome back!* She watched him test her rinse water, then take the pot to the sink, to pump in more cool. He set another pan to heat beside it.

"So where've you been all this time?" she asked again, slipping back into the tub.

"Stumbling around this blasted mountain for the past two hours. Your friend Judy's no mapmaker."

"Before that, I mean. What made you so late?"

"It rained all the way across Kentucky, then Missouri, too, and I wasn't feeling too…spry. I holed up in a hayloft for a couple of days." Tag brought a chair over to sit beside the tub, then lifted the pot of water off the stove. She reached for it, but he shook his head. "Allow me, babe."

His hand slid around the nape of her neck to support her. She sighed and closed her eyes, going luxuriously limp as he trickled hot water through her hair. "Mmm…nice." Still holding her, Tag set the pot aside. Candlelight flickered red beyond her eyelids. She gasped as his mouth came out of the dark down onto hers. She opened to him and leaned back, giving herself completely to his hold, their tongues dancing a liquid dance of yearning and promise.

He drew back at last, brushed his lips across her cheek. "What you do to me, Susannah…"

"Oh, you ain't seen nothin' yet." She opened her eyes to see him pouring too much shampoo into his palm. "Hey, wait, I've already—"

"Oh? Well, can't let it go to waste." He rubbed it into her hair. "Shut those blue eyes."

She smiled and obeyed, letting him lather her hair, his fingers massaging her scalp, scrubbing tiny, delicious circles down the back of her slippery neck. Oh, he had her in a lather, all right. Sudsy, soapy foreplay, his fingers gliding down her temples, tracing the arc of her eyebrows, the line of her nose, teasing her lips till she smiled blindly against them. The hand supporting her neck eased backward, tipping her back. Feeling his eyes move over her, she trembled, then sighed with pure pleasure while his fingers caressed her neck, soaped her shoulders, then skated uphill and down along the very tops of her breasts, tantalizing, hesitating… *Oh, what are you waiting for?* She caught his wrist and drew his hand down over her skin, shuddered as a soapy fingertip rolled slowly round and round her nipple. "Yeah…"

"You are so beautiful!" he whispered somewhere above her.

"Rinse me off, Tag. I need t'see you."

"Not just yet." His finger traced a slippery figure eight to her other breast, then drew arabesques of soapy delight, spiraling lazily inward till his fingertip reached the peak of sensation—a starburst of heat.

She murmured deep in her throat as her hips rocked entreatingly. "Tag…" *You're torturing me, you Yankee devil!*

And he wasn't done yet. He whispered something dark and wordless as his fingertip wandered down her middle, stopped to delve into her navel, making her laugh and squirm and rock again.

"Oh, just you *wait* till I get hold of you!" she muttered breathlessly.

"You'll get your chance, babe, I promise." He rubbed his face across her breast, then back again, his beard scratching. She whimpered and caught the back of his head, held him pressed against her, her skin roughening to goose bumps.

He laughed and pulled back out of her hands. "Wait. Be still."

He wanted to be in charge, was in charge. She swallowed tremulously and nodded, then slowly went limp in his hold, letting him do unto her... She let out one high, singing note as his fingers found the precise center of her desire. Then, "Oh, yeah, oh...oh..."

He knew the sweet spot when he found it, homing in on it as her voice rose half an urgent octave. And he knew to take his time no matter how she begged, sending her round and round, spiraling inward into her own dark red delight, Tag following, somehow knowing, his touch so knowing and owning...till there was no way to resist him, no way at all, and no reason to— *"Ohhhhh!"* Sobbing deep in her throat, she reached for him blindly. *Oh, yes!* The hand behind her nape slid down to her back and he brought her upright. She threw her arms around his neck and shuddered against him. "Oh, Tag!"

HE LAY ON SOFTNESS, dimly aware of sunlight beyond his lids, a warm weight draped across his chest, soothing the aches within. After a while Tag opened his eyes and saw gold, firelight, sun sizzling along threads of finest copper. He sighed in wonder. Susannah. She'd caught him in a net of enchantment, spun from her own silky hair. Hauled up from the cold, dark depths to sunlight, he lay captured and dazzled and spent, content as he'd never been before in his life. *Is this what they mean by happy?*

The contrast with the past few days of pain and wondering, lying huddled and shivering in a leaky barn, worrying she wouldn't be there for him when and if he ever found the strength to reach her, desperately needing her warmth in the cold dark and she not there—to stumble from that to this... *Heaven, I've died and gone to...* He smiled and slept.

HE WOKE LATER as the mattress shifted and a weight settled beside him. Feeling the butterfly brush of her fingers through his chest hair, he smiled blindly. "The doctor's...not in." It had been nothing but one emergency after another, all night long. Though given a little mouth-to-mouth resuscitation maybe he could rise to one last... He opened his eyes to find her scowling at his chest. Her fingers stroked down to a spot that made him wince.

"They did this to you?" she demanded, drawl husky with outrage.

"No, that was you, babe. Last night."

"I did *not*..." She glanced up, realized he was teasing and laughed. "Wise guy." Her smile faded and she turned back to the damage. "Didn't realize in the dark. I wouldn't have..."

"Hurray for the dark." He stroked her bare knee. She was wearing a long-sleeved white shirt and nothing more as far as he could tell. He lifted a shirttail to be sure, grinned as she sniffed and tweaked it out of his grasp. Ms. Prim in the daylight, a killer after-hours. *Oh, Susannah Mack, what you do to me!*

She swore softly to herself as her fingertips found another injury. "Those bastards! One more thing I owe him."

"Colton?" He didn't want to think about Colton, old grievances or pains. He wanted coffee, then food, then more sleep, then Susannah again. Once you'd made it to heaven, why hash over the bad times?

"Who else?" she muttered, and rose abruptly off the bed. "It's gettin' to be quite a long list."

He groaned and pulled a pillow across his eyes. "Must be a Texas thing, feuds..."

"Yankees have no sense of justice? Of...of honor?"

"That's *just* what I mean, Lambchops." He tossed the pillow aside. "Here it is almost the year 2000, and you guys are still fighting the Civil War? You don't hear Yankees fretting about Southerners.''

''Uh-huh. It's a whole lot easier t'forgive when you're on the winnin' side.'' She lifted a battered coffeepot off the woodstove, poured a mugful, and brought it back to the bed. ''So...maybe I'll forgive Stephen once I've beaten him. When I'm standin' in the winner's circle at the Kentucky Derby, a blanket of roses round my Payback colt.'' Her eyes were wide and innocent as she stopped by the bed.

He sighed and hitched himself backward to lean against the headboard. ''You just don't quit, woman.''

''Nope.'' She stepped up onto the mattress, all long, bare golden legs and swaying shirttails, then knelt gracefully astride him, careful to support all her weight on those slender horsewoman's thighs. Smiling her slow, wicked smile, she raised the mug to his lips. ''Coffee?''

''*Who* won that war?''

CHAPTER TWENTY

BUT THOUGH ANOTHER battle was brewing in their apparently unending war, Susannah chose not to take advantage. For two days she observed a strict truce while Tag built up his strength, leaving him to sleep when he would, then returning with wildflowers from her wanderings on the mountain to cook him biscuits and canned stews on top of the woodburning stove. Or to rub his aching muscles with clever, tantalizing fingers and warm corn oil—the closest thing to medicine she had.

It was more truce than Tag would have chosen. But each time he reached for her, she laughed and slid out of his grasp and swore that with two cracked ribs, he was unfit for service, however he cared to take that.

By late afternoon of the second day, he'd had enough cosseting and enough of her bossing him around. Time to take charge, he told himself, sitting up on the edge of the bed. "Susannah?"

No answer from beyond the door she'd left half ajar. He dressed in the clothes he'd worn since Kentucky. They smelled of soap and sunshine now. She must have washed them. "Susannah?"

Dread beginning to stir, he walked out to the sagging porch. He'd slept most of the day away. He could half imagine Susannah waiting till she was certain he'd recover, then, with honor satisfied—by her own lunatic standards—she'd take Payback's honey and hit the road, hellbent on avenging

Brady and God knew what else. "Susannah?" If she'd left him again...

He glanced toward the ancient privy built in a glade south of the cabin, detoured that way and didn't find her. To the west the sun was a fireball falling to a jagged purple horizon. Its horizontal rays turned the aspen leaves on this mountain to green-gold. "Susannah!" he called again, turning—and caught a flicker of movement where the cabin's alpine meadow met the trees.

As he neared, her hand fluttered above the high grass, then fell. His heart stuttered, then settled to a faster pace. Injured, while he'd been lounging in bed, when he should have been up protecting her? Colton's men had come at last, or the bastard himself? They weren't as safe here as she seemed to think. He ducked under an overhanging branch and into a pocket of sunlight—to find her lying on her stomach, looking down the mountain. Eyes narrowed, she glanced back over her shoulder and put a finger to her lips.

"What—"

"*Hush!*" She patted the ground beside her.

He lay down and peered over the grass. Saw a brook, no more than two feet wide, spilling over rocks, then pausing thirty feet downslope to make a pool dammed by boulders, overhung by aspens, before plunging toward the valley again. Nothing moved beyond it. "He's found us?"

"More than likely. If he heard you yellin'..." She sniffed. "I've been tryin' to get a look at him for days. Goin' by the size of his hoofprints, I'd say he's a—"

He blew out his breath. "We're talking about a *deer?*"

"An elk. Bull for sure."

"You'll drive me *mad,* woman!" One way or the other. She lay with her chin propped on one hand, red-gold silk spilling over her shoulders, the curve in her spine pure poetry. He swallowed and laid one hand on her bottom. She smiled and reached backward. Caught his wrist. "You'll spook the elk."

"Doubtful." He stroked her with just the tips of his fingers, though the palm of his hand began to press down on her softness. Two days since he'd had her and it felt like two years. *Susannah?*

Arching her neck, she refocused her attention downhill, but the corners of her mouth tipped and deepened. He increased his pressure ever so slightly. If she ignored it...

She sighed, a deep, lazy sound, and her hips rocked once, down into the grass, long slender thighs flexing beneath her jeans. His heart leaped and he pressed harder. She made a tiny, humming sound deep in her throat. "You'll scare my elk."

"I bet you two socks you scare him first." He rolled on top of her.

She groaned luxuriously and stretched under his weight, arching her back, the grass swishing as she slowly spread her legs. "I'll *take* that bet and I'll raise you my—"

"Brassiere," he said firmly, his hands sliding around her body. Through her shirt and the silk beneath, her nipples stood hard and eager for his touch, pure magic. Everything green was turning to gold as the sun sank, her hair to silk afire. She moaned and lowered her face into the grass. He swept the fiery silk to one side and laid his mouth on her nape, brushed it slowly down to the tender curve where neck met shoulder. She moaned again and bucked beneath him, reached back and caught his hair with both hands.

Don't ever leave me again! he told her silently, fiercely, his hands hot and heavy upon her. It was starting to scare him, the power she had over him. He needed somehow to even the odds, needed some way to mark her the way she was marking him.

Instinct whispered it knew the way, even while reason told him that his power lasted no longer than it took the echoes of her cries to die out over the mountainside. But if it was even for that long... His hands smoothed down her tapered ribcage, found her belt and unbuckled it.

THE GRASS HAD gone purple with shadows. They hadn't seen the elk, but who'd been looking? From the corner of his eye, Tag could make out a star, diamond dancing on a field of cobalt blue. He kissed the corner of her mouth and started to shift.

"Don't you dare move." Susannah reached behind and pressed him down again.

He laughed and obeyed, but loving had energized him, jolted his brains. Lying with Susannah was pure paradise, but there was a viper in their garden. A viper he had to think about stomping. Ignoring him was no solution. "I've been thinking," he said at last.

She trembled beneath him—laughter. "That's what you've been doin'?"

"Among other things. And I see it this way, babe. We can't stay here much longer. Your ex has got to be hunting us." The cabin belonged to Dana, she'd told him the first morning. It was a prospector's camp from the late 1800s, built on the far flank of the same mountain you could see from the Ribbon R. And Dana knew they were there—had given her permission to use the place via Judy. Which meant that if Colton or his flunkies leaned on Judy or Dana... "Till we unload the sperm, we've got to be a moving target."

Her body went taut beneath him, including the muscles that clamped him directly. He gulped and responded. "We're *not* selling that sperm!" she insisted.

"Oh? Who's the senior partner here?" He brushed his beard across her nape and smiled when she squirmed. He was learning all her hot spots.

"I don't recall agreein' t'that!" Her drawl had gone husky again. "I said I'd share, but—"

"So put it this way, partner. Who's on top?"

She was silent. Stubborn, stubborn...and she'd gone utterly still, her whole body expressing fierce disapproval. He wouldn't have it. He nuzzled her ear and she shivered, then froze again. *But if we can't agree...*

They had to agree. His way was the only way that would work, that could save them, he was sure of it. He brushed his mouth down to the top of her velvety shoulder, then nipped her—and her whole body arched beneath him. He propped his elbows, cupped her breasts and held her to that quivering bow. Deep inside her, he felt himself hardening all over again. "Who's on *top,* Susannah?"

Shuddering, stubborn silence, their locked stillness more erotic than any movement. He dragged his unshaven chin over the same sensitive spot, and she let out a shivering hiss between her teeth. "Who?" he repeated.

"You are," she purred at last, tiger soft. "For now." A sulking tiger.

And what was that proverb about the tiger? That once you'd mounted, you'd better keep riding?

THEY SLEPT THAT NIGHT wrapped in each other's arms—and resumed the battle at dawn. "You're not being practical," he said, straddling a chair while he watched her make biscuits. That she could cook on top of everything else never failed to amaze him. "Suppose we did it your way. Used the sperm on your mare. What are the odds that her colt would win the Kentucky Derby? A thousand to one? Ten thou? How many racehorses are born in this country each year?"

She shrugged impatiently. "Thirty or forty thousand, I'd say. But—"

"And the owner of each and every one of those foals dreams of winning the Derby. How many horses get to run in it? Twelve?"

"More. Twenty at the startin' gate wouldn't be unusual."

Her lips wavered just this side of a pout. She cut the dough with vicious twists of a glass, then grimly precise, arranged the circles in a cast-iron skillet.

She wasn't stupid. She had to see his logic. "So if you beat out forty thousand colts to make it to the Derby—*if,* babe—then your odds are still twenty to one. Yeah, that's what I call a reliable revenge."

She clanged the top down onto the skillet and the skillet onto the stove. "You just don't get it! Sheba's grandmother on her dam's side was a *full* sister to Ruffian. On the other side, her grandsire was Secretariat, bred back to a Nijinsky mare. You pair that with Payback's blood and your odds go *way* up. That's a match made in heaven."

"Has she ever thrown any notable colts?"

"She's never been paired with Payback." She stooped to open the fire door, peer inside, add a stick and slam it again.

"Any winners at all, Lambchops? Mated with any stud?"

She stayed in a crouch, frowning. "Three that would have won, but..."

"But." He reached for a lock of her hair, fingered it, considered reeling her in, then thought better of it. "But?"

"Two of 'em, fillies, might have been Ruffian all over again, but they never made it to the track. Too high-spirited. The colt that showed speed, they gelded. He set a record for six furlongs in his maiden race that still stands, but he had a...tantrum in the starting gate before his second race. Ruptured a tendon and never ran again." She stood and moved to the sink.

More money was made in the breeding shed after a stud's racing career was over than was ever earned on the track, Tag had learned, reading about Payback. The only reason an owner would geld a promising colt up front, foregoing all hope for that eventual jackpot, was... "She throws vicious colts? And even fillies?"

"High-*spirited.*" She tossed her head as she turned and

flashed her eyes at him. "Which is why Payback's her ideal complement. He's a pussycat through and through, and he stamps his get. My colt'll have his temperament."

"Or hers, since it takes two to tango. What if your colt's vicious—sorry—high-spirited, babe? What then?"

She gave him a coolly tolerant smile. "Then that's still my specialty, what I do best, gentling colts. Prepping yearlings for the track. If the right trainer had handled her colts from the start... All that fire and energy and will to win, Tag, it's gotta go somewhere. Either it explodes out—or it explodes in a straight line. You just have t'channel it."

That settled it, then and there. He could see his stubborn lover saddling up a four-legged stick of dynamite, bound and determined to turn it into an amiable equine rocket. Her own will to win colliding with that of a half-ton renegade stallion. *No, thanks.* "How'd you ever come to buy this mare, for Pete's sake?"

Susannah cracked the lid, looking in on the biscuits, then resettled it. "She was the right breeding—Brady thought so, too—and the right price. I could *just* afford her."

"A millionaire's wife, why couldn't you have bought any horse you wanted?" Why had she needed her own broodmare at all when Fleetfoot was stocked to overflowing?

She stood, staring down at the stove, her cheeks flushed by more than its heat, then spun to the sink. "He...didn't like me to have money. Walkin' around money. He gave me whatever he thought I needed, fancy clothes, presents all the time, but..." She shrugged. "And he gave me credit cards, but not the kind where you could get cash off 'em. They had limits."

Limits that Colton, a platinum-card customer himself, must have had to request specially for his wife. "And you put up with that? Let him treat you like a child?" Had her love been so blind that she didn't recognize a control freak in her own bed?

"I..." Her fingers traced the bronze handle of the pump,

powdery green with age. "I hardly noticed, that first year. I had everything I needed or could possibly want. I don't get the wants much, anyway, 'cept for horses and travel. And between his jet and the stables…" She shrugged. "So it took me a while to notice."

"But you put up with it once you did?" God, he wanted—most violently—to shake her. "So how did you buy your broodmare?" Begged Colton for the money? Or—Tag slammed the door hard on the thought of what she might have done to coax it out of him, raw jealousy raking its claws across the far side of that door.

Her fingers moved over the handle again. "I had a bit of money of my own saved up. A coupla thou' from workin' as an exercise girl back at that stable down the road from my dad's. So I took that and started bettin' it at the track, whenever we'd go to watch Stephen's horses run." She looked toward the back window, a wry tilt to her lips in profile. "I'm a pretty good judge of horseflesh."

His anger eased a notch. "And did he know you were betting?"

She turned to face him, surprised. "Oh, no." Her eyes skated to the stove. "My best win ever was one where I bet *against* his horse. He'd have never forgiven that." She reached for her hot pads and homed in on the skillet. "That's why he never knew about my mare. Brady and I bought her at an auction while Stephen was off on one of his business trips. She was bred already, so I worked out a deal with a trainer who wanted the foal. That's where she went after the sale—to Christina Meade's farm out in Washington. She dropped a fine filly in March. Once the baby's weaned, I can move Sheba, or board her there as long as I want."

She carried the skillet to the pine table near the back window, then turned to face him, chin up. "So now you know where to find her. D'you still mean to sell her and take your half?"

This is a test, isn't it? Tag held her eyes as he closed the distance between them, stopped only when they stood toe to toe. To be that near to Susannah was to touch her, steel to magnet, an irrevocable fact of his existence. He palmed her cheek, sliding his fingers up past her ear into silkiness. "No." If Sheba was her act of rebellion, a declaration of freedom, only a fool would try to part them. He'd tamed a hawk once with kindness—or at least sheltered one for a little while, till it healed and flew away. "No, but *you* should sell her." Her lips stopped their slow curve and turned willful. "You won't have much use for her once we've sold the honey."

"We're not—" She stopped as he laid a finger across her mouth.

"We *are*. You owe me, I'm collecting and there's no other way, Susannah. If the guy's really as vengeful as you say he is, d'you think your colt would *live* three years till the Kentucky Derby? You think your mare, once you bred her with Payback's sperm, would live to deliver, if he's that kind of guy?" Her face had gone pale. Tough. If he had to rock her to make her see reason, he would. "Or maybe you're exaggerating. Maybe Colton's not a gentleman psycho. Maybe he's just a spoiled brat, a rich boy who likes to get his way."

"He's…more than that." She bit her lip and looked down.

More, meaning worse? Or more, meaning Colton was wacko, but with redeeming qualities, potential—and that, in spite of everything, she still loved him? Women could be such damn fools! Tag combed his fingers through her hair to the back of her head, gathered a handful and tugged, bringing her face up. "You told me once you were about to leave him?"

"I was. I'd been broodin' for months, wonderin' if there was some way to put it all back together, the way I'd first felt about him." She sighed, eyes distant as a Rocky Mountain sky. "So I went down t'Houston, the end of December, to visit Saskia, girl talk, y'know. She's not much for givin' advice, but one night she asked me if maybe I was bein' stubborn, if maybe the reason I was so down was 'cause I couldn't admit to myself that I'd made a mistake? That my dream of happy-ever-after-with-Stephen was one big, gold-plated dud.''

Bless you, Saskia Mack! ''And you decided?''

''That…she was right. That I'd given us a fair shot and it was time to cut loose. That by the year 2000 I wanted to be over him. Getting on with my own life. So I flew back up to Fleetfoot, meanin' to tell him that night. I knew it'd be ugly—more than ugly. I was sort of…scared, but…'' She paused, groping for words.

''Did he ever…?'' Even the thought was shameful, the words to express it almost impossible to speak. As if the shame was contagious, a disease passed from male to male. And if she said yes, then the violence *would* pass to him. Tag couldn't imagine not avenging her, if Colton had ever laid a hand on her.

''Never.'' She leaned into him, her breasts resting against his chest, her head tipped back to look up at him. ''Not once. He's not like that and I wouldn't have stood still for that.''

Thank God. He let go of her hair and wrapped his arms around her waist. She buried her face against his collarbone. ''But he scared you, baby?''

Her lips caressed him as she shook her head. ''Not at first. Not till almost the end. And even then it was nothing I could ever put my finger on. Just bits and pieces…a story I'd heard…the way I'd see him treat people, sometimes, little people who had no way of fighting back. I hated that, though he treated me all right.''

And for some women that would have been good enough. As long as they were on the inside of Colton's golden circle, why care about the unfortunates on the outside? Tag's arms tightened around her.

''I tried, once or twice at first, to step between him and people, change his mind. We butted heads real bad about a housemaid he fired, but...Stephen had a way of twistin' things. We couldn't just disagree. I was either on his side or I was against him, is how he always saw it. So I started backin' down, goin' my own way, tryin' to make amends for him, when I could. Shuttin' my eyes to way too much, I see now. There was a story this guard told me a few months after I came t'Fleetfoot. I didn't believe it at the time, just couldn't. But lookin' back now..."

She stopped suddenly and glanced up and around, then Tag heard it, too.

A voice calling, thin and far away. "Hey! Anybody home?"

CHAPTER TWENTY-ONE

THEIR VISITOR WAS SEAN, Dana's stepson, looking more excited and less sullen than Tag had ever seen him before. He'd ridden Guapo, the beginner's pony, up from the Ribbon R. Sent by Dana. He gave them her news between mouthfuls of biscuit and strawberry jam. Two men had come calling the night before, asking for either Susannah or Tag. A little man and a big one.

"Murphy and one of his men," Susannah translated grimly.

They'd arrived while Dana was completing dinner, with a half-dozen hungry guests milling around the ranch house. "They tried to rent our whole place, all the cabins. She told them we had no vacancy and they said they'd pay double if she'd cancel the reservations. When she told 'em no again, I guess they got mad. Said she oughtta think about it. Then they asked if they could look around, and they did, the barn and every cabin."

Wonderful. Tag exchanged glances with Susannah. Two women who needed protecting now, but his place was here. "This was yesterday?"

Mouth full, Sean nodded, gulped, then added, "So Sam decided he wanted to play poker all night. He got the mountain bikers in cabin one t'play, and he called some of his friends from town to come up and visit. They played half the night, I guess, in the kitchen. They even let me play till I went bust."

Tag relaxed. *Good man.* "Who's Sam?"

"The new wrangler," Susannah replied softly. "Judy's cousin. He'll take good care of her."

But a wrangler had dudes to mind. He couldn't guard Dana day and night. Tag rubbed his chin while the kid chowed down. Sean was bright, but he had a chip on his shoulder the size of a barn. Some issue that Tag hadn't had the time to pry out of the boy during his brief stay at the dude ranch. Something to do with the death of Sean's father last spring. Somehow he seemed to blame his stepmother. Still.

"I guess it's up to you, then, Sean," he said, which got the kid's attention. "Those guys'll be coming back." They'd probably gone first to Susannah's home ranch in Texas, then finding no trace of her there, were trying here. Dana's refusal would have convinced them they were on the right track.

"Me?" Sean wiped his mouth and sat back, frowning.

"You don't want 'em hassling Dana."

"Mmm." He wriggled sideways in his seat to inspect the cabin.

"Put it this way," Tag said. "Your *dad* wouldn't want them hassling Dana. Or your baby brother or sister, whichever it is, either. Right?" Susannah stirred on his other side. He put a hand over hers and squeezed gently. "Sean?"

"Yeah." The kid bent double to inspect his tennis shoes under the table. Retied the laces on one, then stayed down, fiddling with the other.

"Good. So how cool are you?"

That brought him up again. He locked teary eyes with Tag and muttered, "Cool enough."

Tag allowed a smile and nodded. "So here's what you do, then. When they come, the men'll have questions, and they'll figure a kid's an easy mark. It's up to you to trick 'em. They'll want to talk to you alone, so let them cut you out from the herd. Go fly fishing somewhere where they'll spot you." He cocked an eyebrow and waited.

The kid was there already. "At the bridge! They'd have to drive right by me."

"That's just the place. Don't be friendly, be cool. They'll ask you about Susannah and me. You look away and mumble. Say you're not supposed to talk about it."

"But then they'll know…"

"That's right. They'll figure you've got something to talk about. So they'll offer you money."

"Tag!" Susannah murmured.

"And I don't take it?" Sean asked, his eyes fixed on Tag. Menfolk closing ranks on the frailer sex.

"Right, but you look tempted. If he shows you the money, look at it and count to ten before you shake your head and turn away. Then he'll up his offer, Sean, and *that's* when you take it."

The boy nodded eagerly. "And then I lie? Say you phoned us from Florida or something?"

"Nope, you send 'em straight up here."

"I DON'T LIKE IT," Susannah said as they stood, arms around each other's waists, watching pony and rider disappear over the shoulder of the mountain, bound for the Ribbon R. "And Dana may never forgive you. He's just a kid."

"His father would say he could handle it."

She snorted. "You never met him. How would you know that?"

"A guy thing, babe. I know. Kids want to be useful at that age. Where were you at thirteen?" He turned her around. The sooner they packed and scrammed, the better.

"My dad had just come home from the hospital, after his fall. Saskia was startin' college in Austin, so…"

"So it was you in charge, huh?" Like him, she'd lost her mother early, though hers had died whereas his had run off. And he, at age thirteen, was stealing food for the table when his father remembered to come home and eat, stealing cars when he didn't. "And you came shining through. So will Sean. And this puts Dana in the clear."

"How d'you figure that?"

"You write her a note and date it yesterday. Maybe address it to Sean, and ask him to give it to her when he finds it. Keep it short and sweet. Say thanks for all their hospitality. And that we're headed out to California to stay with a friend of mine. A vet in San Diego. We'll leave it here on the table for Murphy to find."

She nodded, satisfied, except— "Do you have friends in San Diego?"

"Not a one I know of." But there must be a hundred veterinarians in a city that size. If Murphy questioned every one, he and Susannah should have weeks in the clear. Time enough to find a buyer for their honey?

SINCE MURPHY SHOULD be chasing them west, they fled north by east toward Denver. The path down to the trailhead on national parkland, where Susannah had hidden his car among those of a dozen hikers, took more out of Tag than he cared to admit. He let her drive for the first few hours while he leaned back and dozed.

They stopped in Gunnison for cheeseburgers to go, then pushed on, Tag grimly totaling their remaining assets. Fifty-four dollars and change. Plus the pistol he'd taken off Peterson back in Kentucky, which they'd better hock at the first opportunity, since they had no papers to carry it.

Plus two talents they dared not use. Let him apply for a job as a vet, let Susannah show her face at any track or thoroughbred stable, and they risked the word going out. Some reporter picking up the gossip and whipping off a three-paragraph human-interest story: Guess Whatever Happened to the Most Spiteful Woman of the Year and that Fool of a Vet Who Helped Her? If that didn't bring Colton and his men running...

But they had to find cash. He could steal a car, Tag supposed, but he had no connections to sell it. And his old skills were rusty. If he were caught and jailed, who would protect Susannah? He glanced at her sideways. She drove with her window open, her hair blowing back in silken banners, downing her burger with all the gusto of a teenage boy. Her blue eyes were locked on the road ahead, as if the winner's circle at Churchill Downs lay around the next bend. *If I wasn't here to protect her, about a thousand men would line up and beg to take my place.* He frowned and reached to wipe a smear of ketchup off her cheek.

Eyes on the climbing road, she absently kissed his fingers. The anger in him shifted toward resolve. "What would a Payback colt bring, Susannah, if you sold him today?"

"Um…" She geared down as the incline steepened. They were climbing out of the valley in long switchbacks toward Monarch Pass. "Last July at the Keeneland Selected Sale, a Payback colt set a world record. Fourteen million. A new boy in town snapped him up, guy from Colombia, drug-cartel money, everybody was whispering. Went head to head with the Saudi sheik who's usually the top bidder and backed him right down."

"Fourteen million." With money like that, they'd be home free. Could run anywhere in the world, if they had to.

"But that record will fall with this crop of yearlings. The Keeneland auction's in—what—two weeks? Any breeder who sells a Payback colt this year, after…" Her voice trailed away as she rolled up her window.

"After we cut the supply line?" *And why the hell did we do it, babe?* She still hadn't told him.

Her chin took on a defiant tilt and she shrugged. "There's this crop of yearlings, then next year's, then that's…all she wrote. So it's anybody's guess what a promisin' Payback colt will bring on the block this year. Sky's the limit. Twenty million, maybe, for a real looker?"

"And that's where we sell the honey!" he exclaimed as it hit him. "You say the two-year-old auction is in two weeks?" If that was where the big money shopped for its bloodstock, then that was where they'd find their black-market buyer. High rollers, rich enough to flout the rules.

They were climbing above timberline, peaks rising on all sides to the sky, the air thinning, the car laboring, Susannah scowling. "You just don't get it, Tag. I don't care about the money—never did. I just want payback."

"You never heard that living well is the best revenge? Say we sold the honey for sixteen million." It would be more of a gamble for the buyer than a live colt and so worth less, but still. "I say we take the money and run. Half of sixteen million, babe? Take your share of that and live for Brady, too. Bet he'd be the first to tell you that."

"And what would *you* do?" Her eyes flashed contempt as they skated across him and back to the road. "Take your half and run off with your tail between your legs t'that beach shack in Thailand? Eight million should buy you a lifetime supply of dusky maidens."

One hundred-pound, half-crazy Texan would do him nicely, dammit, if only she'd come to her senses.

"I know I owe you, Tag, but I owe him more."

"Brady?"

"*Stephen.* Don't you care at all what he's done? He hurt me, he hurt you, he hurt Saskia, Ike, he put the *big* hurt on Brady. You want me just t'forget about it?"

They'd reached the top of the pass. She pulled into an overlook where half a dozen cars had stopped. Laughing tourists posed for their loved ones' cameras against a breathtaking backdrop of jagged blue horizon, snowy mountains, desert softened by distance. The continental divide, a spine of ice-topped, unforgiving granite, cutting one world into two, the land sloping away green to the Atlantic on one side, arid rocks and range to the Pacific on the other. "Yes," Tag said softly.

"Just that, Susannah. Let's untangle ourselves from this mess, then forget about it. Walk away." *Hand in hand.*

"I can't."

"Won't." He slammed out of the car and stalked to the boulders that marked the edge, glared out over the empty miles. She might think she was free of Colton, but she wasn't. No matter how twisted, revenge was still a form of connection. He didn't want her to hate Colton—he wanted her not to care. He gave a start as she came up behind and slid her arms around his waist.

"Tag?" She stood on tiptoe behind him, her breath warming his ear.

He shrugged and felt her breasts brush his shoulderblades. Already drumming with anger, his pulse surged like a river approaching a cataract. She flattened one hand on his stomach and smoothed it slowly up to his heart. Stopped there.

So much for pretending indifference. He spun out of her embrace, then turned back to the car. Climbed in on the driver's side. She might drive him mad, but he was damned if he'd let her choose their road.

He took it slow as they descended, stopping at every overlook, careful not to overheat the brakes. Ignoring her anxious glances, he let himself cool down, too. If she was going to run her life on raw emotion, he'd have to be cold and logical enough for two. They'd driven halfway down the mountain before he spoke. "What if we gave the honey back to Colton?" *This is a test, Susannah Mack.* "I give up my hope of money, you give up your chance at revenge. How's that for a compromise, partner?"

"You want us just t'roll over? Give in?" From her expression, he might have suggested they skateboard buck naked all the way down from Monarch Pass.

"No," he said, hanging onto his patience. "I'm saying what if we strike a hard bargain? Colton wants the sperm so much, we let him have it. In exchange, we get to live our

own lives unmolested.'' *My life with you, if you'll have me.*
It wasn't what he wanted, starting again from scratch, but he
could do it, if Colton stopped knocking the props out from
under.

"You don't get it at all, Tag! That's not how his mind
works. He doesn't want to bargain, he wants revenge. No,
listen t'me! I started t'tell you back at the cabin 'bout something a guard told me a few months after I married Stephen…''

It had happened one night when Stephen was off on one
of his trips. A young broodmare was slow in delivering. Susannah had spelled the mare's groom all that night, waiting
and watching for the moment to call in the vet. A security
guard she was afraid had a bit of a crush on her had found
her there and hung around, talking and offering her sips of
bourbon from a bottle he shouldn't have been carrying on
duty. "Guess it sort of loosened his lips after a while. He
asked me if I knew about Stephen's tapes, and I said no, what
tapes did he mean?''

He told her that all the guards knew Stephen had a collection of tapes over at the office. Tapes made off the security
cameras.

The hair at the back of Tag's neck rose. *That chair I sat
in, back in the office at Fleetfoot, facing a security camera…*

"He claimed that each tape had a name printed on the
spine. Said he'd snuck a peek at one of em, one night when
he was bored. Tape of a man, sittin' in a chair.'' The man
had been crying. "Tryin' not to, tryin' to make it look like
he was coughing or he had a cold, but it kept breaking out.
He was crying, asking over and over, what Stephen wanted
from him. Why was he wreckin' his life? What had he done
to Stephen to deserve this?''

Tag's hands had turned to blocks of ice, frozen to the
wheel. He'd sat in that very chair! Hadn't cried, but he'd

asked the same question—*What does Colton want from me?*
God, the sick bastard—filming men begging?

''Listenin' to him, the guard, at first it was like one of those
dreams. You know the one where you're tryin' to scream, but
your lungs won't push the air? It was like that, me sittin'
there. I needed to make him shut up, but I couldn't. He bab-
bled on and on. Finally he stopped for a drink and I found
my tongue. Said I didn't believe it for one minute, but even
if he *had* seen something like that, then there must be a good
reason. That the guy must've deserved whatever he got. He
must have done something terrible to Stephen.

''But the guard said no, he'd asked around, and heard from
a guard who was close t'Murphy that the man was one of
four who'd gone to the same private boarding school as Stephen. That the four had bullied Stephen back when he was a
pudgy, nearsighted kid with no friends. So—'' her drawl had
changed to a strained half whisper ''—so when Stephen grew
up and came into his money, he…hunted them down.''

''Had 'em hit, you mean?'' No doubt Murphy could ar-
range that.

She swallowed and shook her head. ''Nothing so easy. He
just…chipped away at 'em, year after year. Loss of a job here,
pay some man to seduce a wife away there, lawsuits and
bankruptcies and accidental housefires. Credit ratings
wrecked, health and tax records screwed up, pets run over,
cars stolen till no insurance company would cover 'em. You
name it, money can buy it. Payback forever and ever, amen.
Or almost forever.''

She'd clamped her hands between her legs. He reached for
one and pulled it over onto his thigh, flattened his hand over
it. ''Meaning?''

''Meaning my guard heard that one of those four had shot
himself a few months after his tape was made.''

If he had any sense at all, he'd stop the car. Hand her the
cannister of sperm and drive off. Leave her to it, whatever

she wanted to do. Because if this was the truth, he didn't need it. Tag twined his fingers through hers and said, "So what did you do once he'd told you?"

She swallowed convulsively. "If I'd believed him, I'd've had t'pack my bags that night. I was in love with my husband, Tag. Hardly knew this guard from Adam—we'd only joked around a few times. So I told myself he was drunk. That he was just running Stephen down t'make himself look good in front of me. That whatever he'd seen, he'd gotten it wrong. He wasn't exactly Einstein. Oh, I wallpapered that night over with every excuse I could find, no matter how flimsy, then I didn't look back."

"You never asked him to show you the tapes?"

"Never saw him again. Somebody reported him drinkin' on the job or maybe being too chummy with me, and that was that. He was gone."

"And you never asked Colton about it?"

She laughed shakily. "Asked the man I thought I loved if he was crazy? I felt so…soiled…having listened to that garbage. I pushed that whole night down and down into the back of my mind, and I never let myself think about it again—till after I'd left Stephen. Till I lost my second job in Austin and I started realizin' that now it was my…payback time."

CHAPTER TWENTY-TWO

LATE THAT AFTERNOON they found a third-rate motel on the edge of Colorado Springs. Susannah made a beeline for the shower and Tag went out on an errand. He lucked into a supplier just before closing time, then hurried back with his package. He'd been worrying about the honey all day.

He found Susannah sitting on their bed, combing out her hair, wrapped in nothing but a towel. "Supper?" she asked hopefully, seeing his package.

"Dry ice." He set it down by the cooler in which the cannister of sperm traveled. She'd kept it packed in ice from Kentucky to the cabin, then stashed the cooler in the creek, trusting the snow-melt to maintain its temperature. But down here in the summer lowlands… "If it thaws, we can kiss our twenty million goodbye."

"We're not—"

"Save it a minute." Tonight they'd have to settle their differences, make a start on the plan he'd formed as they drove. As soon as he'd done this, Tag decided. "How much is in here?" he asked, while he set washrags ready to hand, then lifted the cannister out onto the floor.

She knelt on the bed above him. "Don't know. I didn't dare open it. Brady said they'd been collecting Payback's sperm at night for a week or two. Storing it in the clinic in a Deepfreeze. He'd only found out from one of the medtechs the day I came back from Houston. 'Cause they'd fired the regular night watchman, put one of Murphy's men in his place, in charge of the stud barns at night."

What the hell had Colton been up to? Tag lifted off the lid and clouds of vapor billowed out, the gaseous remains of evaporated dry ice. Mystical, roiling magician's smoke, concealing the treasure within. He waved it aside and bumped heads with Susannah, looking down. The inner container held—his fingertips touched one after another, counting them off—"eight straws." And there were still a few lumps of dry ice in the outer reservoir ring. *Thank you, God!*

Using hand towels to protect his fingers, he stacked the outer ring with dry ice, sealed the lid again, sat back and drew a breath. "Eight." Sperm for artificial insemination was mixed with extender and preservatives, then stored in plastic "straws," ready to be thawed and inserted directly into a mare. "Eight matings."

Susannah refastened her towel over her breasts. "You couldn't dilute each one a bit? Stretch the good times a bit further?"

"Depends on how potent Payback was and how much the temperature has varied since 'harvest.' Some of the sperm will have died already in the freezing."

"And the rest of the teeny suckers have to hang on another eight months."

Too true. Mares in the northern hemisphere came into season in the late winter and early spring. "So, no, this is the recommended dose. It'd be a gamble to try and stretch it."

"Then that leaves four straws for you, and four for me," Susannah said softly—and looked him straight in the eye.

Here we go. "No, I'm afraid it doesn't." He sat beside her, lifted one hand from her lap and rubbed his thumb across the palm. "We're going to be asking some breeder to take an enormous risk, Susannah. To lay down millions on the chance of a Payback colt. And anybody with that kind of money will have brains to match. He'll know that if the first mating doesn't take, he'll need enough sperm for a second try, a third and so on. To make him feel safe, we've got to offer the eight straws as a package deal. It'll be the buyer's bonus if the sperm is still potent enough to impregnate a second mare, or even a third or fourth. But that's fair enough. The only reason to take a high risk is in hopes of an enormous payoff.''

''Money!'' She jerked her hand aside. ''That's all this is to you. All you've cared about from the start. Why you're sittin' here now.''

''That's part of it,'' he said levelly. *But not all, love.* ''Money brings freedom, in case you haven't noticed. Freedom to come and go as you please. To choose work you love, instead of being forced to work some job you hate to keep the wolf from the door. Freedom from lying awake in the dark, wondering if next week you'll have food to eat or a roof over your head. Yeah, I like money in my pocket.'' And they'd need more than pocket change, if they meant to outrun Colton. *No tapes of thee and me crying for his collection, babe, I promise you.* He drew a tentative fingertip down her thigh. *Trust me, Susannah. I'll take care of you.*

She brushed his hand aside. ''You won't be free till your pocket's full of money, Tag? Well, I won't be free till I've settled the score.''

As rockheaded as she was beautiful. Sitting this close to her, he could smell the clean scent of her skin. All his instincts cried that he should simply overpower her resistance, tip her back on the bed and *tell* her how it would be. Show her.

Reason told him that if did that, he'd win this battle—and lose the war. He crossed his arms and flexed, fighting his own strength. ''If that's what you need to be free of all this…'' *To be free to come to me.* ''Then settle the score once and for *all,* Susannah. Whipping Colton's horse in the Derby, you think that'll hurt him?''

Her eyes shifted away from his arms, roamed the room. ''Yeah, I do. You don't know his pride.''

"You don't know *men*, babe, if you think that. Whipping Colton's ass in a horse race? That'll be about as effective as flogging him with your powder puff. And if he holds a grudge against you already, you want to make it worse, humiliating him a second time in front of his own kind?"

"Your way's any better? So we make a few crummy million—so what? How does that punish Stephen?"

"You're thinking like a woman—like a teacher, shaking her finger at the naughty boy. Let's shame Stephen in front of his classmates. Uh-uh, kid, if you want to play with the big guys, you'd better learn to think like one."

"So you're the expert? How would *you* do it?"

"Easy. You don't pick a fight—ever—Lambchops, unless you mean to finish it. If you're going to hit somebody, then you go straight for the knockout punch. No threats, no scolding, no dancing around. You put him down fast—and you make sure he stays down."

She blinked. "How?"

"You take your half of whatever we get for the honey, and you hire yourself a hit man. If you have to have revenge, if you won't be happy till you've had it, then that's the only safe way to take it." She parted her lips to protest, but he rode right over her. "But me, I don't think I'll stick around to watch the fun. It's your ex, baby...and it's *your* quarrel."

Her lips quivered; her eyes glittered with tears. "I don't want him dead, Tag, b-b-but I...I need *payback!*"

"Payback leads to payback leads to payback. That's no way to live. No life I want to lead."

"But—"

"No buts. If that's all that matters to you..." His pulse had risen in spikes till now it hammered at the top of his skull. He yanked the car keys from his pocket and dropped them on the bed. "I'm going out for a bite. Be here or not when I come back, Susannah, but if you are...then we play it my way." *And this, my darling, is most surely a test!*

HE'D BEEN TOO TOUGH on her, Tag told himself, coming back around midnight. The fast food he'd found had hit his stomach like a lump of lead. After he'd eaten, he'd walked around the town, dreading to go back to the room and find her gone. The way he'd hammered on her, he could hardly blame her this time if she'd taken the honey and run. But he'd had to make her see where this idiotic feud would take her in the end. *And I meant every word.* No, he couldn't back down even a little bit. Had to hang tough.

Hanging tough might mean he'd lost her forever.

His steps quickened. *I shouldn't have left her.* And left her the keys. *Fool.* He wanted no part of her childish revenge, but if she'd taken him at his word, run off to find it...

Colton would kill her in the end, if she pushed him far enough. He couldn't just leave her to it. Where she went, he'd have to follow. Tag was almost running as he passed under the blue neon sign, then into the courtyard of the U-shaped motel. He saw his car parked before their room and stopped short. *Thank you, God!*

He closed the door to their unit behind him. By the dim light sifting past the dingy curtains, he could see a huddled lump under the blanket. Susannah didn't stir as he padded to the bathroom, brushed his teeth and showered, then came to bed.

He slid in under the covers and turned toward her. Her breathing sounded as shaky as a child's after a good cry. "Lambchops?"

She jerked away from his touch, then sniffed and lay motionless.

So what was he supposed to do? Coax her out of her pout? Or leave her alone till she'd forgiven him?

But this past hour, he'd thought maybe he'd lost her. To banish that aching emptiness, he needed contact. Hoped she needed it, too. He caught a strand of her hair and fingered it wistfully. "Babe?"

No answer, but then she hadn't told him to go to hell. He slid closer to her warmth. *Susannah, love...*

Still no response. Asleep? No, not with that uneven breathing. Crying? He spooned up against her and reached around to touch her cheeks—dry and hot. Her lashes fluttered like moth wings in the dark. Her mouth trembled, soft and unsmiling.

But as long as she'd allow him to touch her, court her... He smoothed his fingers down her slender throat. Traced one fingertip along her delicate collarbones, back and forth, waiting for a consenting sigh that didn't come. *Babe?* Was this a game of sulking—or the real thing?

Butterfly light, he drew his fingers down the rich, ripe swell of her breast, to brush its peak. Found it waiting for his touch, hard and fever hot. Hard as he was growing. He groaned and cupped her, rose to one elbow to lean over her, brushing her cheek with his lips. ''Susannah?''

''That's all you've wanted from me from the start, isn't it?'' Her drawl was icy with contempt. ''This and money.''

He froze, lips to her skin. *Not true.* Yes, he'd wanted her from the first time he'd laid eyes on her, and yes, he'd wanted repayment for the career she'd wrecked. But some time in the past few weeks, he no longer could remember when, he'd crossed over an unseen line. Into unknown territory where wanting had no beginning, no end in sight. Cupping her softness, he felt her nipple nudge his palm. However cruel her words, her body still responded to him.

He drew his fingers inward, closed on her, cherishing her in a slow, beguiling dance. *Come to me, darlin', come on...*

She shuddered against him, sighed, then slowly rolled over to lie face up to the ceiling.

Halfway round to face him was halfway to forgiving. Tag smiled to himself. They were all right, then. She'd let him *make* it all right. He kissed the side of her mouth and his fingers on her grew bolder.

Nothing. He sat up, leaned over to kiss her breast.

"Go right ahead," she said bitterly. "You've taken everything else you wanted. Be my guest."

He straightened. Started to speak, then closed his mouth. He had no stomach for starting their argument all over again. If she hadn't bought his reasons the first time, why would she buy them now? He let her go and met the dark glitter of her shadowed eyes. "If that's how you feel, then no, thank you." He'd take all of her or he'd take nothing.

He lay down and turned his back on her, pulled the covers to his chin. And lay, his arms aching to hold her, his eyes dry and open, his own hopes taunting him from the blackest corners of the shabby room, till the sun rose at last to release him.

LAST NIGHT'S MISERY had blended straight into this morning's. After a breakfast choked down in silence, Tag laid his plans on the table. Susannah had to admit they were clever. Downright brilliant—the man had a head if he had no heart— but for her they entailed a truckload of pain before the payoff. And she'd never wanted a payoff, only that Stephen should pay.

She should have taken the honey and run last night.

Shoulds had never been her strong point.

So now she was stuck with playing it Tag's way, since he wouldn't back hers. First step was they needed money. Several thousand, he figured, to put on a plausible show. And the only way he could see to raise such a sum in the twelve days before Keeneland was to steal cars and sell them.

She'd pronounced that idea, dumb, dumb, *dumb* and too bad if that hurt his feelings. Hadn't bothered to tell him why, but the thought of Tag being arrested, then dragged off to prison gave her the cold horrors. He might be big and tough and immensely capable, but the stories you heard about prison... *No way, José.* She'd do anything to keep Tag from risking that, even beg and borrow, much as that turned her stomach.

So after breakfast Susannah made a phone call, then returned to Tag, who slouched wearily against the front of their car.

"Willy says that if Jake doesn't come into the store by three, he'll send his boy out to the ranch t'fetch him. Promised he'd have him waitin' there by the phone at six this evening."

Willy ran the store and gas station at the crossroads, some eight miles from the home ranch. Jake stopped in whenever he drove past to pick up a newspaper or the latest gossip. She hadn't dared call her dad's ex-partner at home, since Tag figured there'd be a tap on Jake and Zelda's line, that maybe their phone had been tapped since she first left Fleetfoot.

So to bypass Stephen's real or imagined bugs, she'd call Jake at the store. Ask him if he could raise a few thousand and wire it to her in Denver. He'd never deny her. And if Tag's plans worked out, she could repay him in a few weeks with interest. Still... She'd been raised to lend with a smile, but never to borrow. She'd rather have had three wisdom teeth yanked than ask Jake for money.

"What now?" She wanted to walk straight into Tag's arms and have him hold her. But she held herself erect, eyes aimed over his shoulder. They'd both made their choices. They were partners in crime now, no more than that. "Where to?"

"There's a racetrack near Denver, isn't there?"

There was, but she'd rather stroll barefoot on hot coals than go there. Tag didn't realize what he was asking. She tried to tell him while they drove toward the track at Arapahoe Park. "You don't get it, what I did, gelding Payback. It might amuse Stephen's friends and his enemies—the owners and breeders. A lot of people up in the private boxes wouldn't mind seein' Stephen take it in the teeth, no matter how much they suck up to him. But the pros down in the sheds, the

jocks and the grooms and the trainers—my dad's people... I
show my face at a track, I'll be lucky somebody doesn't dump
a bucket of manure over my head.''

"Not with me there, they won't. I just need you to spread
a few rumors, Susannah.''

Need, yeah. She needed *him*—his smile, his touch, his
arms, his respect. He needed *her* to make a killing. You'd
think after falling for one heartless man, she'd have known
better the next time. She crossed her arms on the window and
leaned out, closed her eyes, let the hot wind blow through
her hair, through her mind.

His knuckles rubbed up her spine. "I still don't see why
you did it.''

She shrugged his hand away. ''You didn't read the tabloids? 'Cause I'm the most spiteful little bitch in America,
why else?''

NO ONE RECOGNIZED HER at first as they strolled through the
sheds behind the track. It was the second-to-last day of a
racemeet. And late in the day, not many people hanging
around. And she'd tucked her hair up under her Stetson.

They stopped outside a stall where a white-haired groom
was icing down the feet of a rangy red colt. Stood watching,
Tag drawing out the man, asking what he was doing and why,
carrying the conversation since the cat had got her tongue.
As if by accident, he brushed her hat off, and her hair came
tumbling down.

The groom straightened and his smile faded. "You're...
Aren't you Ben Mack's girl? The one who...'' He spit even
as she nodded reluctantly. ''Your daddy rode the finest horse
I ever handled, Stormcrow, back in the eighties. What you
did, I reckon your ol' man's whirlin' in his grave.''

What could she say? Ridiculous to let a stranger make her
cry, but she could feel the tears gathering. She shrugged,
tipped up her chin and stalked on. Realized after a moment

that she walked alone and looked back to see that Tag was still leaning over the stall door. Talking.

He caught up to her near the end of the shed. "That worked out well."

"For you, maybe."

He put a hand on her shoulder and drew her toward the next barn. "I told him there was a lot more to the story than ever hit the papers. Then I asked him if he'd heard there was a stash of Payback sperm being offered for sale."

"I guess that pricked up his ears."

"You could say that. He asked who was selling and I said I didn't know for sure. But that I'd heard it on the very best of authority."

"Meanin' me," she said bitterly. She made the rumor look real. Gave the listener the impression that his information came straight from the horse's mouth. Who should know better than Colton's ex-wife? Tag was using her.

They planted his rumor twice more that day, once with a trainer, while they watched the last runners of the day parading in the paddock. Then once in a bar a block from the track, to a table of hard-eyed jockeys.

They quickly developed a method, efficient as it was painful. Susannah's recognition opened up the topic. Once she'd been chastised and fled, Tag would stay behind to defend her—and to drop his rumor, that somewhere out there, someone was selling Payback's sperm. And that the asking price was said to be in the millions.

"They never recognize *you*," she complained as they drove away.

"No man's ever going to notice me, with you around." He brushed a knuckle across her cheek, his smile fading as she grimaced and drew away.

"So what now?" She felt as if she'd taken a hard fall, then had the backrunners ride right over her. She supposed she owed him her help for dragging him into her quarrel in the first place, but Lord, he was taking it out of her hide, strip by strip.

"It's almost six. We find a phone for you, and while you're calling Jake, I'll see if I can sell Peterson's .38."

"Won't the hock shops all be closed?"

"I want another bar, babe, for this. The sleazier the better."

"If you try t'sell it to the wrong guy, if there's a cop undercover, or..."

He swung into a fast-food joint and gave her an amused smile. "Just because you blindsided me in Vermont doesn't mean I was born yesterday, Lambchops. Guys, I can handle." He reached past her to grip her door handle. "I'll be back in an hour or so."

"Don't go!" She had the sudden panicky vision of Tag being beaten up in some dive. Of her sitting here waiting for him, forever and ever. "Jake will send us the money."

Tag shoved open her door. "Hope to God he does, but even so, it won't get here tonight. If you don't want to sleep in the car, we'll need cash."

"The car's fine for a night. Honest."

"I can do better than that." He put her out gently but firmly—and drove away.

Two hours later she looked up from a cold cup of coffee to see him parking out front. She met him coming in the door. "Six thousand! Jake says it'll be at the American Express office tomorrow."

"Way to go, cowgirl!" For an instant it seemed he'd hug her. But neither of them closed that last crucial foot, and the moment passed. "And I got a hundred for the gun. Have you eaten yet?"

They celebrated with T-bones and red wine at a steak house. A meal Stephen would have sneered at, but to her it was a feast. Sighing with contentment, she sat back finally. "What next?"

"How far do you think those rumors we planted will travel?"

She shrugged. "Who knows? It's a small, tight world, horse racing. Some of those jocks will be ridin' in Maryland or Louisiana or California by this weekend. That groom'll tell all the other grooms. Every groom will tell his trainer. Most trainers train for five to ten owners, so they'll pass it on to them, then the owners..." She shrugged. "Word ought t'hit London by midweek, Paris by Friday." She took a sip of wine. "Stephen'll hear some time tomorrow, I'd reckon. Some track reporter'll pick up on it. Call him and ask." She shivered and set the glass down.

"The minute Jake's money comes through, we're outta here," Tag promised. "We'll sell the car to a dealer, then fly from now on. So where do we plant the rumor next? Where will the big money be this weekend?"

"That's easy. Sunday's the Hollywood Gold Cup. A grade-one stakes race for three-year-olds and up. Purse is over a million dollars. The winningest jocks on the best horses will be ridin' there."

"And the best horses belong to the richest owners." Tag smiled. "The Gold Cup it is, then. Murphy should come roaring into Denver late tomorrow or the next day to try to track us down. And we'll be in California."

"One jump ahead," she agreed. If they didn't stumble. "Now tell me again why we're doin' this?" She'd been too hurt and sleep-deprived this morning to follow clearly.

"Buzz, baby." She narrowed her eyes at the endearment, and his smile turned wry. "We want to create the biggest buzz possible, before we hit the Keeneland sale. Not just to raise anticipation, but to make it seem real. The more the honey's talked about beforehand, the more it'll seem to actually exist. When we finally approach our bidders, I don't want them thinking, 'Who the hell are you and what kind of scam is this—stolen stallion sperm? Get outta here!'"

"You want 'em thinking, 'Oh, here you are at last,'" Susannah agreed. "Those guys with the Payback honey."

"Exactly. And I want them to have already imagined what they'd do if they ever got a chance to corner the last of Payback's sperm. Would they grab for the brass ring? How much would they be willing to pay? How would they go about faking a legal mating to fool the Jockey Club?"

"Makes sense." She turned her wineglass on the table, watched the ruby lights glint and go. The man was smart, all right. Leading with his brain where she led with her heart. She'd seen his kindness from the start, but not the cold calculation beneath it.

"We need to start choosing our bidders," Tag said across the table. "I'd like about five. A small enough number that we can keep our auction secret till the bidding's done. A large enough number that we boost the sense of competition. Goes without saying that each one has to have the kind of money that he could risk twenty million and lose it with a smile. And no stuffed shirts. We don't want to invite the kind of people who'd blow the whistle on us to the Jockey Club—or to Colton."

"That lets out the British royals," Susannah said.

"Too true. But can you think of four or five? Best of all, guys who detest each other? The more they'd love to show each other up, the better. A healthy sense of competition is what we want here."

"Competition?" Susannah snorted. "Half the owners I've met through Stephen are saying 'my horse is faster than yours,' when what they're really *playing* is 'guess who's got the biggest Richard?' I can fill you a room with enough deep-pocket testosterone to blow out the walls, easy."

Tag lifted his glass to her in a solemn toast. "Do that and I'll make you a rich woman, Susannah."

"Been there, done that." It wasn't all it was cracked up to be, not by a long shot. She'd settle for happy, but she was beginning to realize that that was a whole lot harder.

CHAPTER TWENTY-THREE

THEY CAUGHT THE RED-EYE Sunday night, flying back from L.A. to Chicago. Tag was jubilant in spite of the shiner he'd acquired. Their rumor had beaten them out to the West Coast. They'd heard whispers of it everywhere they went at Hollywood Park.

Susannah was glum. Everyone who'd recognized her had given her what-for. She might feel a twinge of satisfaction that Tag had shared some of the heat this time—his shiner was the souvenir of a groom who'd identified him as the vet who did the dastardly deed. But satisfaction was canceled out by remorse. If she'd never asked him to help her in the first place, he wouldn't be sitting there turning four shades of eggplant.

On top of guilt she was suffering acute withdrawal pains. No Tag in her bed for three nights running. Not that she couldn't end that situation with one cry of "Is there a doctor in the house?"

But so far she'd managed to bite her tongue. Tag might have stolen her heart and the honey, but she still had her pride. And a few shreds of common sense. Because he'd said it himself. Once they'd pulled off this auction, he was history. A beach bum in Thailand. *Might as well get a head start on getting over him now.*

She glanced at him and scowled. He looked halfway to bum already. "You ever mean t'shave again?" The way those bristles would feel against her skin...

"Not till after Keeneland. I'll let it grow in for another day or so, then shape it."

She nodded. Once they reached the bluegrass, the game changed. No more swanning around, begging to be recognized. In Stephen's backyard, their profiles better be lower than low. "Guess I'll get a haircut in Chicago tomorrow," she said. "Something really short…"

"Don't." He looked almost comically stricken. "I like it the way it is."

Tough. "Above the ears and sort of conservative punk," she added solemnly. "Maybe dyed black with a streak of burgundy?"

His dismay faded as their eyes held, memories sizzling between them. Hurt and challenge and wary question. He reached for a curl that kissed her cheek. "Would that fit in at the parties?"

So now they were back to business—all he cared about, in the end. She tossed her head to pull free. "Should." The last few days before the Keeneland Selected Sale, it was nothing but party, party, party as hopeful breeders courted million-dollar buyers. "Not for the local ladies. But for the call girls anything goes, as long as it's sexy." With such a congregation of heavy hitters in need of nightly entertainment, working girls flew in from New York, Miami, L.A., London. That would be her cover. She'd be welcome anywhere, taken seriously nowhere. "I'll fit in better than you with that shiner," she added spitefully.

"Don't be so sure. I'm going to look suave with a black eyepatch." He glanced up as the beverage cart approached. "A drink?

"I picked up a rumor back at Hollywood, as well as dropped ours," Tag continued after the cart had passed. He was absorbed in trying to rip open one of those tiny packets of peanuts. "Could Colton be hurting, money-wise? Word's out that he might be going bankrupt. That *he's* the one who's selling Payback's honey, to try to pay off some loan he owes.''

"No idea. He never told me boo about his finances." She bit her lip thoughtfully. "I've never known the man t'skimp. His motto was always 'see it, want it, buy three.' Though now you mention it, when I left Fleetfoot he was tryin' to raise a whoppin' sum of money. I never knew for what."

"Does he own Fleetfoot free and clear?" Tag offered her the nuts.

She shook her head. "Doesn't own it at all. The farm's in a trust to be passed down to little blond, blue-eyed Coltons forever and ever. He gets paid a yearly allowance by the trust. He lives at the farm for free, with property taxes and maintenance paid from estate revenues. All Stephen owns himself is the jet and the horses and his Miami mansion."

"Must be tough." Tag munched peanuts and frowned into space. "Two hundred thoroughbreds, you told me once. Could he mortgage those?"

"Sure. Bluegrass banks'll take a horse for collateral." She stood, withdrew her Stetson from the overhead, where it nestled next to the honey, then sat again. "But my guess is that's all wild speculation. Once we started the rumor rollin' 'bout Payback sperm for sale, people needed a reason *why* it's for sale—and made one up to suit." She let her seat back all the way, then settled her hat over her eyes. "G'night."

For just a moment, she had the sensation that something very large and very warm loomed over her. She smelled peanuts and wrinkled her nose. Pulled her brim lower and turned to face the aisle.

"'Night," he said softly at her back.

THEY SLEPT THAT NIGHT in an airport hotel. In a room with two beds. Then spent half the next day refining Susannah's list of prospective bidders, then seeking their addresses with the help of a database at a Chicago public library. Without much success. Multimillionaires weren't usually listed in the phone book. And since only one of Susannah's candidates was an American, their task was that much harder.

Sheik Misha'al al Sabik was the easiest to trace, since the racing magazines had followed the man for years. But as well as his original estate in Saudi Arabia, he had another in France, another in Ireland, a fourth in Wyoming, a fifth in Argentina. "Not that we can count on him being at home anywhere," Susannah said. "Another man with his own jet. He could have taken a notion to eat snails in Paris or go hawking in Afghanistan this week."

"You've met him?"

"Oh, yeah. I sat next to him at lunch in the clubhouse before the Derby last year. A very nice guy. We laughed a lot." Tag had stopped looking so pleased. Good. She got heartburn herself every time she thought about dusky Thai maidens. "But his head bodyguard was the *real* charmer," she added, turning the knife.

One turn too many. Tag frowned and coolly went back to business. "Bodyguards—do they all have them?"

"Generally. Villanova never goes anywhere without half-a-dozen heavies. I don't know if they're status symbols where he comes from—machismo—or just your basic necessity." Villanova was the Colombian who'd bought the world-record Payback colt at the last summer sales. Drug-cartel money, it was whispered, and what better way to launder it than at the track?

"Sheik Misha'al usually travels with two or three. Our English tabloid king always runs in a pack, but you can't tell his friends from his hired thugs. Kawabata has what he calls a personal assistant, little guy maybe an inch or two taller than me, carries a laptop. Probably can break bricks with his pinkie. Our movie star, he has a few to keep the fans at bay."

"Wonderful." Tag stared blankly at the computer screen, listing only an agent's address in L.A. for their actor. "We can't let them keep *us* at bay. Looks like we'll have to do our inviting in person, Susannah.''

"I'd figured that already." There were just too many addresses and too little time. "So we hand-deliver at the Keeneland preview parties."

"Under Colton's nose."

THEY WENT THEIR separate ways for the rest of that day, then rendezvoused at O'Hare for a commuter flight. Waiting for her by the ticket counter, Tag felt a tap on his shoulder and turned. Blinked.

"Well?" She cocked her head and a glossy mane, one shade lighter than black, tumbled over her shoulder.

Knockout! Not that she hadn't been before, but every man was a sucker for novelty. Susannah Mack as a sleek brunette—my, oh, my! Her eyes had gone from blue to storm-cloud violet. Mascara turned her lashes to inky thickets and somehow she'd darkened her eyebrows. Her lipstick was the color of a ripe plum, and her lips looked swollen from kissing. He wanted to pick her up and carry her off to a private lounge—or a phone booth, all else failing. "So, you didn't cut it." He turned her around, just an excuse to touch her.

"Decided to go for the expensive look. Classic call girl. Sheik Misha'al wouldn't look twice at a tart."

Hadn't met the guy and already he was hating him. "So what's in the boxes?" He nodded at her shopping bags.

She took his arm with a smugly mysterious smile. "Wait and see."

THEY FLEW FROM O'HARE to Cincinnati, spent the night, then bought a used car in the morning. Painful—their working cash was more than halved already—but necessary. Couldn't rent a car these days without a credit card. Thanks to Colton, neither of them had one, nor would have dared use it if they had. And wheels might yet be needed for a quick getaway.

From Cincinnati they drove to Lexington. They scouted the hotels by car, Susannah pointing out the swankiest ones that catered to the horse crowd, ate supper in the darkest booth of a backstreet diner, then drove twenty miles out into the country to Cam's place. The real Cam, this time, Susannah's and Brady's friend from Fleetfoot.

"You sure he'll take us in?" he asked as they parked out front of a white frame farmhouse at the end of a rutted lane. They hadn't called in advance, in case Colton really was bugging her friends.

Already out of the car, she nodded, then stopped at the sound of barking. Tag stepped out hurriedly as big, shadowy shapes came bounding out of the dark, bellowing their arrival. "Easy, guys."

She left him out in the driveway with the pack—two hounds, a Lab cross and a Rotweiler—while she went on toward a light that had switched on around back, escorted by a growling little Jack Russell.

She called him a few minutes later. Tag walked around back, the dogs bumping his knees, whacking him with their tails, grabbing for his sleeves to lead him on. If Cam took them in, at least they could sleep soundly at night. The security staff was first rate.

An old man stood beside Susannah on the back stoop. Nearly as wide as she was tall, he was dressed in striped pajamas and a dressing gown. Cam took Tag's measure over an armful of blankets and pillows, then gave him a surly nod upon introduction. "Past my bed time," he said curtly. "Breakfast is at six or you'll feed yourselves." He plopped the bedding onto Tag's outstretched arms and banged back into the house.

"Is he always this friendly?" Tag muttered while she led him off through the dark, lighting their way with a flashlight Cam had given her.

"Heart of gold," Susannah assured him. "It's just that he's a morning person. All those years trainin', risin' at dawn."

"Oh." Her flashlight played over a looming structure. "That's the guesthouse?"

"Mmm, more or less." She shoved at a heavy sliding door, and the warm, earthy smells of a stable drifted out. A goat bleated a sleepy greeting. Something big stomped a hoof and snorted.

"The places I've seen with you, Susannah Mack," he marveled, sitting on a bale of hay in the loft while she whipped a blanket into the air, then laid it out neatly over a mound of fragrant straw. Not that he was complaining. Either through stinginess or because he'd assumed they were a couple, Cam had given them only two blankets. And she was using them to make one bed. Better Susannah in his arms in a stable than the cushiest of king-size mattresses to himself at the Plaza.

Still, Susannah felt compelled to defend Cam. "He's got his reasons to be careful." Colton's men had searched Cam's farm from attic to pigpens the morning after Tag and she had escaped with the sperm cannister, she told him while she worked. Then returned two days later to do it again.

"Why the hell didn't he call the police?" Tag might prefer to settle his own fights himself, but an old man beset by bullies...

Susannah snorted. "In Fayette County, the horse is king. After mining, nothing brings in more money to Kentucky. The sheriff would have taken one look at the Fleetfoot name on the guards' truck and backed right back down Cam's driveway." And if Cam had tried to press a complaint, Colton would have countered with some trumped-up charge of embezzlement. "Cam was a trainer at Fleetfoot, you know. Started with Stephen's dad back in the sixties and worked there ever since."

Except that he'd been laid off back in March. "I didn't know that," she murmured, coming to take the pillows from

Tag's arms. "Looks like he's sort of scroungin' t'get by now."

"Was that some sort of revenge on you, his firing?"

She shrugged. "Hard t'say. Maybe not. He said Stephen laid off three of his trainers the same day."

"Out of how many?"

"Five." She took the flashlight and left—there was a bathroom just inside the farmhouse back door that they were welcome to use, she'd told him. Tag sat in the fragrant dark and thought. Three out of five trainers laid off? *Sounds like a cost-cutting measure to me.* Maybe the rumors about hard times at Fleetfoot Farm were true.

"WHAT THE *HELL* WAS THAT?" Heart thundering, Tag jerked bolt upright. Bloody murder—and close at hand. He sat in a hayloft, golden light dappling the straw and his blankets. And Susannah had turned into a brunette, if he wasn't still dreaming.

"Lancelot." She yawned, sat up and stretched delectably.

His heart shifted smoothly from shock to lust—she'd stayed on her own side of the blanket all night long, he remembered now—then staggered as the racket started again. A donkey, he realized, braying up the dawn.

"Cam's burro," Susannah added as she stood, her T-shirt brushing the tops of her thighs. "He's got a weakness for hoofed critters."

Tag met the collection after a pancake breakfast served up by Cam in his kitchen. The old man was as amiable at six in the morning as he'd been grumpy at ten at night. Tag accompanied him on his rounds while Susannah borrowed his shower. They fed the four goats, slopped the pig and piglets, inspected the llamas, admired three kinds of African antelope and a tame white-tailed deer. Tag stopped in dismay when they reached Lancelot. "What happened to him?'' One of the burro's lop ears hung down at a dreadful angle and was smeared with dried blood.

Cam shrugged burly shoulders. ''Damned if I know. Randy old devil. If it moves he'll hump it, is why the name. Probably went after my lady llama again. She doesn't care for him.''

''We can't leave him like that,'' Tag protested as Cam made to pass on.

''Got to. Can't afford vet bills these days. Susannah tell you her jerk-off husband fired me?''

''Ex-husband.'' Tag rubbed the burro's soft muzzle, then yanked his hand back as the jack bared its yellow teeth. ''Did she tell you I was a vet?''

That announcement was good for a full day's work. All five dogs had ear mites, it turned out. Cam had the medicine, but they wiggled and complained so, he hadn't yet applied it. And the sheep needed dipping. And he supposed Tag could tackle the burro, if he insisted. Cam had no painkiller on the premises, but give Lancelot three or four rum-and-cokes—stiff ones—and he'd mellow right out.

Cam and Susannah departed for Cam's lady friend, who lived with her mother a few miles away. They'd agreed that the cannister of sperm would be safest in the freezer in her basement. Tag stayed behind to practice skills he'd wondered if he'd ever need again.

When they returned late that afternoon, he was trimming the last knot. Susannah admired his handiwork, twenty-two stitches, while Lancelot gave her the evil eye over the rim of the feedbag that served as his improvised muzzle. Four rum-and-cokes had slowed him down and no doubt dulled the pain, but they hadn't improved his jackass temperament. Tag wore a set of toothmarks on one hip to attest to that.

''Nice,'' Susannah murmured, stroking the jack's other

long ear. She glanced up at him shyly. "You really miss this, don't you?"

It showed that much? Tag nodded, then busied himself collecting his sewing kit.

"I'm sorry." She touched his shoulder, then withdrew her hand as he turned. "If it wasn't for me…"

"I wouldn't have had all kinds of adventures." Been reviled, bankrupt, shot at, beaten up. Fallen crazy in love. "Life's one big trade-off, babe."

Accompanying him up to the farmhouse, she told him about her day's work. She'd left Cam with his sweetheart and driven in to Lexington. Had reserved them a suite at the best hotel for Tuesday, the last night of the sale, then found a do-it-yourself print shop, where she'd printed out their bidders' invitations. While Tag unbuttoned his sweaty shirt and laid it over a chair back, she showed him a box of cream-colored cards.

"Perfect," he applauded. She'd set out the information they'd agreed upon in an elegantly simple script. At first glance the note looked like an invitation to an exclusive wedding.

"And I phoned Alix's office. Her assistant said you can find her tonight, five t'six, at her house, loading up supplies for a dinner party."

Alix Waltham was *the* fashionable caterer of the bluegrass. She'd catered events at Fleetfoot, and all the surrounding farms, for years. It had been Susannah's idea that Tag apply for a job as banquet waiter. "Alix is always on the lookout for studly types t'carry the canapés around."

"You really think she'll hire me?" he worried now. "Seems awfully short notice for breaking in new staff."

"Dude…" Eyes on his torso, Susannah drifted closer. She stopped, just out of reach. "Alix is as man-crazy as they come. You wear your tuxedo and that eyepatch t'night and—" She scowled.

"And?" he challenged softly. Was she jealous?

She shrugged and swung away. "This is the *dumbest* damned scheme! I hate it! We should've stuck with my plan."

Tag opened the bathroom door. "Too late now, babe. We're in the backstretch and running for home."

She sniffed. "You know how many things can go wrong in the last furlong?"

CHAPTER TWENTY-FOUR

IT WAS LONG AFTER midnight when Tag groped his way up the stairs to the loft, scuffed wearily through the hay, then eased under the covers.

"Where have you *been?*" Susannah snarled and rolled to the far side of the blanket. "We waited supper forever b'fore we gave up and ate. I've been wonderin' if maybe Murphy was back in town, had nailed you..."

"Alix was short of help tonight. So I stayed and worked the party." A sit-down dinner for forty at a breeder's farm on the far side of Lexington.

"Huh!" She fussed with the covers, then added, "Late party."

"We had to clean up and decamp afterward." He'd never think of catering as a pretend-job for bored housewives again. "And I spilled some soup on my shirt at the last minute. Alix was nice enough to take me back to her place and throw it in the wash before the stain set."

Susannah snorted. "You mean *she* spilled it on you?"

"No, I—" Well, Alix *had* been handing the container to him, though he'd have sworn it was his butterfingers that— "Don't be silly. The only woman I know who's that devious is you."

"Huh!" She rolled over again, jerking most of the blanket off him. "If that's what you think, then you'd better stick t'cats and parakeets, doctor, cause you sure don't know women."

Doctor. He stirred and hardened, a conditioned reflex by

now whenever she said the word. "Susannah...?" Naturally he found Alix attractive—any man would. And he'd been flattered when she'd suggested he stay the night. But what he wanted—who he wanted—was here. He braced himself up on his elbows, staring down at her swaddled shape. *Just one goodnight kiss?*

"Don't even think about it!"

Woman believed in payback, all right. He reclaimed his half of the blanket with one yank, turned his back on her—then blinked as it hit him. Jealous, by God! He fell asleep smiling.

SUNDAY. The first session of the sale was Monday night and they'd yet to deliver a single invitation. But tonight was their best shot. Alix was catering *the* event of the summer, a party for four hundred plus at the estate of the top consignor of the Keeneland sale. Most of their prospects should be there, Susannah assured him, as she delivered him to the caterer's office. Alix's team was driving out to the farm to do the prep on-site.

"And what'll you do today?" Tag asked, leaning back in his window to say goodbye. She'd hadn't said four words to him at breakfast. But she'd dressed with care in English riding boots, skin-tight creamy jodhpurs and a dark-green silk shirt with its top two buttons undone. Any fox hunter would take one look, grab his quirt and cry "Tally-ho!"

"Mooch around the Keeneland racecourse. Today's the last full day to preview the yearlings. With any luck, I'll run into some of our prospects out in the barns. Sheik Misha'al is bound t'be making the rounds."

"Won't he be at the party tonight?"

"Not likely. He's a strict Muslim, doesn't approve of drinking."

All kinds of manly virtues, blast the man. "Are you sure

Keeneland's such a good idea? What are the chances you'll bump into Colton?''

She gave him a breezy smile. ''I'll keep my eyes peeled.''

''But—'' He straightened hastily as the car rolled away, Susannah waving a mocking farewell over her shoulder. *Be careful, hotshot,* he begged her silently, and trudged off to a day of turning radishes into roses.

A MODEST LITTLE get-together for four hundred of the world's richest. If you crossed the barbecue scene from *Gone with the Wind* with the last night of the Republican Presidential Convention, then threw in a smidgin of Mardi Gras and a dash of United Nations cocktail party, it would look like this, Tag decided as he maneuvered his silver tray around the mansion's ballroom, offering Dom Perignon to all and sundry. The party had been in full cry for two hours but showed no signs of letting up. New arrivals kept sailing in the front door, dropping their wraps on the overworked butler and his crew of maids, then plunging into the thick of it with cries of ''Darling! Babs! Well, Rudy, I never…!''

Music and voices meshed in a humming din—deep-South drawls, Japanese murmurs, Oxford arrogance, Irish banter, oil-patch twangs, Wall Street jargon, Hollywood buzzwords. But whatever flavor of English the guests spoke, the topic was horses. And Colton. And the delicious, *scandalous* rumor that someone, somewhere, was selling a cache of Payback sperm! That reps of the Jockey Club had called Stephen Colton on the carpet today to demand an explanation and that he'd denied everything.

Tag's ears were flapping frantically. He could edge up on any conversation—no one looked at him twice. His serving tray stamped him as just a piece of moving furniture—but he never caught more than a phrase before the next fat cat looked up, spied the flutes of bubbly and snapped his fingers for service. And each and every one of them wanted serving yesterday. He'd been right all those years ago, stealing cars from these overgrown brats. Tag's teeth were clenched from smiling politely, his ribs ached from the weight of the loaded tray, and he wondered where the hell Susannah was. If Murphy had nabbed her this afternoon... Or maybe the sheik had whisked her off on his magic carpet?

He jumped as someone bumped his bottom. Whirled to find Katy, one of the canapé team, grinning at him over her shoulder. "I just had to pass it on," she confessed. "The creeps know you can't fight back with your hands full. I'm pinched black and blue." She nodded across the room toward the grand staircase that swept up to a second-floor gallery, where a Dixieland band added to the hubbub. "The boys up there say they're getting awfully dry, if you'd be so kind."

Coming back down the stairs, Tag spotted her at last. Susannah, swaying in through the French doors that opened onto the back terrace, overlooking the striped tents out on the lawn. The backyard was barbecue pits, carriage rides, barn tours and a rock band for the younger set.

And oh, Susannah! Some fairy's wand had turned his cowgirl into a sophisticate. She'd kept it simple—a dress of midnight blue silk that could have passed for French lingerie, not that any man with a breath left in his body would complain. High heels to match and smoky sheer stockings with a dark seamline hugging each gorgous calf. She wore her hair up in a simple twist that showed off her swan neck and the sparkly blue earrings dangling from her ears. Even as he watched, three men homed in on her from three different directions. She batted her inky lashes just as a woman moved to the foot of Tag's vantage point and waved up at him.

"Yoo-hoo, handsome? Could you bring some of that bubbly down here?"

Once he hit ground level, he lost track of her. Tag went back to the kitchen to refill his tray, then returned, pausing on the fringe of the crush. Find a cluster of men, four-deep, and at its center he'd be sure to—

"Taggart, honey!"

He turned to see Alix Waltham bearing down on him with her model's toothy smile and her hungry eyes. Woman who cooked like a dream yet she never looked as if she got enough to eat. Go figure. He raised the tray an inch to keep her off, but she reached right over it. "That *tie!*" She pulled it loose and began to retie it, murmuring as she worked, "You are the beau of the ball, honey! I can't tell you how many ol' biddies have asked me if we offer brunch in bed. And every one of 'em wants that 'pirate in a tuxedo' to serve it."

He smiled weakly, mumbled thanks as she finished the knot, then patted his beard. "Gotta go, Alix." She was starting to grate on his nerves. He plunged into the crowd, then slowed down, scanning for Susannah—and spotted her standing under a potted palm near the foot of the staircase. Glaring at him. What was her beef?

"Hittin' it off with the boss lady, I see," she purred when he stopped beside her.

"We aim to please. And where the hell have you been?"

"Oh, here and there. Mixin' and minglin'." She selected a crystal flute from his tray.

"How nice for you, Lambchops. And me up to my eye-patch in crudités and canapés and cannibal bluehairs."

"Poor pitiful you! Whose idea was this, anyway?"

"True." And why were they fighting? It wasn't Susannah he was mad at. It was every man in the room who was stripping her with his eyes. "How'd your day go?"

"I bagged the actor! He was looking over a *fine* Mr. Prospector colt with his bloodstock agent. I just sidled up and laid it on him."

"Excellent. Have you spotted any of our targets here?" He had two of their invitations tucked in an inner pocket, but since he didn't know the faces that went with the names…

''See that crowd over there, under the gallery?'' She nodded to a knot of suits and boisterous laughter back in the
shadows. ''That's Reardon, the tabloid-king. And I hear he's
branchin' out into American casinos. He was always tryin' to
get Stephen t'invest in some deal or other.''

''Will he recognize you?''

She rubbed the rim of her glass along her lips and
shrugged. ''Doubt it. The man never looks higher than a
woman's headlights.'' She tipped her glass and emptied it,
smacked the glass down on his tray. ''So let's go see.''

''Hey, wait!'' he called as she sashayed off, but the band
broke into a rousing rendition of Dixie and she failed to hear
him. He started after her. *How d'you plan to invite him without an invitation?* he wanted to ask. She carried no purse,
perhaps had forgotten it somewhere in her mingling?

''Hey, you! Waiter! Over here!'' A frat-boy type lifted a
hand and snapped his fingers, then turned back to his admiring circle.

Living well is the best revenge, Tag reminded himself as
he swerved obediently. Or maybe Susannah *had* something.
Dumping his whole tray on this pompous jerk's head seemed
infinitely more tempting.

Once he'd served Frat-boy's circle, he followed in Susannah's wake, ignoring all but the most plaintive cries. *Where
are you, babe?* He could see her target, a circle of tweeds
and pinstripes, fanning out now to face the wall. *What the
hell?* He edged sideways and saw her through a gap in the
masculine blockade.

Susannah said something to the man in the loudest tweed,
fluttered her lashes—and extended one long, silk-clad leg out
before her like a dancer. *Susannah?* As Tag stared, she inched
her dress up her smoky thigh. Her audience stood mesmer-
ized. The hem crept past the darker top of her stocking—to
reveal a shocking-white square of vellum. One of their invitations, tucked beneath her garter strap.

She slipped it free. Slid the hem back down her thigh with a caressing, suggestive slowness. With a soft word and a killer smile, she placed the envelope in the publisher's hands. He stood like a jacklighted deer, clutching the card.

She patted his arm and walked past him straight at Tag. Without slowing, she lifted a glass off his tray—"Whew!"—and sailed on.

He caught up with her ten minutes later out on the terrace as she edged away from a clone of Colonel Sanders. She put her empty glass on his tray and chose another, drawling, "Presentation is all."

"You're starting to scare me."

"Only startin'?" They parted, she to mix, he to serve. He collected more snippets of gossip. In the library a group of cigar-smoking, bourbon-sipping old hardboots waved off his champagne with disdain, but not before he heard that Colton had sold his Learjet and now leased something smaller.

Another professed himself not surprised. Colton wasn't the horseman his daddy had been—the boy played at breeding, rather than studied it, lived it. Colton hadn't paired the bloodlines that resulted in Payback, whatever he claimed. That had been his old man's doing, the last year of his life. And since that superstud's well had run dry...

A third man chimed in, claiming he'd heard Colton had mortgaged everything on four feet at Fleetfoot to invest in some Indian casino.

Casinos! Every man bristled and the conversation swerved to the cursed casinos, cutting into the take at every track in the country, purses going down, idiot bettors opting for slot machines rather than horses.

At that point, Tag bumped a chair and its occupant looked up at him pointedly. "You need something, son?"

"No, sir." He left the room with alacrity and jubilation. It wasn't just another rumor, launched by his own. For whatever reason, Colton seemed to be on the skids. Now if there was just some way to grease them. Without his millions, Colton didn't worry Tag at all.

He stepped out onto the crowded terrace, looking for Susannah, but no luck. He turned toward the tents—and saw her almost running up the lawn. "Stephen!" she hissed, catching his arm and drawing him back into the ballroom. "He's back there! Out in the main tent with a blond model on each arm. Identical twins." She grimaced.

"You okay?" He wanted to take her in his arms. No way while he balanced twenty glasses filled to the winking brim. "Did he see you?"

"I...I'm not sure. I was concentratin' on our Mr. Kawabata—I'd just slipped him his invitation. Then I turned around and there Stephen was—bang—right across the tent."

Tag glanced over her shoulder. No sign of pursuit that he could see. "What about Murphy?"

"Didn't spot him." She bit her lip. "Think I'll go powder my nose."

"You okay, babe?" he asked again.

"Yeah...just rattled me a little. It was so *weird,* seein' him after so long. I don't know if he's changed or I've changed, but he sure didn't look the same."

"Any regrets, babe?"

She snorted. "Only regret is you losin' my .45! All I could think was what he'd done to Brady, and yet he wasn't fit to black Brady's old boots. What was God *thinkin'* to permit that?"

"Here." Tag handed her the tray. She took it automatically and frowned up at him, her eyes bright with tears. "I don't know what He was thinking, but *I* think..." Tag framed her upturned face with his hands. Drew a breath to tell her for the first time that he loved her—and someone rapped him on the shoulder.

"If you *don't* mind, we'll take some champagne over here?"

"Right away." He shared a wry smile with Susannah as he took back his tray. "I think He broke the mold after he made you, Lambchops."

"Thank you," she whispered, and turned away—froze—and swung back. "Villanova's just comin' in the door!"

Mr. Drug Cartel. "The one with the redhead?" The extraordinary redhead. Surrounded by half a dozen ugly-looking customers.

"Yeah." She licked her lips. "Could you do him, Tag? He sort of...scares me."

"Consider it done," he said, then growled under his breath as someone rapped on his shoulder again. "*Co*ming."

That bunch of bubbly-suckers cleared his tray. He detoured to the kitchen to find that Alix was now pushing burgundy, since they'd killed the 200 bottles of Dom Perignon. Bearing a tray of that, he set off in chase of Villanova. Found his group out on the terrace, eying the tents.

He stopped to set his load on the limestone balustrade, pulled an invitation from his inner pocket, held it flat against the underside of the tray and moved on. Twelve feet out from Villanova he hit a wall of muscle—two bodyguards. Big men with eyes like the dots on dice and sneers beneath their mustaches. Bulges in their coats they didn't even try to hide. "Sir?" He extended the tray invitingly.

The younger man took two glasses and held them to the older man's nose. He sniffed, considered, then nodded, and junior took them back to his master and lady. "None for you?" Receiving no response from Snake Eyes, Tag started around him.

"No." A soft Spanish "no," the o shortened to half a syllable.

"Very good." Tag rotated his envelope out from under the tray. "Then if you'd give this to your boss?"

The guard stared from the card to Tag's face, then back again. Took it between the tips of two fingers. "Alberto?" A third man appeared at his elbow. He passed the card backward. *"Para el patrón."*

"Thanks." Tag eased a step backward, then stopped as Snake Eyes' grip on his tray tightened. He smiled inquiringly.

Snake Eyes did know how to smile, after all. It wasn't pretty. Behind him, Villanova received the note, glanced at Tag, then ripped it open. Read it—and laughed aloud. Said something in machine-gun Spanish to the third bodyguard, who then returned.

"He say, where you get this?"

"A man paid me to deliver it to your boss." It was the story he and Susannah had devised if anyone asked. They were just lowly, know-nothing gofers for the mysterious sperm sellers. "I don't know who he was, never saw him before," he added, anticipating the next questions. "He left the party about an hour ago."

This was relayed to Villanova, who stood, staring at him, tapping the card against his lips. If he ever needed to buy Tag a coffin, he'd know his size to the inch. Thank God Susannah had left this one to him! Tag counted to twenty and felt a bead of sweat trickle down his ribs. Villanova dipped his handsome head in an ironic salute, said, *"Gracias,"* and tucked the card in an inner pocket of his beautiful suit.

The bodyguard turned the tray, turning Tag away with it. He left, half expecting a boot in the rear as he went. *That may have been a mistake, Susannah, inviting a king cobra to our party.* Crossing Colton looked like child's play in comparison.

And speaking of which... Back inside, Tag scanned the room for Susannah's ex. No sign of him or his twin blondes, which was just as well. They'd never met face-to-face, and now he wore a beard and an eyepatch, but if Colton really had a tape from his visit to Fleetfoot and played it occasionally... The hair at his nape stirred as he pictured it, Colton sitting there gloating, playing his tape collection. *Does he make popcorn?*

"Did you connect?" Susannah demanded, materializing at his elbow.

"Yeah, and I'm sort of wishing I hadn't. Villanova's bad news, babe."

"Comes off him in waves," she agreed, and picked up a glass of burgundy. "But if it's money you want..." She gasped, then stood, plum-colored lips ajar, eyes wide and widening.

"What is it?" A group was coming in the front door. No one he knew.

"I don't *believe* it! Son of a *bitch!*"

"Who? What?"

"Fidel Ortega!" She scooped a second glass off his tray.

"Who's he, babe? Susannah?"

She didn't spare him a glance. "Man who started it all. Must be here drummin' up business." She started across the room.

An old lover to have a pull on her like that? In the group that had just entered, there was a slight, dark man wearing an immaculate white summer suit. That one? He was handsome enough in a dandyish way.

Holding her glasses aloft like a dancer, Susannah glided on. He'd seen her move like that. When? Where? The image slotted in, superimposed over her midnight blue form like a moving double image. *Susannah stalking through the grass like a tigress, tire iron swinging at her side, toward him and the guard who held him.* "Crap!" He started after her—and a woman stepped into his path.

"Oh, *lovely,* what have we here? Is it merlot?"

"Burgundy." He ground his teeth as she chose a glass, rejected it and found a fuller one. He ducked around her and hit a wall of backs, a dozen laughing people encircling one gesturing raconteur. He worked around them, peering desperately over shoulders for Susannah—and saw her.

Halfway up the staircase to the gallery, she looked like a virgin priestess in some ancient rite, offerings of wine held on high as she mounted the temple steps. He stopped, drew a breath. *So I was wrong.* There was nothing up there to hunt, unless she meant to do in the band. Or the courting couple that stood along the carved balustrade.

Susannah reached the top, turned and glided on. Midway around the gallery she stopped, set a glass on the railing each side of her, looked down.

Inviting someone to join her? Ortega? And she didn't seem to give a damn that Tag was watching their reunion. She put a hand to her ear and when it came away, something sparkled in her fingers. She leaned out, poised and watching—then tossed. Blue sparks flew through the air.

Tag growled under his breath. Across the room, the man in the white summer suit stooped to pick up the earring, stood and turned, scanning upward. He stiffened—and above him, as their eyes connected, Susannah smiled.

She'd never smiled for Tag like that. She licked her luscious lips, beckoned with one finger. The man moved like a sleepwalker, closer, Romeo to Juliet's balcony. *Damn you, Susannah. If this is the real you, then who did I fall in love with?*

Ortega paused, gazing upward. Her lips moved, but apparently he couldn't hear her. He moved closer yet, put a hand to his chest in a gesture of "Who, me?"

Susannah nodded, reached up to her other ear, pulled off its earring, and dropped it straight down. Ortega grinned, stepped forward and stooped for it—as Susannah lifted one of her glasses and tipped.

Red wine cascaded down. Spattered on white linen. The noise in the ballroom dropped by half.

Ortega let out a yell and straightened, stared up—and Susannah emptied her second glass full in his face.

In the sudden, stupefied silence, the sound of wine splashing on flesh was deafening. *Obscene.*

A woman shrieked. A man laughed aloud. Ortega stood as if pole-axed, waiting to fall, striped with wine red as blood. Susannah threw her glass and it shattered at his feet. As she snatched up the other, he yelped and ducked under the gallery.

She stood for a moment more, her gaze sweeping the goggling crowd below. Blue norther eyes in a wintry blast. Cold enough to freeze the champagne in every glass, to freeze horse troughs from Churchill Downs to Miami. She stepped backward and faded into the shadows.

CHAPTER TWENTY-FIVE

IT WAS AFTER TWO in the morning when Tag groped his way up the barn stairs. *Susannah, you crazy bitch, are you there?*

He'd found the car waiting for him at Alix's office, keys on its seat, with no note of explanation. Either she'd caught a taxi out to Cam's farm or she was gone again. *And this time good riddance!* He needed a revenge-crazy lunatic in his life like he needed a hole in his head.

A light switched on above, beamed across the rafters, and for the first time in hours he drew a full breath. "Susannah." Devil in a blue dress. Still clothed but for her heels, she sat cross-legged in the center of their blanket, holding the flashlight. Eyes wide as a barn owl. Chin defiant.

He stopped when he loomed over her. "Want to say anything before I strangle you?"

The tip of her tongue skated across her lips. "Sorry?"

"Sorry. Oh, good! Great! That covers it, huh?" He'd helped the apopleptic butler and his outraged staff comb the entire upstairs mansion for her, all the while praying she'd escaped down the back stairs. Knowing that if they found her he'd have to punch out half a dozen men to extract her. After that he'd taken a tongue-lashing from a nearly hysterical Alix, who deemed the wrecking of her party a professional catastrophe. How *dare* he go AWOL when she needed him for cleanup? For support?

But a thousand times worse than all that, he'd lived for four hours wondering if he'd ever see Susannah again—and if he could keep his hands off her lovely neck if he did.

"Yeah, sorry makes it all fine again. You realize you may have wrecked everything? If anyone recognized you... If word gets back to Colton..."

"I know, I know." She braced her arms behind her and leaned back to look up. "I'm sorry, but I just—"

"Had to have payback? What was it this time, Lambchops? He cut you off in traffic once? Or was that the curtain scene in some old lovers' quarrel?"

"Lovers? Ha! Fidel Ortega?"

Well, thank heavens for small mercies. He kicked off his shoes and sat, facing her. "Talk. You said he started it all? Started what?"

"Everything." She stared beyond him into the shadows. "I told you I'd gone down t'Houston, to have a heart-to-heart with Saskia..." Anxious to face the breakup with Stephen and be done with it, she'd flown back to Fleetfoot one day earlier than expected. Had arrived in time for a late supper— to find that Stephen had a guest. He and Murphy were dining with a man she'd never met before, a Miami Cuban, Fidel Ortega. A business associate, Stephen had explained, which as usual explained nothing.

But she didn't care anymore. All Ortega was to her was a charming impediment. No way did she want an audience when she spoke with Stephen. She'd picked at her meal, then left the men to their cigars and brandy. But halfway up the stairs, she'd decided to ask Stephen to cut his evening short. She needed to lift this burden off her heart and be done with it.

She'd opened the door to the library, then stopped. "The room's L-shaped—they didn't see me. They were into business already. Ortega was sayin' that his fee was five per cent, half up front, half on payout of the insurance. Stephen said that was no problem, he had one and a half million in his safe, right there. Ortega could count it while they waited.

"Whatever they were talking about, I knew Stephen

wouldn't take kindly to my interrupting.'' So she'd given up and gone to her room, switched on the lights and a few minutes later, heard the first pebbles hit her windowpane. Drawing back the drapes, she'd spotted Brady gesturing frantically from the bushes. She'd laughed and gone down to him by the back stairs, expecting that he had a new horse to show her. Or a new girlfriend to brag about.

No such good news. He'd dragged her off to his truck to talk, then driven her to the stud barn. ''He asked me if I knew who Ortega was, and when I said no, he told me. Around the racetracks and horseshow rings of the country, Fidel Ortega was known as Fido's Delight by those in the know. Because when you see him around a stable, you know the dogs will be eatin' high tomorrow. Ortega turns horses to dogmeat. He's a horse hitman.''

''*What?*''

''He kills horses for their owners. Say a guy buys a promising yearling, pays one million for him and insures for the same. And it turns out his colt can't outrun a sick turtle. Can't resell him now for what he paid. Everybody knows his track record. So...the colt dies. Breaks his leg in some stable accident and has to be put down. Or dies of a heart attack. Least that's what the vet thinks. And the owner collects one million dollars from his insurance.''

They stared at each other. ''And Ortega takes five percent as his fee?''

''Five percent. All it takes is a crowbar to break bones. Or a customized extension cord to electrocute, which looks the same as a heart attack, Brady told me. Or an injection of filth if the owner wants the death to look like colic. And a man with no heart. No heart at all t'be able to *do* that.'' She shivered violently.

Tag reached for her and pulled her into his lap. *Not crazy at all, then!* He'd done her every kind of injustice. Not crazy, just too full of passion and heart for her own good. ''So a fee of one and a half million up front, plus the same on completion, makes three million. Colton was hiring him to kill a horse insured for sixty million, then, if Ortega's cut was five percent?''

''Right.'' She shivered again and leaned back into his warmth. ''And there was only one horse at Fleetfoot insured for sixty million. Brady had spotted Ortega driving through the gates, and once he saw him, he knew *some* horse would die that night. And since Stephen had fired the regular night man at the stud barns a few weeks back, a real horseman who wouldn't have stood for that, then that meant the one t'die would be a stallion. And Brady had learned just that morning that they'd been taking Payback's honey at night. Once I told him what I'd heard, we knew the target.''

He tightened his arms around her. ''But why not sell Payback if Colton needed the money? Why'd he have to kill him?''

''Cause years back he'd sold fifty lifetime breeding rights in Payback, for a million dollars apiece—and he'd already spent that money. If Stephen sold Pookums, the breeders owning those rights would *still* own that portion of his matings. The new buyer could only buy the right to send fifty mares to Payback each year. That's figuring a hundred mares a season, which is way too many for most studs.''

''So he'd be worth roughly thirty million to a new buyer. Got it.'' It made more sense to kill the stallion and realize fifty-seven million, after Ortega's cut. More sense, if you had no heart. He kissed the side of her mouth. ''So you took him and ran.''

It was all she and Brady could think to do. She knew from sad experience that there was no winning arguments with Stephen. And to go to the county sheriff, where it would be the word of a Texas nobody against the hometown millionaire? The hit was clearly scheduled for that very night. Stephen must have planned it thinking she'd be in Houston, would never even know Ortega had come calling.

They decided to spirit Payback away to someplace safe, then find someone big and powerful enough to protect him from Stephen.

A famous track writer or maybe someone in the Jockey Club. Susannah had taken Brady's truck, which had a hitch to pull a horse trailer. Brady had stayed behind to distract the guard at the security board, then flip the switch for the farm's back gate, so she could drive through without raising the alarm.

And to guard her back, Tag realized. The old man had had guts.

He was supposed to follow in her car. "When he never came, I got scared and drove on. Brady had friends with a stable up near Saratoga. He'd figured we could hide Pookums there while we straightened things out. I didn't know their names or the town, but I headed that direction, anyway."

By then she hadn't slept in more than twenty-four hours. "I took a wrong turn somewhere, ended up in Vermont. Decided I'd better push on to Canada, but I was nearly out of gas." She had no cash. Had depended on Brady to bring some. She tried to use her credit cards, only to find they'd been canceled. And by using them, perhaps she'd pinpointed her location? "I thought about letting Pookums run free, t'run for his life, but he's an old softie. The minute his stomach growled, he'd amble up to somebody's barn and demand his oats. Stephen would get him back in no time and then— *whack.*

"So all I could think t'do was reduce his value to zero." If Payback wasn't worth sixty million, wasn't worth anything at all, then Stephen had no reason to kill him.

"So that's about that," Susannah murmured. She slid out of his lap and knelt beside him, looking up. "Once you'd done it, I phoned the Boston Globe, told 'em I had a story

they'd kill for. Then I drove t'Boston. Traded Brady's spare
tire at a filling station for gas t'get there, wishing I'd thought
of that before. Gave a news conference so the whole world
would know Payback was worthless. And the insurance company, Lloyd's of London.

"But—" Tears streamed down her face "—I was so frantic, tryin' to save Payback, I never even thought about *you*.
That Stephen might..."

He pulled her down on the blanket and lay beside her,
stroking the tears off her cheeks. "Susannah Mack, I'm glad
you found me, instead of Canada."

She laughed through her tears. "R-really? Truly? After all
I've put you through?"

"Really, truly. I wouldn't have missed this ride for the
world." He kissed the tip of her nose. "But why didn't you
tell me? Why didn't you tell the world why you'd done it?"

"I don't know." She nestled under his chin, molding her
body to his. "At first 'cause it was none of the world's business. I was so *ashamed* of Stephen. I didn't want to wave his
dirty laundry on the nightly news, I just wanted t'forget about
it. I'd stopped him and that was all that counted. Then...after
he'd had me thrown in jail in Boston for horse theft and he
came t'visit—"

"He *what?*" Tag sought her chin, tipped her face till he
could see her eyes.

"Late that night. Man has his own jet, y'know." She wiped
her lashes and smiled. "Came to see me in my cell and tell
me that Brady was dead."

His heart, already racing with her nearness, soared into
overdrive. "He...saw you behind bars—his own wife—and
he wouldn't go your bail?" He might have to kill the bastard
after all.

"Yeah." She didn't seem to find it so remarkable. "He
said I couldn't prove anything, anyway, without Brady t'back
me. And he said if I ever said 'boo' about it t'anybody, he'd

sue me back to the Stone Age for slander. Or maybe he'd send Ortega after me.''

"He said that." *You are dogmeat, Colton.* And soon, since Tag hadn't Susannah's patience. *Revenge by the year 2000, at the very latest.*

"Yeah." She shrugged. "Anyway, it was done. I didn't much care. At that point I figured I'd done what I'd set out to do—save Payback. All I wanted to do was crawl home t'Texas and mourn Brady.''

He kissed her eyes, her nose, her drowsy, tear-salty smile. "Susannah Mack, you amaze me." *I want you to amaze me for the rest of my life.*

"You know the rest," she murmured when their lips parted. "When I saw Ortega tonight, something snapped. Only reason he'd be at that party is to drum up business. Glad I didn't have a gun, 'cause maybe I would have shot him.''

He kissed her again. "From now on, why don't you just point—and leave the payback to me?''

Tears spilled silver down her cheeks as she laughed. She was as worn out as he was.

"Turn over," he commanded softly. She turned and he worked the zipper down her supple spine. Skinned her gradually out of her dress, stopping to kiss each inch of bare skin as it appeared. Lying limp as a sleepy tiger, she murmured in wordless delight. Let him touch…admire…cherish. He skimmed the dress off her ankles and tossed it over a bale. She wore black lace lingerie she must have bought in Chicago, including a garter belt and—*bless you, darling*—she'd put the bikini panties on over her belt. He tugged them down her long legs and sailed them into the shadows.

"Mmm." She smiled and reached for one of her garter clips.

He caught her hand—"no *way*"—lifted it, kissed it, pressed it down into the blanket above her head. Settled down over her and felt her arch to meet him. Susannah in silk stockings was his idea of heaven.

LONG AFTER SUSANNAH had fallen asleep in the midst of a purring little laugh, Tag lay, her silky head pillowed on his shoulder, staring up at the shadowed rafters. Thinking…frowning. His last doubt had been canceled, but still their future looked iffy.

Consider it from Colton's point of view. Tag didn't doubt now that Colton had loved her in his own fashion. And she'd betrayed him. Publicly. With the whole world gleefully watching. Also tricked him out of sixty million dollars, a sum he'd been so desperate to obtain he'd been willing to cash in his finest stallion.

Is he ever going to forgive and forget?

Colton, the king of revenge? *So the question is, will twenty million be enough to outrun him?* Looks like he's overreached himself and maybe he's going down, but how soon? And is that soon enough if he's willing to spend his last dime to pay back Susannah?

So think, Taggart. His heart faltered—

Hawww hee-haw, hee-haw!

—then resumed its steady beat. Just Lancelot down below, singing up the sun. Slowly Tag smiled—and slept.

He rose before Susannah and had a talk with Cam. The old man agreed, she was better out of the way. If even one person had recognized her last night and word got around, Colton's men might well search Cam's farm again. And the Keeneland racecourse would be swarming with his men. Because once Colton realized they were in town, then the rest became obvious. He'd guess the when and how of the rumored sale of Payback's honey, if not the where.

It took some strenuous arm-twisting, however, to make Susannah see it Tag's way. "It's your own fault," he pointed out finally. "The price you pay for nailing Ortega. Now you

have to lie low till our auction and leave the rest to me.'' Tag
would find Sheik Misha'al and deliver their last invitation.
Susannah would spend the next two days helping Cam break
a yearling for a small time breeder in western Kentucky.

"Meet me at our hotel room, 10 p.m. Tuesday,'' he
warned, kissing her one last time through the window of
Cam's truck. "No later, no sooner.''

"You're getting mighty damned bossy,'' she muttered. "I
still think—''

He put his lips to her ear and whispered, "Turnabout is
fair play, Lambchops. Last night it was *you* on top, so today…'' She was both scowling and blushing as he waved her
down the drive. He missed her already. But he hadn't ten
minutes to spare in the next thirty-six hours to pine. First he
had to drive to Lexington, and if he couldn't find what he
needed there, then it was on to Louisville. And then came the
hard part.

THE KEENELAND SELECTED Sale. Not unlike a four-legged
Miss Universe contest, Tag thought, standing in the three-
deep crowd along the walls of the sales pavillion. Every yearling was a beauty. The auction house accepted only the finest
thoroughbred fillies and colts in the country, rejecting two of
every three applicants, making their final selection on a point
system based on pedigree and conformation.

And every yearling was a contestant, with the yearly crown
going to the horse that went for the top price of the two-day
auction—or better yet, that established a new world's record.
The previous record had been broken twice tonight already,
each time for a Payback colt. When the winning bid of 26
million dollars had lit up on the electronic board above the
auctioneer, the audience had gone wild. Even the other rail
birds, who had no intention of bidding, had yelled and applauded. Watching fat cats drop millions—not Tag's kind of
sport.

Still he was happy to see how shrewdly Susannah had chosen their marks. In the first hour of the auction, five yearlings had topped a million dollars. Two of those had gone to Mr. Kawabata, their Japanese industrialist—and he'd wrested both of them from Jackson Tate, their Hollywood high roller. Reardon, the English tabloid king, had taken the third. Then all five of their invitees had leaped to bid on the two Payback colts, along with a dozen others. Villanova had taken both, the first one for a world-record 21 million. The second, the spitting image of Payback himself, for 26 million. Each time the auctioneer had named Sheik Misha'al al Sabik as the second highest bidder.

Now if only Tag could locate that gentleman. The auction moved so fast—a new horse every three minutes or so—it had taken him a good half hour to realize that all bidders weren't necessarily sitting in the amphitheatre. The two auctioneers wore button earphones, as did the six bid spotters who worked the aisles of the pavillion, scanning for the discreetly raised finger or the cool nod that signified a bid, then relaying that figure back to the auctioneer.

Apparently there were other spotters elsewhere in the building, as well. According to the auctioneer, the winning bid for the last colt had come in from the walking ring directly behind the pavillion, where buyers could watch the horses in action as their handlers prepared them for their grand entrance into the sales ring.

To compound his confusion, the auctioneer named the winning bidder only if given permission to do so. And sometimes the buyer didn't bid. Bloodstock agents were hired guns, paid to advise on equine purchases and sometimes to do the actual bidding on their client's behalf.

The gavel cracked. The colt in the ring shied and tried to rear, but his green-coated handler brought him quickly to earth and led him toward the exit door on the left. "Sold to the BBA for $950,000,'' declared the auctioneer as the next glossy thoroughbred entered, stage right.

"What's BBA?" Tag asked the man at his elbow, a friendly, knowledgeable guy who'd helped Tag sort out some of his confusion.

"British Bloodstock Agency."

"Bidding for whom?"

His acquaintance shrugged. "Could be anybody. Sheik Maktoum from Dubai, that Saudi sheik—Misha'al—or even the Pope. Word'll leak out in a day or two."

Too late. He needed to hand the sheik his invitation tonight.

"Would you bid four, four, who'll make it four for this *fine*-lookin' animal?" the auctioneer chanted. "Got four million, four million five, now who'll bid five, would you bid five, would you *do* it? *Thank* you, Five, would you bid six, sir? I need six, I got six, would you bid seven? Seven? Who'll go for seven? Now *look,* folks, the Lord loves a cheerful giver, so who'll give me seven? Got *seven,* now eight, would you go eight, would you do it? Could you live with yourself if you *don't* do it?" The bidding was slowing and had narrowed to a man in a Stetson up front—Tag saw it dip a second before the price jumped—and someone else on the far side of the arena. *Crack!* "Eight million five, an Oscar-winning colt if *I* ever saw one to Mr. Jackson Tate!''

The audience cheered the celebrity and his purchase, and the next beauty minced in. A Payback filly. Who went three minutes later for ten million to Reardon, though another bidder had pushed him all the way. A bidder that Tag couldn't spot anywhere in the pavillion. Susannah's reclusive Saudi? Bidding from where?

"Hip number sixty-nine," intoned the announcer as the next colt entered the ring, referring to the numbered tag attached to his gleaming flank. "A son of Paid in Full, winner of the Belmont and Preakness, and son of the great Payback himself, Triple Crown winner, five-time Eclipse horse of the…''

Paid in Full, now Fleetfoot Farm's top stallion. He couldn't hold a candle to his own sire, Susannah had explained—he was a good horse, but not a wonder horse. He was the reason Colton had harvested Payback's sperm, Tag had finally realized. Paid in Full would have been credited with siring eight colts that were really his own half siblings if Brady hadn't snatched Payback's honey and run. *One more debt Colton will chalk up to me and Susannah.*

Crack! The Paid in Full colt went for a mere $2,500,000. ''That should make Colton happy,'' muttered a man just ahead of Tag.

His companion snorted. ''Make his bank happy, you mean. I heard he's two months behind on his interest payments.''

Tag had heard more than that while he'd been scouting the Keeneland library for Sheik Misha'al. He'd eavesdropped on a couple of old hardboots, voices raised over their third round of mint juleps, one of whom had sworn that Colton had invested sixty million dollars last February. Start-up money, to back an Indian casino, one of Reardon's schemes. A scheme that never got off the ground. Because the governor of the state for which the casino had been planned had sensed which way the political winds were blowing and had spun like a weathercock, coming out against gambling despite all the tribe's desperate lobbying. The casino was stalled for years if not forever.

So that was why Colton had needed sixty million. Had the casino gone through, anyone owning a piece of the action would have made billions. With his plan to liquidate Payback thwarted, Colton must have found some other way to raise the money, intending to pay off his debts with casino dollars. But the best-laid plans of mice and men…

Crack! ''Sold to Sheik Misha'al for six million, five.''

''Where *is* that guy?'' Tag demanded of his neighbor. ''Or

is he even in Kentucky?'' Perhaps all his purchases were being bought by an agent?

"Oh, he's here someplace, all right," drawled the other. "You drove in to Keeneland by the main gates?" Tag nodded. "Then if you looked toward the airport—" the Lexington airport, he meant, which abutted the racecourse "—you'd have seen a 747 parked on the back runway? Arabic printing on its side? That plane belongs to the Doobey brothers, we call 'em, Sheik Maktoum and his two brothers, from Dubai.''

"That's not the sheik I'm after." The Maktoums bought up the Northern Dancer bloodlines, Susannah had explained. Their prospect, Sheik Misha'al al Sabik, was a Saudi, and his breeding program favored Payback's lineage.

"Yeah. But if you look beyond the Maktoums' 747, you'll see a French jet, painted sun yellow, no writing on it anywhere. That's how al Sabik travels."

If the man owned his own jet, he definitely belonged at their private auction. Tag decided to check the walking ring out back—then changed his mind as he approached the exit at the rear of the pavillion. Murphy stood beside the door, arms crossed, icy eyes scanning the crowd. Tag drifted backward into the spectators. Damn. He was pinned here till Murphy moved on. There was no way to sneak past him to reach the far exit.

He stayed pinned the whole night. Watched in fuming frustration while the elusive Sheik Misha'al bought one of the remaining Paid in Full colts, and Villanova scarfed up the last son of Payback—for the top bid of the night. Also the top bid of the 20th century. Twenty-nine million dollars.

TUESDAY NIGHT, one hour to go till their private auction. Tag knocked on their hotel room door, then unlocked it—and Susannah ran into his arms. "Ooof! Watch the ribs!" he gasped as she hugged him.

"Where have you *been?*" she demanded. "I've been

chewin' my nails to the elbow, wonderin' if—'' She pulled his head down and kissed him hard.

Lip-locked, Tag groped behind him and shut the door. He leaned back against it, cradling her between his legs. "Missed you," he murmured against her mouth, then plumbed her honeyed depths. She shuddered against him and his hands moved to her hips, lifting her up onto tiptoe. He glanced beyond her head at a couch. Fifty minutes left—did they dare? No, there was one last phone call to make and he couldn't make it from here. "Rain check, baby," he murmured against her lips, then, *"ow!"*

Her arms eased and she lifted her head. "Your ribs still hurtin'?"

Every last inch of him ached. And that bodyguard last night had been the final straw. After the auction he'd bribed a baggage handler at the Lexington airport to let him slip through a side door and walk out to Sheik Misha'al's sun-yellow jet.

The bodyguard had come sailing out of the dark to blindside him. With a gun pressed to the back of Tag's head and his nose scraping concrete, they'd had a long, earnest conversation. Luckily the guy had been an American, since Tag knew not one word of Arabic, and he'd had a sense of humor. He'd finally accepted the invitation, opened it to check for bombs, read it, then laughed and marched Tag back to the terminal. He'd promised the sheik would see it.

Everything depended on that promise.

Tag prowled the suite checking their arrangements while he told her the story. Susannah hadn't wasted her time upon arrival. Refreshments sat waiting on a side table, a bottle of Chivas Regal and a bottle of water for the drinkers, an insulated carafe of espresso for the sheik. She'd arranged the couch and four chairs in a semicircle facing the desk, which would serve as their auction pulpit. On the desk a phone sat ready. Beside the desk stood an extra-large wine chiller filled with cubed ice—and the gleaming sperm container.

"Perfect," he applauded. She looked perfect, too, conservatively elegant in a blue-gray day dress and heels. They'd agreed that this had to look like a class act. Their high rollers might not have any scruples about bidding in a black-market auction, but let them catch one whiff of tackiness and they'd be gone. *We're selling sizzle here, as well as steak.*

"What if nobody comes?" she dithered, tagging his heels into the bedroom. "This feels like that first party I threw at Fleetfoot. I was so scared everybody would snub Stephen for marryin' me..."

He smiled at her over his shoulder and led the way out onto a balcony. Four stories directly below, a swimming pool shimmered turquoise with underwater lights. "But they came, didn't they?"

"Oh, yeah, they all came. I found out as long as you had money, they'd overlook 'bout anything."

"And tonight we're offering something rarer than money." While he dressed in the tuxedo he'd rented, he told her about Keeneland. "Villanova bought every Payback colt, though the Sheik and Reardon snapped at his heels the whole way."

"Hard t'believe there's somebody with more money than the sheik," Susannah murmured, watching him dress. "But I guess cocaine trumps even Saudi oil wells. Running drugs must be like owning the federal mint."

"Yep. And it looks like Villanova means to corner the market on the last of Payback's bloodlines." Which put them in the catbird seat tonight. Villanova hungry, the sheik and the others frustrated.

Susannah's eyes narrowed. "What is *that?*" She crossed the room to touch the bruise just below his ribs.

"Souvenir from the airport." He turned away and buttoned his shirt.

"A bodyguard with *hooves?*"

"Oh, that's Lancelot, then." He snatched his tie off the bureau.

She laughed. "How's his poor ear?"

"Couldn't be better. Would you tie this for me, babe?" Then it was time to go downstairs.

CHAPTER TWENTY-SIX

11:50 P.M. Concealed in a phone booth across the lobby, Tag watched their high rollers gather, as per instructions, by the fountain. Kawabata with his assistant arrived first, looked around expectantly, then burst into laughter as Jackson Tate joined him. The millionaires bowed deeply to each other while their seconds traded curt nods. Reardon was next to appear, escorted by three thugs, instead of the one bodyguard that their note had specified. Tag wasn't surprised.

The lobby doors opened again and a tall, athletic type entered, his eyes scanning the room. Sheik Misha'al's American bodyguard. Ignoring the men by the fountain, he circled the lobby's perimeter. His eyes met Tag's as he passed the phone booth, but his steps didn't slow. Reaching the lobby doors again, he spoke into a microphone clipped to his lapel.

Two men stepped out of a side corridor that led to the first-floor rooms. Both of them looked decidedly mideastern and the one limping in the lead, midforties, bearded and darkly handsome in spite of his lame leg, clad in the best of understated English tailoring, had to be the sheik. He joined his fellow bidders with an austere smile that made the first three look like frat boys in search of a beer blast.

The lobby doors swung wide and four men fanned out to either side—the toughs to the right stopping short as they confronted the sheik's man. At the desk across the room, the night clerk goggled. There was a brief, icy exchange of words, then three of Villanova's honchos stalked on to cover the other points of the compass, while their leader, Snake Eyes from the party, remained beside the American.

Tag glanced at his watch, then lifted the phone and dialed the number he'd called that morning. By the time he hung up, two minutes later, Villanova had joined the other bidders and all five were comparing notes. He had precisely thirty minutes to make this happen.

He lost more than five, conveying his guests to the suite. Too many bodyguards to fit in one elevator. They went up in two groups, Tag parking the first half at the top of the shaft while he went down for the rest. Once they were reassembled, Villanova's heavies backed him against a wall of the corridor and gave him a patting down he wouldn't have permitted a doctor.

Teeth gritted, he smiled blandly throughout, then led them to the suite, shedding excess guards en route. Villanova's man watched the elevator, Reardon's extras took the two side corridors, the Sheik's second man and one of the Colombians took the door to the stairwell. Villanova's third man stationed himself at the door to the suite.

Tag unlocked the door and held it wide. There was a moment of paralysis as five multimillionaires pondered precedence, then Jackson Tate laughed aloud. "Guys, let's not stand here sucking our thumbs all night! I've got this hot babe waiting for me back in my room and she's not the kind of girl who…" He disappeared beyond the door and the others jostled after him.

Tag turned to Villanova's man. He hadn't planned on this. "Would you like to come inside?"

The man showed his teeth, but it wasn't a smile. Shook his head no.

There was no time left to argue. He'd just have to pray. Tag entered the suite to find bodyguards solemnly trooping in and out of the bedroom—checking under the bed for assassins, he supposed, while Susannah served drinks to their masters and settled them into their chairs. She handed Sheik Misha'al his cup of coffee, laughed at something he said, then joined Tag behind their desk with a speaking glance.

"Thank you for coming," Tag said to call them to attention. As Susannah had promised, there was enough testosterone assembled in this room to blow the doors off. He had to dominate this meeting or lose it. "I assume that by attending this auction tonight, you each have agreed to abide by the rules we stated in our invitation?"

Ten pairs of eyes studied him coldly. The guards stood behind their clients along the wall. The breeders sat sipping their scotch or coffee. Not men who cared to think they were bound by any rule.

"You each have a minimum of forty million available in an Asian account, which can be wired to our numbered account *tonight,* in case you're the high bidder," Tag specified, looking for signs of dissent. Last week he had opened an account with a bank in Hong Kong, which at this hour would be open for business. He scanned the five faces, found no disagreement and continued. "Each of you has agreed that win or lose, he will keep the outcome of this auction entirely confidential."

This time Kawabata and Reardon nodded, then the others, except for Villanova, and that was probably just machismo. Mr. Drug Cartel wasn't the type to squeal to any authority, be it cops or Jockey Club. Any problems he had, he'd settle himself, his midnight eyes assured Tag.

"All right, gentlemen, tonight we're offering eight straws of Payback sperm, in prime condition, which should be enough, conservatively speaking, to impregnate one mare. If you're a lucky man, you might get as many as four foals." But every one of these five would consider himself fortune's favorite. "Susannah, if you'll do the honors?"

Each bidder was given a chance to peer through the clouds

of white gas and count the straws. She capped the cannister and returned it to the ice. "Now. If you're ready to begin—"

"One question," said Reardon, the Englishman. "Whom do you represent?"

Tag smiled. "You don't need to know that."

"Oh, but we do," said Villanova. His voice was like the purr of a big animal, soft with amusement. It didn't match his bottomless eyes. "Because if this sperm is not *precisely* as described—viable and coming from Payback...then I'll need to know who to...see about that." The other bidders murmured grim agreement, while behind the Colombian, there was a soft *click!*

Snake Eyes held an open switchblade. Ignoring his audience, he cleaned a fingernail, nodded to himself, then the blade vanished behind brown, deft fingers.

"Understood." Tag glanced at Susannah. *Follow me, babe.* "We represent Mr. Stephen Colton in this transaction."

She blinked. Her long delicate throat moved as she swallowed, then she turned to smile at the men—as Kawabata snorted. "How can this be? Everyone here knows that this woman is Colton's ex-wife! And everyone knows the divorce was...bitter."

Susannah's smile was cool, contemptuous, utterly assured. "*Do* they? Things aren't always what they seem."

"Now that's a proposition I'll buy any night of the week," Jackson Tate observed with a laugh. "Gentlemen, we're all gamblers or we wouldn't be here. Let's get on with this, shall we? It's time to ante up or bow out."

Bless you. "For the opening bid we'll need a minimum of five million," Tag said quickly, and the actor lifted a forefinger. "Good. Am I bid six?"

"Six," growled Reardon, "but I'm with Villanova. If this is a scam..."

Tag shook his head. "I have six. Am I—"

"Seven," said Sheik Misha'al. He smiled at Susannah.

The bidding was up to eleven million, Villanova in the lead, when something thumped against the hallway door. Everyone swung around, the guards reaching into their unbuttoned jackets.

"I have eleven," Tag insisted. "Am I bid twelve?"

Nobody turned, he was losing them—lost them entirely as someone rapped on the door. Three hard, imperious knocks.

"The Jockey Club!" muttered Mr. Kawabata, who had yet to bid. He broke into excited Japanese and stood, turning to his assistant.

"Who'll give me twelve?" Tag said in a louder voice.

Rap. Rap. Rap.

"Whoever he is, he means to join the party." Jackson Tate strode over to the door, setting off a frenzy among the bodyguards—some of them moving between their clients and the door, all of them drawing their guns as the actor threw the bolt. "Well, *well!*" Tate laughed and backed away from the swinging door.

Stephen Colton walked into the room, followed by a wobbling Colombian—who was held upright by the much smaller man at his back. Murphy. The Irishman shoved his prisoner at Snake Eyes, who cursed, caught him and slammed him against a wall. With a woozy smile, the guard slid down the paneling and sat.

"Sorry to keep you waiting, gentlemen," Colton drawled, surveying the assembly.

He was bigger than he'd looked on TV and tougher than Tag would have expected, behind his boyish charm. More than a pretty boy, with eyes as flat and pale as his own hired killer's, behind those gold wire rims. Those wintry eyes moved from the bidders, to the container of sperm, to his ex-wife's white face. "Susannah, we have to talk." He glanced back at the bidders. "Gentlemen, if you'll excuse us a moment?"

She swallowed convulsively, nodded—and lifted the container from the ice. Walked with it into the bedroom like a sleepwalker returning to bed. Tag followed. Colton brought up the rear and closed the door behind them.

Susannah stood backed against the glass door to the balcony. She held the cannister clasped to her breast. Her eyes were enormous, wounded and searching. Tag met them for a second, then hung his head.

Colton chuckled. "So you started without me."

Not meeting his eyes, Tag shrugged. "Didn't think they'd wait."

"You tipped him off?" Susannah's voice was a humming growl trapped halfway between anguish and rage. Her hand blindly caressed the top of the cannister. *"Tag?"*

"What's the high bid?" Colton demanded, ignoring her completely.

"Eleven from Villanova."

"You *did!* Oh, you money-grubbing, double-crossing Yankee Judas!"

"I'm sorry, babe." Turning his back on Colton's jeering laughter, Tag tried to reach her with his eyes. *Trust me, darlin'.* "The more I thought about it, the more this seemed the only way. I've cut a deal for both of us. Colton's promised to give us both a truce—no more revenge, no more hunting us down. We can live our own lives after tonight. And we get one-fourth of whatever the sperm brings. That'll be enough for me to finance a new clinic and you take the rest." He held out his hand and eased toward her. *Come to me.* "Sometimes it's smartest to think small."

"Small thoughts from a *small* man!" she cried bitterly. "And I thought I loved you?" Her fingers twirled the top of the cannister and spun it free.

"Susannah, *no!*" Dear God, all his plans! He leaped for her as she elbowed the sliding door open, Colton swearing and lunging at his heels.

"Lying bastard! Keep *away* from me!" She threw the top.

Tag ducked, and steel clanged off bone beside him. Colton put a hand slowly to his head, smiled uncertainly, sat on the bed. "Susannah, don't!" But she'd slipped through the gap and out onto the balcony. "Wait!" Tag paused in the doorway.

She leaned far out over the railing, the eight plastic straws clutched between her hands like a bundle of brittle sticks. "You're just one more lying, money-grubbin', selfish *b-bastard!*" she sobbed, looking back at him over her shoulder.

God, if she leaned any further he'd lose *her,* and he wasn't sure if she'd hit pavement or swimming pool. "Susannah...darling..." He eased up behind her. "That's the last of Payback you've got there."

"A lot *you* care! This is nothin' but money to you!"

"But to you it's the last of Payback, whoever it goes to." He edged closer. "Maybe eight more of his foals to run in the world, babe? If you don't drown 'em." Behind him, he heard the glass door slide back. Colton. She must have heard him, too. She sobbed and leaned further out over the drop. "You can pay us both back or you can save the last of Payback—which'll it be?" Tag reached around her on both sides and caught her wrists. "Babe?"

"*Bastard!*" She shuddered against him.

He put his lips to her ear and murmured, "Trust me, Lambchops. Don't do this."

She shuddered and whispered again, "You *heartless* bastard!"

"Got her?" Colton demanded behind them.

"I got her." But after this, would he ever have her again? Tag kissed the tears on her cheek. "Give 'em to me. Please, darling?" She slowly let go. Still holding her, he handed the straws back over his shoulder to Colton—whose laughing groan of relief was music to Tag's ears. *You need this money, don't you, Colton? And you need it bad.*

He drew Susannah back from the railing. Hooked an arm around her waist and led her back inside. She wouldn't look up at him. "You think you made a deal with the devil, then you better think again," she murmured on a note of dazed indifference.

"Susannah, how *can* you say that?" Colton laughed and Tag met his merciless eyes, bright with mirth and victory.

We'll see.

Colton repacked the straws in their container and left the room. Tag stayed to wet a cloth in the bathroom sink and wipe her face. Sitting on the bed, she stared right through him. "Let's go watch the end," he said finally, and brushed her cheek with his knuckles. She flinched and another tear rolled down her nose.

He would have given his right arm to comfort her—but not their future. "Come on, babe." He led her out the door to the sitting room.

Where the auction was coming to an end. "Who'll give me twenty-two million?" Colton demanded.

Villanova glanced at the sheik and smirked. The Arab frowned into space. "Twenty-two million for a horse not even born yet?" He shook his head ever so slightly and Susannah made a small painful noise. His dark eyes swung to her, to her ex-husband, to the container of sperm, then back to Colton. "What if we added a—how do you say it?—a sweetener to this deal? Payback himself."

"Payback?" Colton said blankly at the same moment Villanova snorted.

"The Arabian mare that I've ridden for sixteen years has earned her retirement. Would Payback make a riding horse now that he's gelded? Have *you* ever sat him?"

Colton started to shake his head as Susannah said, "*I* have." Her eyes spoke to the sheik alone. "He rides like a dream. He's like riding the wind!" Her fingers twined together and squeezed.

Villanova shook his head. "And he has no balls! What do I need a nag without *cojones*, eh? No, we bid for the sperm here."

"But I'll be happy to discuss a separate deal," Colton interjected smoothly. "Now, final offers for Payback's sperm? We stand at twenty-two million. Going once?"

The sheik glanced again at Villanova and the Colombian grinned. His message was clear. He could go on all night, stack millions up to the moon. The Arab shrugged and sat back in his chair. "Going twice, going three times and *sold* to Señor Villanova," Colton announced. "The very last of Payback and a bargain at the price! Thank you all, gentlemen."

Tag put his lips to Susannah's ear. "Go pack for both of us, babe. You have three minutes, then we blow this joint."

She looked up at him, unsmiling, then stalked into the bedroom. To pack or simply wash her hands of him? While he waited to see, Tag crossed the room and introduced himself to the sheik's head bodyguard.

"Trace Sutton," the American said in an undertone as they shook.

"Trace, Susannah and I need a favor, and I believe your boss would approve." Tag spoke hurriedly, while Murphy stared at them from the hallway door, his pale eyes full of promise.

Tag walked back toward the desk in time to hear the sheik say, "One hundred thousand, then. My van will collect him tomorrow morning at six."

Colton turned to Villanova. "Here's the number of my account to which you can wire. If you'd care to do that now?" It wasn't a question. Tag plucked Colton's sleeve as Villanova picked up the phone. "About Susannah's and my cut?"

Laughter trembled in the Kentuckian's voice, twitched the corners of his lips. "What about it?" His eyes switched beyond Tag to where Susannah stood holding a suitcase. "This is the best you could do, babycakes? *This* clown?"

"You're breaking your promise?" Tag asked evenly.

Susannah groaned and turned away. Walked toward the door—then stopped when she saw Murphy.

Colton's voice dropped to a vicious whisper. "I'm breaking that one, Taggart, and I'm making another! You haven't seen the last of me. You look back and I'll be there for the rest of your miserable life, sucker. You'll curse the day you were ever born!" He raised his voice. "Susannah, wait!"

"*Ha!* In your sorry dreams." She started straight for Murphy.

The sheik murmured something to his bodyguard and they moved in behind her. If he missed this train, he'd never make it out that door, Tag realized, turning back to Colton. "Goodbye." He followed the others straight past a helplessly glowering Murphy and out the door to freedom.

"See you soon!" Colton called after them. "*Real* soon."

"WHAT WAS THAT ABOUT?" Trace Sutton asked as they walked the gauntlet past Villanova's surly men. The other bidders had gone on ahead, taking their spare guards with them.

Tag drew a breath. "A very long story. A never-ending grudge. But thanks for the safe conduct—I don't think we would've walked out of there without you."

Ahead of Tag and the two bodyguards, Susannah and the sheik were discussing Payback—his intelligence, his heart, his gaits, his sense of humor. Tag moved up on Susannah's left. She glanced up at him and her smile faded to coldness.

"Then he shall see the home of his ancestors," the Arab declared.

"Who?" Tag inquired. If this guy thought he was going to charm Susannah away without a fight, he'd better think again.

"Payback," the Sheik explained, looking not at all annoyed by the interruption. "All thoroughbreds trace their lineage back to three Arabian stallions in the eighteenth century, surely you know? That is why I come to Kentucky, to reclaim the best of them. They are my people's heritage. We should have the very best of the best, the swiftest and the most beautiful. A man should ride no less."

They entered the elevator and Tag pressed the buttons. As the doors closed, he said, "In that case, sir, I wonder if you'd care to stop by our room for a moment? I have something you'll want to see."

"But..." Susannah said, then paused.

Sheik Misha'al's eyes were dark as Villanova's, but far from empty. Intelligence and humor stirred in their depths. He dipped his head. "The night is young."

The elevator stopped at the second floor. Tag took Susannah's elbow and steered her along the corridor, the others following. And at least now she would look at him. "What the devil are you up to?" she whispered.

Tag simply smiled. "Here we are." He unlocked the door to a room, not half so grand as their suite upstairs, but it had a refrigerator. The Arab guard stayed in the corridor. Sutton shut the door behind his boss and leaned against it. Tag opened the refrigerator—and drew out a stainless steel cannister. He set it on the bed.

"Son of a blue-bottomed baboon!" Susannah murmured reverently. She dropped on the mattress beside it and stared up at him.

Tag opened the cannister. Smoke billowed in mystic clouds. He waved it aside and lifted out...eight straws. "If you'd still like to buy the last of the very best, sir, then here it is. Prime Payback sperm."

The Sheik narrowed his eyes. "The other cannister contained no sperm?"

"I didn't say that." Tag capped the container.

They measured each other. The Arab stroked his trim beard. "What is your price?"

"For six of these straws, we need a flat ten million, plus some other considerations." If they couldn't survive—couldn't thrive—on five million apiece, they were spoiled brats, which they were not. "Additionally we each need a salaried job for five years on one of your estates—the same estate." He glanced down at Susannah, found her eyes bright with tears, a smile starting to tremble. "You'll find us useful. Susannah's a crack yearling trainer and I'm a veterinarian. Not a large-animal doctor, but I can learn. We'll want reasonable salaries and board, stabling for Susannah's broodmare—and your complete protection from Stephen Colton for five years."

Tag gave Colton that long to self-destruct, though five years was probably generous. After that—a bankrupt Colton, stripped of his hired killers, of all his means to hound and buy misery? That man Tag could handle, if it ever came to that. He didn't think it would.

"That should be no problem," said the sheik. "But the other two straws, they are not for sale?"

Meeting Susannah's eyes, Tag shook his head. "Those two chances belong to Susannah. She has this mare…"

"A granddaughter to a full sister of Ruffian," she murmured, almost singing it, and the Sheik nodded as if he understood completely.

And I hope to God her foal takes after Payback, with his pussycat temperament, Tag prayed. Or that Susannah was the miracle worker she thought she was. Whichever, he owed her that chance. Would have to grit his teeth and simply hope for the best. You couldn't clip the wings of a hawk, then expect to hold her love.

"Those conditions are all easy enough and acceptable," said Misha'al. "But should *this* deal prove to be a swindle…"

"Then you have us as hostage," Tag said. "
to deliver your Payback colt—or colts—myself i

The sheik nodded. "Then we have a deal—o
conditions. First, Susannah explains to me why Payback was stolen and gelded."

She looked up, bit her lip, slowly nodded. "I'll do that, sir, but not tonight if you don't mind."

"Of course. And second—" he turned to Tag "—you tell me what was in the original cannister."

"Eight straws of prime…burro sperm. Eleven months after insemination, Villanova's finest mares will be dropping half-thoroughbred mules."

Susannah's hands flew to her mouth as the Sheik threw back his head and laughed aloud. He swung to a grinning Sutton to share the joke, then turned back, still laughing delightedly. "You sold Sergio Villanova *burro* sperm?"

"No." Tag shook his head. "I didn't. Colton did."

"You sly, Yankee *devil!*" Susannah flung her arms around him and hugged him tight.

He bit back a yelp and glanced over her head at the men. They got the entire joke. Villanova's finest mares would drop their long-eared, short-legged, braying babies in the spring after next. And as small and tight as the racing world was, Tag doubted the Colombian would be able to keep his humiliation a secret. Given Villanova's savage sense of machismo and what a man must do to uphold it, a few days after that, Colton would be running for his life. Would learn once and for all that vengeance came home to roost in the bitter end.

"So…" The Sheik glanced at his watch, then looked up and smiled to find Tag offering him the cannister. He tucked it under one arm. "My van collects Payback tomorrow morning at six, then we fly for France. You may sleep aboard tonight or…" He smiled as Tag shook his head and his eyes flicked toward Susannah. The sheik nodded.

"Then you should join us at dawn. I'll leave Rashid outside your— No, he'll wait down the hall, at the elevators, though I don't think there should be trouble tonight? Good, but all the same…"

Outside the door, Tag shook hands with both men. "Thank you."

Sheik Misha'al patted the cannister. "Horses are for beauty. For speed. To light a man's soul. You've chosen a guardian who knows that. Now…we bid you goodnight."

SUSANNAH SAT WAITING for him on the bed, arms braced behind her, no smile on her face. He shut the door and waited by it. Said finally, "I'm sorry."

"I about *died* when Stephen walked in and I thought you'd double-crossed me." She knuckled a tear off inky lashes. "The sound you heard was my heart breakin'."

"Susannah, I'm *so* sorry, but you wear your heart on your sleeve. If I'd told you before, Colton would have taken one look at your face and known he was walking into a trap."

"I know, I know, but still…" She shook her head slowly. "Burro sperm." A smile tugged at her lips. "I know the who, but how'd you *ever?*"

"It was nothing, really. All it took was a few items from a veterinary-supply house, about eight rum-and-cokes over two days to keep him in a party mood, and a lady llama to tease him."

"Talk about tough love!" She held out her arms and he came to stand before her. She unbuttoned his shirt and laughed up at him. "So that's all these bruises and bite marks…" She kissed a bruise below his ribcage, smiled up at him when he shivered. "So that's the how. But the why?"

"The more I thought about it, after you told me everything, I thought you did deserve some sort of…payback. You used the word justice, once."

"For Brady, yeah…" She hooked her fingers over his belt,

kissed his stomach again. "Payback by the year 2000. Boy, did you deliver!"

He smoothed a hand through her hair. "So is it enough now? Do you think Brady would be satisfied?" *Can we get on with the rest of our lives, love?*

"*Satisfied?*" She laughed up at him. "You hear that sound up there?" She nodded at the ceiling. "That's Brady and my dad up in heaven, falling off clouds, they're laughing so hard. Brady always did have a soft spot for mules."

Tag set one knee on the mattress, between hers. "And you, love, are you satisfied?"

Owl-eyed and suddenly solemn, Susannah shook her head. "Nope. But if our jet leaves at dawn, you have a few hours to fix that—" a wicked smile curled and grew "—*Doctor* Taggart."

He tipped her back on the bed and followed her down. "Rest of my life to fix that."

HARLEQUIN SUPERROMANCE®

**From April to June 1999,
read about three women whose
New Millennium resolution is**

By the Year 2000: *Revenge?*

The Wrong Bride by Judith Arnold.
Available in April 1999.
Cassie Webster loves Phillip Keene and expected to marry
him—but it turns out he's marrying someone else. So
Cassie shows up at his wedding…to prove he's got
The Wrong Bride.

Don't Mess with Texans by Peggy Nicholson.
Available in May 1999.
Susannah Mack Colton is out to get revenge on her
wealthy—and nasty—ex-husband. But in the process
she gets entangled with a handsome veterinarian,
complicating *his* life, too. Because that's what happens
when you *"Mess with Texans"!*

If He Could See Me Now by Rebecca Winters.
Available in June 1999.
The Rachel Maynard of today isn't the Rachel of ten
years ago. Now a lovely and accomplished woman,
she's looking for sweet revenge—and a chance to win
the love of the man who'd once rejected her.
If He Could See Me Now…

Available at your favorite retail outlet.

HARLEQUIN®
Makes any time special ™

If you enjoyed what you just read,
then we've got an offer you can't resist!

Take 2 bestselling love stories FREE!

Plus get a FREE surprise gift!

Clip this page and mail it to Harlequin Reader Service®

IN U.S.A.	IN CANADA
3010 Walden Ave.	P.O. Box 609
P.O. Box 1867	Fort Erie, Ontario
Buffalo, N.Y. 14240-1867	L2A 5X3

YES! Please send me 2 free Harlequin Superromance® novels and my free surprise gift. Then send me 4 brand-new novels every month, which I will receive months before they're available in stores. In the U.S.A., bill me at the bargain price of $3.57 plus 25¢ delivery per book and applicable sales tax, if any*. In Canada, bill me at the bargain price of $3.96 plus 25¢ delivery per book and applicable taxes**. That's the complete price and a savings of over 10% off the cover prices—what a great deal! I understand that accepting the 2 free books and gift places me under no obligation ever to buy any books. I can always return a shipment and cancel at any time. Even if I never buy another book from Harlequin, the 2 free books and gift are mine to keep forever. So why not take us up on our invitation. You'll be glad you did!

134 HEN CNET
334 HEN CNEU

Name	(PLEASE PRINT)	
Address	Apt.#	
City	State/Prov.	Zip/Postal Code

* Terms and prices subject to change without notice. Sales tax applicable in N.Y.
** Canadian residents will be charged applicable provincial taxes and GST.
  All orders subject to approval. Offer limited to one per household.
® are registered trademarks of Harlequin Enterprises Limited.

SUP99   ©1998 Harlequin Enterprises Limited

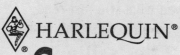

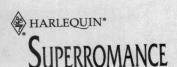

#840 IF HE COULD SEE ME NOW • Rebecca Winters
By the Year 2000: Satisfaction!
Rachel Maynard was rejected by her best friend's handsome brother,
Nikos Athas, and now—years later—she's determined to win his love.
Except that when she meets his older brother, Stasio, she realizes she's not
in love with Nikos at all. Because *real* satisfaction can only come from
being loved by a man of strength, passion and honor—a man like Stasio.

#841 WINTER SOLDIER • Marisa Carroll
In Uniform
When Lieutenant Leah Gentry goes overseas as part of a team that
will provide medical care for those in need, she figures she'll spend
long days doing fulfilling work. What she *doesn't* expect is to fall for
Dr. Adam Sauder. *Or* to return home pregnant with his child.

#842 SECOND TO NONE • Muriel Jensen
The Delancey Brothers
What's a tough cop doing in a place like this? Mike Delancey was one of
the best hostage negotiators in Texas. But he left it all behind to work in the
winery he and his brothers inherited. He was ready for a change but nothing
could have prepared him for Veronica Callahan—a woman with a *very*
interesting past.

#843 TRIAL COURTSHIP • Laura Abbot
Life is a trial for nine-year-old Nick Porter. His grandparents make him
eat broccoli and nag him about his clothes. Aunt Andrea's a great guardian,
but she's always on him about school and manners and stuff. At least there's
Tony. For a grown-up, he's *way* cool. Nick's seen how Tony and Andrea
look at each other. Maybe if he's lucky, Tony and Andrea will get together
and Nick'll get what he *really* wants—a family!

#844 FAMILY PRACTICE • Bobby Hutchinson
Emergency
Dr. Michael Forsythe's marriage is in trouble. He and his wife, Polly, have
not been able to cope with a devastating loss or offer each other the comfort
and reassurance they both need. It takes another crisis—and the unsettling
presence of a four-year-old child—to rekindle the deep love they still share.

#845 ALL-AMERICAN BABY • Peg Sutherland
Hope Springs
To heiress Melina Somerset—pregnant and on the run—the town of
Hope Springs looks like an ideal place to start over. Unfortunately, her
safety depends on a man she met months ago when she was living under an
assumed name. But this Ash Thorndyke is nothing like the man she used to
know. She'd loved that man enough to carry his child. *This* one she's not
sure she can trust.